THE WORKS OF
WILLIAM MAKEPEACE
THACKERAY

VOLUME XVI

Roundabout Papers

Second Funeral
of Napoleon

FIFTY-SIX PHOTOGRAVURES AND
ILLUSTRATIONS FROM ORIGINAL
DRAWINGS BY THACKERAY,
FREDERICK WALKER, R.A.,
GEORGE DU MAURIER,
FRANK DICKSEE, R.A.,
RICHARD DOYLE,
ETC.

P. F. COLLIER & SON
Publishers   New York

ROUNDABOUT PAPERS.

CONTENTS.

ROUNDABOUT PAPERS.

iv CONTENTS.

THE SECOND FUNERAL OF NAPOLEON.

ROUNDABOUT PAPERS.

ON A LAZY IDLE BOY.

I HAD occasion to pass a week in the autumn in the little old town of Coire or Chur, in the Grisons, where lies buried that very ancient British king, saint, and martyr, Lucius,* who founded the Church of St. Peter, which stands opposite the house No. 65, Cornhill. Few people note the church now-a-days, and fewer ever heard of the saint. In the cathedral at Chur, his statue appears surrounded by other sainted persons of his family. With tight red breeches, a Roman habit, a curly brown beard, and a neat little gilt crown and sceptre, he stands, a very comely and cheerful image: and, from what I may call his peculiar position with regard to No. 65, Cornhill, I beheld this figure of St. Lucius with more interest than I should have bestowed upon personages who, hierarchically, are, I daresay, his superiors.

The pretty little city stands, so to speak, at the end of the world—of the world of to-day, the world of rapid motion, and rushing railways, and the commerce and intercourse of men. From the northern gate, the iron road stretches away to Zürich, to Basel, to Paris, to home. From the old southern barriers, before which a little river rushes, and around which stretch the crumbling bat-

---

*Stow quotes the inscription, still extant, "from the table fast chained in St. Peter's Church, Cornhill;" and says "he was after some chronicle buried at London, and after some chronicle buried at Glowcester"—but, oh! these incorrect chroniclers! when Alban Butler, in the "Lives of the Saints," v. xii., and Murray's "Handbook," and the Sacristan at Chur, all say Lucius was killed there, and I saw his tomb with my own eyes!

tlements of the ancient town, the road bears the slow diligence or lagging vetturino by the shallow Rhine, through
the awful gorges of the Via Mala, and presently over the
Splügen to the shores of Como.

I have seldom seen a place more quaint, pretty, calm,
and pastoral, than this remote little Chur. What need
have the inhabitants for walls and ramparts, except to
build summer-houses, to trail vines, and hang clothes to
dry? No enemies approach the great mouldering gates:
only at morn and even, the cows come lowing past them,
the village maidens chatter merrily round the fountains,
and babble like the ever-voluble stream that flows under
the old walls. The schoolboys, with book and satchel, in
smart uniforms, march up to the gymnasium, and return
thence at their stated time. There is one coffee-house
in the town, and I see one old gentleman goes to it.
There are shops with no customers seemingly, and the lazy
tradesmen look out of their little windows at the single
stranger sauntering by. There is a stall with baskets of
queer little black grapes and apples, and a pretty brisk
trade with half a dozen urchins standing round. But, beyond this, there is scarce any talk or movement in the
street. There's nobody at the book-shop. "If you will
have the goodness to come again in an hour," says the
banker, with his mouthful of dinner at one o'clock, "you
can have the money." There is nobody at the hotel, save
the good landlady, the kind waiters, the brisk young cook
who ministers to you. Nobody is in the Protestant church
—(oh! strange sight, the two confessions are here at peace!)
—nobody in the Catholic church: until the sacristan, from
his snug abode in the cathedral close, espies the traveller
eyeing the monsters and pillars before the old shark-toothed
arch of his cathedral, and comes out (with a view to remu-
neration possibly) and opens the gate, and shows you the
venerable church, and the queer old relics in the sacristy,
and the ancient vestments (a black velvet cope, amongst
other robes, as fresh as yesterday, and presented by that
notorious "pervert," Henry of Navarre and France), and

the statue of St. Lucius who built St. Peter's Church, opposite No. 65, Cornhill.

What a quiet, kind, quaint, pleasant, pretty old town! Has it been asleep these hundreds and hundreds of years, and is the brisk young Prince of the Sidereal Realms in his screaming car drawn by his snorting steel elephant coming to waken it? Time was when there must have been life and bustle and commerce here. Those vast, venerable walls were not made to keep out cows, but men-at-arms led by fierce captains, who prowled about the gates, and robbed the traders as they passed in and out with their bales, their goods, their pack-horses, and their wains. Is the place so dead that even the clergy of the different denominations can't quarrel? Why, seven or eight, or a dozen, or fifteen hundred years ago (they haven't the register, over the way, up to that remote period. I daresay it was burnt in the fire of London)—a dozen hundred years ago, when there was some life in the town, St. Lucius was stoned here on account of theological differences, after founding our church in Cornhill.

There was a sweet pretty river walk we used to take in the evening, and mark the mountains round glooming with a deeper purple; the shades creeping up the golden walls; the river brawling, the cattle calling, the maids and chatterboxes round the fountains babbling and bawling; and several times in the course of our sober walks, we overtook a lazy slouching boy, or hobbledehoy, with a rusty coat, and trowsers not too long, and big feet trailing lazily one after the other, and large lazy hands dawdling from out the tight sleeves, and in the lazy hands a little book, which my lad held up to his face, and which I daresay so charmed and ravished him, that he was blind to the beautiful sights around him; unmindful, I would venture to lay any wager, of the lessons he had to learn for to-morrow; forgetful of mother waiting supper, and father preparing a scolding;—absorbed utterly and entirely in his book.

What was it that so fascinated the young student, as he stood by the river shore? Not the *Pons Asinorum*. What

book so delighted him, and blinded him to all the rest of
the world, so that he did not care to see the apple-woman
with her fruit, or (more tempting still to sons of Eve) the
pretty girls with their apple cheeks, who laughed and prattled round the fountain? What was the book? Do you
suppose it was Livy, or the Greek grammar? No; it was
a Novel that you were reading, you lazy, not very clean,
good-for-nothing, sensible boy! It was D'Artagnan lock-
ing up General Monk in a box, or almost succeeding in
keeping Charles the First's head on. It was the prisoner
of the Château d'If cutting himself out of the sack fifty
feet under water (I mention the novels I like best myself—novels without love or talking, or any of that sort of
nonsense, but containing plenty of fighting, escaping, robbery, and rescuing)—cutting himself out of the sack, and
swimming to the island of Montecristo. O Dumas! O thou
brave, kind, gallant old Alexandre! I hereby offer thee
homage, and give thee thanks for many pleasant hours. I
have read thee (being sick in bed) for thirteen hours of a
happy day, and had the ladies of the house fighting for the
volumes. Be assured that lazy boy was reading Dumas
(or I will go so far as to let the reader here pronounce the
eulogium, or insert the name of his favourite author); and
as for the anger, or it may be, the reverberations of his
schoolmaster, or the remonstrances of his father, or the
tender pleadings of his mother that he should not let the
supper grow cold—I don't believe the scapegrace cared one
fig. No! Figs are sweet, but fictions are sweeter.

Have you ever seen a score of white-bearded, white-robed
warriors, or grave seniors of the city, seated at the gate of
Jaffa or Beyrout, and listening to the story-teller reciting
his marvels out of "Antar" or the "Arabian Nights?" I
was once present when a young gentleman at table put a
tart away from him, and said to his neighbour, the Younger
Son (with rather a fatuous air), "I never eat sweets."

"Not eat sweets! and do you know why?" says T.

"Because I am past that kind of thing," says the young
gentleman.

"Because you are a glutton and a sot!" cries the elder (and Juvenis winces a little). "All people who have natural, healthy appetites, love sweets; all children, all women, all Eastern people, whose tastes are not corrupted by gluttony and strong drink." And a plateful of raspberries and cream disappeared before the philosopher.

You take the allegory? Novels are sweets. All people with healthy literary appetites love them—almost all women;—a vast number of clever, hard-headed men. Why, one of the most learned physicians in England said to me only yesterday, "I have just read "So-and-So" for the second time" (naming one of Jones's exquisite fictions). Judges, bishops, chancellors, mathematicians, are notorious novel readers; as well as young boys and sweet girls, and their kind, tender mothers. Who has not read about Eldon, and how he cried over novels every night when he was not at whist?

As for that lazy naughty boy at Chur, I doubt whether *he* will like novels when he is thirty years of age. He is taking too great a glut of them now. He is eating jelly until he will be sick. He will know most plots by the time he is twenty, so that *he* will never be surprised when the Stranger turns out to be the rightful earl,—when the old waterman, throwing off his beggarly gabardine, shows his stars and the collars of his various orders, and clasping Antonia to his bosom, proves himself to be the prince, her long-lost father. He will recognize the novelist's same characters, though they appear in red-heeled pumps and *ailes-de-pigeon*, or the garb of the nineteenth century. He will get weary of sweets, as boys of private schools grow (or used to grow, for I have done growing some little time myself, and the practice may have ended too)—as private schoolboys used to grow tired of the pudding before their mutton at dinner.

And pray what is the moral of this apologue? The moral I take to be this: the appetite for novels extending to the end of the world; far away in the frozen deep, the sailors reading them to one another during the endless night;—far away under the Syrian stars, the solemn sheikhs and elders hearkening to the poet as he recites his tales; far away in the Indian camps, where the soldiers listen to ——'s tales, or ——'s, after the hot day's march; far away in little Chur yonder, where the lazy boy pores over the fond volume, and drinks it in with all his eyes;—the demand being what we know it is, the merchant must supply it, as he will supply saddles and pale ale for Bombay or Calcutta.

But as surely as the cadet drinks too much pale ale, it will disagree with him; and so surely, dear youth, will too much novels cloy on thee. I wonder, do novel writers themselves read many novels? If you go into Gunter's, you don't see those charming young ladies (to whom I present my most respectful compliments) eating tarts and ices, but at the proper even-tide they have good plain wholesome tea and bread-and-butter. Can anybody tell me does the author of the "Tale of Two Cities" read novels? does the author of the "Tower of London" devour romances? does the dashing "Harry Lorrequer" delight in "Plain or Ringlets" or "Sponge's Sporting Tour?" Does the veteran, from whose flowing pen we had the books which delighted our young days, "Darnley," and "Richelieu," and "Delorme,"* relish the works of Alexandre the Great, and thrill over the "Three Musqueteers?" Does the accomplished author of the "Caxtons" read the other tales in "Blackwood?" (For example, that ghost-story printed last August, and which for my part, though I read it in the public reading-room at the Pavilion Hotel at Folkestone, I protest frightened me so that I scarce dared look over my shoulder.) Does "Uncle Tom" admire "Adam Bede;" and does the author of the "Vicar of Wrexhill" laugh over the "Warden" and the "Three Clerks?" Dear youth of ingenuous countenance and ingenuous pudor! I make no doubt that the eminent parties above named all partake of

---

* By the way, what a strange fate is that which befell the veteran novelist! He was appointed her Majesty's Consul-General in Venice, the only city in Europe where the famous "Two Cavaliers" cannot by any possibility be seen riding together.

novels in moderation—eat jellies—but mainly nourish themselves upon wholesome roast and boiled.

Here, dear youth aforesaid! our *Cornhill Magazine* owners strive to provide thee with facts as well as fiction; and though it does not become them to brag of their Ordinary, at least they invite thee to a table where thou shalt sit in good company. That story of the "Fox" was written by one of the gallant seamen who sought for poor Franklin under the awful Arctic Night: that account of China is told by the man of all the empire most likely to know of what he speaks: those pages regarding Volunteers come from an honoured hand that has borne the sword in a hundred famous fields, and pointed the British guns in the greatest siege in the world.

Shall we point out others? We are fellow-travellers, and shall make acquaintance as the voyage proceeds. In the Atlantic steamers, on the first day out (and on high and holidays subsequently), the jellies set down on table are richly ornamented; *medioque in fonte leporum* rise the American and British flags nobly emblazoned in tin. As the passengers remark this pleasing phenomenon, the Captain no doubt improves the occasion by expressing a hope, to his right and left, that the flag of Mr. Bull and his younger Brother may always float side by side in friendly emulation. Novels having been previously compared to jellies—here are two (one perhaps not entirely saccharine, and flavoured with an *amari aliquid* very distasteful to some palates)—two novels under two flags, the one that ancient ensign which has hung before the well-known booth of "Vanity Fair;" the other that fresh and handsome standard which has lately been hoisted on "Barchester Towers." Pray, sir, or madam, to which dish will you be helped?

So have I seen my friends Captain Lang and Captain Comstock press their guests to partake of the fare on that memorable "First day out," when there is no man, I think, who sits down but asks a blessing on his voyage, and the good ship dips over the bar, and bounds away into the blue water.

ON TWO CHILDREN IN BLACK.

MONTAIGNE and Howel's Letters are my bedside books. If I wake at night, I have one or other of them to prattle me to sleep again. They talk about themselves forever, and don't weary me. I like to hear them tell their old stories over and over again. I read them in the dozy hours, and only half remember them. I am informed that both of them tell coarse stories. I don't heed them. It was the custom of their time, as it is of Highlanders and Hottentots, to dispense with a part of dress which we all wear in cities. But people can't afford to be shocked either at Cape Town or at Inverness every time they meet an individual who wears his national airy raiment. I never knew the "Arabian Nights" was an improper book until I happened once to read it in a "family edition." Well, *qui s'excuse*. * * * Who, pray, has accused me as yet? Here am I smothering dear good old Mrs. Grundy's objections, before she has opened her mouth. I love, I say, and scarce ever tire of hearing, the artless prattle of those two dear old friends, the Perigourdin gentleman and the priggish little Clerk of King Charles's Council. Their egotism in nowise disgusts me. I hope I shall always like to hear men, in reason, talk about themselves. What subject does a man know better? If I stamp on a friend's corn, his outcry is genuine—he confounds my clumsiness in the accents of truth. He is speaking about himself, and expressing his emotion of grief or pain in a manner perfectly authentic and veracious. I have a story of my own, of a wrong done to me by somebody, as far back as the year 1838: whenever I think of it, and have had a couple glasses of wine, I *cannot* help telling it. The toe is stamped upon: the pain is just as keen as ever: I cry out, and perhaps utter imprecatory language. I told the story only last Wednesday at dinner:—

"Mr. Roundabout," says a lady sitting by me, "how comes it that in your books there is a certain class (it may be of men, or it may be of women, but that is not the question in point)—how comes it, dear sir, there is a certain class of persons whom you always attack in your writings, and savagely rush at, goad, poke, toss up in the air, kick, and trample on?"

I couldn't help myself. I knew I ought not to do it. I told her the whole story, between the entrées and the roast. The wound began to bleed again. The horrid pang was there, as keen and as fresh as ever. If I live half as long as Tithonus, that crack across my heart can never be cured. There are wrongs and griefs that *can't* be mended. It is all very well of you, my dear Mrs. G., to say that this spirit is unchristian, and that we ought to forgive and forget, and so forth. How can I forget at will? How forgive? I can forgive the occasional waiter, who broke my beautiful old decanter at that very dinner. I am not going to do him any injury. But all the powers on earth can't make that claret-jug whole.

So, you see, I told the lady the inevitable story. I was egotistical. I was selfish, no doubt; but I was natural, and was telling the truth. You say you are angry with a man for talking about himself. It is because you yourself are selfish, that that other person's Self does not interest you. Be interested by other people and with their affairs. Let them prattle and talk to you, as I do my dear old egotists just mentioned. When you have had enough of them, and sudden hazes come over your eyes, lay down the volume; pop out the candle, and *dormez bien*. I should like to write a nightcap book—a book that you can muse over, that you can smile over, that you can yawn over—a book of which you can say, "Well, this man is so and so and so and so; but he has a friendly heart (although some wiseacres have painted him as black as Bogey), and you may trust what he says." I should like to touch you sometimes with a reminiscence that shall waken your sympathy, and make you say, *Io anchè* have so thought, felt, smiled, suf-

fered.   Now, how is this to be done except by egotism?
Linea recta brevissima.   That right line "I" is the very
shortest, simplest, straightforwardest means of communication between us, and stands for what it is worth and no
more.   Sometimes authors say, "The present writer has
often remarked;" or, "The undersigned has observed;"
or, "Mr. Roundabout presents his compliments to the gentle reader, and begs to state," etc.: but "I" is better and
straighter than all these grimaces of modesty: and although
these are Roundabout Papers, and may wander who knows
whither, I shall ask leave to maintain the upright and simple perpendicular.   When this bundle of egotisms is bound
up together, as they may be one day, if no accident prevents this tongue from wagging, or this ink from running,
they will bore you very likely; so it would to read through
Howel's Letters from beginning to end, or to eat up the
whole of a ham: but a slice on occasion may have a relish:
a dip into the volume at random and so on for a page or
two: and now and then a smile; and presently a gape; and
the book drops out of your hand; and so, *bon soir*, and
pleasant dreams to you.   I have frequently seen men at
clubs asleep over their humble servant's works, and am
always pleased.   Even at a lecture I don't mind, if they
don't snore.   Only the other day when my friend A. said,
"You've left off that Roundabout business, I see; very glad
you have," I joined in the general roar of laughter at the
table.   I don't care a fig whether Archilochus likes the
papers or no.   You don't like partridge, Archilochus, or
porridge, or what not?   Try some other dish.   I am not
going to force mine down your throat, or quarrel with you
if you refuse it.   Once in America a clever and candid
woman said to me, at the close of a dinner, during which
I had been sitting beside her, "Mr. Roundabout, I was told
I should not like you; and I don't."   "Well, ma'am,"
says I, in a tone of the most unfeigned simplicity, "I don't
care."   And we became good friends immediately, and
esteemed each other ever after.

So, my dear Archilochus, if you come upon this paper,

and say, "Fudge!" and pass on to another, I for one shall not be in the least mortified. If you say, "What does he mean by calling this paper 'On Two Children in Black,' when there's nothing about people in black at all, unless the ladies he met (and evidently bored) at dinner, were black women? What is all this egotistical pother? A plague on his I's!" My dear fellow, if you read Montaigne's "Essays," you must own that he might call almost any one by the name of any other, and that an essay on the Moon or an essay on Green Cheese would be as appropriate a title as one of his on Coaches, on the Art of Discoursing, or Experience, or what you will. Besides, if I *have* a subject (and I have), I claim to approach it in a roundabout manner.

You remember Balzac's tale of the "Peau de Chagrin," and how every time the possessor used it for the accomplishment of some wish the fairy *peau* shrank a little and the owner's life correspondingly shortened? I have such a desire to be well with my public that I am actually giving up my favourite story. I am killing my goose, I know I am. I can't tell my story of the children in black after this; after printing it, and sending it through the country. When they are gone to the printer's these little things become public property. I take their hands. I bless them. I say, "Good-by, my little dears." I am quite sorry to part with them : but the fact is, I have told all my friends about them already, and don't dare to take them about with me any more.

Now every word is true of this little anecdote, and I submit that there lies in it a most curious and exciting little mystery. I am like a man who gives you the last bottle of his '25 claret. It is the pride of his cellar; he knows it, and he has a right to praise it. He takes up the bottle, fashioned so slenderly—takes it up tenderly, cants it with care, places it before his friends, declares how good it is, with honest pride, and wishes he had a hundred dozen bottles more of the same wine in his cellar. *Si quid novisti,* &c., I shall be very glad to hear from you. I protest and vow I am giving you the best I have.

Well, who those little boys in black were, I shall never probably know to my dying day. They were very pretty little men, with pale faces, and large, melancholy eyes; and they had beautiful little hands, and little boots, and the finest little shirts, and black paletots lined with the richest silk; and they had picture-books in several languages, English, and French, and German, I remember. Two more aristocratic-looking little men I never set eyes on. They were travelling with a very handsome, pale lady in mourning, and a maid-servant dressed in black, too; and on the lady's face there was the deepest grief. The little boys clambered and played about the carriage, and she sate watching. It was a railway-carriage from Frankfort to Heidelberg.

I saw at once that she was the mother of those children, and going to part from them. Perhaps I have tried parting with my own, and not found the business very pleasant. Perhaps I recollect driving down (with a certain trunk and carpet-bag on the box) with my own mother to the end of the avenue, where we waited—only a few minutes—until the whirring wheels of that "Defiance" coach were heard rolling towards us as certain as death. Twang goes the horn; up goes the trunk; down come the steps. Bah! I see the autumn evening: I hear the wheels now: I smart the cruel smart again: and, boy or man, have never been able to bear the sight of people parting from their children.

I thought these little men might be going to school for the first time in their lives; and mamma might be taking them to the doctor, and would leave them with many fond charges, and little wistful secrets of love, bidding the elder to protect his younger brother, and the younger to be gentle, and to remember to pray to God always for his mother, who would pray for her boy too. Our party made friends with these young ones during the little journey; but the poor lady was too sad to talk except to the boys now and again, and sate in her corner, pale, and silently looking at them.

The next day, we saw the lady and her maid driving in the direction of the railway station, *without the boys.* The parting had taken place, then. That night they would sleep among strangers. The little beds at home were vacant, and poor mother might go and look at them. Well, tears flow, and friends part, and mothers pray every night all over the world. I daresay we went to see Heidelberg Castle, and admired the vast shattered walls, and quaint gables; and the Neckar running its bright course through that charming scene of peace and beauty; and ate our dinner, and drank our wine with relish. The poor mother would eat but little *Abendessen* that night; and, as for the children—that first night at school—hard bed, hard words, strange boys bullying and laughing, and jarring you with their hateful merriment—as for the first night at a strange school, we most of us remember what *that* is. And the first is not the *worst*, my boys, there's the rub. But each man has his share of troubles, and, I suppose, you must have yours.

From Heidelberg we went to Baden-Baden: and I daresay, saw Madame de Schlangenbad and Madame de la Cruche-cassée, and Count Punter, and honest Captain Blackball. And whom should we see in the evening, but our two little boys, walking on each side of a fierce, yellow-faced, bearded man! We wanted to renew our acquaintance with them, and they were coming forward quite pleased to greet us. But the father pulled back one of the little men by his paletot, gave a grim scowl, and walked away. I can see the children now looking rather frightened away from us and up into the father's face, or the cruel uncle's—which was he? I think he was the father. So this was the end of them. Not school as I at first had imagined. The mother was gone, who had given them the heaps of pretty books, and the pretty studs in the shirts, and the pretty silken clothes, and the tender—tender cares; and they were handed to this scowling practitioner of Trente et Quarante. Ah! this is worse than school. Poor little men! poor mother sitting by the vacant little beds! We saw the children once or twice after, always in Scowler's company; but we did not dare to give each other any marks of recognition.

From Baden we went to Basle, and thence to Lucerne, and so over the St. Gothard into Italy. From Milan we went to Venice; and now comes the singular part of my story. In Venice there is a little court of which I forget the name: but in it is an apothecary's shop, whither I went to buy some remedy for the bites of certain animals which abound in Venice. Crawling animals, skipping animals, and humming, flying animals; all three will have at you at once; and one night nearly drove me into a strait-waistcoat. Well, as I was coming out of the apothecary's with the bottle of spirits of hartshorn in my hand (it really does do the bites a great deal of good), whom should I light upon but one of my little Heidelberg-Baden boys!

I have said how handsomely they were dressed as long as they were with their mother. When I saw the boy at Venice, who perfectly recognized me, his only garb was a wretched yellow cotton gown. His little feet, on which I had admired the little shiny boots, were *without shoe or stocking*. He looked at me, ran to an old hag of a woman, who seized his hand; and with her he disappeared down one of the thronged lanes of the city.

From Venice we went to Trieste (the Vienna railway at that time was only opened as far as Laybach, and the magnificent Semmering Pass was not quite completed). At a station, between Laybach and Graetz, one of my companions alighted for refreshment, and came back to the carriage saying:—

"There's that horrible man from Baden, with the two little boys."

Of course, we had talked about the appearance of the little boy at Venice, and his strange altered garb. My companion said they were pale, wretched-looking, and *dressed quite shabbily*.

I got out at several stations, and looked at all the carriages. I could not see my little men. From that day to this I have never set eyes on them. That is all my story. Who were they? What could they be? How can you explain that mystery of the mother giving them up; of the remarkable splendour and elegance of their appearance while under her care; of their bare-footed squalor in Venice a month afterwards; of their shabby habiliments at Laybach? Had the father gambled away his money and sold their clothes? How came they to have passed out of the hands of a refined lady (as she evidently was, with whom I first saw them) into the charge of quite a common woman like her with whom I saw one of the boys at Venice? Here is but one chapter of the story. Can any man write the next, or that preceding the strange one on which I happened to light? Who knows? the mystery may have some quite simple solution. I saw two children, attired like little princes, taken from their mother and consigned to other care; and a fortnight afterwards, one of them barefooted and like a beggar. Who will read this riddle of The Two Children in Black?

ON RIBBONS.

THE uncle of the present Sir Louis N. Bonaparte, K.G.,
&c., inaugurated his reign as Emperor over the neighbouring nation by establishing an Order, to which all citizens
of his country, military, naval, and civil—all men most
distinguished in science, letters, arts, and commerce—were
admitted. The emblem of the Order was but a piece of
ribbon, more or less long or broad, with a toy at the end
of it. The Bourbons had toys and ribbons of their own,
blue, black, and all-coloured; and on their return to do-
minion such good old Tories would naturally have preferred
to restore their good old Orders of Saint Louis, Saint Es-
prit, and Saint Michel; but France had taken the ribbon
of the Legion of Honour so to her heart that no Bourbon
sovereign dared to pluck it thence.

In England, until very late days, we have been accustomed rather to pooh-pooh national Orders, to vote ribbons
and crosses tinsel gewgaws, foolish foreign ornaments, and
so forth. It is known how the Great Duke (the breast of
whose own coat was plastered with some half-hundred
decorations) was averse to the wearing of ribbons, medals,
clasps, and the like, by his army. We have all of us read
how uncommonly distinguished Lord Castlereagh looked at
Vienna, where he was the only gentleman present without
any decoration whatever. And the Great Duke's theory
was, that clasps and ribbons, stars and garters, were good
and proper ornaments for himself, for the chief officers of
his distinguished army, and for gentlemen of high birth,
who might naturally claim to wear a band of garter blue
across their waistcoats; but that for common people your
plain coat, without stars and ribbons, was the most sensible
wear.

And no doubt you and I are as happy, as free, as comfortable; we can walk and dine as well; we can keep the

winter's cold out as well, without a star on our coats, as
without a feather in our hats.   How often we have laughed
at the absurd mania of the Americans for dubbing their
senators, members of Congress, and States' representatives,
Honourable!   We have a right to call *our* privy councillors
Right Honourable, our lords' sons Honourable, and so
forth; but for a nation as numerous, well educated, strong,
rich, civilized, free as our own, to dare to give its distinguished citizens titles of honour—monstrous assumption of
low-bred arrogance and *parvenue* vanity!   Our titles are
respectable, but theirs absurd.   Mr. Jones, of London, a
chancellor's son, and a tailor's grandson, is justly honourable, and entitled to be Lord Jones at his noble father's
decease: but Mr. Brown, the senator from New York, is a
silly upstart for tacking Honourable to his name, and our
sturdy British good sense laughs at him.   Who has not
laughed (I have myself) at Honourable Nahum Dodge,
Honourable Zeno Scudder, Honourable Hiram Boake, and
the rest?   A score of such queer names and titles I have
smiled at in America.   And, *mutato nomine?*   I meet a
born idiot, who is a peer and born legislator.   This drivelling noodle and his descendants through life are your natural superiors and mine—your and my children's superiors.
I read of an alderman kneeling and knighted at court: I
see a gold-stick waddling backwards before majesty in a
procession, and if we laugh, don't you suppose the Americans laugh too?

Yes, stars, garters, orders, knighthoods, and the like,
are folly.   Yes, Bobus, citizen and soap-boiler, is a good
man, and no one laughs at him or good Mrs. Bobus, as they
have their dinner at one o'clock.   But who will not jeer at
Sir Thomas on a melting day, and Lady Bobus, at Margate, eating shrimps in a donkey-chaise?   Yes, knighthood
is absurd: and chivalry an idiotic superstition: and Sir
Walter Manny was a zany: and Nelson, with his flaming
stars and cordons, splendent upon a day of battle, was a
madman: and Murat, with his crosses and orders, at the
head of his squadrons charging victorious, was only a crazy

mountebank, who had been a tavern-waiter, and was puffed up with absurd vanity about his dress and legs. And the men of the French line at Fontenoy, who told Messieurs de la Garde to fire first, were smirking French dancing-masters; and the Black Prince, waiting upon his royal prisoner, was acting an inane masquerade; and Chivalry is naught; and Honour is humbug; and Gentlemanhood is an extinct folly; and Ambition is madness; and desire of distinction is criminal vanity; and glory is bosh; and fair fame is idleness; and nothing is true but two and two; and the colour of all the world is drab; and all men are equal; and one man is as tall as another; and one man is as good as another—and a great dale betther, as the Irish philosopher said.

Is this so? Titles and badges of honour are vanity; and in the American Revolution you have his Excellency General Washington sending back, and with proper spirit sending back, a letter in which he is not addressed as Excellency and General. Titles are abolished; and the American Republic swarms with men claiming and bearing them. You have the French soldier cheered and happy in his dying agony, and kissing with frantic joy the chief's hand who lays the little cross on the bleeding bosom. At home you have the dukes and earls jobbing and intriguing for the Garter; the military knights grumbling at the civil knights of the Bath; the little ribbon eager for the collar; the soldiers and seamen from India and the Crimea marching in procession before the queen, and receiving from her hands the cross bearing her royal name. And, remember, there are not only the cross wearers, but all the fathers and friends; all the women who have prayed for their absent heroes; Harry's wife, and Tom's mother, and Jack's daughter, and Frank's sweetheart, each of whom wears in her heart of hearts afterwards the badge which son, father, lover, has won by his merit; each of whom is made happy and proud, and is bound to the country by that little bit of ribbon.

I have heard, in a lecture about George the Third, that,

at his accession, the king had a mind to establish an order
for literary men. It was to have been called the Order of
Minerva—I suppose with an Owl for a badge. The knights
were to have worn a star of sixteen points, and a yellow
ribbon; and good old Samuel Johnson was talked of as
President, or Grand Cross, or Grand Owl, of the society.
Now about such an order as this there certainly may be
doubts. Consider the claimants, the difficulty of settling
their claims, the rows and squabbles amongst the candi-
dates, and the subsequent decision of posterity! Dr. Beat-
tie would have ranked as first poet, and twenty years after
the sublime Mr. Hayley would, no doubt, have claimed the
Grand Cross. Mr. Gibbon would not have been eligible on
account of his dangerous freethinking opinions; and her
sex, as well as her republican sentiments, might have interfered with the knighthood of the immortal Mrs. Catha-
rine Macaulay. How Goldsmith would have paraded the
ribbon at Madame Cornelys's, or the Academy dinner!
How Peter Pindar would have railed at it! Fifty years
later, the noble Scott would have worn the Grand Cross
and deserved it; but Gifford would have had it; and Byron, and Shelley, and Hazlitt, and Hunt would have been
without it; and had Keats been proposed as officer, how
the Tory prints would have yelled with rage and scorn!
Had the star of Minerva lasted to our present time——but
I pause, not because the idea is dazzling, but too awful.
Fancy the claimants, and the row about their precedence!
Which philosopher shall have the grand cordon?—which
the collar?—which the little scrap no bigger than a butter-
cup? Of the historians—A, say,—and C, and F, and G,
and S, and T,—which shall be Companion and which Grand
Owl? Of the poets, who wears, or claims, the largest and
brightest star? Of the novelists, there is A, and B and C
D; and E (star of first magnitude, newly discovered), and
F (a magazine of it), and fair G, and H, and I, and brave
old J, and charming K, and L, and M, and N, and O (fair
twinklers), and I am puzzled between three P's—Peacock,
Miss Pardoe, and Paul Pry—and Queechy, and R, and S,

and T, *mère et fils*, and very likely U, O gentle reader, for who has not written his novel now-a-days?—who has not a claim to the star and straw-coloured ribbon?—and who shall have the biggest and largest? Fancy the struggle! Fancy the squabble! Fancy the distribution of prizes!

Who shall decide on them? Shall it be the sovereign? shall it be the minister for the time being? and has Lord Palmerston made a deep study of novels? In this matter the late ministry, to be sure, was better qualified; but even then, grumblers who had not got their canary cordons, would have hinted at professional jealousies entering the cabinet; and, the ribbons being awarded, Jack would have scowled at his because Dick had a broader one; Ned been indignant because Bob's was as large: Tom would have thrust his into the drawer, and scorned to wear it at all. No—no: the so-called literary world was well rid of Minerva and her yellow ribbon. The great poets would have been indifferent, the little poets jealous, the funny men furious, the philosophers satirical, the historians supercilious, and, finally, the jobs without end. Say, ingenuity and cleverness are to be rewarded by State tokens and prizes—and take for granted the Order of Minerva is established—who shall have it? A great philosopher? no doubt, we cordially salute him G.C.M. A great historian? G.C.M. of course. A great engineer? G.C.M. A great poet? received with acclamation G.C.M. A great painter? oh! certainly, G.C.M. If a great painter, why not a great novelist? Well, pass, great novelist, G.C.M. But if a poetic, a pictorial, a story-telling or music-composing artist, why not a singing artist? Why not a basso-profondo? Why not a primo tenore? And if a singer, why should not a ballet-dancer come bounding on the stage with his cordon, and cut capers to the music of a row of decorated fiddlers? A chemist puts in his claim for having invented a new colour; an apothecary for a new pill; the cook for a new sauce; the tailor for a new cut of trowsers. We have brought the star of Minerva down from the breast to the pantaloons. Stars and garters! can we go any farther; or shall we give the shoemaker the yellow ribbon of the order for his shoetie?

When I began this present Roundabout excursion, I think I had not quite made up my mind whether we would have an Order of all the Talents or not: perhaps I rather had a hankering for a rich ribbon and gorgeous star, in which my family might like to see me at parties in my best waistcoat. But then the door opens, and there come in, and by the same right too, Sir Alexis Soyer! Sir Alessandro Tamburini! Sir Agostino Velluti! Sir Antonio Paganini (violinist)! Sir Sandy McGuffog (piper to the most noble the Marquis of Farintosh)! Sir Alcide Flicflac (premier danseur of H.M. Theatre)! Sir Harley Quin and Sir Joseph Grimaldi (from Covent Garden)! They have all the yellow ribbon. They are all honourable, and clever, and distinguished artists. Let us elbow through the rooms, make a bow to the lady of the house, give a nod to Sir George Thrum, who is leading the orchestra, and go and get some champagne and seltzer-water from Sir Richard Gunter, who is presiding at the buffet. A national decoration might be well and good: a token awarded by the country to all its *bene-merentibus :* but most gentlemen with Minerva stars would, I think, be inclined to wear very wide breast-collars to their coats. Suppose yourself, brother penman, decorated with this ribbon, and looking in the glass, would you not laugh? Would not wife and daughters laugh at that canary-coloured emblem?

But suppose a man, old or young, of figure ever so stout, thin, stumpy, homely, indulging in looking-glass reflections with that hideous ribbon and cross called V. C. on his coat, would he not be proud? and his family, would not they be prouder? For your nobleman there is the famous old blue garter and star, and welcome. If I were a marquis—if I had thirty—forty thousand a year (settle the sum, my dear Alnaschar, according to your liking), I should consider myself entitled to my seat in parliament and to my garter. The garter belongs to the Ornamental Classes. Have you seen the new magnificent *Pavo Spicifer* at the Zoological

Gardens, and do you grudge him his jewelled coronet and
the azure splendour of his waistcoat? I like my lord mayor
to have a gilt coach; my magnificent monarch to be surrounded by magnificent nobles : I huzzay respectfully when
they pass in procession. It is good for Mr. Briefless (50,
Pump Court, fourth floor,) that there should be a lord
chancellor, with a gold robe and fifteen thousand a year.
It is good for a poor curate that there should be splendid
bishops at Fulham and Lambeth : their lordships were poor
curates once, and have won, so to speak, their ribbon. Is
a man who puts into a lottery to be sulky because he does
not win the twenty thousand pounds prize? Am I to fall
into a rage, and bully my family when I come home, after
going to see Chatsworth or Windsor, because we have only
two little drawing-rooms? Welcome to your garter, my
lord, and shame upon him *qui mal y pense.*

So I arrive in my roundabout way near the point towards
which I have been trotting ever since we set out.

In a voyage to America, some nine years since, on the
seventh or eighth day out from Liverpool, Captain L——
came to dinner at eight bells as usual, talked a little to the
persons right and left of him, and helped the soup with his
accustomed politeness. Then he went on deck, and was
back in a minute, and operated on the fish, looking rather
grave the while.

Then he went on deck again; and this time was absent,
it may be, three or five minutes, during which the fish disappeared, and the *entrées* arrived, and the roast beef. Say
ten minutes passed—I can't tell after nine years.

Then L—— came down with a pleased and happy countenance this time, and began carving the sirloin: "We
have seen the light," he said. "Madam, may I help you
to a little gravy, or a little horse-radish?" or what not?

I forget the name of the light; nor does it matter. It
was a point of Newfoundland for which he was on the look-
out, and so well did the *Canada* know where she was, that,
between soup and beef, the captain had sighted the headland by which his course was lying.

And so through storm and darkness, through fog and midnight, the ship had pursued her steady way over the pathless ocean and roaring seas, so surely that the officers who sailed her knew her place within a minute or two, and guided us with a wonderful providence safe on our way. Since the noble Cunard Company has run its ships, but one accident, and that through the error of a pilot, has happened on the line.

By this little incident (hourly of course repeated, and trivial to all sea-going people) I own I was immensely moved, and never can think of it but with a heart full of thanks and awe. We trust our lives to these seamen, and how nobly they fulfil their trust! They are, under heaven, as a providence for us. Whilst we sleep, their untiring watchfulness keeps guard over us. All night through that bell sounds at its season, and tells how our sentinels defend us. It rang when the *Amazon* was on fire, and chimed its heroic signal of duty, and courage, and honour. Think of the dangers these seamen undergo for us: the hourly peril and watch; the familiar storm; the dreadful iceberg; the long winter nights when the decks are as glass, and the sailor has to climb through icicles to bend the stiff sail on the yard. Think of their courage and their kindnesses in cold, in tempest, in hunger, in wreck! "The women and children to the boats," says the captain of the *Birkenhead*, and, with the troops formed on the deck, and the crew obedient to the word of glorious command, the immortal ship goes down. Read the story of the *Sarah Sands*:—

SARAH SANDS

"The screw steam-ship *Sarah Sands*, 1,330 registered tons, was chartered by the East India Company in the autumn of 1858, for the conveyance of troops to India. She was commanded by John Squire Castle. She took out a part of the 54th Regiment, upwards of 350 persons, besides the wives and children of some of the men, and the families of some of the officers. All went well till the 11th

November, when the ship had reached lat. 14 S., long. 56 E., upwards of 400 miles from the Mauritius.

"Between three and four P.M. on that day a very strong smell of fire was perceived arising from the after-deck, and upon going below into the hold, Captain Castle found it to be on fire, and immense volumes of smoke arising from it. Endeavours were made to reach the seat of the fire, but in vain; the smoke and heat were too much for the men. There was, however, no confusion. Every order was obeyed with the same coolness and courage with which it was given. The engine was immediately stopped. All sail was taken in, and the ship brought to the wind, so as to drive the smoke and fire, which was in the after-part of the ship, astern. Others were, at the same time, getting fire-hoses fitted and passed to the scene of the fire. The fire, however, continued to increase, and attention was directed to the ammunition contained in the powder magazines, which were situated one on each side the ship immediately above the fire. The starboard magazine was soon cleared. But by this time the whole of the after-part of the ship was so much enveloped in smoke that it was scarcely possible to stand, and great fears were entertained on account of the port magazine. Volunteers were called for, and came immediately, and, under the guidance of Lieutenant Hughes, attempted to clear the port magazine, which they succeeded in doing, with the exception, as was supposed, of one or two barrels. It was most dangerous work. The men became overpowered with the smoke and heat, and fell; and several, while thus engaged, were dragged up by ropes, senseless.

"The flames soon burst up through the deck, and running rapidly along the various cabins, set the greater part on fire.

"In the meantime Captain Castle took steps for lowering the boats. There was a heavy gale at the time, but they were launched without the least accident. The soldiers were mustered on deck;—there was no rush to the boats; —and the men obeyed the word of command as if on parade. The men were informed that Captain Castle did not despair of saving the ship, but that they must be prepared to leave her if necessary. The women and children were lowered into the port lifeboat, under the charge of Mr. Very, third officer, who had orders to keep clear of the ship until recalled.

"Captain Castle then commenced constructing rafts of spare spars. In a short time, three were put together, which would have been capable of saving a great number of those on board. Two were launched overboard, and safely moored alongside, and then a third was left across the deck forward, ready to be launched.

"In the meantime the fire had made great progress. The whole of the cabins were one body of fire, and at about 8.30 P.M. flames burst through the upper deck, and shortly after the mizen rigging caught fire. Fears were entertained of the ship paying off, in which case the flames would have been swept forwards by the wind; but fortunately the after-braces were burnt through, and the main-yard swung round, which kept the ship's head to wind. About nine P.M., a fearful explosion took place in the port magazine, arising, no doubt, from the one or two barrels of powder which it had been impossible to remove. By this time the ship was one body of flame, from the stern to the main rigging, and thinking it scarcely possible to save her, Captain Castle called Major Brett (then in command of the troops, for the colonel was in one of the boats) forward, and, telling him that he feared the ship was lost, requested him to endeavour to keep order amongst the troops till the last, but, at the same time, to use every exertion to check the fire. Providentially, the iron bulkhead in the after-part of the ship withstood the action of the flames, and here all efforts were concentrated to keep it cool.

"No person," says the captain, "can describe the manner in which the men worked to keep the fire back; one party were below, keeping the bulkhead cool, and when several were dragged up senseless, fresh volunteers took their places, who were, however, soon in the same state. At about ten P.M., the maintopsail-yard took fire. Mr.

Welch, one quartermaster, and four or five soldiers, went
aloft with wet blankets, and succeeded in extinguishing it,
but not until the yard and mast were nearly burnt through.
The work of fighting the fire below continued for hours,
and about midnight it appeared that some impression was
made; and after that, the men drove it back, inch by inch,
until daylight, when they had completely got it under.
The ship was now in a frightful plight.   The after-part
was literally burnt out—merely the shell remaining—the
port quarter blown out by the explosion: fifteen feet of
water in the hold."   .

"The gale still prevailed, and the ship was rolling and
pitching in a heavy sea, and taking in large quantities of
water abaft: the tanks, too, were rolling from side to side
in the hold.

"As soon as the smoke was partially cleared away, Captain Castle got spare sails and blankets aft to stop the leak,
passing two hawsers round the stern, and setting them up.
The troops were employed baling and pumping.   This continued during the whole morning.

"In the course of the day the ladies joined the ship.   The
boats were ordered alongside, but they found the sea too
heavy to remain there.   The gig had been abandoned during the night, and the crew, under Mr. Wood, fourth
officer, had got into another of the boats.   The troops were
employed the remainder of the day baling and pumping,
and the crew securing the stern.   All hands were employed during the following night baling and pumping, the
boats being moored alongside, where they received some
damage.   At daylight, on the 13th, the crew were employed
hoisting the boats, the troops were working manfully
baling and pumping.   Latitude at noon, 13 deg. 12 min.
south.   At five P.M., the foresail and foretopsail were set,
the rafts were cut away, and the ship bore for the Mauritius.   On Thursday, the 19th, she sighted the island of
Rodrigues, and arrived at Mauritius on Monday the 23rd."

The Nile and Trafalgar are not more glorious to our

country, are not greater victories than these won by our merchant seamen. And if you look in the captains' reports of any maritime register, you will see similar acts recorded every day. I have such a volume for last year, now lying before me. In the second number, as I open it at hazard, Captain Roberts, master of the ship *Empire*, from Shields to London, reports how on the 14th ult. (the 14th December, 1859), he, "being off Whitby, discovered the ship to be on fire between the main hold and boilers: got the hose from the engine laid on, and succeeded in subduing the fire; but only apparently; for at seven the next morning, the *Dudgeon* bearing S.S.E. seven miles' distance, the fire again broke out, causing the ship to be enveloped in flames on both sides of midships: got the hose again into play and all hands to work with buckets to combat with the fire. Did not succeed in stopping it till four P.M., to effect which, were obliged to cut away the deck and top sides, and throw overboard part of the cargo. The vessel was very much damaged and leaky: determined to make for the Humber. Ship was run on shore, on the mud, near Grimsby harbour, with five feet of water in her hold. The donkey-engine broke down. The water increased so fast as to put out the furnace fires and render the ship almost unmanageable. On the tide flowing, a tug towed the ship off the mud, and got her into Grimsby to repair."

On the 2nd of November, Captain Strickland, of the *Purchase* brigantine, from Liverpool to Yarmouth, U. S., "encountered heavy gales from W. N. W to W. S. W., in lat. 43° N., long. 34° W., in which we lost jib, foretopmast, staysail, topsail, and carried away the foretopmast stays, bobstays and bowsprit, headsails, cut-water and stern, also started the wood ends, which caused the vessel to leak. Put her before the wind and sea, and hove about twenty-five tons of cargo overboard to lighten the ship forward. Slung myself in a bowline, and by means of thrusting 2½-inch rope in the opening, contrived to stop a great portion of the leak.

"*December 16th.*—The crew, continuing night and day

at the pumps, could not keep the ship free; deemed it prudent for the benefit of those concerned to bear up for the nearest port. On arriving in lat. 48° 45′ N., long. 23° W., observed a vessel with a signal of distress flying. Made towards her, when she proved to be the barque *Carleton*, water-logged. The captain and crew asked to be taken off. Hove to, and received them on board, consisting of thirteen men : and their ship was abandoned. We then proceeded on our course, the crew of the abandoned vessel assisting all they could to keep my ship afloat. We arrived at Cork harbour on the 27th ult."

Captain Coulson, master of the brig *Othello*, reports that his brig foundered off Portland, December 27;—encountering a strong gale, and shipping two heavy seas in succession, which hove the ship on her beam-ends. "Observing no chance of saving the ship, took to the long boat, and within ten minutes of leaving her saw the brig founder. We were picked up the same morning by the French ship *Commerce de Paris*, Captain Tombarel."

Here, in a single column of a newspaper, what strange, touching pictures do we find of seamen's dangers, vicissitudes, gallantry, generosity! The ship on fire—the captain in the gale slinging himself in a bowline to stop the leak—the Frenchman in the hour of danger coming to his British comrade's rescue—the brigantine, almost a wreck, working up to the barque with the signal of distress flying, and taking off her crew of thirteen men : "We then proceeded on our course, *the crew of the abandoned vessel assisting all they could to keep my ship afloat.*" What noble, simple words! What courage, devotedness, brotherly love! Do they not cause the heart to beat, and the eyes to fill?

This is what seamen do daily, and for one another. One lights occasionally upon different stories. It happened, not very long since, that the passengers by one of the great ocean steamers were wrecked, and, after undergoing the most severe hardships, were left, destitute and helpless, at a miserable coaling port. Amongst them were old men, ladies, and children. When the next steamer arrived, the passengers by that steamer took alarm at the haggard and miserable appearance of their unfortunate predecessors, and actually *remonstrated with their own captain, urging him not to take the poor creatures on board.* There was every excuse, of course. The last-arrived steamer was already dangerously full: the cabins were crowded; there were sick and delicate people on board—sick and delicate people who had paid a large price to the company for room, food, comfort, already not too sufficient. If fourteen of us are in an omnibus, will we see three or four women outside and say, "Come in, because this is the last 'bus, and it rains?" Of course not: but think of that remonstrance, and of that Samaritan master of the *Purchase* brigantine!

In the winter of '53, I went from Marseilles to Civita Vecchia, in one of the magnificent P. and O. ships, the *Valetta*, the master of which subsequently did distinguished service in the Crimea. This was his first Mediterranean voyage, and he sailed his ship by the charts alone, going into each port as surely as any pilot. I remember walking the deck at night with this most skilful, gallant, well-bred, and well-educated gentleman, and the glow of eager enthusiasm with which he assented, when I asked him whether he did not think a RIBBON or ORDER would be welcome or useful in his service.

Why is there not an ORDER OF BRITANNIA for British seamen? In the Merchant and the Royal Navy alike, occur almost daily instances and occasions for the display of science, skill, bravery, fortitude in trying circumstances, resource in danger. In the First Number of the *Cornhill Magazine*, a friend contributed a most touching story of the M'Clintock expedition, in the dangers and dreadful glories of which he shared; and the writer was a merchant captain. How many more are there (and, for the honour of England, may there be many like him!)—gallant, accomplished, high-spirited, enterprising masters of their noble profession! Can our fountain of Honour not be brought to such men? It plays upon captains and colonels in seemly profusion. It pours forth not illiberal rewards upon doctors and judges. It sprinkles mayors and aldermen. It bedews a painter now and again. It has spirted a baronetcy upon two, and bestowed a coronet upon one noble man of letters. Diplomatists take their Bath in it as of right; and it flings out a profusion of glittering stars upon the nobility of the three kingdoms. Cannot Britannia find a ribbon for her sailors? The Navy, royal or mercantile, is *a service*. The command of a ship, or the conduct of her, implies danger, honour, science, skill, subordination, good faith. It may be a victory, such as that of the *Sarah Sands;* it may be discovery, such as that of the *Fox;* it may be heroic disaster, such as that of the *Birkenhead;* and in such events merchant seamen, as well as royal seamen, take their share.

Why is there not, then, an Order of Britannia? One day a young officer of the *Euryalus* may win it; and, having just read the memoirs of LORD DUNDONALD, I know who ought to have the first Grand Cross.

ON SOME LATE GREAT VICTORIES.

On the 18th day of April last I went to see a friend in a neighbouring Crescent, and on the steps of the next house beheld a group something like that here depicted. A news-

boy had stopped in his walk, and was reading aloud the journal which it was his duty to deliver; a pretty orange girl, with a heap of blazing fruit, rendered more brilliant by one of those great blue papers in which oranges are now artfully wrapped, leant over the railing and listened; and opposite the *nympham discentem* there was a capering and

acute-eared young satirist of a crossing-sweeper, who had
left his neighbouring professional avocation and chance of
profit, in order to listen to the tale of the little news-boy.

That intelligent reader, with his hand following the line
as he read it out to his audience, was saying:—"And—now
—Tom—coming up smiling—after his fall—dee—delivered
a rattling clinker upon the Benicia Boy's—potato-trap— •
but was met by a—punisher on the nose—which," &c.,
&c.; or words to that effect. Betty at 52 let me in, while
the boy was reading his lecture; and, having been some
twenty minutes or so in the house and paid my visit, I took
leave.

The little lecturer was still at work on the 51 doorstep,
and his audience had scarcely changed their position. Having read every word of the battle myself in the morning, I
did not stay to listen further; but if the gentleman who
expected his paper at the usual hour that day experienced
delay and a little disappointment I shall not be surprised.

I am not going to expatiate on the battle. I have read
in the correspondent's letter of a Northern newspaper, that
in the midst of the company assembled the reader's humble
servant was present, and in a very polite society, too, of
"poets, clergymen, men of letters, and members of both
Houses of Parliament." If so, I must have walked to the
station in my sleep, paid three guineas in a profound fit of
mental abstraction, and returned to bed unconscious, for I
certainly woke there about the time when history relates
that the fight was over. I do not know whose colours I
wore—the Benician's, or those of the Irish champion; nor
remember where the fight took place, which, indeed, no
somnambulist is bound to recollect. Ought Mr. Sayers to
be honoured for being brave, or punished for being naughty?
By the shade of Brutus the elder, I don't know.

In George II.'s time, there was a turbulent navy lieutenant (Handsome Smith he was called—his picture is at
Greenwich now, in brown velvet, and gold and scarlet; his
coat handsome, his waistcoat exceedingly handsome; but
his face by no means the beauty)—there was, I say, a tur-

bulent young lieutenant who was broke on a complaint of the French ambassador, for obliging a French ship of war to lower her topsails to his ship at Spithead. But, by the King's orders, Tom was next day made Captain Smith. Well, if I were absolute king, I would send Tom Sayers to the mill for a month, and make him Sir Thomas on coming out of Clerkenwell. You are a naughty boy, Tom! but then, you know, we ought to love our brethren, though ever so naughty. We are moralists, and reprimand you; and you are hereby reprimanded accordingly. But in case England should ever have need of a few score thousand champions, who laugh at danger; who cope with giants; who, stricken to the ground, jump up and gaily rally, and fall, and rise again, and strike, and die rather than yield— in case the country should need such men, and you should know them, be pleased to send lists of the misguided persons to the principal police stations, where means may some day be found to utilize their wretched powers, and give their deplorable energies a right direction. Suppose, Tom, that you and your friends are pitted against an immense invader—suppose you are bent on holding the ground, and dying there, if need be—suppose it is life, freedom, honour, home, you are fighting for, and there is a death-dealing sword or rifle in your hand, with which you are going to resist some tremendous enemy who challenges your championship on your native shore? Then, Sir Thomas, resist him to the death, and it is all right: kill him, and heaven bless you. Drive him into the sea, and there destroy, smash, and drown him; and let us sing *Laudamus*. In these national cases, you see, we override the indisputable first laws of morals. Loving your neighbour is very well, but suppose your neighbour comes over from Calais and Boulogne to rob you of your laws, your liberties, your newspaper, your parliament (all of which *some* dear neighbours of ours have given up in the most self-denying manner): suppose any neighbour were to cross the water and propose this kind of thing to us? Should we not be justified in humbly trying to pitch him into the water? If it were the King of Belgium himself we must do so. I mean that fighting, of course, is wrong; but that there are occasions when, &c.—I suppose I mean that that one-handed fight of Sayers is one of the most spirit-stirring little stories ever told: and, with every love and respect for Morality—my spirit says to her, "Do, for goodness' sake, my dear madam, keep your true, and pure, and womanly, and gentle remarks for another day. Have the great kindness to stand a *leetle* aside, and just let us see one or two more rounds between the men. That little man with the one hand powerless on his breast facing yonder giant for hours, and felling him, too, every now and then! It is the little *Java* and the *Constitution* over again."

I think it is a most fortunate event for the brave Heenan, who has acted and written since the battle with a true warrior's courtesy, and with a great deal of good logic too, that the battle was a drawn one. The advantage was all on Mr. Sayers's side. Say a young lad of sixteen insults me in the street, and I try and thrash him, and do it. Well, I have thrashed a young lad. You great, big tyrant, couldn't you hit your own size? But say the lad thrashes me? In either case I walk away discomfited: but in the latter, I am positively put to shame. Now, when the ropes were cut from that death-grip, and Sir Thomas released, the gentleman of Benicia was confessedly blind of one eye, and speedily afterwards was blind of both. Could Mr. Sayers have held out for three minutes, for five minutes, for ten minutes more? He says he could. So we say *we* could have held out, and did, and had beaten off the enemy at Waterloo, even if the Prussians hadn't come up. The opinions differ pretty much according to the nature of the opinants. I say the Duke and Tom could have held out, that they meant to hold out, that they did hold out, and that there has been fistifying enough. That crowd which came in and stopped the fight ought to be considered like one of those divine clouds which the gods send in Homer:

> Apollo shrouds
> The godlike Trojan in a veil of clouds.

It is the best way of getting the godlike Trojan out of the scrape, don't you see? The *nodus* is cut; Tom is out of chancery; the Benicia boy not a bit the worse, nay, better than if he had beaten the little man. He has not the humiliation of conquest. He is greater, and will be loved more hereafter by the gentle sex. Suppose he had overcome the godlike Trojan? Suppose he had tied Tom's corpse to his cab-wheels, and driven to Farnham, smoking the pipe of triumph? Faugh! the great, hulking conqueror! Why did you not hold your hand from yonder hero? Everybody, I say, was relieved by that opportune appearance of the British gods, protectors of native valour, who interfered, and "withdrew" their champion.

Now, suppose six-feet-two conqueror, and five-feet-eight beaten; would Sayers have been a whit the less gallant and meritorious? If Sancho had been allowed *really* to reign in Barataria, I make no doubt that, with his good sense and kindness of heart, he would have devised some means of rewarding the brave vanquished, as well as the brave victors in the Baratarian army, and that a champion who had fought a good fight would have been a knight of King Don Sancho's orders, whatever the upshot of the combat had been. Suppose Wellington overwhelmed on the plateau of Mont St. John; suppose Washington attacked and beaten at Valley Forge—and either supposition is quite easy—and what becomes of the heroes? They would have been as brave, honest, heroic, wise; but their glory, where would it have been? Should we have had their portraits hanging in our chambers? have been familiar with their histories? have pondered over their letters, common lives, and daily sayings? There is not only merit, but luck which goes to making a hero out of a gentleman. Mind, please you, I am not saying that the hero is after all not so very heroic; and have not the least desire to grudge him his merit because of his good fortune.

Have you any idea whither this Roundabout Essay on some late great victories is tending? Do you suppose that by those words I mean Trenton, Brandywine, Salamanca,

Vittoria, and so forth? By a great victory I can't mean
that affair at Farnham, for it was a drawn fight. Where
then are the victories, pray, and when are we coming to
them?

My good sir, you will perceive that in this Nicæan discourse I have only as yet advanced as far as this—that a
hero, whether he wins or loses, is a hero; and that if a fellow will but be honest and courageous, and do his best, we
are for paying all honour to him. Furthermore, it has
been asserted that Fortune has a good deal to do with the
making of heroes; and thus hinted for the consolation of
those who don't happen to be engaged in any stupendous
victories, that, had opportunity so served, they might have
been heroes too. If you are not, friend, it is not your
fault, whilst I don't wish to detract from any gentleman's
reputation who is. There. My worst enemy can't take
objection to that. The point might have been put more
briefly perhaps; but, if you please, we will not argue that
question.

Well, then. The victories which I wish especially to
commemorate in this the last article of our first volume, are
the six great, complete, prodigious, and undeniable victories, achieved by the corps which the editor of the CORN-
HILL MAGAZINE has the honour to command. When I
seemed to speak disparagingly but now of generals, it was
that chief I had in my I (if you will permit me the expression), I wished him not to be elated by too much prosperity; I warned him against assuming heroic imperatorial
airs, and cocking his laurels too jauntily over his ear. I
was his conscience, and stood on the splash-board of his
triumph-car, whispering, " *Hominem memento te.* " As we
rolled along the way, and passed the weathercocks on the
temples, I saluted the symbol of the goddess Fortune with
a reverent awe. " We have done our little endeavour," I
said, bowing my head, " and mortals can do no more. But
we might have fought bravely, and *not* won. We might
have cast the coin, calling ' Head,' and lo! Tail might
have come uppermost." O thou Ruler of Victories!—thou

awarder of Fame!—thou Giver of Crowns (and shillings)—
if thou hast smiled upon us, shall we not be thankful?
There is a Saturnine philosopher, standing at the door of
his book-shop, who, I fancy, has a pooh-pooh expression as
the triumph passes. (I can't see quite clearly for the laurels, which have fallen down over my nose.) One hand is
reining in the two white elephants that draw the car; I
raise the other hand up to—to the laurels, and pass on,
waving him a graceful recognition. Up the Hill of Lud-
gate—around the Pauline Square—by the side of Chepe—
until it reaches our own Hill of Corn—the procession
passes. The Imperator is bowing to the people; the captains of the legions are riding round the car, their gallant
minds struck by the thought, "Have we not fought as well
as yonder fellow, swaggering in the chariot, and are we not
as good as he?" Granted, with all my heart, my dear
lads. When your consulship arrives, may you be as fortunate. When these hands, now growing old, shall lay down
sword and truncheon, may you mount the car, and ride to
the temple of Jupiter. Be yours the laurel then. *Neque
me myrtus dedecet,* looking cosily down from the arbour
where I sit under the arched vine.

I fancy the Imperator standing on the steps of the temple (erected by Titus) on the Mons Frumentarius, and addressing the citizens: "Quirites!" he says, "in our campaign of six months, we have been engaged six times, and
in each action have taken near upon a *hundred thousand
prisoners.* Go to! What are other magazines compared
to our magazine? (Sound, trumpeter!) What banner is
there like that of Cornhill? You, philosopher yonder?"
(he shirks under his mantle). "Do you know what it is to
have a hundred and ten thousand readers? A hundred
thousand readers? a hundred thousand *buyers!*" (Cries of
No!—Pooh! Yes, upon my honour! Oh, come! and murmurs of applause and derision)—"I say more than a hundred thousand purchasers—and I believe *as much as a million* readers!" (Immense sensation.) "To these have we
said an unkind word? We have enemies; have we hit

them an unkind blow? Have we sought to pursue party
aims, to forward private jobs, to advance selfish schemes?
The only persons to whom wittingly we have given pain
are some who have volunteered for our corps—and of these
volunteers we have had *thousands.*" (Murmurs and grum-
bles.) "What commander, citizens, could place all these
men—could make officers of all these men?" (cries of No
—no! and laughter)—"could say, 'I accept this recruit,
though he is too short for our standard, because he is poor
and has a mother at home who wants bread?' could enrol
this other, who is too weak to bear arms, because he says,
'Look sir, I shall be stronger anon?' The leader of such
an army as ours must select his men, not because they are
good and virtuous, but because they are strong and capable.
To these our ranks are ever open, and in addition to the
warriors—who surround me"—(the generals look proudly
conscious)—"I tell you, citizens, that I am in treaty with
other and most tremendous champions, who will march by
the side of our veterans to the achievement of fresh victories. Now, blow trumpets! Bang, ye gongs! and drummers, drub the thundering skins! Generals and chiefs, we
go to sacrifice to the gods."

Crowned with flowers, the captains enter the temple, the
other Magazines walking modestly behind them. The people huzza; and, in some instances, kneel and kiss the
fringes of the robes of the warriors. The Philosopher
puts up his shutters, and retires into his shop, deeply
moved. In ancient times, Pliny (*apud* Smith) relates it
was the custom of the Imperator "to paint his whole body
a bright red;" and, also, on ascending the Hill, to have
some of the hostile chiefs led aside "to the adjoining prison, and put to death." We propose to dispense with both
these ceremonies.

THORNS IN THE CUSHION.

In the Essay with which our first Number closed, the CORNHILL MAGAZINE was likened to a ship sailing forth on her voyage, and the captain uttered a very sincere prayer for her prosperity. The dangers of storm and rock; the vast outlay upon ship and cargo, and the certain risk of the venture, gave the chief officer a feeling of no small anxiety; for who could say from what quarter danger might arise, and how his owner's property might be imperilled? After a six months' voyage, we with very thankful hearts could acknowledge our good fortune: and, taking up the apologue in the Roundabout manner, we composed a triumphal procession in honour of the Magazine, and imagined the Imperator thereof riding in a sublime car to return thanks in the Temple of Victory. Cornhill is accustomed to grandeur and greatness, and has witnessed, every ninth of November, for I don't know how many centuries, a prodigious annual pageant, chariot progress, and flourish of trumpetry; and our publishing office being so very near the Mansion-House, I am sure the reader will understand how the idea of pageant and procession came naturally to my mind. The imagination easily supplied a gold coach, eight cream-coloured horses of your true Pegasus breed, huzzaing multitudes, running footmen, and clanking knights in armour, a chaplain and a sword-bearer with a muff on his head, scowling out of the coach-window, and a Lord Mayor all crimson, fur, gold chain, and white ribbons, solemnly occupying the place of state. A playful fancy could have carried the matter farther, could have depicted the feast in the Egyptian Hall, the ministers, chief-justices, and right reverend prelates taking their seats round about his lordship, the turtle and other delicious viands, and Mr. Toole behind the central throne, bawling out to the assembled guests and dignitaries: "My Lord So-and-so, my Lord What-d'ye-call-

'em, my Lord Etcætera, the Lord Mayor pledges you all in a loving cup." Then the noble proceedings come to an end; Lord Simper proposes the ladies; the company rises from table, and adjourns to coffee and muffins. The carriages of the nobility and guests roll back to the West. The Egyptian Hall, so bright just now, appears in a twilight glimmer, in which waiters are seen ransacking the dessert, and rescuing the spoons. His lordship and the Lady Mayoress go into their private apartments. The robes are doffed, the collar and white ribbons are removed. The Mayor becomes a man, and is pretty surely in a fluster about the speeches which he has just uttered; remembering too well now, wretched creature, the principal points which he *didn't* make when he rose to speak. He goes to bed to headache, to care, to repentance, and, I daresay, to a dose of something which his body-physician has prescribed for him. And there are ever so many men in the city who fancy that man happy!

Now, suppose that all through that 9th of November his lordship has had a racking rheumatism, or a toothache, let us say, during all dinner time—through which he has been obliged to grin and mumble his poor old speeches. Is he enviable? Would you like to change with his lordship? Suppose that bumper which his golden footman brings him, instead i'fackins of ypocras or canary, contains some abomination of senna? Away! Remove the golden goblet, insidious cup-bearer! You now begin to perceive the gloomy moral which I am about to draw.

Last month we sang the song of glorification, and rode in the chariot of triumph. It was all very well. It was right to huzzay, and be thankful, and cry, Bravo, our side! and besides, you know, there was the enjoyment of thinking how pleased Brown, and Jones, and Robinson (our dear friends) would be at this announcement of success. But now that the performance is over, my good sir, just step into my private room, and see that it is not all pleasure—this winning of successes. Cast your eye over those newspapers, over those letters. See what the critics say of your harmless jokes, neat little trim sentences, and pet waggeries! Why, you are no better than an idiot; you are drivelling; your powers have left you; this always overrated writer is rapidly sinking to, &c.

This is not pleasant; but neither is this the point. It may be the critic is right, and the author wrong. It may be that the archbishop's sermon is not so fine as some of those discourses twenty years ago which used to delight the faithful in Granada. Or it may be (pleasing thought!) that the critic is a dullard, and does not understand what he is writing about. Everybody who has been to an exhibition has heard visitors discoursing about the pictures before their faces. One says, "This is very well;" another says, "This is stuff and rubbish;" another cries, "Bravo! this is a masterpiece:" and each has a right to his opinion. For example, one of the pictures I admired most at the Royal Academy is by a gentleman on whom I never, to my knowledge, set eyes. This picture is No. 346, *Moses*, by Mr. S. Solomon. I thought it had a great intention. I thought it finely drawn and composed. It nobly represented, to my mind, the dark children of the Egyptian bondage, and suggested the touching story. My newspaper says: "Two ludicrously ugly women, looking at a dingy baby, do not form a pleasing object;" and so goodby, Mr. Solomon. Are not most of our babies served so in life? and doesn't Mr. Robinson consider Mr. Brown's cherub an ugly, squalling little brat? So cheer up, Mr. S. S. It may be the critic who discoursed on your baby is a bad judge of babies. When Pharaoh's kind daughter found the child, and cherished and loved it, and took it home, and found a nurse for it, too, I daresay there were grim, brick-dust-coloured chamberlains, or some of the tough, old, meagre, yellow princesses at court, who never had children themselves, who cried out, "Faugh! the horrid little squalling wretch!" and knew he would never come to good; and said, "Didn't I tell you so?" when he assaulted the Egyptian.

Never mind then, Mr. S. Solomon, I say, because a critic

pooh-poohs your work of art—your Moses—your child—
your foundling. Why, did not a wiseacre in *Blackwood's*
Magazine lately fall foul of "Tom Jones?" O hypercritic!
So, to be sure, did good old Mr. Richardson, who could
write novels himself—but you, and I, and Mr. Gibbon, my
dear sir, agree in giving our respect, and wonder, and admiration, to the brave old master.

In these last words I am supposing the respected reader
to be endowed with a sense of humour, which he may or
may not possess; indeed, don't we know many an honest
man who can no more comprehend a joke, than he can turn
a tune. But I take for granted, my dear sir, that you are
brimming over with fun—you mayn't make jokes, but
you could if you would—you know you could; and in your
quiet way you enjoy them extremely. Now many people
neither make them, nor understand them when made, nor
like them when understood, and are suspicious, testy, and
angry with jokers. Have you ever watched an elderly
male or female—an elderly "party," so to speak, who begins to find out that some young wag of the company is,
"chaffing" him? Have you ever tried the sarcastic or
Socratic method with a child? Little simple he or she, in
the innocence of the simple heart, plays some silly freak,
or makes some absurd remark, which you turn to ridicule.
The little creature dimly perceives that you are making fun
of him, writhes, blushes, grows uneasy, bursts into tears,
—upon my word it is not fair to try the weapon of ridicule
upon that innocent young victim. The awful objurgatory
practice he is accustomed to. Point out his fault, and lay
bare the dire consequences thereof: expose it roundly, and
give him a proper, solemn, moral whipping—but do not attempt to *castigare ridendo*. Do not laugh at him writhing,
and cause all the other boys in the school to laugh. Remember your own young days at school, my friend—the
tingling cheeks, burning ears, bursting heart, and passion
of desperate tears, with which you looked up, after having
performed some blunder, whilst the doctor held you to
public scorn before the class, and cracked his great clumsy

jokes upon you—helpless, and a prisoner! Better the block itself, and the lictors, with their fasces of birch-twigs, than the maddening torture of those jokes!

Now with respect to jokes—and the present company of course excepted—many people, perhaps most people, are as infants. They have little sense of humour. They don't like jokes. Raillery in writing annoys and offends them. The coarseness apart, I think I have met very, very few women who liked the banter of Swift and Fielding. Their simple, tender natures revolt at laughter. Is the satyr always a wicked brute at heart, and are they rightly shocked at his grin, his leer, his horns, hoofs, and ears? *Fi donc, le vilain monstre,* with his shrieks, and his capering crooked legs! Let him go and get a pair of well-wadded black silk stockings, and pull them over those horrid shanks; put a large gown and bands over beard and hide; and pour a dozen of lavender-water into his lawn handkerchief, and cry, and never make a joke again. It shall all be highly-distilled poesy, and perfumed sentiment, and gushing eloquence; and the foot *shan't* peep out, and a plague take it. Cover it up with the surplice. Out with your cambric, dear ladies, and let us all whimper together.

Now, then, hand on heart, we declare that it is not the fire of adverse critics which afflicts or frightens the editorial bosom. They may be right; they may be rogues who have a personal spite; they may be dullards who kick and bray as their nature is to do, and prefer thistles to pineapples; they may be conscientious, acute, deeply learned, delightful judges, who see your joke in a moment, and the profound wisdom lying underneath. Wise or dull, laudatory or otherwise, we put their opinions aside. If they applaud, we are pleased: if they shake their quick pens, and fly off with a hiss, we resign their favours and put on all the fortitude we can muster. I would rather have the lowest man's good word than his bad one, to be sure; but as for coaxing a compliment, or wheedling him into good-humour, or stopping his angry mouth with a good dinner, or accepting his contributions for a certain Magazine, for fear of his barking or snapping elsewhere—*allons donc !* These shall not be our acts. Bow-wow, Cerberus! Here shall be no sop for thee, unless—unless Cerberus is an uncommonly good dog, when we shall bear no malice because he flew at us from our neighbour's gate.

What, then, is the main grief you spoke of as annoying you—the toothache in the Lord Mayor's jaw, the thorn in the cushion of the editorial chair? It is there. Ah! it stings me now as I write. It comes with almost every morning's post. At night I come home, and take my letters up to bed (not daring to open them), and in the morning I find one, two, three thorns on my pillow. Three I extracted yesterday; two I found this morning. They don't sting quite so sharply as they did; but a skin is a skin, and they bite, after all, most wickedly. It is all very fine to advertise on the Magazine, "Contributions are only to be sent to 65, Cornhill, and not to the Editor's private residence." My dear sir, how little you know man- or woman-kind, if you fancy they will take that sort of warning! How am I to know (though, to be sure, I begin to know now) as I take the letters off the tray, which of those envelopes contains a real *bona fide* letter, and which a thorn? One of the best invitations this year I mistook for a thorn-letter, and kept it without opening. This is what I call a thorn-letter:—

"CAMBERWELL, *June 4.*

"SIR,—May I hope, may I entreat, that you will favour me by perusing the enclosed lines, and that they may be found worthy of insertion in the *Cornhill Magazine?* We have known better days, sir. I have a sick and widowed mother to maintain, and little brothers and sisters who look to me. I do my utmost as a governess to support them. I toil at night when they are at rest, and my own hand and brain are alike tired. If I could add but *a little* to our means by my pen, many of my poor invalid's wants might be supplied, and I could procure for her comforts to which she is now a stranger. Heaven knows it is not for want of *will* or for want of *energy* on my part, that she is now in ill-health, and our little household almost without bread. Do—do cast a kind glance over my poem, and if you can help us, the widow, the orphans will bless you! I remain, sir, in anxious expectancy,

"Your faithful servant,   S. S. S."

And enclosed is a little poem or two, and an envelope with its penny stamp—Heaven help us!—and the writer's name and address.

Now you see what I mean by a thorn. Here is the case put with true female logic. "I am poor; I am good; I am ill; I work hard; I have a sick mother and hungry brothers and sisters dependent on me. You can help us if you will." And then I look at the paper, with the thousandth part of a faint hope that it may be suitable, and I find it won't do: and I knew it wouldn't do: and why is this poor lady to appeal to my pity and bring her poor little ones kneeling to my bedside, and calling for bread which I can give them if I choose? No day passes but that argument *ad misericordiam* is used. Day and night that sad voice is crying out for help. Thrice it appealed to me yesterday. Twice this morning it cried to me: and I have no doubt when I go to get my hat, I shall find it with its piteous face and its pale family about it, waiting for me in the hall. One of the immense advantages which women have over our sex is, that they actually like to read these letters. Like letters? O mercy on us! Before I was an editor I did not like the postman much:—but now!

A very common way with these petitioners is to begin with a fine flummery about the merits and eminent genius of the person whom they are addressing. But this artifice, I state publicly, is of no avail. When I see *that* kind of herb, I·know the snake within it, and fling it away before it has time to sting. Away, reptile, to the waste-paper basket, and thence to the flames!

But of these disappointed people, some take their disappointment and meekly bear it. Some hate and hold you

C

their enemy because you could not be their friend. Some, furious and envious, say: "Who is this man who refuses what I offer, and how dares he, the conceited coxcomb, to deny my merit?"

Sometimes my letters contain not mere thorns, but bludgeons. Here are two choice slips from that noble Irish oak, which has more than once supplied alpeens for this meek and unoffending skull:—

"THEATRE ROYAL, DONNYBROOK.

"SIR,—I have just finished reading the first portion of your Tale, 'Lovel the Widower,' and am much surprised at the unwarrantable strictures you pass therein on the *corps de ballet*.

"I have been for more than ten years connected with the theatrical profession, and I beg to assure you that the majority of the *corps de ballet* are virtuous, well-conducted girls, and, consequently, that snug cottages are not taken for them in the Regent's Park.

"I also have to inform you that theatrical managers are in the habit of speaking good English, possibly better English than authors.

"You either know nothing of the subject in question, or you assert a wilful falsehood.

"I am happy to say that the characters of the *corps de ballet*, as also those of actors and actresses, are superior to the snarlings of dyspeptic libellers, or the spiteful attacks and *brutum fulmen* of ephemeral authors.

"I am, sir, your obedient servant,
"The Editor of the *Cornhill Magazine*.   A. B. C."

"THEATRE ROYAL, DONNYBROOK.

"SIR,—I have just read, in the *Cornhill Magazine* for January, the first portion of a Tale written by you, and entitled 'Lovel the Widower.'

"In the production in question you employ all your malicious spite (and you have great capabilities that way) in trying to degrade the character of the *corps de ballet*. When you imply that the majority of ballet-girls have villas taken for them in the Regent's Park, *I say you tell a deliberate falsehood.*

Haveing been brought up to the stage from infancy, and, though now an actress, haveing been seven years principal dancer at the opera, I am competent to speak on the subject. I am only surprised that so vile a libeller as yourself should be allowed to preside at the Dramatic Fund dinner on the 22nd instant. I think it would be much better if you were to reform your own life, instead of telling lies of those who are immeasurably your superiors.

" Yours in supreme disgust.

"A. D."

The signatures of the respected writers are altered, and for the site of their Theatre Royal an adjacent place is named, which (as I may have been falsely informed) used to be famous for quarrels, thumps and broken heads. But, I say, is this an easy chair to sit on, when you are liable to have a pair of such shillelaghs flung at it? And, prithee, what was all the quarrel about? In the little history of "Lovel the Widower" I described, and brought to condign punishment, a certain wretch of a ballet-dancer, who lived splendidly for awhile on ill-gotten gains, had an accident, and lost her beauty, and died poor, deserted, ugly, and every way odious. In the same page, other little ballet-dancers are described, wearing homely clothing, doing their duty, and carrying their humble savings to the family at home. But nothing will content my dear correspondents but to have me declare that the majority of ballet-dancers have villas in the Regent's Park, and to convict me of "deliberate falsehood." Suppose, for instance, I had chosen to introduce a red-haired washerwoman into a story? I might get an expostulatory letter saying, " Sir, in stating that the majority of washerwomen are red-haired, you are a liar! and you had best not speak of ladies who are immeasurably your superiors." Or suppose I had ventured to describe an illiterate haberdasher? One of the craft might write to

me, "Sir, in describing haberdashers as illiterate, you utter
a wilful falsehood.   Haberdashers use much better English
than authors."   It is a mistake, to be sure.   I have never
said what my correspondents say I say.   There is the text
under their noses, but what if they choose to read it their
own way?   "Hurroo, lads! Here's for a fight.   There's
a bald head peeping out of the hut.   There's a bald head!
It must be Tim Malone's."   And whack! come down both
the bludgeons at once.

Ah me! we wound where we never intended to strike;
we create anger where we never meant harm; and these
thoughts are the thorns in our Cushion.   Out of mere ma-
lignity, I suppose, there is no man who would like to make
enemies.   But here, in this editorial business, you can't do
otherwise: and a queer, sad, strange, bitter thought it is,
that must cross the mind of many a public man: "Do
what I will, be innocent or spiteful, be generous or cruel,
there are A and B, and C and D, who will hate me to the
end of the chapter—to the chapter's end—to the Finis of
the page—when hate, and envy, and fortune, and disappointment shall be over."

ON SCREENS IN DINING-ROOMS

A GRANDSON of the late Rev. Dr. Primrose (of Wake-field, vicar) wrote me a little note from his country living this morning, and the kind fellow had the precaution to write "No thorn" upon the envelope, so that ere I broke the seal, my mind might be relieved of any anxiety lest the letter should contain one of those lurking stabs which are so painful to the present gentle writer. Your epigraph, my dear P., shows your kin' and artless nature; but don't you see it is of no use? People who are bent upon assas-sinating you in the manner mentioned will write "No thorn" upon their envelopes too; and you open the case, and presently out flies poisoned stiletto, which springs into a man's bosom, and makes the wretch howl with an-guish. When the bailiffs are after a man, they adopt all sorts of disguises, pop out on him from all conceivable cor-ners, and tap his miserable shoulder. His wife is taken ill; his sweetheart, who remarked his brilliant, too brill-iant appearance at the Hyde Park review, will meet him at Cremorne, or where you will. The old friend who has owed him that money these five years will meet him at so-and-so and pay. By one bait or other the victim is hooked, netted, landed, and down goes the basket-lid. It is not your wife, your sweetheart, your friend, who is going to pay you. It is Mr. Nab the bailiff. *You* know——you are caught. You are off in a cab to Chancery Lane.

You know, I say? *Why* should you know? I make no manner of doubt you never were taken by a bailiff in your life. I never was. I have been in two or three debtors' prisons, but not on my own account. Goodness be praised! I mean you can't escape your lot; and Nab only stands here metaphorically as the watchful, certain, and untiring officer of Mr. Sheriff Fate. Why, my dear Primrose, this morning along with your letter comes another, bearing the well-known superscription of another old friend, which I open without the least suspicion, and what do I find? A few lines from my friend Johnson, it is true, but they are written on a page covered with feminine handwriting. "Dear Mr. Johnson," says the writer, "I have just been perusing with delight a most charming tale by the Archbishop of Cambray. It is called 'Telemachus;' and I think it would be admirably suited to the *Cornhill Magazine*. As you know the editor, will you have the great kindness, dear Mr. Johnson, to communicate with him *personally* (as that is much better than writing in a roundabout way to Cornhill, and waiting goodness knows how long for an answer), and stating my readiness to translate this excellent and instructive story? I do not wish to breathe *a word* against, 'Lovel Parsonage,' 'Framley the Widower,' or any of the novels which have appeared in the *Cornhill Magazine*, but I *am sure* 'Telemachus' is as good as new to English readers, and in point of interest and morality *far*," &c., &c., &c.

There it is. I am stabbed through Johnson. He has lent himself to this attack on me. He is weak about women. Other strong men are. He submits to the common lot, poor fellow. In my reply I do not use a word of unkindness. I write him back gently, that I fear "Telemachus" won't suit us. He can send the letter on to his fair correspondent. But however soft the answer, I question whether the wrath will be turned away. Will there not be a coolness between him and the lady? and is it not possible that henceforth her fine eyes will look with darkling glances upon the pretty orange cover of our Magazine?

Certain writers, they say, have a bad opinion of women. Now am I very whimsical in supposing that this disappointed candidate will be hurt at her rejection, and angry or cast down according to her nature? "Angry, indeed!" says Juno, gathering up her purple robes and royal raiment. "Sorry, indeed!" cries Minerva, lacing on her corslet again, and scowling under her helmet. (I imagine the well-known Apple case has just been argued and decided.) "Hurt, forsooth! Do you suppose *we* care for the opinion of that hobnailed lout of a Paris? Do you suppose that I, the Goddess of Wisdom, can't make allowances for mortal ignorance, and am so base as to bear malice against a poor creature who knows no better? You little know the goddess nature when you dare to insinuate that our divine minds are actuated by motives so base. A love of justice influences *us*. We are above mean revenge. We are too magnanimous to be angry at the award of such a judge in favour of such a creature." And rustling out their skirts, the ladies walk away together. This is all very well. You are bound to believe them. They are actuated by no hostility: not they. They bear no malice—of course not. But when the Trojan war occurs presently, which side will they take? many brave souls will be sent to Hades. Hector will perish. Poor old Priam's bald numskull will be cracked, and Troy town will burn, because Paris prefers golden-haired Venus to ox-eyed Juno and grey-eyed Minerva.

The last Essay of this Roundabout Series, describing the griefs and miseries of the editorial chair, was written, as the kind reader will acknowledge, in a mild and gentle, not in a warlike or satirical spirit. I showed how cudgels were applied; but, surely, the meek object of persecution hit no blows in return. The beating did not hurt much, and the person assaulted could afford to keep his good-humour; indeed, I admired that brave though illogical little actress, of the T. R. D–bl–n, for her fiery vindication of her profession's honour. I assure her I had no intention to tell l—s—well, let us say, monosyllables—about my superiors: and I wish her nothing but well, and when Macmahon (or shall it be Mulligan?) *Roi d'Irlande,* ascends his throne, I hope she may be appointed professor of English to the princesses of the royal house. *Nuper*— in former days—I too have militated; sometimes, as I now think, unjustly; but always, I vow, without personal rancour. Which of us has not idle words to recall, flippant jokes to regret? Have you never committed an imprudence? Have you never had a dispute, and found out that you were wrong? So much the worse for you. Woe be to the man *qui croit toujours avoir raison.* His anger is not a brief madness, but a permanent mania. His rage is not a fever-fit, but a black poison inflaming him, distorting his judgment, disturbing his rest, embittering his cup, gnawing at his pleasure, causing him more cruel suffering than ever he can inflict on his enemy. *O la belle morale!* As I write it, I think about one or two little affairs of my own. There is old Dr. Squaretoso (he certainly was very rude to me, and that's the fact); there is Madame Pomposa (and certainly her ladyship's behaviour was about as cool as cool could be). Never mind, old Squaretoso: never mind, Madame Pomposa! Here is a hand. Let us be friends, as we once were, and have no more of this rancour.

I had hardly sent that last Roundabout Paper to the printer (which, I submit, was written in a pacable and not unchristian frame of mind), when Saturday came, and with it, of course, my *Saturday Review.* I remember at New York coming down to breakfast at the hotel one morning, after a criticism had appeared in the *New York Herald,* in which an Irish writer had given me a dressing for a certain lecture on Swift. Ah! my dear little enemy of the T. R. D., what were the cudgels in *your* little *billet-doux* compared to those noble New York shillelaghs? All through the Union, the literary sons of Erin have marched *alpeen-stock* in hand, and in every city of the States they call each other and everybody else the finest names. Having come to breakfast, then, in the public room, I sit down, and see —that the nine people opposite have all got *New York Heralds* in their hands. One dear little lady, whom I knew, and who sate opposite, gave a pretty blush, and popped her paper under the table-cloth. I told her I had had my whipping already in my own private room, and begged her to continue her reading. I may have undergone agonies, you see, but every man who has been bred at an English public school comes away from a private interview with Dr. Birch with a calm, even a smiling face.

And this is not impossible, when you are prepared. You screw your courage up—you go through the business. You come back and take your seat on the form, showing not the least symptom of uneasiness or of previous unpleasantries. But to be caught suddenly up, and whipped in the bosom of your family—to sit down t> breakfast, and cast your innocent eye on a paper, and find, before you are aware, that the *Saturday Monitor* or *Black Monday Instructor* has hoisted you and is laying on—that is indeed a trial. Or perhaps the family has looked at the dreadful paper beforehand, and weakly tries to hide it. "Where is the *Instructor*, or the *Monitor?*" say you. "Where is that paper?" says mamma to one of the young ladies. Lucy hasn't it. Fanny hasn't seen it. Emily thinks that the governess has it. At last, out it is brought, that awful paper! Papa is amazingly tickled with the article on Thomson; thinks that show up of Johnson is very lively; and now—heaven be good to us!—he has come to the critique on himself:—"Of all the rubbish which we have had from Mr. Tomkins, we do protest and vow that this last cartload is" &c. Ah, poor Tomkins!—but most of all, ah! poor Mrs. Tomkins, and poor Emily, and Fanny, and Lucy, who have to sit by and see *paterfamilias* put to the torture!

Now, on this eventful Saturday, I did not cry, because it was not so much the Editor as the Publisher of the *Cornhill Magazine* who was brought out for a dressing; and it is wonderful how gallantly one bears the misfortunes of one's friends. That a writer should be taken to task about his books, is fair, and he must abide the praise or the censure. But that a publisher should be criticised for his dinners, and for the conversation which did *not* take place there,—is this tolerable press practice, legitimate joking, or honourable warfare? I have not the honour to know my next-door neighbour, but I make no doubt that he receives his friends at dinner; I see his wife and children pass constantly; I even know the carriages of some of the people who call upon him, and could tell their names. Now, suppose his servants were to tell mine what the doings are next door, who comes to dinner, what is eaten and said, and I were to publish an account of these transactions in a newspaper, I could assuredly get money for the report; but ought I to write it, and what would you think of me for doing so?

And suppose, Mr. Saturday Reviewer—you *censor morum*, you who pique yourself (and justly and honourably in the main) upon your character of gentleman, as well as of writer,—suppose, not that you yourself invent and indite absurd twaddle about gentlemen's private meetings and transactions, but pick this wretched garbage out of a New York street, and hold it up for your readers' amusement —don't you think, my friend, that you might have been better employed? Here, in my *Saturday Review*, and in an American paper subsequently sent to me, I light, astonished, on an account of the dinners of my friend and publisher, which are described as "tremendously heavy," of the conversation (which does not take place), and of the guests assembled at the table. I am informed that the proprietor of the *Cornhill*, and the host on these occasions, is "a very good man, but totally unread;" and that on my asking him whether Dr. Johnson was dining behind the screen, he said, "God bless my soul, my dear sir, there's no person by the name of Johnson here, nor any one behind the screen," and that a roar of laughter cut him short. I am informed by the same New York correspondent that I have touched up a contributor's article; that I once said to a literary gentleman, who was proudly pointing to an anonymous article as his writing, "Ah! I thought I recognized *your hoof* in it." I am told by the same authority that the *Cornhill Magazine* "shows symptoms of being on the wane," and having sold nearly a hundred thousand copies, he (the correspondent) "should think forty thousand was now about the mark." Then the graceful writer passes on to the dinners, at which it appears the Editor of the Magazine "is the great gun, and comes out with all the geniality in his power."

Now suppose this charming intelligence is untrue? Sup-

pose the publisher (to recall the words of my friend the
Dublin actor of last month) is a gentleman to the full as
well informed as those whom he invites to his table? Suppose he never made the remark, beginning—"God bless my
soul, my dear sir," &c., nor anything resembling it? Suppose nobody roared with laughing? Suppose the Editor
of the *Cornhill Magazine* never "touched up" one single
line of the contribution which bears "marks of his hand?"
Suppose he never said to any literary gentleman, "I recognized *your hoof*" in any periodical whatever? Suppose
the 40,000 subscribers, which the writer to New York
"considered to be about the mark," should be between 90,-
000 and 100,000 (and as he will have figures, there they
are). Suppose this back-door gossip should be utterly
blundering and untrue, would any one wonder? Ah! if
we had only enjoyed the happiness to number this writer
among the contributors to our Magazine, what a cheerfulness and easy confidence his presence would impart to our
meetings! He would find that "poor Mr. Smith" had
heard that recondite anecdote of Dr. Johnson behind the
screen; and as for "the great gun of those banquets," with
what geniality should not I "come out" if I had an amiable companion close by me, dotting down my conversation
for the *New York Times!*

Attack our books, Mr. Correspondent, and welcome.
They are fair subjects for just censure or praise. But woe
be to you, if you allow private rancours or animosities to
influence you in the discharge of your public duty. In the
little court where you are paid to sit as judge, as critic,
you owe it to your employers, to your conscience, to the
honour of your calling, to deliver just sentences; and you
shall have to answer to heaven for your dealings, as surely
as my Lord Chief Justice on the Bench. The dignity of
letters, the honour of the literary calling, the slights put
by haughty and unthinking people upon literary men,—
don't we hear outcries upon these subjects raised daily?
As dear Sam Johnson sits behind the screen, too proud to
show his threadbare coat and patches among the more pros-

perous brethren of his trade, there is no want of dignity in
him, in that homely image of labour ill-rewarded, genius
as yet unrecognized, independence sturdy and uncomplain-
ing.   But Mr. Nameless, behind the publisher's screen un-
invited, peering at the company and the meal, catching
up scraps of the jokes, and noting down the guests' behaviour and conversation,—what a figure his is!   *Allons*, Mr.
Nameless!   Put up your notebook; walk out of the hall;
and leave gentlemen alone who would be private, and wish
you no harm.

TUNBRIDGE TOYS

I WONDER whether those little silver pencil-cases with a moveable almanack at the butt-end are still favourite implements with boys, and whether pedlars still hawk them about the country? Are there pedlars and hawkers still, or are rustics and children grown too sharp to deal with them? Those pencil-cases, as far as my memory serves me, were not of much use. The screw, upon which the moveable almanack turned, was constantly getting loose. The 1 of the table would work from its moorings, under Tuesday or Wednesday, as the case might be, and you would find, on examination, that Th. or W. was the 23½ of the month (which was absurd on the face of the thing), and in a word your cherished pencil-case an utterly unreliable timekeeper. Nor was this a matter of wonder. Consider the position of a pencil-case in a boy's pocket. You had hard-bake in it; marbles, kept in your purse when the money was all gone; your mother's purse knitted so fondly and supplied with a little bit of gold, long since—prodigal little son!—scattered amongst the swine—I mean amongst brandy-balls, open tarts, three-cornered puffs, and similar abominations. You had a top and string; a knife; a piece of cobbler's wax; two or three bullets; a *Little Warbler;* and I, for my part, remember, for a considerable period, a brass-barrelled pocket-pistol (which would fire beautifully, for with it I shot off a button from Butt Major's jacket);— with all these things, and ever so many more, clinking and rattling in your pockets, and your hands, of course, keeping them in perpetual movement, how could you expect your moveable almanack not to be twisted out of its place now and again—your pencil-case to be bent—your liquorice water not to leak out of your bottle over the cobbler's wax, your bull's-eyes not to ram up the lock and barrel of your pistol, and so forth?

In the month of June, thirty-seven years ago, I bought one of those pencil-cases from a boy whom I shall call Hawker, and who was in my form. Is he dead? Is he a millionaire? Is he a bankrupt now? He was an immense screw at school, and I believe to this day that the value of the thing for which I owed and eventually paid three-and-sixpence, was in reality not one-and-nine.

I certainly enjoyed the case at first a good deal, and amused myself with twiddling round the moveable calendar. But this pleasure wore off. The jewel, as I said, was not paid for, and Hawker, a large and violent boy, was exceedingly unpleasant as a creditor. His constant remark was, " When are you going to pay me that three-and-sixpence? What sneaks your relations must be? They come to see you. You go out to them on Saturdays and Sundays, and they never give you anything! Don't tell *me*, you little humbug!" and so forth. The truth is that my relations were respectable; but my parents were making a tour in Scotland; and my friends in London, whom I used to go and see, were most kind to me, certainly, but somehow never tipped me. That term, of May to August, 1823, passed in agonies then, in consequence of my debt to Hawker. What was the pleasure of a calendar pencil-case in comparison with the doubt and torture of mind occasioned by the sense of the debt, and the constant reproach in that fellow's scowling eyes and gloomy, coarse reminders? How was I to pay off such a debt out of sixpence a week? ludicrous! Why did not some one come to see me, and tip me? Ah! my dear sir, if you have any little friends at school, go and see them, and do the natural thing by them. You won't miss the sovereign. You don't know what a blessing it will be to them. Don't fancy they are too old—try 'em. And they will remember you, and bless you in future days; and their gratitude shall accompany your dreary after life; and they shall meet you kindly when thanks for kindness are scant. O mercy! shall I ever forget that sovereign you gave me, Captain Bob? or the agonies of being in debt to Hawker? In that very term, a relation of mine was going to India. I actually was fetched from school in order to take leave of him. I am afraid I told Hawker of this circumstance. I own I speculated upon my friend's giving me a pound. A pound? Pooh! A relation going to India, and deeply affected at parting from his darling kinsman, might give five pounds to the dear fellow! * * * There was Hawker when I came back—of course there he was. As he looked in my scared face, his turned livid with rage. He muttered curses, terrible from the lips of so young a boy. My relation, about to cross the ocean to fill a lucrative appointment, asked me with much interest about my progress at school, heard me construe a passage of Eutropius, the pleasing Latin work on which I was then engaged; gave me a God bless you, and sent me back to school; upon my word of honour, without so much as a half-crown! It is all very well, my dear sir, to say that boys contract habits of expecting tips from their parents' friends, that they become avaricious, and so forth. Avaricious! fudge! Boys contract habits of tart and toffee eating, which they do not carry into after life. On the contrary, I wish I *did* like 'em. What raptures of pleasure one could have now for five shillings, if one could but pick it off the pastrycook's tray! No. If you have any little friends at school, out with your half-crowns, my friend, and impart to those little ones the little fleeting joys of their age.

Well, then. At the beginning of August, 1823, Bartle-my-tide holidays came, and I was to go to my parents, who were at Tunbridge Wells. My place in the coach was taken by my tutor's servants—Bolt-in-Tun, Fleet Street, seven o'clock in the morning, was the word. My Tutor, the Rev. Edward P——, to whom I hereby present my best compliments, had a parting interview with me: gave me my little account for my governor: the remaining part of the coach-hire; five shillings for my own expenses; and some five-and-twenty shillings on an old account which had been overpaid, and was to be restored to my family.

Away I ran and paid Hawker his three-and-six. Ouf!

what a weight it was off my mind! (He was a **Norfolk** boy, and used to go home from Mrs. Nelson's Bell Inn, Aldgate—but that is not to the point.)   The next morning, of course, we were an hour before the time.   I and another boy shared a hackney-coach; two-and-six: porter for putting luggage on coach, threepence.   I had no more money of my own left.   Rasherwell, my companion, went into the Bolt-in-Tun coffee-room, and had a good breakfast.   I couldn't; because, though I had five-and-twenty shillings of my parents' money, I had none of my own, you see.

I certainly intended to go without breakfast, and still remember how strongly I had that resolution in my mind. But there was that hour to wait.   A beautiful August morning—I am very hungry.   There is Rasherwell "tucking" away in the coffee-room.   I pace the street, as sadly almost as if I had been coming to school, not going thence. I turned into a court by mere chance—I vow it was by mere chance—and there I see a coffee-shop with a placard in the window, *Coffee Twopence. Round of buttered toast, Twopence.*   And here am I hungry, penniless, with five-and-twenty shillings of my parents' money in my pocket.

What would you have done?   You see I had had my money, and spent it in that pencil-case affair.   The five-and-twenty shillings were a trust—by me to be handed over.

But then would my parents wish their only child to be actually without breakfast?   Having this money, and being so hungry, so *very* hungry, mightn't I take ever so little? Mightn't I at home eat as much as I chose?

Well, I went into the coffee-shop, and spent fourpence. I remember the taste of the coffee and toast to this day—a peculiar, muddy, not-sweet-enough, most fragrant coffee— a rich, rancid, yet not-buttered-enough, delicious toast. The waiter had nothing.   At any rate, fourpence I know was the sum I spent.   And the hunger appeased, I got on the coach a guilty being.

At the last stage,—what is its name?   I have forgotten in seven-and-thirty years,—there is an inn with a little green and trees before it; and by the trees there is an open carriage. It is our carriage. Yes, there are Prince and Blucher, the horses; and my parents in the carriage. Oh! how I had been counting the days until this one came! Oh! how happy had I been to see them yesterday! But there was that fourpence. All the journey down the toast had choked me, and the coffee poisoned me.

I was in such a state of remorse about the fourpence, that I forgot the maternal joy and caresses, the tender paternal voice. I pull out the twenty-four shillings and eightpence with a trembling hand.

"Here's your money," I gasp out, "which Mr. P. owes you, all but fourpence. I owed three-and-sixpence to Hawker out of my money for a pencil-case, and I had none left, and I took fourpence of yours, and had some coffee at a shop."

I suppose I must have been choking whilst uttering this confession.

"My dear boy," says the governor, "why didn't you go and breakfast at the hotel?"

"He must be starved," says my mother.

I had confessed; I had been a prodigal; I had been taken back to my parents' arms again. It was not a very great crime as yet, or a very long career of prodigality; but don't we know that a boy who takes a pin which is not his own, will take a thousand pounds when occasion serves, bring his parents' grey heads with sorrow to the grave, and carry his own to the gallows? Witness the career of Dick Idle, upon whom our friend Mr. Sala has been discoursing. Dick only began by playing pitch-and-toss on a tombstone: playing fair, for what we know: and even for that sin he was promptly caned by the beadle. The bamboo was ineffectual to cane that reprobate's bad courses out of him. From pitch-and-toss he proceeded to manslaughter if necessary: to highway robbery; to Tyburn and the rope there. Ah! heaven be thanked, my parents' heads are still above the grass, and mine still out of the noose.

As I look up from my desk, I see Tunbridge Wells Com-

mon and the rocks, the strange familiar place which I remember forty years ago.   Boys saunter over the green with
stumps and cricket-bats.   Other boys gallop by on the rid-
ing-master's hacks.   I protest it is *Cramp, Riding Master,*
as it used to be in the reign of George IV., and that Cen-
taur Cramp must be at least a hundred years old.   Yonder
comes a footman with a bundle of novels from the library.
Are they as good as *our* novels?   Oh! how delightful they
were!   Shades of Valancour, awful ghost of Manfroni,
how I shudder at your appearance!   Sweet image of Thaddeus of Warsaw, how often has this almost infantile hand
tried to depict you in a Polish cap and richly embroidered
tights!   And as for Corinthian Tom in light blue pantaloons and Hessians, and Jerry Hawthorn from the country,
can all the fashion, can all the splendour of real life which
these eyes have subsequently beheld, can all the wit I have
heard or read in later times, compare with your fashion,
with your brilliancy, with your delightful grace, and sparkling vivacious rattle?

Who knows?   They *may* have kept those very books at
the library still—at the well-remembered library on the
Pantiles, where they sell that delightful, useful Tunbridge
ware.   I will go and see.   I went my way to the Pantiles,
the queer little old-world Pantiles, where, a hundred years
since, so much good company came to take its pleasure.
Is it possible, that in the past century, gentlefolks of the
first rank (as I read lately in a lecture on George II. in the
Cornhill Magazine) assembled here and entertained each
other with gaming, dancing, fiddling, and tea?   There are
fiddlers, harpers, and trumpeters performing at this moment in a weak little old balcony, but where is the fine
company?   Where are the earls, duchesses, bishops, and
magnificent embroidered gamesters?   A half dozen of children and their nurses are listening to the musicians; an old
lady or two in a poke bonnet passes, and for the rest, I see
but an uninteresting population of native tradesmen.   As
for the library, its window is full of pictures of burly theo-
logians, and their works, sermons, apologues, and so forth.

Can I go in and ask the young ladies at the counter for "Manfroni, or the One-Handed Monk," and "Life in London, or the Adventures of Corinthian Tom, Jeremiah Hawthorn, Esq., and their friend Bob Logic?"—absurd. I turn away abashed from the casement—from the Pantiles —no longer Pantiles, but Parade. I stroll over the common and survey the beautiful purple hills around, twinkling with a thousand bright villas, which have sprung up over this charming ground since first I saw it. What an admirable scene of peace and plenty! What a delicious air breathes over the heath, blows the cloud shadows across it, and murmurs through the full-clad trees! Can the world show a land fairer, richer, more cheerful? I see a portion of it when I look up from the window at which I write. But fair scene, green woods, bright terraces gleaming in sunshine, and purple clouds swollen with summer rain—nay, the very pages over which my head bends—disappear from before my eyes. They are looking backwards, back into forty years off, into a dark room, into a little house hard by on the Common here, in the Bartlemy-tide holidays. The parents have gone to town for two days: the house is all his own, his own and a grim old maidservant's, and a little boy is seated at night in the lonely drawing-room, poring over "Manfroni, or the One-Handed Monk," so frightened that he scarcely dares to turn round.

DE JUVENTUTE.

Our last Paper of this veracious and roundabout series related to a period which can only be historical to a great number of readers of this Magazine. Four I saw at the station to-day with orange-covered books in their hands, who can but have known George IV. by books, and statues, and pictures. Elderly gentlemen were in their prime, old men in their middle age, when he reigned over us. His image remains on coins; on a picture or two hanging here and there in a Club or old-fashioned dining-room; on horse-back, as at Trafalgar Square, for example, where I defy any monarch to look more uncomfortable. He turns up in sundry memoirs and histories which have been published of late days; in Mr. Massey's History; in the Buckingham and Grenville Correspondence; and gentlemen who have accused a certain writer of disloyalty are referred to those volumes to see whether the picture drawn of George is over-charged. Charon has paddled him off; he has mingled with the crowded republic of the dead. His effigy smiles from a canvas or two. Breechless he bestrides his steed in Trafalgar Square. I believe he still wears his robes at Madame Tussaud's (Madame herself having quitted Baker Street and life, and found him she modelled t'other side the Stygian stream). On the head of a five-shilling piece we still occasionally come upon him, with St. George, the dragon-slayer, on the other side of the coin. Ah me! did this George slay many dragons? Was he a brave, heroic champion, and rescuer of virgins? Well! well! have you and I overcome all the dragons that assail *us?* come alive and victorious out of all the caverns which we have entered in life, and succoured, at risk of life and limb, all poor distressed persons in whose naked limbs the dragon Pov-erty is about to fasten his fangs, whom the dragon Crime is poisoning with his horrible breath, and about to crunch up and devour? O my royal liege! O my gracious prince and warrior! *You* a champion to fight that monster? Your feeble spear ever pierce that slimy paunch or plated back? See how the flames come gurgling out of his red-hot brazen throat! What a roar! Nearer and nearer he trails, with eyes flaming like the lamps of a railroad engine. How he squeals, rushing out through the darkness of his tunnel! Now he is near. Now he is *here*. And now— what?—lance, shield, knight, feathers, horse and all? O horror, horror! Next day, round the monster's cave, there lie a few bones more. You who wish to keep yours in your skins, be thankful that you are not called upon to go out and fight dragons. Be grateful that they don't sally out and swallow you. Keep a wise distance from their caves, lest you pay too dearly for approaching them. Remember that years passed, and whole districts were ravaged, before the warrior came who was able to cope with the devouring monster. When that knight *does* make his appearance, with all my heart let us go out and welcome him with our best songs, huzzahs, and laurel wreaths, and eagerly recognize his valour and victory. But he comes only seldom. Countless knights were slain before St. George won the battle. In the battle of life are we all going to try for the honours of championship? If we can do our duty, if we can keep our place pretty honourably through the combat, let us say, *Laus Deo!* at the end of it, as the firing ceases, and the night falls over the field.

The old were middle-aged, the elderly were in their prime, then, thirty years since, when yon royal George was still fighting the dragon. As for you, my pretty lass, with your saucy hat and golden tresses tumbled in your net, and you, my spruce young gentleman in your mandarin's cap (the young folks at the country-place where I am staying are so attired), your parents were unknown to each other, and wore short frocks and short jackets, at the date of this five-shilling piece. Only to-day I met a dog-cart crammed with children—children with mustachios and mandarin caps, children with saucy hats and hair-nets—children in

short frocks and knickerbockers (surely the prettiest boy's
dress that has appeared these hundred years)—children
from twenty years of age to six; and father, with mother
by his side, driving in front—and on father's countenance
I saw that very laugh which I remember perfectly in the
time when this crown-piece was coined—in *his* time, in
King George's time, when we were school-boys seated on
the same form.   The smile was just as broad, as bright, as
jolly, as I remember it in the past—unforgotten, though
not seen or thought of, for how many decades of years, and
quite and instantly familiar, though so long out of sight.

Any contemporary of that coin who takes it up and reads
the inscription round the laurelled head, "Georgius IV.
Britanniarum Rex. Fid. Def. 1823," if he will but look
steadily enough at the round, and utter the proper incanta-
tion, I daresay may conjure back his life there.   Look well,
my elderly friend, and tell me what you see?   First, I see
a Sultan, with hair, beautiful hair, and a crown of laurels
round his head, and his name is Georgius Rex. Fid. Def.,
and so on.   Now the Sultan has disappeared; and what is
that I see?   A boy,—a boy in a jacket.   He is at a desk;
he has great books before him, Latin and Greek books and
dictionaries.   Yes, but behind the great books, which he
pretends to read, is a little one, with pictures, which he is
really reading.   It is—yes, I can read now—it is the
"Heart of Mid Lothian," by the author of "Waverley"—
or, no, it is "Life in London, or the Adventures of Corinthian Tom, Jeremiah Hawthorn, and their friend Bob
Logic," by Pierce Egan; and it has pictures—oh! such
funny pictures!   As he reads, there comes behind the boy
a man, a dervish, in a black gown, like a woman, and a
black square cap, and he has a book in each hand, and he
seizes the boy who is reading the picture-book, and lays his
head upon one of his books, and smacks it with the other.
The boy makes faces, and so that picture disappears.

Now the boy has grown bigger.   *He* has got on a black
gown and cap, something like the dervish.   He is at a
table, and ever so many bottles on it, and fruit, and tobac-

co; and other young dervishes come in. They seem as if they were singing. To them enters an old moollah, he takes down their names, and orders them all to go to bed. What is this? a carriage, with four beautiful horses all galloping —a man in red is blowing a trumpet. Many young men are on the carriage—one of them is driving the horses. Surely they won't drive into that—ah! they have all disappeared? And now I see one of the young men alone. He is walking in a street—a dark street—presently a light comes to a window. There is the shadow of a lady who passes. He stands there till the light goes out. Now he is in a room scribbling on a piece of paper, and kissing a miniature every now and then. They seem to be lines each pretty much of a length. I can read *heart, smart, dart ; Mary, fairy ; Cupid, stupid ; true, you ;* and never mind what more. Bah! it is bosh. Now see, he has got a gown on again, and a wig of white hair on his head, and he is sitting with other dervishes in a great room full of them, and on a throne in the middle is an old Sultan in scarlet, sitting before a desk, and he wears a wig too—and the young man gets up and speaks to him. And now what is here? He is in a room with ever so many children, and the miniature hanging up. Can it be a likeness of that woman who is sitting before that copper urn, with a silver vase in her hand, from which she is pouring hot liquor into cups? Was *she* ever a fairy? She is as fat as a hippopotamus now. He is sitting on a divan by the fire. He has a paper on his knees. Read the name of the paper. It is the *Superfine Review.* It inclines to think that Mr. Dickens is not a true gentleman, that Mr. Thackeray is not a true gentleman, and that when the one is pert and the other is arch, we, the gentlemen of the *Superfine Review,* think, and think rightly, that we have some cause to be indignant. The great cause why modern humour and modern sentimentalism repel us, is that they are unwarrantably familiar. Now, Mr. Sterne, the *Superfine Reviewer* thinks, "was a true sentimentalist, because he was *above all things* a true gentleman." The flattering inference is obvious:

let us be thankful for having an elegant moralist watching over us, and learn, if not too old, to imitate his highbred politeness and catch his unobtrusive grace. If we are unwarrantably familiar, we know who is not. If we repel by pertness, we know who never does. If our language offends, we know whose is always modest. O pity! The vision has disappeared off the silver, the images of youth and the past are vanishing away! We who have lived before railways were made, belong to another world. In how many hours could the Prince of Wales drive from Brighton to London, with a light carriage built expressly, and relays of horses longing to gallop the next stage? Do you remember Sir Somebody, the coachman of the Age, who took our half-crown so affably? It was only yesterday; but what a gulph between now and then? *Then* was the old world. Stage-coaches, more or less swift, riding-horses, pack-horses, highwaymen, knights in armour, Norman invaders, Roman legions, Druids, Ancient Britons, painted blue, and so forth—all these belong to the old period. I will concede a halt in the midst of it, and allow that gunpowder and printing tended to modernize the world. But your railroad starts the new era, and we of a certain age belong to the new time and the old one. We are of the time of chivalry as well as the Black Prince or Sir Walter Manny. We are of the age of steam. We have stepped out of the old world on to Brunel's vast deck, and across the waters *ingens patet tellus*. Towards what new continent are we wending? to what new laws, new manners, new politics, vast new expanses of liberties unknown as yet, or only surmised? I used to know a man who had invented a flying-machine. "Sir," he would say, "give me but five hundred pounds, and I will make it. It is so simple of construction that I tremble daily lest some other person should light upon and patent my discovery." Perhaps faith was wanting; perhaps the five hundred pounds. He is dead, and somebody else must make the flying-machine. But that will only be a step forward on the journey already begun since we quitted the old world. There it lies on the other side of yonder embankments. You young folks have never seen it: and Waterloo is to you no more than Agincourt, and George IV. than Sardanapalus. We elderly people have lived in that prærailroad world, which has passed into limbo and vanished from under us. I tell you it was firm under our feet once, and not long ago. They have raised those railroad embankments up, and shut off the old world that was behind them. Climb up that bank on which the irons are laid, and look to the other side —it is gone. There *is* no other side. Try and catch yesterday. Where is it? Here is a *Times* newspaper, dated Monday 26th, and this is Tuesday 27th. Suppose you deny there was such a day as yesterday?

We who lived before railways, and survive out of the ancient world, are like Father Noah and his family out of the Ark. The children will gather round and say to us patriarchs, "Tell us, grandpapa, about the old world." And we shall mumble our old stories; and we shall drop off one by one; and there will be fewer and fewer of us, and these very old and feeble. There will be but ten prærailroadites left: then three—then two—then one—then O! If the hippopotamus had the least sensibility (of which I cannot trace any signs either in his hide or his face), I think he would go down to the bottom of his tank, and never come up again. Does he not see that he belongs to bygone ages, and that his great hulking barrel of a body is out of place in these times? What has he in common with the brisk young life surrounding him? In the watches of the night, when the keepers are asleep, when the birds are on one leg, when even the little armadillo is quiet, and the monkeys have ceased their chatter,—he, I mean the hippopotamus, and the elephant, and the long-necked giraffe, perhaps may lay their heads together and have a colloquy about the great silent antediluvian world which they remember, where mighty monsters floundered through the ooze, crocodiles basked on the banks, and dragons darted out of the caves and waters before men were made to slay them. We who lived before railways—are antediluvians

—we must pass away. We are growing scarcer every day; and old—old—very old relicts of the times when George was still fighting the Dragon.

Not long since, a company of horse-riders paid a visit to our watering-place. We went to see them, and I bethought me that young Walter Juvenis, who was in the place, might like also to witness the performance. A pantomime is not always amusing to persons who have attained a certain age; but a boy at a pantomime is always amused and amusing, and, to see his pleasure, is good for most hypochondriacs.

We sent to Walter's mother, requesting that he might join us, and the kind lady replied that the boy had already been at the morning performance of the equestrians, but was most eager to go in the evening likewise. And go he did; and laughed at all Mr. Merryman's remarks, though he remembered them with remarkable accuracy, and insisted upon waiting to the very end of the fun, and was only induced to retire just before its conclusion by representations that the ladies of the party would be incommoded if they were to wait and undergo the rush and trample of the crowd round about. When this fact was pointed out to him, he yielded at once, though with a heavy heart, his eyes looking longingly towards the ring as we retreated out of the booth. We were scarcely clear of the place, when we heard "God save the King," played by the equestrian band, the signal that all was over. Our companion entertained us with scraps of the dialogue on our way home —precious crumbs of wit which he had brought away from that feast. He laughed over them again as we walked under the stars. He has them now, and takes them out of the pocket of his memory, and crunches a bit, and relishes it with a sentimental tenderness, too, for he is, no doubt, back at school by this time; the holidays are over; and Doctor Birch's young friends have reassembled.

Queer jokes, which caused a thousand simple mouths to grin! As the jaded Merryman uttered them to the old gentleman with the whip, some of the old folks in the audi-

ence, I daresay, indulged in reflections of their own.
There was one joke—I utterly forget it—but it began with
Merryman saying what he had for dinner. He had mutton for dinner, at one o'clock, after which "he had to
come to business." And then came the point. Walter
Juvenis, Esq., Rev. Doctor Birch's, Market Rodborough,
if you read this, will you please send me a line, and let
me know what was the joke Mr. Merryman made about
having his dinner? *You* remember well enough. But
do I want to know? Suppose a boy takes a favourite,
long-cherished lump of cake out of his pocket, and offers
you a bite? *Merci!* The fact is, I *don't* care much about
knowing that joke of Mr. Merryman's.

But whilst he was talking about his dinner, and his mutton, and his landlord, and his business, I felt a great interest about Mr. M. in private life—about his wife, lodgings,
earnings, and general history, and I daresay was forming
a picture of those in my mind:—wife cooking the mutton;
children waiting for it; Merryman in his plain clothes,
and so forth; during which contemplation the joke was
uttered and laughed at, and Mr. M., resuming his professional duties, was tumbling over head and heels. Do not
suppose I am going, *sicut est mos*, to indulge in moralities
about buffoons, paint, motley, and mountebanking. Nay,
Prime Ministers rehearse their jokes; Opposition leaders
prepare and polish them; Tabernacle preachers must arrange
them in their mind before they utter them. All I mean
is, that I would like to know any one of these performers
thoroughly, and out of his uniform: that preacher, and
why in his travels this and that point struck him; wherein
lies his power of pathos, humour, eloquence;—that Minister of State, and what moves him, and how his private
heart is working;—I would only say that, at a certain time
of life certain things cease to interest: but about *some*
things when we cease to care, what will be the use of life,
sight, hearing? Poems are written, and we cease to admire. Lady Jones invites us, and we yawn; she ceases to
invite us, and we are resigned. The last time I saw a bal-

let at the opera—oh! it is many years ago—I fell asleep in
the stalls, wagging my head in insane dreams, and I hope
affording amusement to the company, while the feet of five
hundred nymphs were cutting flicflacs on the stage at a
few paces' distance.   Ah, I remember a different state of
things!   *Credite posteri.*   To see those nymphs—gracious
powers, how beautiful they were!   That leering, painted,
shrivelled, thin-armed, thick-ankled old thing, cutting
dreary capers, coming thumping down on her board out of
time—*that* an opera-dancer?   Pooh!   My dear Walter, the
great difference between *my* time and yours, who will enter
life some two or three years hence, is that, now, the dancing women and singing women are ludicrously old, out of
time, and out of tune; the paint is so visible, and the dinge
and wrinkles of their wretched old cotton stockings, that I
am surprised how anybody can like to look at them.   And
as for laughing at *me* for falling asleep, I can't understand
a man of sense doing otherwise.   In *my* time, *à la bonne
heure*.   In the reign of George IV., I give you my honour,
all the dancers at the opera were as beautiful as Houris.
Even in William IV.'s time, when I think of Duvernay
prancing in as the Bayadère,—I say it was a vision of loveliness such as mortal eyes can't see now-a-days.   How well
I remember the tune to which she used to appear!   Kaled
used to say to the Sultan, "My lord, a troop of those dancing and singing gurls called Bayadères approaches," and,
to the clash of cymbals, and the thumping of my heart, in
she used to dance!   There has never been anything like it
—never.   There never will be—I laugh to scorn old people
who tell me about your Noblet, your Montessu, your Ves-
tris, your Parisot—pshaw, the senile twaddlers!   And the
impudence of the young men, with their music and their
dancers of to-day!   I tell you the women are dreary old
creatures.   I tell you one air in an opera is just like
another, and they send all rational creatures to sleep.   Ah,
Ronzi de Begnis, thou lovely one!   Ah, Caradori, thou
smiling angel!   Ah, Malibran!   Nay, I will come to modern times, and acknowledge that Lablache was a very good

singer thirty years ago (though Porto was the boy for me): and then we had Ambrogetti, and Curioni, and Donzelli, a rising young singer.

But what is most certain and lamentable is the decay of stage beauty since the days of George IV. Think of Sontag! I remember her in "Otello" and the "Donna del Lago" in '28. I remember being behind the scenes at the opera (where numbers of us young fellows of fashion used to go), and seeing Sontag let her hair fall down over her shoulders previous to her murder by Donzelli. Young fellows have never seen beauty like *that*, heard such a voice, seen such hair, such eyes. Don't tell *me!* A man who has been about town since the reign of George IV., ought he not to know better than you young lads who have seen nothing? The deterioration of women is lamentable; and the conceit of the young fellows more lamentable still, that they won't see this fact, but persist in thinking their time as good as ours.

Bless me! when I was a lad, the stage was covered with angels, who sang, acted, and danced. When I remember the Adelphi, and the actresses there: when I think of Miss Chester, and Miss Love, and Mrs. Serle at Sadler's Wells, and her forty glorious pupils—of the Opera and Noblet, and the exquisite young Taglioni, and Pauline Leroux, and a host more! One much-admired being of those days I confess I never cared for, and that was the chief *male* dancer—a very important personage then, with a bare neck, bare arms, a tunic, and a hat and feathers, who used to divide the applause with the ladies, and who has now sunk down a trap-door for ever. And this frank admission ought to show that I am not your mere twaddling *laudator temporis acti*—your old fogey who can see no good except in his own time.

They say that claret is better now-a-days, and cookery much improved since the days of *my* monarch—of George IV. *Pastry Cookery* is certainly not so good. I have often eaten half-a-crown's worth (including, I trust, ginger-beer) at our school pastrycook's, and that is a proof that the pastry must have been very good, for could I do as much now? I passed by the pastrycook's shop lately, having occasion to visit my old school. It looked a very dingy old baker's; misfortunes may have come over him—those penny tarts certainly did *not* look so nice as I remember them: but he may have grown careless as he has grown old (I should judge him to be now about ninety-six years of age) and his hand may have lost its cunning.

Not that we were not great epicures. I remember how we constantly grumbled at the quantity of the food in our master's house—which on my conscience I believe was excellent and plentiful—and how we tried once or twice to eat him out of house and home. At the pastrycook's we may have over-eaten ourselves (I have admitted half-a-crown's worth for my own part, but I don't like to mention the *real* figure for fear of perverting the present generation of boys by my monstrous confession)—we may have eaten too much, I say. We did; but what then? The school apothecary was sent for: a couple of small globules at night, a trifling preparation of senna in the morning, and we had not to go to school, so that the draught was an actual pleasure.

For our amusements, besides the games in vogue, which were pretty much in old times as they are now (except cricket, *par exemple*—and I wish the present youth joy of their bowling, and suppose Armstrong and Whitworth will bowl at them with light field-pieces next), there were novels—ah! I trouble you to find such novels in the present day! O "Scottish Chiefs," didn't we weep over you! O "Mysteries of Udolfo," didn't I and Briggs minor draw pictures out of you, as I have said? This was the sort of thing: this (see opposite page) was the fashion in *our* day. Efforts, feeble indeed, but still giving pleasure to us and our friends. "I say, old boy, draw us Vivaldi tortured in the Inquisition," or "Draw us Don Quixote and the windmills, you know," amateurs would say, to boys who had a love of drawing. "Peregrine Pickle" we liked, our fathers admiring it, and telling us (the sly old boys) it was capital fun; but I think I was rather bewildered by it, though "Roderick Random" was and remains delightful. I don't remember having Sterne in the school library, no doubt be-

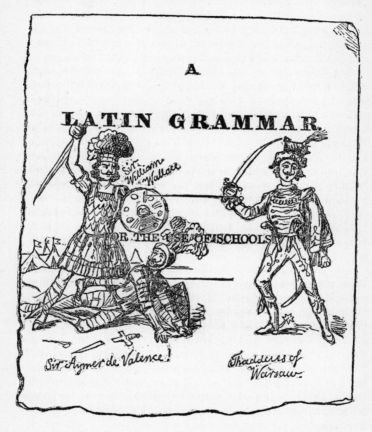

cause the works of that divine were not considered decent for young people. Ah! not against thy genius, O father of Uncle Toby and Trim, would I say a word in disrespect. But I am thankful to live in times when men no longer have the temptation to write so as to call blushes on women's cheeks, and would shame to whisper wicked allusions to honest boys. Then, above all, we had WALTER SCOTT, the kindly, the generous, the pure—the companion of what countless delightful hours; the purveyor of how much happiness; the friend whom we recall as the constant benefactor of our youth! How well I remember the type and the brownish paper of the old duodecimo "Tales of My Landlord!" I have never dared to read the "Pirate," and the "Bride of Lammermoor," or "Kenilworth," from that day to this, because the finale is unhappy, and people die, and are murdered at the end. But "Ivanhoe," and "Quentin Durward!" Oh! for a half-holiday, and a quiet corner, and one of those books again! Those books, and perhaps those eyes with which we read them; and, it may be, the brains behind the eyes! It may be the tart was good; but how fresh the appetite was! If the gods would give me the desire of my heart, I should be able to write a story which boys would relish for the next few dozen of centuries. The boy-critic loves the story: grown up, he loves the author who wrote the story. Hence the kindly tie is established between writer and reader, and lasts pretty nearly for life. I meet people now who don't care for Walter Scott, or the "Arabian Nights;" I am sorry for them, unless they in their time have found *their* romancer—their charming Scheherazade. By the way, Walter, when you are writing, tell me who is the favourite novelist in the fourth form now? Have you got any things so good and kindly as dear Miss Edgeworth's "Frank?" It used to belong to a fellow's sisters generally; but though he pretended to despise it, and said, "Oh, stuff for girls!" he read it; and I think there were one or two passages which would try my eyes now, were I to meet with the little book.

As for Thomas and Jeremiah (it is only my witty way of calling Tom and Jerry), I went to the British Museum the other day on purpose to get it; but somehow, if you will press the question so closely, on reperusal, Tom and Jerry

is not so brilliant as I had supposed it to be. The pictures
are just as fine as ever; and I shook hands with broad-
backed Jerry Hawthorn and Corinthian Tom with delight,
after many years' absence. But the style of the writing,
I own, was not pleasing to me; I even thought it a little
vulgar—well! well! other writers have been considered
vulgar—and as a description of the sports and amusements
of London in the ancient times, more curious than amusing.

But the pictures!—oh! the pictures are noble still!
First, there is Jerry arriving from the country, in a green
coat and leather gaiters, and being measured for a fashionable suit at Corinthian House, by Corinthian Tom's tailor.
Then away for the career of pleasure and fashion. The
park! delicious excitement! The theatre! the saloon!! the
green-room!!! Rapturous bliss—the opera itself! and then
perhaps to Temple Bar, to *knock down a Charley* there!
There are Jerry and Tom, with their tights and little
cocked hats, coming from the opera—very much as gentlemen in waiting on royalty are habited now. There they
are at Almack's itself, amidst a crowd of high-bred personages, with the Duke of Clarence himself looking at them
dancing. Now, strange change, they are in Tom Cribb's
parlour, where they don't seem to be a whit less at home
than in fashion's gilded halls: and now they are at New-
gate, seeing the irons knocked off the malefactors' legs
previous to execution. What hardened ferocity in the
countenance of the desperado in yellow breeches! What
compunction in the face of the gentleman in black (who, I
suppose, has been forging), and who clasps his hands, and
listens to the chaplain! Now we haste away to merrier
scenes: to Tattersall's (ah! gracious powers! what a funny
fellow that actor was who performed Dicky Green in that
scene at the play!); and now we are at a private party, at
which Corinthian Tom is waltzing (and very gracefully,
too, as you must confess) with Corinthian Kate, whilst Bob
Logic, the Oxonian, is playing on the piano!

"After," the text says, "*the Oxonian* had played several
pieces of lively music, he requested as a favour that Kate

and his friend Tom would perform a waltz. Kate without
any hesitation immediately stood up. Tom offered his
hand to his fascinating partner, and the dance took place.
The plate conveys a correct representation of the 'gay
scene' at that precise moment. The anxiety of *the Oxo-*

nian to witness the attitudes of the elegant pair had nearly
put a stop to their movements. On turning round from
the pianoforte and presenting his comical *mug*, Kate could
scarcely suppress a laugh."

And no wonder; just look at it now (as I have copied it
to the best of my humble ability), and compare Master

Logic's countenance and attitude with the splendid elegance of Tom! Now every London man is weary and *blasé*. There is an enjoyment of life in these young bucks of 1823 which contrasts strangely with our feelings of 1860. Here, for instance, is a specimen of their talk and walk. " ' If,' says Logic—' if *enjoyment* is your *motto*, you may make the most of an evening at Vauxhall, more than at any other place in the metropolis. It is all free and easy. Stay as long as you like, and depart when you think proper.'— ' Your description is so flattering,' replied JERRY, ' that I do not care how soon the time arrives for us to start.' LOGIC proposed a ' *bit of a stroll* ' in order to get rid of an hour or two, which was immediately accepted by Tom and Jerry. A *turn* or two in Bond Street, a *stroll* through Piccadilly, a *look in* at TATTERSALL'S, a *ramble* through Pall Mall, and a *strut* on the Corinthian path, fully occupied the time of our heroes until the hour for dinner arrived, when a few glasses of TOM'S rich wines soon put them on the *qui vive*. VAUXHALL was then the object in view, and the TRIO started, bent upon enjoying the pleasures which this place so amply affords."

How nobly those inverted commas, those italics, those capitals, bring out the writer's wit and relieve the eye! They are as good as jokes, though you mayn't quite perceive the point. Mark the varieties of lounge in which the young men indulge—now a *stroll*, then a *look in*, then *a ramble*, and presently *a strut*. When George, Prince of Wales, was twenty, I have read in an old Magazine, "the Prince's lounge " was a peculiar manner of walking which the young bucks imitated. At Windsor George III. had *a cat's path*—a sly early walk which the good old king took in the gray morning before his household was astir. What was the Corinthian path here recorded? Does any antiquary know? And what were the rich wines which our friends took, and which enabled them to enjoy Vauxhall? Vauxhall is gone, but the wines which could occasion such a delightful perversion of the intellect as to enable it to enjoy ample pleasures there, what were they?

So the game of life proceeds, until Jerry Hawthorn, the rustic, is fairly knocked up by all this excitement and is forced to go home, and the last picture represents him getting into the coach at the White Horse Cellar, he being one of six inside; whilst his friends shake him by the hand; whilst the sailor mounts on the roof; whilst the Jews hang round with oranges, knives, and sealing-wax: whilst the guard is closing the door.   Where are they now, those sealing-wax vendors? where are the guards? where are the jolly teams? where are the coaches? and where the youth that climbed inside and out of them; that heard the merry horn which sounds no more; that saw the sun rise over Stonehenge; that rubbed away the bitter tears at night after parting as the coach sped on the journey to school and London; that looked out with beating heart as the milestones flew by, for the welcome corner where began home and holidays?

It is night now: and here is home.   Gathered under the quiet roof elders and children lie alike at rest.   In the midst of a great peace and calm, the stars look out from the heavens.   The silence is peopled with the past; sorrowful remorses for sins and shortcomings—memories of passionate joys and griefs rise out of their graves, both now alike calm and sad.   Eyes, as I shut mine, look at me, that have long ceased to shine.   The town and the fair landscape sleep under the starlight, wreathed in the autumn mists.   Twinkling among the houses a light keeps watch here and there, in what may be a sick chamber or two.   The clock tolls sweetly in the silent air.   Here is night and rest.   An awful sense of thanks makes the heart swell, and the head bow, as I pass to my room through the sleeping house, and feel as though a hushed blessing were upon it.

ON A JOKE I ONCE HEARD FROM THE LATE THOMAS HOOD

THE good-natured reader who has perused some of these rambling papers has long since seen (if to see has been worth his trouble) that the writer belongs to the old-fashioned classes of this world, loves to remember very much more than to prophesy, and though he can't help being carried onward, and downward, perhaps, on the hill of life, the swift milestones marking their forties, fifties—how many tens or lustres shall we say?—he sits under Time, the white-wigged charioteer, with his back to the horses, and his face to the past, looking at the receding landscape and the hills fading into the grey distance. Ah me! those grey, distant hills were green once, and *here*, and covered with smiling people! As we came *up* the hill there was difficulty, and here and there a hard pull to be sure, but strength, and spirits, and all sorts of cheery incident and companionship on the road; there were the tough struggles (by Heaven's merciful will) overcome, the pauses, the faintings, the weakness, the lost way, perhaps, the bitter weather, the dreadful partings, the lonely night, the passionate grief—towards these I turn my thoughts as I sit and think in my hobby-coach under Time, the silver-wigged charioteer. The young folks in the same carriage meanwhile are looking forwards. Nothing escapes their keen eyes—not a flower at the side of a cottage garden, nor a bunch of rosy-faced children at the gate: the landscape is all bright, the air brisk and jolly, the town yonder looks beautiful, and do you think they have learned to be difficult about the dishes at the inn?

Now, suppose Paterfamilias on his journey with his wife and children in the sociable, and he passes an ordinary brick house on the road with an ordinary little garden in

the front, we will say, and quite an ordinary knocker to
the door, and as many sashed windows as you please, quite
common and square, and tiles, windows, chimney-pots,
quite like others; or suppose, in driving over such and such
a common, he sees an ordinary tree, and an ordinary donkey browsing under it, if you like—wife and daughter look
at these objects without the slightest particle of curiosity
or interest. What is a brass knocker to them but a lion's
head, or what not? and a thorn-tree with a pool beside it,
but a pool in which a thorn and a jackass are reflected?

But you remember how once upon a time your heart used
to beat, as you beat on that brass knocker, and whose eyes
looked from the window above? You remember how by
that thorn-tree and pool, where the geese were performing
a prodigious evening concert, there might be seen, at a certain hour, somebody in a certain cloak and bonnet, who
happened to be coming from a village yonder, and whose
image has flickered in that pool? In that pool, near the
thorn? Yes, in that goose-pool, never mind how long ago,
when there were reflected the images of the geese—and two
geese more. Here, at least, an oldster may have the advantage of his young fellow travellers, and so Putney
Heath or the New Road may be invested with a halo of
brightness invisible to them, because it only beams out of
his own soul.

I have been reading the Memorials of Hood by his children,* and wonder whether the book will have the same
interest for others and for younger people, as for persons
of my own age and calling. Books of travel to any country become interesting to us who have been there. Men
revisit the old school, though hateful to them, with ever so
much kindliness and sentimental affection. There was the
tree, under which the bully licked you: here the ground
where you had to fag out on holidays, and so forth. In a
word, my dear sir, *You* are the most interesting subject to
yourself, of any that can occupy your worship's thoughts.
I have no doubt, a Crimean soldier, reading a history of

* "Memorials of Thomas Hood." Moxon. 1860. 2 vols.

that siege, and how Jones and the gallant 99th were ordered
to charge or what not, thinks, "Ah, yes, we of the 100th
were placed so and so, I perfectly remember." So with
this memorial of poor Hood, it may have, no doubt, a
greater interest for me than for others, for I was fighting,
so to speak, in a different part of the field, and engaged,
a young subaltern in the Battle of Life, in which Hood
fell, young still, and covered with glory. "The Bridge of
Sighs" was his Corunna, his heights of Abraham—sickly,
weak, wounded, he fell in the full blaze and fame of that
great victory.

What manner of man was the genius who penned that
famous song? What like was Wolfe, who climbed and
conquered on those famous heights of Abraham? We all
want to know details regarding men who have achieved famous feats, whether of war, or wit, or eloquence, or endurance, or knowledge. His one or two happy and heroic
actions take a man's name and memory out of the crowd
of names and memories. Henceforth he stands eminent.
We scan him: we want to know all about him; we walk
round and examine him, are curious, perhaps, and think
are we not as strong and tall and capable as yonder champion; were we not bred as well, and could we not endure
the winter's cold as well as he? Or we look up with all
our eyes of admiration; will find no fault in our hero: declare his beauty and proportions perfect; his critics envious
detractors, and so forth. Yesterday, before he performed
his feat, he was nobody. Who cared about his birthplace,
his parentage, or the colour of his hair? To-day, by some
single achievement, or by a series of great actions to which
his genius accustoms us, he is famous, and antiquarians
are busy finding out under what schoolmaster's ferule he
was educated, where his grandmother was vaccinated, and
so forth. If half a dozen washing-bills of Goldsmith's
were to be found to-morrow, would they not inspire a general interest, and be printed in a hundred papers? I lighted
upon Oliver, not very long since, in an old Town and Country Magazine, at the Pantheon masquerade, "in an old Eng-

lish habit." Straightway my imagination ran out to meet
him, to look at him, to follow him about. I forgot the
names of scores of fine gentlemen of the past age, who were
mentioned besides. We want to see this man who has
amused and charmed us; who has been our friend, and
given us hours of pleasant companionship and kindly
thought. I protest when I came, in the midst of those
names of people of fashion, and beaux, and demireps, upon
those names " *Sir J. R-yn-lds, in a domino ; Mr. Cr-d-ck
and Dr. G-ldsm-th, in two old English dresses,*" I had, so
to speak, my heart in my mouth. What, *you* here, my
dear Sir Joshua? Ah, what an honour and privilege it is
to see you! This is Mr. Goldsmith? And very much, sir,
the ruff and the slashed doublet become you! O Doctor!
what a pleasure I had and have in reading the " Animated
Nature." How *did* you learn the secret of writing the
decasyllable line, and whence that sweet wailing note of
tenderness that accompanies your song? Was Beau Tibbs
a real man, and will you do me the honour of allowing me
to sit at your table at supper? Don't you think you know
how he would have talked? Would you not have liked to
hear him prattle over the champagne?

Now, Hood is passed away—passed off the earth as much
as Goldsmith or Horace. The times in which he lived,
and in which very many of us lived and were young, are
changing or changed. I saw Hood once as a young man,
at a dinner which seems almost as ghostly now as that
masquerade at the Pantheon (1772), of which we were
speaking anon. It was at a dinner of the Literary Fund,
in that vast apartment which is hung round with the portraits of very large Royal Freemasons, now unsubstantial
ghosts. There at the end of the room was Hood. Some
publishers, I think, were our companions. I quite remember his pale face; he was thin and deaf, and very silent;
he scarcely opened his lips during the dinner, and he made
one pun. Some gentleman missed his snuff-box, and Hood
said,——(the Freemasons' Tavern was kept, you must remember, by Mr. CUFF in those days, not by its present pro-

prietors). Well, the box being lost, and asked for, and
CUFF (remember that name) being the name of the landlord,
Hood opened his silent jaws and said   *   *   *   Shall I
tell you what he said? It was not a very good pun, which
the great punster then made. Choose your favourite pun
out of " Whims and Oddities," and fancy that was the joke
which he contributed to the hilarity of our little table.

Where those asterisks are drawn on the page, you must
know a pause occurred, during which I was engaged with
"Hood's Own," having been referred to the book, by this
life of the author which I have just been reading. I am
not going to dissert on Hood's humour; I am not a fair
judge. Have I not said elsewhere that there are one or
two wonderfully old gentlemen still alive who used to give
me tips when I was a boy? I can't be a fair critic about
them. I always think of that sovereign, that rapture of
raspberry tarts, which made my young days happy. Those
old sovereign-contributors may tell stories ever so old, and
I shall laugh; they may commit murder, and I shall believe it was justifiable homicide. There is my friend
Baggs, who goes about abusing me, and of course our dear
mutual friends tell me. Abuse away, *mon bon !* You
were so kind to me when I wanted kindness, that you may
take the change out of that gold now, and say I am a cannibal and negro, if you will. Ha, Baggs! Dost thou
wince as thou readest this line? Does guilty conscience
throbbing at thy breast tell thee of whom the fable is narrated? Puff out thy wrath, and, when it has ceased to
blow, my Baggs shall be to me as the Baggs of old—the
generous, the gentle, the friendly.

No, on second thoughts, I am determined I will not repeat that joke which I heard Hood make. He says he
wrote these jokes with such ease that he sent manuscripts
to the publishers faster than they could acknowledge the
receipt thereof. I won't say that they were all good jokes,
or that to read a great book full of them is a work at
present altogether jocular. Writing to a friend respecting
some memoir of him which had been published, Hood says,

" You will judge how well the author knows me, when he says my mind is rather serious than comic." At the time when he wrote these words, he evidently undervalued his own serious power, and thought that in punning and broadgrinning lay his chief strength. Is not there something touching in that simplicity and humility of faith? "To make laugh is my calling," says he; "I must jump, I must grin, I must tumble, I must turn language head over heels, and leap through grammar;" and he goes to his work humbly and courageously, and what he has to do that does he with all his might, through sickness, through sorrow, through exile, poverty, fever, depression—there he is, always ready to his work, and with a jewel of genius in his pocket! Why, when he laid down his puns and pranks, put the motley off, and spoke out of his heart, all England and America listened with tears and wonder! Other men have delusions of conceit and fancy themselves greater than they are, and that the world slights them. Have we not heard how Liston always thought he ought to play Hamlet? Here is a man with a power to touch the heart almost unequalled, and he passes days and years in writing "Young Ben he was a nice young man," and so forth. To say truth, I have been reading in a book of "Hood's Own" until I am perfectly angry. "You great man, you good man, you true genius and poet," I cry out, as I turn page after page. "Do, do, make no more of these jokes, but be yourself, and take your station."

When Hood was on his deathbed, Sir Robert Peel, who only knew of his illness, not of his imminent danger, wrote to him a noble and touching letter, announcing that a pension was conferred on him :

"I am more than repaid," writes Peel, "by the personal satisfaction which I have had in doing that for which you return me warm and characteristic acknowledgments.

"You perhaps think that you are known to one, with such multifarious occupations as myself, merely by general reputation as an author; but I assure you that there can be little, which you have written and acknowledged, which I have not read; and that there are few, who can appreciate and admire more than myself, the good sense and good feeling which have taught you to infuse so much fun and merriment into writings correcting folly and exposing absurdities, and yet never trespassing beyond those limits within which wit and facetiousness are not very often confined. You may write on with the consciousness of independence, as free and unfettered, as if no communication had ever passed between us. I am not conferring a private obligation upon you, but am fulfilling the intentions of the legislature, which has placed at the disposal of the Crown a certain sum (miserable, indeed, in amount) to be applied to the recognition of public claims on the bounty of the Crown. If you will review the names of those, whose claims have been admitted on account of their literary, or scientific eminence, you will find an ample confirmation of the truth of my statement.

"One return, indeed, I shall ask of you,—that you will give me the opportunity of making your personal acquaintance."

And Hood, writing to a friend, enclosing a copy of Peel's letter, says: "Sir R. Peel came from Burleigh on Tuesday night, and went down to Brighton on Saturday. If he had written by post, I should not have had it till to-day. So he sent his servant with the enclosed on *Saturday night;* another mark of considerate attention." He is frightfully unwell, he continues, his wife says he looks *quite green:* but ill as he is, poor fellow, "his well is not dry. He has pumped out a sheet of Christmas fun, is drawing some cuts, and shall write a sheet more of his novel."

O sad, marvellous picture of courage, of honesty, of patient endurance, of duty struggling against pain! How noble Peel's figure is standing by that sick bed! how generous his words, how dignified and sincere his compassion! And the poor dying man, with a heart full of natural grat-

itude towards his noble benefactor, must turn to him and
say—"If it be well to be remembered by a minister, it is
better still not to be forgotten by him in a 'hurly Burleigh!'" Can you laugh? Is not the joke horribly
pathetic from the poor dying lips? As dying Robin Hood
must fire a last shot with his bow—as one reads of Catholics on their death-beds putting on a Capuchin dress to
go out of the world—here is poor Hood at his last hour
putting on his ghastly motley, and uttering one joke more.

He dies, however, in dearest love and peace with his
children, wife, friends; to the former especially his whole
life had been devoted, and every day showed his fidelity,
simplicity, and affection. In going through the record of
his most pure, modest, honourable life, and living along
with him, you come to trust him thoroughly and feel that
here is a most loyal, affectionate, and upright soul, with
whom you have been brought into communion. Can we
say as much of all lives of all men of letters? Here is one
at least without guile, without pretension, without schem-
ing, of a pure life, to his family and little modest circle of
friends tenderly devoted.

And what a hard work, and what a slender reward! In
the little domestic details with which the book abounds,
what a simple life is shown to us! The most simple little
pleasures and amusements delight and occupy him. You
have revels on shrimps; the good wife making the pie;
details about the maid, and criticisms on her conduct;
wonderful tricks played with the plum-pudding—all the
pleasures centring round the little humble home. One
of the first men of his time, he is appointed editor of a
magazine at a salary of 300*l.* per annum, signs himself
exultingly "Ed. N. M. M." and the family rejoice over the
income as over a fortune. He goes to a Greenwich dinner
—what a feast and rejoicing afterwards!

"Well, we drank 'the Boz' with a delectable clatter,
which drew from him a good warm-hearted speech.
* * * He looked very well, and had a younger brother

along with him. * * * Then we had songs. Barham
chanted a Robin Rood ballad, and Cruikshank sang a burlesque ballad of Lord H——; and somebody, unknown to
me, gave a capital imitation of a French showman. Then
we toasted Mrs. Boz, and the chairman, and Vice, and the
Traditional Priest sang the 'Deep deep sea,' in his deep
deep voice; and then we drank to Proctor, who wrote the
said song; also Sir J. Wilson's good health, and Cruikshank's, and Ainsworth's: and a Manchester friend of the
latter sang a Manchester ditty, so full of trading stuff,
that it really seemed to have been not composed, but manu-
factured. Jerdan, as Jerdanish as usual on such occasions
—you know how paradoxically he is *quite at home* in
dining out. As to myself, I had to make my *second maiden
speech,* for Mr. Monckton Milnes proposed my health in
terms my modesty might allow me to repeat to *you*, but my
memory won't. However I ascribed the toast to my notoriously bad health, and assured them that their wishes had
already improved it—that I felt a brisker circulation—a
more genial warmth about the heart, and explained that
a certain trembling of my hand was not from palsy, or my
old ague, but an inclination in my hand to shake itself with
every one present. Whereupon I had to go through the
friendly ceremony with as many of the company as were
within reach, besides a few more who came express from
the other end of the table. *Very* gratifying, wasn't it?
Though I cannot go quite so far as Jane, who wants me to
have that hand chopped off, bottled, and preserved in
spirits. She was sitting up for me, very anxiously, as
usual when I go out, because I am so domestic and steady,
and was down at the door before I could ring at the gate,
to which Boz kindly sent me in his own carriage. Poor
girl! what *would* she do if she had a wild husband instead
of a tame one? "

And the poor anxious wife is sitting up, and fondles the
hand which has been shaken by so many illustrious men!
The little feast dates back only eighteen years, and yet

somehow it seems as distant as a dinner at Mr. Thrale's,
or a meeting at Will's.

Poor little gleam of sunshine! very little good cheer en-
livens that sad simple life.   We have the triumph of the
magazine: then a new magazine projected and produced:
then illness and the last scene, and the kind Peel by the
dying man's bedside, speaking noble words of respect and
sympathy, and soothing the last throbs of the tender honest
heart.

I like, I say, Hood's life even better than his books, and
I wish, with all my heart, *Monsieur et cher confrère*, the
same could be said for both of us, when the ink-stream of
our life hath ceased to run.   Yes: if I drop first, dear
Baggs, I trust you may find reason to modify some of the
unfavourable views of my character, which you are freely
imparting to our mutual friends.   What ought to be the
literary man's point of honour now-a-days?   Suppose,
friendly reader, you are one of the craft, what legacy would
you like to leave to your children?   First of all (and by
Heaven's gracious help) you would pray and strive to give
them such an endowment of love, as should last certainly
for all their lives, and perhaps be transmitted to their children.   You would (by the same aid and blessing) keep
your honour pure, and transmit a name unstained to those
who have a right to bear it.   You would,—though this
faculty of giving is one of the easiest of the literary man's
qualities—you would, out of your earnings, small or great,
be able to help a poor brother in need, to dress his wounds,
and, if it were but twopence, to give him succour.   Is the
money which the noble Macaulay gave to the poor lost to
his family?   God forbid.   To the loving hearts of his kindred is it not rather the most precious part of their inheri-
tance?   It was invested in love and righteous doing, and it
bears interest in heaven.   You will, if letters be your vo-
cation, find saving harder than giving and spending.   To
save be your endeavour too, against the night's coming
when no man may work; when the arm is weary with the
long day's labour; when the brain perhaps grows dark;

when the old, who can labour no more, want warmth and rest, and the young ones call for supper.

I copied a little galley-slave from a quaint old silver spoon which we purchased in a curiosity-shop at the Hague. It is one of the gift-spoons so common in Holland, and which have multiplied so astonishingly of late years at our dealers' in old silverware. Along the stem of the spoon are written the words: "Anno 1609, *Bin ick aldus ghekledt gheghaen*"—"In the year 1609 I went thus clad." The good Dutchman was released from his Algerine captivity (I imagine his figure looks like that of a slave amongst the Moors), and in his thank-offering to some god-child at home, he thus piously records his escape.

Was not poor Cervantes also a captive amongst the Moors? Did not Fielding, and Goldsmith, and Smollett, too, die at the chain as well as poor Hood? Think of Fielding going on board his wretched ship in the Thames, with scarce a hand to bid him farewell; of brave Tobias Smollett, and his life, how hard, and how poorly rewarded; of Goldsmith, and the physician whispering, "Have you something on your mind?" and the wild, dying eyes answering, Yes. Notice how Boswell speaks of Goldsmith, and the splendid contempt with which he regards him. Read Hawkins on Fielding, and the scorn with which Dandy Walpole and Bishop Hurd speak of him. Galley-slaves doomed to tug the oar and wear the chain, whilst my lords and dandies take their pleasure, and hear fine music and disport with fine ladies in the cabin!

But stay. Was there any cause for this scorn? Had some of these great men weaknesses which gave inferiors advantage over them? Men of letters cannot lay their hands on their hearts, and say, "No, the fault was fortune's, and the indifferent world's, not Goldsmith's nor Fielding's." There was no reason why Oliver should always be thriftless; why Fielding and Steele should sponge upon their friends; why Sterne should make love to his neighbours' wives. Swift, for a long time, was as poor as any wag that ever laughed: but he owed no penny to his neighbours: Addison, when he wore his most threadbare coat, could hold his head up, and maintain his dignity: and, I dare vouch, neither of those gentlemen, when they were ever so poor, asked any man alive to pity their condition, and have a regard to the weaknesses incidental to the literary profession. Galley-slave, forsooth! If you are sent to prison for some error for which the law awards that sort of laborious seclusion, so much the more shame for you. If you are chained to the oar a prisoner of war, like Cervantes, you have the pain, but not the shame, and the friendly compassion of mankind to reward you. Galley-slaves, indeed! What man has not his oar to pull? There is that wonderful old stroke-oar in the Queen's galley. How many years has he pulled? Day and night, in rough water or smooth, with what invincible vigour and surprising gaiety he plies his arms. There is in the same *Galère Capitaine* that well-known, trim figure, the bow oar; how he tugs, and with what a will! How both of them have been abused in their time! Take the Lawyer's galley, and that dauntless octogenarian in command; when has *he* ever complained or repined about his slavery? There is the Priest's galley—black and lawn sails—do any mariners out of Thames work harder? When lawyer, and statesman, and divine, and writer are snug in bed, there is a ring at the poor Doctor's bell. Forth he must go, in rheumatism or snow; a galley-slave bearing his galley-pots to quench the flames of fever, to succour mothers and young children in their hour of peril, and, as gently and soothingly as may be, to carry the hopeless patient over to the silent shore. And have we not just read of the actions of the Queen's galleys, and their brave crews in the Chinese waters? Men not more worthy of human renown and honour to-day in their victory, than last year in their glorious hour of disaster. So with stout hearts may we ply the oar, messmates all, till the voyage is over, and the Harbour of Rest is found.

ROUND ABOUT THE CHRISTMAS TREE.

THE kindly Christmas tree, from which I trust every gentle reader has pulled a bonbon or two, is yet all aflame whilst I am writing, and sparkles with the sweet fruits of its season. You young ladies, may you have plucked pretty giftlings from it; and out of the cracker sugar-plum which you have split with the captain or the sweet young curate may you have read one of those delicious conundrums which the confectioners introduce into the sweetmeats, and which apply to the cunning passion of love. Those riddles are to be read at *your* age, when I daresay they are amusing. As for Dolly, Merry, and Bell, who are standing at the tree, they don't care about the love-riddle part, but understand the sweet-almond portion very well. They are four, five, six years old. Patience, little people! A dozen merry Christmases more, and you will be reading those wonderful love-conundrums, too. As for us elderly folks, we watch the babies at their sport, and the young people pulling at the branches: and instead of finding bonbons or sweeties in the packets which *we* pluck off the boughs, we find enclosed Mr. Carnifex's review of the quarter's meat; Mr. Sartor's compliments, and little statement for self and the young gentlemen; and Madame de Sainte-Crinoline's respects to the young ladies, who encloses her account, and will send on Saturday, please; or we stretch our hand out to the educational branch of the Christmas tree, and there find a lively and amusing article from the Rev. Henry Holyshade, containing our dear Tommy's exceedingly moderate account for the last term's school expenses.

The tree yet sparkles, I say. I am writing on the day before Twelfth Day, if you must know; but already ever so many of the fruits have been pulled, and the Christmas lights have gone out. Bobby Miseltow, who has been

E

staying with us for a week (and who has been sleeping mysteriously in the bath-room), comes to say he is going away to spend the rest of the holidays with his grandmother—and I brush away the manly tear of regret as I part with the dear child. " Well, Bob, good-by, since you *will* go. Compliments to grandmamma. Thank her for the turkey. Here's——" (*A slight pecuniary transaction takes place at this juncture, and Bob nods and winks, and puts his hand in his waistcoat pocket.*) " You have had a pleasant week? "

BOB. " Haven't I ! " (*And exit, anxious to know the amount of the coin which has just changed hands.*)

He is gone, and as the dear boy vanishes through the door (behind which I see him perfectly), I too cast up a little account of our past Christmas week. When Bob's holidays are over, and the printer has sent me back this manuscript, I know Christmas will be an old story. All the fruit will be off the Christmas tree then; the crackers will have cracked off; the almonds will have been crunched; and the sweet-bitter riddles will have been read; the lights will have perished off the dark green boughs; the toys growing on them will have been distributed, fought for, cherished, neglected, broken. Ferdinand and Fidelia will each keep out of it (be still, my gushing heart!) the remembrance of a riddle read together, of a double-almond munched together, and the moiety of an exploded cracker. * * * The maids, I say, will have taken down all that holly stuff and nonsense about the clocks, lamps, and looking-glasses, the dear boys will be back at school, fondly thinking of the pantomime-fairies whom they have seen; whose gaudy gossamer wings are battered by this time; and whose pink cotton (or silk is it?) lower extremities are all dingy and dusty. Yet but a few days, Bob, and flakes of paint will have cracked off the fairy flower-bowers, and the revolving temples of adamantine lustre will be as shabby as the city of Pekin. When you read this, will Clown still be going on lolling his tongue out of his mouth, and saying, " How are you to-morrow? " To-morrow, indeed! He must be almost ashamed of himself (if that cheek is still capable of the blush of shame) for asking the absurd question. To-morrow, indeed! To-morrow the diffugient snows will give place to Spring; the snowdrops will lift their heads; Ladyday may be expected, and the pecuniary duties peculiar to that feast; in place of bonbons, trees will have an eruption of light green knobs; the whitebait season will bloom * * * as if one need go on describing these vernal phenomena, when Christmas is still here, though ending, and the subject of my discourse!

We have all admired the illustrated papers, and noted how boisterously jolly they become at Christmas time. What wassail bowls, robin-redbreasts, waits, snow landscapes, bursts of Christmas song! And then to think that these festivities are prepared months before—that these Christmas pieces are prophetic! How kind of artists and poets to devise the festivities beforehand, and serve them pat at the proper time! We ought to be grateful to them, as to the cook who gets up at midnight and sets the pudding a-boiling, which is to feast us at six o'clock. I often think with gratitude of the famous Mr. Nelson Lee—the author of I don't know how many hundred glorious pantomimes—walking by the summer wave at Margate, or Brighton perhaps, revolving in his mind the idea of some new gorgeous spectacle of faëry, which the winter shall see complete. He is like cook at midnight (*si parva licet*). He watches and thinks. He pounds the sparkling sugar of benevolence, the plums of fancy, the sweetmeats of fun, the figs of—well, the figs of fairy fiction, let us say, and pops the whole in the seething cauldron of imagination, and at due season serves up THE PANTOMIME.

Very few men in the course of nature can expect to see *all* the pantomimes in one season, but I hope to the end of my life I shall never forego reading about them in that delicious sheet of the *Times* which appears on the morning after Boxing-day. Perhaps reading is even better than seeing. The best way, I think, is to say you are ill, lie in bed, and have the paper for two hours, reading all the way

down from Drury Lane to the Britannia at Hoxton. Bob
and I went to two pantomimes. One was at the Theatre
of Fancy, and the other at the Fairy Opera, and I don't
know which we liked the best.

At the Fancy, we saw "Harlequin Hamlet, or Daddy's
Ghost and Nunky's Pison," which is all very well—but,
gentlemen, if you don't respect Shakspeare, to whom will
you be civil? The palace and ramparts of Elsinore by
moon and snowlight is one of Loutherbourg's finest efforts.
The banqueting-hall of the palace is illuminated: the peaks
and gables glitter with the snow: the sentinels march
blowing their fingers with the cold—the freezing of the
nose of one of them is very neatly and dexterously arranged:
the snow-storm rises: the winds howl awfully along the
battlements: the waves come curling, leaping, foaming to
shore. Hamlet's umbrella is whirled away in the storm.
He and his two friends stamp on each other's toes to keep
them warm. The storm-spirits rise in the air, and are
whirled howling round the palace and the rocks. My
eyes! what tiles and chimney-pots fly hurtling through the
air! As the storm reaches its height (here the wind instruments come in with prodigious effect, and I compliment
Mr. Brumby and the violoncellos)—as the snow-storm rises
(queek, queek, queek, go the fiddles, and then thrumpty
thrump comes a pizzicato movement in Bob Major, which
sends a shiver into your very boot-soles), the thunderclouds deepen (bong, bong, bong, from the violoncellos).
The forked lightning quivers through the clouds in a zigzag scream of violins—and look, look, look! as the froth-
ing, roaring waves come rushing up the battlements, and
over the reeling parapet, each hissing wave becomes a ghost,
sends the gun-carriages rolling over the platform, and
plunges howling into the water again.

Hamlet's mother comes on to the battlements to look for
her son. The storm whips her umbrella out of her hands,
and she retires screaming in pattens.

The cabs on the stand in the great market-place at Elsinore are seen to drive off, and several people are drowned.

The gas-lamps along the street are wrenched from their foundations, and shoot through the troubled air. Whish, rush, hish! how the rain roars and pours! The darkness becomes awful, always deepened by the power of the music —and see—in the midst of a rush, and whirl, and scream of spirits of air and wave—what is that ghastly figure moving hither? It becomes bigger, bigger, as it advances down the platform—more ghastly, more horrible, enormous! It is as tall as the whole stage. It seems to be advancing on the stalls and pit, and the whole house screams with terror, as the GHOST OF THE LATE HAMLET comes in, and begins to speak. Several people faint, and the light-fingered gentry pick pockets furiously in the darkness.

In the pitchy darkness, this awful figure throwing his eyes about, the gas in the boxes shuddering out of sight, and the wind-instruments bugling the most horrible wails, the boldest spectator must have felt frightened. But hark! what is that silver shimmer of the fiddles! Is it—can it be—the gray dawn peeping in the stormy east? The ghost's eyes look blankly towards it, and roll a ghastly agony. Quicker, quicker ply the violins of Phœbus Apollo. Redder, redder grow the orient clouds. Cockadoodloodloo! crows that great cock which has just come out on the roof of the palace. And now the round sun himself pops up from behind the waves of night. Where is the ghost? He is gone! Purple shadows of morn "slant o'er the snowy sward," the city wakes up in life and sunshine, and we confess we are very much relieved at the disappearance of the ghost. We don't like those dark scenes in pantomimes.

After the usual business, that Ophelia should be turned into Columbine was to be expected; but I confess I was a little shocked when Hamlet's mother became Pantaloon, and was instantly knocked down by Clown Claudius. Grimaldi is getting a little old now, but for real humour there are few clowns like him. Mr. Shuter, as the grave-digger, was chaste and comic, as he always is, and the scene-painters surpassed themselves.

"Harlequin Conqueror and the Field of Hastings," at

the other house, is very pleasant too. The irascible William is acted with very great vigour by Snoxall, and the battle of Hastings is a good piece of burlesque. Some trifling liberties are taken with history, but what liberties will not the merry genius of pantomime permit himself? At the battle of Hastings, William is on the point of being defeated by the Sussex volunteers, very elegantly led by the always pretty Miss Waddy (as Haco Sharpshooter), when a shot from the Normans kills Harold. The fairy Edith hereupon comes forward, and finds his body, which straightway leaps up a live harlequin, whilst the Conqueror makes an excellent clown, and the Archbishop of Bayeux a diverting pantaloon, &c. &c. &c.

Perhaps these are not the pantomimes we really saw; but one description will do as well as another. The plots, you see, are a little intricate and difficult to understand in pantomimes; and I may have mixed up one with another. That I was at the theatre on Boxing-night is certain—but the pit was so full that I could only see fairy legs glittering in the distance, as I stood at the door. And if I was badly off, I think there was a young gentleman behind me worse off still. I own that he has good reason (though others have not) to speak ill of me behind my back, and hereby beg his pardon.

Likewise to the gentleman who picked up a party in Piccadilly, who had slipped and fallen in the snow, and was there on his back, uttering energetic expressions; that party begs to offer thanks, and compliments of the season.

Bob's behaviour on New Year's day, I can assure Dr. Holyshade, was highly creditable to the boy. He had expressed a determination to partake of every dish which was put on the table; but after soup, fish, roast beef, and roast-goose, he retired from active business until the pudding and mince-pies made their appearance, of which he partook liberally, but not too freely. And he greatly advanced in my good opinion by praising the punch, which was of my own manufacture, and which some gentlemen present (Mr. O'M—g—n, amongst others) pronounced to be too weak.

Too weak! A bottle of rum, a bottle of Madeira, half a bottle of brandy, and two bottles and a half of water—*can* this mixture be said to be too weak for any mortal? Our young friend amused the company during the evening, by exhibiting a two-shilling magic-lantern, which he had purchased, and likewise by singing "Sally, come up!" a quaint, but rather monotonous melody, which I am told is sung by the poor negro on the banks of the broad Mississip.

What other enjoyments did we proffer for the child's amusement during the Christmas week? A great philosopher was giving a lecture to young folks at the British Institution. But when this diversion was proposed to our young friend Bob, he said, "Lecture? No, thank you. Not as I knows on," and made sarcastic signals on his nose. Perhaps he is of Dr. Johnson's opinion about lectures: "Lectures, sir! what man would go to hear that imperfectly at a lecture, which he can read at leisure in a book?" *I* never went, of my own choice, to a lecture; that I can vow. As for sermons, they are different; I delight in them, and they cannot, of course, be too long.

Well, we partook of yet other Christmas delights besides pantomime, pudding, and pie. One glorious, one delightful, one most unlucky and pleasant day, we drove in a brougham, with a famous horse, which carried us more quickly and briskly than any of your vulgar railways, over Battersea Bridge, on which the horse's hoofs rung as if it had been iron; through suburban villages, plum-caked with snow; under a leaden sky, in which the sun hung like a red-hot warming-pan; by pond after pond, where not only men and boys, but scores after scores of women and girls, were sliding, and roaring, and clapping their lean old sides with laughter, as they tumbled down, and their hobnailed shoes flew up in the air; the air frosty with a lilac haze, through which villas, and commons, and churches, and plantations glimmered. We drive up the hill, Bob and I; we make the last two miles in eleven minutes; we pass that poor, armless man who sits there in the cold, following you with his eyes. I don't give anything, and Bob looks disappointed. We are set down neatly at the gate, and a horse-holder opens the brougham door. I don't give anything; again disappointment on Bob's part. I pay a shilling apiece, and we enter into the glorious building, which is decorated for Christmas, and straightway forgetfulness on Bob's part of everything but that magnificent scene. The enormous edifice is all decorated for Bob and Christmas. The stalls, the columns, the fountains, court, statues, splendours, are all crowned for Christmas. The delicious negro is singing his Alabama choruses for Christmas and Bob. He has scarcely done, when, Tootarootatoo! Mr. Punch is performing his surprising actions, and hanging the beadle. The stalls are decorated. The refreshment tables are piled with good things; at many fountains "MULLED CLARET" is written up in appetizing capitals. "Mulled claret—oh, jolly! How cold it is!" says Bob; I pass on. "It's only three o'clock," says Bob. "No, only three," I say, meekly. "We dine at seven," sighs Bob, "and it's so-o-o coo-old." I still would take no hints. No claret, no refreshment, no sandwiches, no sausage-rolls for Bob. At last I am obliged to tell him all. Just before we left home, a little Christmas bill popped in at the door and emptied my purse at the threshold. I forgot all about the transaction, and had to borrow half-a-crown from John Coachman to pay for our entrance into the palace of delight. *Now* you see, Bob, why I could not treat you on that second of January when we drove to the palace together; when the girls and boys were sliding on the ponds at Dulwich; when the darkling river was full of floating ice, and the sun was like a warming-pan in the leaden sky.

One more Christmas sight we had, of course; and that sight I think I like as well as Bob himself at Christmas, and at all seasons. We went to a certain garden of delight, where, whatever your cares are, I think you can manage to forget some of them, and muse, and be not unhappy; to a garden beginning with a Z, which is as lively as Noah's ark; where the fox has brought his brush, and the cock has brought his comb, and the elephant has brought his trunk, and the kangaroo has brought his bag, and the condor his old white wig and black satin hood. On this day it was so cold that the white bears winked their pink eyes, as they plapped up and down by their pool, and seemed to say, "Aha, this weather reminds us of dear home!" "Cold! bah! I have got such a warm coat," says brother Bruin, "I don't mind;" and he laughs on his pole, and clucks down a bun. The squealing hyænas gnashed their teeth and laughed at us quite refreshingly at their window; and, cold as it was, Tiger, Tiger, burning bright, glared at us red-hot through his bars, and snorted blasts of hell. The woolly camel leered at us quite kindly as he paced round his ring on his silent pads. We went to our favourite places. Our dear wambat came up, and had himself scratched very affably. Our fellow-creatures in the monkey-room held out their little black hands, and piteously asked us for Christmas alms. Those darling alligators on their rock winked at us in the most friendly way. The solemn eagles sate alone, and scowled at us from their peaks; whilst little Tom Ratel tumbled over head and heels for us in his usual diverting manner. If I have cares in my mind, I come to the Zoo, and fancy they don't pass the gate. I recognize my friends, my enemies, in countless cages. I entertained the eagle, the vulture, the old billy-goat, and the black-pated, crimson-necked, blear-eyed, baggy, hook-beaked, old marabou stork yesterday at dinner; and when Bob's aunt came to tea in the evening, and asked him what he had seen, he stepped up to her gravely, and said—

"First I saw the white bear, then I saw the black,
    Then I saw the camel with a hump upon his back.
Chorus of }
Children. } Then I saw the camel with a HUMP upon his back!
    Then I saw the grey wolf, with mutton in his maw;
    Then I saw the wambat waddle in the straw;
    Then I saw the elephant with his waving trunk,
    Then I saw the monkeys—mercy, how unpleasantly
        they——smelt!"

There. No one can beat that piece of wit, can he, Bob? And so it is all over; but we had a jolly time, whilst you were with us, hadn't we? Present my respects to the doctor; and I hope, my boy, we may spend another merry Christmas next year.

ON A CHALK-MARK ON THE DOOR.

ON the doorpost of the house of a friend of mine, a few inches above the lock, is a little chalk-mark, which some sportive boy in passing has probably scratched on the pillar. The doorsteps, the lock, handle, and so forth, are kept decently enough; but this chalk-mark, I suppose some three inches out of the housemaid's beat, has already been on the door for more than a fortnight, and I wonder whether it will be there whilst this paper is being written, whilst it is at the printer's, and, in fine, until the month passes over? I wonder whether the servants in that house will read these remarks about the chalk-mark? That the *Cornhill Magazine* is taken in in that house I know. In fact I have seen it there. In fact I have read it there. In fact I have written it there. In a word, the house to which I allude is mine—the "editor's private residence," to which, in spite of prayers, entreaties, commands, and threats, authors, and ladies especially, *will* send their communications, although they won't understand that they injure their own interests by so doing; for how is a man who has his own work to do, his own exquisite inventions to form and perfect—Maria to rescue from the unprincipled Earl—the atrocious General to confound in his own machinations—the angelic Dean to promote to a bishopric, and so forth—how is a man to do all this, under a hundred interruptions, and keep his nerves and temper in that just and equable state in which they ought to be when he comes to assume the critical office? As you will send here, ladies, I must tell you you have a much worse chance than if you forward your valuable articles to Cornhill. Here your papers arrive, at dinner-time, we will say. Do you suppose that is a pleasant period, and that we are to criticize you between the *ovum* and *malum*, between the soup and the dessert? I have touched, I think, on this subject before. I

say again, if you want real justice shown you, don't send
your papers to the private residence. At home, for instance, yesterday, having given strict orders that I was to
receive nobody, "except on business," do you suppose a
smiling young Scottish gentleman, who forced himself into
my study, and there announced himself as agent of a Cattle-food Company, was received with pleasure? There, as
I sate in my arm-chair, suppose he had proposed to draw a
couple of my teeth, would I have been pleased? I could
have throttled that agent. I daresay the whole of that
day's work will be found tinged with a ferocious misanthropy, occasioned by my clever young friend's intrusion.
Cattle-food, indeed! As if beans, oats, warm mashes, and
a ball, are to be pushed down a man's throat just as he is
meditating on the great social problem, or (for I think it
was my epic I was going to touch up) just as he was about
to soar to the height of the empyrean!

Having got my cattle-agent out of the door, I resume my
consideration of that little mark on the doorpost, which is
scored up as the text of the present little sermon; and
which I hope will relate, not to chalk, nor to any of its
special uses or abuses (such as milk, neck-powder, and the
like), but to servants. Surely ours might remove that un-
seemly little mark? Suppose it were on my coat, might I
not request its removal? I remember, when I was at
school, a little careless boy, upon whose forehead an ink
mark remained, and was perfectly recognizable for three
weeks after its first appearance. May I take any notice of
this chalk-stain on the forehead of my house? Whose
business is it to wash that forehead? and ought I to fetch
a brush and a little hot water, and wash it off myself?

Yes. But that spot removed, why not come down at
six, and wash the doorsteps? I daresay the early rising
and exercise would do me a great deal of good. The housemaid, in that case, might lie in bed a little later, and have
her tea and the morning paper brought to her in bed: then,
of course, Thomas would expect to be helped about the boots
and knives; cook about the saucepans, dishes, and what not;

the lady's-maid would want somebody to take the curl-papers out of her hair, and get her bath ready. You should have a set of servants for the servants, and these under-servants should have slaves to wait on them. The king commands the first lord in waiting to desire the second lord to intimate to the gentleman usher to request the page of the antechamber to entreat the groom of the stairs to implore John to ask the captain of the buttons to desire the maid of the still-room to beg the housekeeper to give out a few more lumps of sugar, as his Majesty has none for his coffee, which probably is getting cold during the negotiation. In our little Brentfords we are all kings, more or less. There are orders, gradations, hierarchies, everywhere. In your house and mine there are mysteries unknown to us. I am not going into the horrid old question of "followers." I don't mean cousins from the country, love-stricken police-men, or gentlemen in mufti from Knightsbridge Barracks; but people who have an occult right on the premises; the uncovenanted servants of the house; grey women who are seen at evening with baskets flitting about area-railings; dingy shawls which drop you furtive curtseys in your neighbourhood; demure little Jacks, who start up from behind boxes in the pantry. Those outsiders wear Thomas's crest and livery, and call him "Sir;" those silent women address the female servants as "Mum," and curtsey before them, squaring their arms over their wretched lean aprons. Then, again, those *servi servorum* have dependents in the vast, silent, poverty-stricken world outside your comfortable kitchen fire, in the world of darkness, and hunger, and miserable cold, and dank, flagged cellars, and huddled straw, and rags, in which pale children are swarming. It may be your beer (which runs with great volubility) has a pipe or two which communicates with those dark caverns where hopeless anguish pours the groan, and would scarce see light but for a scrap or two of candle which has been whipped away from your worship's kitchen. Not many years ago—I don't know whether before or since that white mark was drawn on the door—a lady occupied the confidential place of housemaid in this "private residence," who brought a good character, who seemed to have a cheerful temper, whom I used to hear clattering and bumping overhead or on the stairs long before daylight—there, I say, was poor Camilla, scouring the plain, trundling and brushing, and clattering with her pans and brooms, and humming at her work. Well, she had established a smuggling communication of beer over the area frontier. This neat-handed Phyllis used to pack up the nicest baskets of my provender, and convey them to somebody outside—I believe, on my conscience, to some poor friend in distress. Camilla was consigned to her doom. She was sent back to her friends in the country; and when she was gone we heard of many of her faults. She expressed herself, when displeased, in language that I shall not repeat. As for the beer and meat, there was no mistake about them. But *après?* Can I have the heart to be very angry with that poor jade for helping another poorer jade out of my larder? On your honour and conscience, when you were a boy, and the apples looked temptingly over Farmer Quarringdon's hedge, did you never——? When there was a grand dinner at home, and you were sliding, with Master Bacon, up and down the stairs, and the dishes came out, did you ever do such a thing as just to——? Well, in many and many a respect servants are like children. They are under domination. They are subject to reproof, to ill-temper, to petty exactions, and stupid tyrannies, not seldom. They scheme, conspire, fawn, and are hypocrites. "Little boys should not loll on chairs." "Little girls should be seen, and not heard;" and so forth. Have we not almost all learnt these expressions of old foozles: and uttered them ourselves when in the square-toed state? The Eton master, who was breaking a lance with our Paterfamilias of late, turned on Paterfamilias, saying, He knows not the nature and exquisite candour of well-bred English boys. Exquisite fiddlestick's end, Mr. Master! Do you mean for to go for to tell us that the relations between young gentlemen and their schoolmasters are entirely frank and cordial; that the lad

is familiar with the man who can have him ﬂogged; never
shirks his exercises; never gets other boys to do his verses;
never does other boys' verses; never breaks bounds; never
tells fibs—I mean the fibs permitted by scholastic honour?
Did I know of a boy who pretended to such a character, I
would forbid my scapegraces to keep company with him.
Did I know a schoolmaster who pretended to believe in the
existence of many hundred such boys in one school at one
time, I would set that man down as a baby in knowledge
of the world. "Who was making that noise?" "I don't
know, sir."—And he knows it was the boy next him in
school. "Who was climbing over that wall?" "I don't
know, sir."—And it is in the speaker's own trousers, very
likely, the glass bottle-tops have left their cruel scars.
And so with servants. "Who ate up the three pigeons
which went down in the pigeon-pie at breakfast this morning?" "O dear me! sir, it was John, who went away last
month?"—or, "I think it was Miss Mary's canary-bird,
which got out of the cage, and is so fond of pigeons, it
never can have enough of them." Yes, it *was* the canary-
bird; and Eliza saw it; and Eliza is ready to vow she did.
These statements are not true; but please don't call them
lies. This is not lying; this is voting with your party.
You *must* back your own side. The servants' hall stands
by the servants' hall against the dining-room. The schoolboys don't tell tales of each other. They agree not to
choose to know who has made the noise, who has broken
the window, who has eaten up the pigeons, who has picked
all the plovers' eggs out of the aspic, how it is that liqueur
brandy of Gledstanes is in such porous glass bottles—and
so forth. Suppose Brutus had a footman, who came and
told him that the butler drank the Curaçoa, which of these
servants would you dismiss?—the butler, perhaps, but the
footman certainly.

No. If your plate and glass are beautifully bright, your
bell quickly answered, and Thomas ready, neat, and good-
humoured, you are not to expect absolute truth from him.
The very obsequiousness and perfection of his service pre-

vents truth.   He may be ever so unwell in mind or body, and he must go through his service—hand the shining plate, replenish the spotless glass, lay the glittering fork—never laugh when you yourself or your guests joke—be profoundly attentive, and yet look utterly impassive—exchange a few hurried curses at the door with that unseen slavey who ministers without, and with you be perfectly calm and polite.   If you are ill, he will come twenty times in an hour to your bell; or leave the girl of his heart—his mother, who is going to America—his dearest friend, who has come to say farewell—his lunch, and his glass of beer just freshly poured out—any or all of these, if the door-bell rings, or the master call out "Thomas" from the hall.   Do you suppose you can expect absolute candour from a man whom you may order to powder his hair?   As between the Rev. Henry Holyshade and his pupil, the idea of entire unreserve is utter bosh; so the truth as between you and Jeames or Thomas, or Mary the housemaid, or Betty the cook, is relative, and not to be demanded on one side or the other. Why, respectful civility is itself a lie, which poor Jeames often has to utter or perform to many a swaggering vulgarian, who should black Jeames's boots, did Jeames wear them and not shoes.   There is your little Tom, just ten, ordering the great, large, quiet, orderly young man about —shrieking calls for hot water—bullying Jeames because the boots are not varnished enough, or ordering him to go to the stables, and ask Jenkins why the deuce Tomkins hasn't brought his pony round—or what you will.   There is mamma rapping the knuckles of Pincot the lady's-maid, and little miss scolding Martha, who waits up five-pair of stairs in the nursery.   Little miss, Tommy, papa, mamma, you all expect from Martha, from Pincot, from Jenkins, from Jeames, obsequious civility and willing service.   My dear, good people, you can't have truth too.   Suppose you ask for your newspaper, and Jeames says, "I'm reading it, and jest beg not to be disturbed;" or suppose you ask for a can of water, and he remarks, "You great, big, 'ulking fellar, ain't you big enough to bring it hup yourself?"

what would your feelings be? Now, if you made similar proposals or requests to Mr. Jones next door, this is the kind of answer Jones would give you. You get truth habitually from equals only; so my good Mr. Holyshade, don't talk to me about the habitual candour of the young Etonian of high birth, or I have my own opinion of *your* candour or discernment when you do. No. Tom Bowling is the soul of honour and has been true to Black-eyed Syousan since the last time they parted at Wapping Old Stairs; but do you suppose Tom is perfectly frank, familiar, and above-board in his conversation with Admiral Nelson, K.C.B.? There are secrets, prevarications, fibs, if you will, between Tom and the Admiral—between your crew and *their* captain. I know I hire a worthy, clean, agreeable, and conscientious male or female hypocrite, at so many guineas a year, to do so and so for me. Were he other than hypocrite I would send him about his business. Don't let my displeasure be too fierce with him for a fib or two on his own account.

Some dozen years ago, my family being absent in a distant part of the country, and my business detaining me in London, I remained in my own house with three servants on board wages. I used only to breakfast at home; and future ages will be interested to know that this meal used to consist, at that period, of tea, a penny roll, a pat of butter, and, perhaps, an egg. My weekly bill used invariably to be about fifty shillings; so that as I never dined in the house, you see, my breakfast, consisting of the delicacies before mentioned, cost about seven shillings and threepence per diem. I must, therefore, have consumed daily—

	s.	*d.*
A quarter of a pound of tea (say), ...	1	3
A penny roll (say), ...	1	0
One pound of butter (say), ...	1	3
One pound of lump-sugar, ...	1	0
A new-laid egg, ...	2	9

Which is the only possible way I have for making out the sum.

Well, I fell ill while under this regimen, and had an illness which, but for a certain doctor, who was brought to me by a certain kind friend I had in those days, would, I think, have prevented the possibility of my telling this interesting anecdote now a dozen years after. Don't be frightened, my dear madam; it is not a horrid, sentimental account of a malady you are coming to—only a question of grocery. This illness, I say, lasted some seventeen days, during which the servants were admirably attentive and kind; and poor John, especially, was up at all hours, watching night after night—amiable, cheerful, untiring, respectful, the very best of Johns and nurses.

Twice or thrice in the seventeen days I may have had a glass of *eau sucrée*—say a dozen glasses of *eau sucrée*—certainly not more. Well, this admirable, watchful, cheerful, tender, affectionate John brought me in a little bill for seventeen pounds of sugar consumed during the illness— "Often 'ad sugar and water; always was a callin' for it," says John, wagging his head quite gravely. You are dead, years and years ago, poor John—so patient, so friendly, so kind, so cheerful to the invalid in the fever. But confess, now, wherever you are, that seventeen pounds of sugar to make six glasses of *eau sucrée* was a *little* too strong, wasn't it, John? Ah, how frankly, how trustily, how bravely he lied, poor John! One evening, being at Brighton, in the convalescence, I remember John's step was unsteady, his voice thick, his laugh queer—and having some quinine to give me, John brought the glass to me—not to my mouth, but struck me with it pretty smartly in the eye, which was not the way in which Dr. Elliotson had intended his prescription should be taken. Turning that eye upon him, I ventured to hint that my attendant had been drinking. Drinking! I never was more humiliated at the thought of my own injustice than at John's reply. "Drinking! Sulp me! I have had ony one pint of beer with my dinner at one o'clock!"—and he retreats, holding on by a chair. These are fibs, you see, appertaining to the situation. John is drunk. "*Sulp* him, he has only had an 'alf-pint of beer with his dinner six hours ago; " and none of his fellow-servants will say otherwise. Polly is smuggled on board ship. Who tells the lieutenant when he comes his rounds? Boys are playing cards in the bedroom. The out-lying fag announces master coming—out go candles—cards popped into bed—boys sound asleep. Who had that light in the dormitory? Law bless you! the poor dear innocents are every one snoring. Every one snoring, and every snore is a lie told through the nose! Suppose one of your boys or mine is engaged in that awful crime, are we going to break our hearts about it? Come, come. We pull a long face, waggle a grave head, and chuckle within our waist-coats.

Between me and those fellow-creatures of mine who are sitting in the room below, how strange and wonderful is the partition! We meet at every hour of the daylight, and are indebted to each other for a hundred offices of duty and comfort of life; and we live together for years, and don't know each other. John's voice to me is quite differ-ent from John's voice when it addresses his mates below. If I met Hannah in the street with a bonnet on, I doubt whether I should know her. And all these good people with whom I may live for years and years, have cares, in-terests, dear friends and relatives, mayhap schemes, pas-sions, longing hopes, tragedies of their own, from which a carpet and a few planks and beams utterly separate me. When we were at the seaside, and poor Ellen used to look so pale, and run after the postman's bell, and seize a let-ter in a great scrawling hand, and read it, and cry in a corner, how should we know that the poor little thing's heart was breaking? She fetched the water, and she smoothed the ribbons, and she laid out the dresses, and brought the early cup of tea in the morning, just as if she had had no cares to keep her awake. Henry (who lived out of the house) was the servant of a friend of mine who lived in chambers. There was a dinner one day, and Henry waited all through the dinner. The champagne was properly iced, the dinner was excellently served; every guest was attended to; the dinner disappeared; the dessert was set; the claret was in perfect order, carefully decanted, and more ready. And then Henry said, "If you please, sir, may I go home?" He had received word that his house was on fire; and, having seen through his dinner, he wished to go and look after his children, and little sticks of furniture. Why, such a man's livery is a uniform of honour. The crest on his button is a badge of bravery.

Do you see—I imagine I do myself—in these little instances, a tinge of humour? Ellen's heart is breaking for handsome Jeames of Buckley Square, whose great legs are kneeling, and who has given a lock of his precious powdered head, to some other than Ellen. Henry is preparing the sauce for his master's wild-ducks while the engines are squirting over his own little nest and brood. Lift these figures up but a story from the basement to the ground-floor, and the fun is gone. We may be *en pleine tragédie*. Ellen may breathe her last sigh in blank verse, calling down blessings upon Jeames the profligate who deserts her. Henry is a hero, and epaulettes are on his shoulders. *Atqui sciebat*, &c., whatever tortures are in store for him, he will be at his post of duty.

You concede, however, that there is a touch of humour in the two tragedies here mentioned. Why? Is it that the idea of persons at service is somehow ludicrous? Perhaps it is made more so in this country by the splendid appearance of the liveried domestics of great people. When you think that we dress in black ourselves, and put our fellow-creatures in green, pink, or canary-coloured breeches; that we order them to plaster their hair with flour, having brushed that nonsense out of our own heads fifty years ago; that some of the most genteel and stately among us cause the men who drive their carriages to put on little Albino wigs, and sit behind great nosegays—I say I suppose it is this heaping of gold lace, gaudy colours, blooming plushes, on honest John Trot, which makes the man absurd in our eyes, who need be nothing but a simple reputable citizen and in-door labourer. Suppose, my dear sir, that you yourself were suddenly desired to put on a full dress, or even undress, domestic uniform with our friend Jones's crest repeated in varied combinations of button on your front and back? Suppose, madam, your son were told, that he could not go out except in lower garments of carnation or amber-coloured plush—would you let him? * * * But as you justly say, this is not the question, and besides it is a question fraught with danger, sir; and radicalism, sir; and subversion of the very foundations of the social fabric, sir. * * * Well, John, we won't enter on your great domestic question. Don't let us disport with Jeames's dangerous strength, and the edge-tools about his knife-board: but with Betty and Susan who wield the playful mop, and set on the simmering kettle. Surely you have heard Mrs. Toddles talking to Mrs. Doddles about their mutual maids? Miss Susan must have a silk gown, and Miss Betty must wear flowers under her bonnet when she goes to church if you please, and did you ever hear such impudence? The servant in many small establishments is a constant and endless theme of talk. What small wage, sleep, meal, what endless scouring, scolding, tramping on messages fall to that poor Susan's lot; what indignation at the little kindly passing word with the grocer's young man, the pot-boy, the chubby butcher! Where such things will end, my dear Mrs. Toddles, I don't know. What wages they will want next, my dear Mrs. Doddles, &c.

Here, dear ladies, is an advertisement which I cut out of the *Times* a few days since, expressly for you:

A LADY is desirous of obtaining a SITUATION for a very respectable young woman as HEAD KITCHEN-MAID under a man-cook. She has lived four years under a very good cook and housekeeper. Can make ice, and is an excellent baker. She will only take a place in a very good family, where she can have the opportunity of improving herself, and, if possible, staying for two years. Apply by letter to, &c. &c.

There, Mrs. Toddles, what do you think of that, and did you ever? Well, no, Mrs. Doddles. Upon my word now,

Mrs. T., I don't think I ever did. A respectable young woman—as head kitchen-maid—under a man-cook, will only take a place in a very good family, where she can improve, and stay two years. Just note up the conditions, Mrs. Toddles, mum, if you please, mum, and *then* let us see :—

1. This young woman is to be HEAD kitchen-maid, that is to say, there is to be a chorus of kitchen-maids, of which the Y. W. is to be chief.

2. She will only be situated under a man-cook. (A) ought he to be a French cook; and (B), if so, would the lady desire him to be a Protestant?

3. She will only take a place in a *very good family*. How old ought the family to be, and what do you call good? that is the question. How long after the Conquest will do? Would a banker's family do, or is a baronet's good enough? Best say what rank in the peerage would be sufficiently high. But the lady does not say whether she would like a high church or a low church family. Ought there to be unmarried sons, and may they follow a profession? and please say how many daughters; and would the lady like them to be musical? And how many company dinners a week? Not too many, for fear of fatiguing the upper kitchen-maid; but sufficient, so as to keep the upper kitchen-maid's hand in. [N.B.—I think I can see a rather bewildered expression on the countenance of Mesdames Doddles and Toddles as I am prattling on in this easy bantering way.]

4. The head kitchen-maid wishes to stay for two years, and improve herself under the man-cook, and having of course sucked the brains (as the phrase is) from under the chef's nightcap, then the head kitchen-maid wishes to go.

And upon my word, Mrs. Toddles, mum, I will go and fetch the cab for her. The cab? Why not her ladyship's own carriage and pair, and the head coachman to drive away the head kitchen-maid? You see she stipulates for everything—the time to come; the time to stay; the family she will be with; and as soon as she has improved herself enough, of course the upper kitchen-maid will step into the carriage and drive off.

Well, upon my word and conscience, if things are coming to *this* pass, Mrs. Toddles, and Mrs. Doddles, mum, I think I will go upstairs and get a basin and a sponge, and then downstairs and get some hot water; and then I will go and scrub that chalk-mark off my own door with my own hands.

It is wiped off, I declare! After ever so many weeks! Who has done it? It was just a little roundabout mark, you know, and it was there for days and weeks, before I ever thought it would be the text of a Roundabout Paper.

ON BEING FOUND OUT.

At the close (let us say) of Queen Anne's reign, when I was a boy at a private and preparatory school for young gentlemen, I remember the wiseacre of a master ordering us all, one night, to march into a little garden at the back of the house, and thence to proceed one by one into a tool or hen house (I was but a tender little thing just put into short clothes, and can't exactly say whether the house was for tools or hens), and in that house to put our hands into a sack which stood on a bench, a candle burning beside it. I put my hand into the sack. My hand came out quite black. I went and joined the other boys in the schoolroom; and all their hands were black too.

By reason of my tender age (and there are some critics who, I hope, will be satisfied by my acknowledging that I am a hundred and fifty-six next birthday) I could not understand what was the meaning of this night excursion—this candle, this tool-house, this bag of soot. I think we little boys were taken out of our sleep to be brought to the ordeal. We came, then, and showed our little hands to the master; washed them or not—most probably, I should say, not—and so went bewildered back to bed.

Something had been stolen in the school that day; and Mr. Wiseacre having read in a book of an ingenious method of finding out a thief by making him put his hand into a sack (which, if guilty, the rogue would shirk from doing), all we boys were subjected to the trial. Goodness knows what the lost object was, or who stole it. We all had black hands to show to the master. And the thief, whoever he was, was not Found Out that time.

I wonder if the rascal is alive—an elderly scoundrel he must be by this time; and a hoary old hypocrite, to whom an old schoolfellow presents his kindest regards—parenthetically remarking what a dreadful place that private

school was; cold, chilblains, bad dinners, not enough victuals, and caning awful!—Are you alive still, I say, you
nameless villain, who escaped discovery on that day of
crime? I hope you have escaped often since, old sinner. Ah, what a lucky thing it is, for you and me, my
man, that we are *not* found out in all our peccadilloes;
and that our backs can slip away from the master and the
cane!

Just consider what life would be, if every rogue was
found out, and flogged *coram populo!* What a butchery,
what an indecency, what an endless swishing of the rod!
Don't cry out about my misanthropy. My good friend
Mealymouth, I will trouble you to tell me, do you go to
church? When there, do you say, or do you not, that you
are a miserable sinner? and saying so, do you believe or
disbelieve it? If you are a M. S , don't you deserve correction, and aren't you grateful if you are to be let off? I
say again, what a blessed thing it is that we are not all
found out!

Just picture to yourself everybody who does wrong being
found out, and punished accordingly. Fancy all the boys
in all the school being whipped; and then the assistants,
and then the head master (Dr. Badford let us call him).
Fancy the provost-marshal being tied up, having previously
superintended the correction of the whole army. After
the young gentlemen have had their turn for the faulty exercises, fancy Dr. Lincolnsinn being taken up for certain
faults in *his* Essay and Review. After the clergyman has
cried his peccavi, suppose we hoist up a bishop, and give
him a couple of dozen! (I see my Lord Bishop of Double-
Gloucester sitting in a very uneasy posture on his right
reverend bench.) After we have cast off the bishop, what
are we to say to the Minister who appointed him? My
Lord Cinqwarden, it is painful to have to use personal correction, to a boy of your age; but really * * * *Siste
tandem, carnifex!* The butchery is too horrible. The
hand drops powerless, appalled at the quantity of birch
which it must cut and brandish. I am glad we are not all

found out, I say again; and protest, my dear brethren, against our having our deserts.

To fancy all men found out and punished is bad enough; but imagine all women found out in the distinguished social circle in which you and I have the honour to move. Is it not a mercy that a many of these fair criminals remain unpunished and undiscovered? There is Mrs. Longbow, who is for ever practising, and who shoots poisoned arrows, too; when you meet her you don't call her liar, and charge her with the wickedness she has done, and is doing? There is Mrs. Painter, who passes for a most respectable woman, and a model in society. There is no use in saying what you really know regarding her and her goings on. There is Diana Hunter—what a little, haughty prude it is; and yet *we* know stories about her which are not altogether edifying. I say it is best, for the sake of the good, that the bad should not all be found out. You don't want your children to know the history of that lady in the next box, who is so handsome, and whom they admire so? Ah me, what would life be if we were all found out, and punished for all our faults? Jack Ketch would be in permanence; and then who would hang Jack Ketch?

They talk of murderers being pretty certainly found out. Psha! I have heard an authority awfully competent vow and declare that scores and hundreds of murders are committed, and nobody is the wiser. That terrible man mentioned one or two ways of committing murder, which he maintained were quite common, and were scarcely ever found out. A man, for instance, comes home to his wife, and * * * but I pause—I know that this Magazine has a very large circulation. Hundreds and hundreds of thousands—why not say a million of people at once?— well, say a million, read it. And amongst these countless readers, I might be teaching some monster how to make away with his wife without being found out, some fiend of a woman how to destroy her dear husband. I will *not* then tell this easy and simple way of murder, as communicated to me by a most respectable party in the confidence of private intercourse. Suppose some gentle reader were to try this most simple and easy receipt—it seems to me almost infallible—and come to grief in consequence, and be found out and hanged? Should I ever pardon myself for having been the means of doing injury to a single one of our esteemed subscribers? The prescription whereof I speak—that is to say, whereof I *don't* speak—shall be buried in this bosom. No, I am a humane man. I am not one of your Bluebeards to go and say to my wife, "My dear! I am going away for a few days to Brighton. Here are all the keys of the house. You may open every door and closet, except the one at the end of the oak-room opposite the fireplace, with the little bronze Shakspeare on the mantelpiece (or what not)." I don't say this to a woman—unless, to be sure, I want to get rid of her—because, after such a caution, I know she'll peep into the closet. I say nothing about the closet at all. I keep the key in my pocket, and a being whom I love, but who, as I know, has many weaknesses, out of harm's way. You toss up your head, dear angel, drub on the ground with your lovely little feet, on the table with your sweet rosy fingers, and cry, "O sneerer! You don't know the depth of woman's feeling, the lofty scorn of all deceit, the entire absence of mean curiosity in the sex, or never, never would you libel us so!" "Ah, Delia! dear, dear Delia! It is because I fancy I *do* know something about you (not all, mind—no, no; no man knows that).—Ah, my bride, my ringdove, my rose, my poppet—choose, in fact, whatever name you like—bulbul of my grove, fountain of my desert, sunshine of my darkling life, and joy of my dungeoned existence, it is because I *do* know a little about you that I conclude to say nothing of that private closet, and keep my key in my pocket. You take away that closet-key then, and the house-key. You lock Delia in. You keep her out of harm's way and gadding, and so she never *can* be found out.

And yet by little strange accidents and coincidents how we are being found out every day! You remember that

old story of the Abbé Kakatoes, who told the company at
supper one night how the first confession he ever received
was from a murderer, let us say.   Presently enters to supper the Marquis de Croquemitaine.   "Palsambleu, abbé!"
says the brilliant marquis, taking a pinch of snuff, "are
you here?   Gentlemen and ladies!   I was the abbé's first
penitent, and I made him a confession which I promise you
astonished him."

To be sure how queerly things are found out!   Here is
an instance.   Only the other day I was writing in these
Roundabout Papers about a certain man, whom I facetiously
called Baggs, and who had abused me to my friends, who
of course told me.   Shortly after that paper was published
another friend, Sacks, let us call him, scowls fiercely at me
as I am sitting in perfect good-humour at the club, and
passes on without speaking.   A cut.   A quarrel.   Sacks
thinks it is about him that I was writing; whereas, upon
my honour and conscience, I never had him once in my
mind, and was pointing my moral from quite another man.
But don't you see, by this wrath of the guilty-conscienced
Sacks, that he had been abusing me too?   He has owned
himself guilty, never having been accused.   He has winced
when nobody thought of hitting him.   I did but put the
cap out, and madly butting and chafing, behold my friend
rushes to put his head into it!   Never mind, Sacks, you
are found out; but I bear you no malice, my man.

And yet to be found out, I know from my own experience, must be painful and odious, and cruelly mortifying to
the inward vanity.   Suppose I am a poltroon, let us say.
With fierce moustache, loud talk, plentiful oaths, and an
immense stick, I keep up nevertheless a character for courage.   I swear fearfully at cabmen and women; brandish
my bludgeon, and perhaps knock down a little man or two
with it; brag of the images which I break at the shooting-
gallery, and pass amongst my friends for a whiskery fire-
eater, afraid of neither man nor dragon.   Ah, me!   Suppose some brisk little chap steps up and gives me a caning
in St. James's Street, with all the heads of my friends

looking out of all the club windows? My reputation is gone. I frighten no man more. My nose is pulled by whipper-snappers, who jump up on a chair to reach it. I am found out. And in the days of my triumphs, when people were yet afraid of me, and were taken in by my swagger, I always knew that I was a lily-liver, and expected that I should be found out some day.

That certainty of being found out must haunt and depress many a bold braggadocio spirit. Let us say it is a clergyman, who can pump copious floods of tears out of his own eyes and those of his audience. He thinks to himself, "I am but a poor swindling, chattering rogue. My bills are unpaid. I have jilted several women whom I have promised to marry. I don't know whether I believe what I preach, and I know I have stolen the very sermon over which I have been snivelling. Have they found me out?" says he, as his head drops down on the cushion.

Then your writer, poet, historian, novelist, or what not. The *Beacon* says that "Jones's work is one of the first order." The *Lamp* declares that "Jones's tragedy surpasses every work since the days of Him of Avon." The *Comet* asserts that "J.'s 'Life of Goody Twoshoes' is a $\kappa\tau\tilde{\eta}\mu\alpha$ $\grave{\epsilon}\varsigma$ $\grave{\alpha}\epsilon\grave{\imath}$, a noble and enduring monument to the fame of that admirable Englishwoman," and so forth. But then Jones knows that he has lent the critic of the *Beacon* five pounds; that his publisher has a half-share in the *Lamp;* and that the *Comet* comes repeatedly to dine with him. It is all very well. Jones is immortal until he is found out; and then down comes the extinguisher, and the immortal is dead and buried. The idea (*dies iræ!*) of discovery must haunt many a man, and make him uneasy, as the trumpets are puffing in his triumph. Brown, who has a higher place than he deserves, cowers before Smith, who has found him out. What is a chorus of critics shouting "Bravo?"—a public clapping hands and flinging garlands? Brown knows that Smith has found him out. Puff, trumpets! Wave, banners! Huzzay, boys, for the immortal Brown! "This is all very well," B. thinks (bowing the while, smil-

ing, laying his hand to his heart); "but there stands Smith
at the window: *he* has measured me; and some day the
others will find me out too." It is a very curious sensation
to sit by a man who has found you out, and who, as you
know, has found you out, or, *vice versâ*, to sit with a man
whom *you* have found out. His talent? Bah! His virtue?
We know a little story or two about his virtue, and he
knows we know it. We are thinking over friend Robinson's antecedents, as we grin, bow, and talk; and we are
both humbugs together. Robinson a good fellow, is he?
You know how he behaved to Hicks? A good-natured
man, is he? Pray, do you remember that little story of
Mrs. Robinson's black eye? How men have to work, to
talk, to smile, to go to bed, and try and sleep, with this
dread of being found out on their consciences! Bardolph,
who has robbed a church, and Nym, who has taken a purse,
go to their usual haunts, and smoke their pipes with their
companions. Mr. Detective Bullseye appears, and says,
"Oh, Bardolph! I want you about that there pyx business!" Mr. Bardolph knocks the ashes out of his pipe,
puts out his hands to the little steel cuffs, and walks away
quite meekly. He is found out. He must go. "Good-
by, Doll Tearsheet! Good-by, Mrs. Quickly, ma'am!"
The other gentlemen and ladies *de la société* look on and
exchange mute adieux with the departing friends. And an
assured time will come when the other gentlemen and ladies will be found out too.

What a wonderful and beautiful provision of nature it
has been that, for the most part, our womankind are not
endowed with the faculty of finding us out! *They* don't
doubt, and probe, and weigh, and take your measure.
Lay down this paper, my benevolent friend and reader, go
into your drawing-room now, and utter a joke ever so old,
and I wager sixpence the ladies there will all begin to
laugh. Go to Brown's house, and tell Mrs. Brown and the
young ladies what you think of him, and see what a welcome you will get! In like manner, let him come to your
house, and tell *your* good lady his candid opinion of you,

and fancy how she will receive him! Would you have your wife and children know you exactly for what you are, and esteem you precisely at your worth? If so, my friend, you will live in a dreary house, and you will have but a chilly fireside. Do you suppose the people round it don't see your homely face as under a glamour, and, as it were, with a halo of love round it? You don't fancy you *are*, as you seem to them? No such thing, my man. Put away that monstrous conceit, and be thankful that *they* have not found you out.

ON A HUNDRED YEARS HENCE.

WHERE have I just read of a game played at a country house? The party assembles round a table with pens, ink, and paper. Some one narrates a tale containing more or less incidents and personages. Each person of the company then writes down, to the best of his memory and ability, the anecdote just narrated, and finally the papers are to be read out. I do not say I should like to play often at this game, which might possibly be a tedious and lengthy pastime, not by any means so amusing as smoking a cigar in the conservatory; or even listening to the young ladies playing their piano-pieces; or to Hobbs and Nobbs lingering round the bottle and talking over the morning's run with the hounds; but surely it is a moral and ingenious sport. They say the variety of narratives is often very odd and amusing. The original story becomes so changed and distorted that at the end of all the statements you are puzzled to know where the truth is at all. As time is of small importance to the cheerful persons engaged in this sport, perhaps a good way of playing it would be to spread it over a couple of years. Let the people who played the game in '60 all meet and play it once more in '61, and each write his story over again. Then bring out your original and compare notes. Not only will the stories differ from each other, but the writers will probably differ from themselves. In the course of the year the incidents will grow or will dwindle strangely. The least authentic of the statements will be so lively or so malicious, or so neatly put, that it will appear most like the truth. I like these tales and sportive exercises. I had begun a little print collection once. I had Addison in his nightgown in bed at Holland House, requesting young Lord Warwick to remark how a Christian should die. I had Cambronne clutching his cocked-hat, and uttering the immortal *la Garde meurt et ne se rend pas.* I had the *Vengeur* going down, and all the crew hurraying like madmen. I had Alfred toasting the muffin; Curtius (Haydon) jumping into the gulf; with extracts from Napoleon's bulletins, and a fine authentic portrait of Baron Munchausen.

What man who has been before the public at all has not heard similar wonderful anecdotes regarding himself and his own history? In these humble essaykins I have taken leave to egotize. I cry out about the shoes which pinch me, and, as I fancy, more naturally and pathetically than if my neighbour's corns were trodden under foot. I prattle about the dish which I love, the wine which I like, the talk I heard yesterday—about Brown's absurd airs—Jones's ridiculous elation when he thinks he has caught me in a blunder (a part of the fun, you see, is that Jones will read this, and will perfectly well know that I mean him, and that we shall meet and grin at each other with entire politeness). This is not the highest kind of speculation, I confess, but it is a gossip which amuses some folks. A brisk and honest small-beer will refresh those who do not care for the frothy outpourings of heavier taps. A two of clubs may be a good, handy little card sometimes, and able to tackle a king of diamonds, if it is a little trump. Some philosophers get their wisdom with deep thought and out of ponderous libraries; I pick up my small crumbs of cogitation at a dinner-table; or from Mrs. Mary and Miss Louisa, as they are prattling over their five o'clock tea.

Well, yesterday at dinner Jucundus was good enough to tell me a story about myself, which he had heard from a lady of his acquaintance, to whom I send my best compliments. The tale is this. At nine o'clock on the evening of the 31st of November last, just before sunset, I was seen leaving No. 96, Abbey Road, St. John's Wood, leading two little children by the hand, one of them in a nankeen pelisse, and the other having a mole on the third finger of his left hand (she thinks it was the third finger, but is quite sure it was the left hand). Thence I walked with them to Charles Boroughbridge's, pork and sausage

man, No. 29, Upper Theresa Road. Here, whilst I left
the little girl innocently eating a polony in the front shop,
I and Boroughbridge retired with the boy into the back
parlour, where Mrs. Boroughbridge was playing cribbage.
She put up the cards and boxes, took out a chopper and a
napkin, and we cut the little boy's little throat (which he
bore with great pluck and resolution), and made him into
sausage-meat by the aid of Purkis's excellent sausage-ma-
chine.   The little girl at first could not understand her
brother's absence, but, under the pretence of taking her to
see Mr. Fechter in "Hamlet," I led her down to the New
River at Sadler's Wells, where a body of a child in a nankeen pelisse was subsequently found, and has never been
recognized to the present day.   And this Mrs. Lynx can
aver, because she saw the whole transaction with her own
eyes, as she told Mr. Jucundus.

I have altered the little details of the anecdote somewhat.   But this story is, I vow and declare, as true as Mrs.
Lynx's.   Gracious goodness! how do lies begin?   What
are the averages of lying?   Is the same amount of lies told
about every man, and do we pretty much all tell the same
amount of lies?   Is the average greater in Ireland than in
Scotland, or *vice versâ*—among women than among men?
Is this a lie I am telling now?   If I am talking about you,
the odds are, perhaps, that it is.   I look back at some
which have been told about me, and speculate on them with
thanks and wonder.   Dear friends have told them of me,
have told them to me of myself.   Have they not to and of
you, dear friend?   A friend of mine was dining at a large
dinner of clergymen, and a story, as true as the sausage
story above given, was told regarding me, by one of those
reverend divines, in whose frocks sit some anile chatterboxes, as any man, who knows this world, knows.   They
take the privilege of their gown.   They cabal, and tattle,
and hiss, and cackle comminations under their breath.   I
say the old women of the other sex are not more talkative
or more mischievous than some of these.   "Such a man
ought not to be spoken to," says Gobemouche, narrating

the story—and such a story! "And I am surprised he is admitted into society at all." Yes, dear Gobemouche, but the story wasn't true; and I had no more done the wicked deed in question than I had run away with the Queen of Sheba.

I have always longed to know what that story was (or what collection of histories), which a lady had in her mind to whom a servant of mine applied for a place, when I was breaking up my establishment once, and going abroad. Brown went with a very good character from us, which, indeed, she fully deserved after several years' faithful service. But when Mrs. Jones read the name of the person out of whose employment Brown came, "That is quite sufficient," says Mrs. Jones. "You may go. I will never take a servant out of *that* house." Ah, Mrs. Jones, how I should like to know what that crime was, or what that series of villanies, which made you determine never to take a servant out of my house? Do you believe in the story of the little boy and the sausages? Have you swallowed that little minced infant? Have you devoured that young Polonius? Upon my word you have maw enough. We somehow greedily gobble down all stories in which the characters of our friends are chopped up, and believe wrong of them without inquiry. In a late serial work written by this hand, I remember making some pathetic remarks about our propensity to believe ill of our neighbours—and I remember the remarks, not because they were valuable, or novel, or ingenious, but because, within three days after they had appeared in print, the moralist who wrote them, walking home with a friend, heard a story about another friend, which story he straightway believed, and which story was scarcely more true than that sausage fable which is here set down. *O mea culpâ, mea maxima culpa!* But though the preacher trips, shall not the doctrine be good? Yea, brethren! Here be the rods. Look you, here are the scourges. Choose me a nice long, swishing, buddy one, light and well-poised in the handle, thick and bushy at the tail. Pick me out a whipcord thong with some dainty knots in it—and now—we all deserve it—whish, whish, whish! Let us cut into each other all round.

A favourite liar and servant of mine was a man I once had to drive a brougham. He never came to my house, except for orders, and once when he helped to wait at dinner so clumsily that it was agreed we would dispense with his further efforts. The (job) brougham horse used to look dreadfully lean and tired, and the livery-stable keeper complained that we worked him too hard. Now, it turned out that there was a neighbouring butcher's lady who liked to ride in a brougham; and Tomkins lent her ours, drove her cheerfully to Richmond and Putney, and, I suppose, took out a payment in mutton-chops. We gave this good Tomkins wine and medicine for his family when sick—we supplied him with little comforts and extras which need not now be remembered—and the grateful creature rewarded us by informing some of our tradesmen whom he honoured with his custom, "Mr. Roundabout? Lor bless you! I carry him up to bed drunk every night in the week." He, Tomkins, being a man of seven stone weight, and five feet high; whereas his employer was—but here modesty interferes, and I decline to enter into the avoirdupois question.

Now, what was Tomkins' motive for the utterance and dissemination of these lies? They could further no conceivable end or interest of his own. Had they been true stories, Tomkins' master would still, and reasonably, have been more angry than at the fables. It was but suicidal slander on the part of Tomkins—must come to a discovery—must end in a punishment. The poor wretch had got his place under, as it turned out, a fictitious character. He might have stayed in it, for of course Tomkins had a wife and poor innocent children. He might have had bread, beer, bed, character, coats, coals. He might have nestled in our little island, comfortably sheltered from the storms of life; but we were compelled to cast him out, and send him driving, lonely, perishing, tossing, starving, to sea—to drown. To drown? There be other modes of death whereby rogues die. Good-by, Tomkins. And so the night-cap is put on, and the bolt is drawn for poor T.

Suppose we were to invite volunteers amongst our respected readers to send in little statements of the lies which they know have been told about themselves; what a heap of correspondence, what an exaggeration of malignities, what a crackling bonfire of incendiary falsehoods, might we not gather together! And a lie once set going, having the breath of life breathed into it by the father of lying, and ordered to run its diabolical little course, lives with a prodigious vitality. You say, "*Magna est veritas et prœvalebit.*" Psha! Great lies are as great as great truths, and prevail constantly, and day after day. Take an instance or two out of my own little budget. I sit near a gentleman at dinner, and the conversation turns upon a certain anonymous literary performance which at the time is amusing the town. "Oh," says the gentleman, "everybody knows who wrote that paper: it is Momus's." I was a young author at the time, perhaps proud of my bantling: "I beg your pardon," I say, "it was written by your humble servant." "Indeed!" was all that the man replied, and he shrugged his shoulders, turned his back, and talked to his other neighbour. I never heard sarcastic incredulity more finely conveyed than by that "indeed." "Impudent liar," the gentleman's face said, as clear as face could speak. Where was Magna Veritas, and how did she prevail then? She lifted up her voice, she made her appeal, and she was kicked out of court. In New York I read a newspaper criticism one day (by an exile from our shores who has taken up his abode in the Western Republic), commenting upon a letter of mine which had appeared in a contemporary volume, and wherein it was stated that the writer was a lad in such and such a year, and, in point of fact, I was, at the period spoken of, nineteen years of age. "Falsehood, Mr. Roundabout," says the noble critic, "you were then not a lad; you were then six-and-twenty years of age." You see he knew better than papa and mamma and parish register. It was easier for him to think and say I lied, on a twopenny matter connected with my own affairs, than to imagine he was mistaken. Years ago, in a time when we were very mad wags, Arcturus and myself met a gentleman from China who knew the language. We began to speak Chinese against him. We said we were born in China. We were two to one. We spoke the mandarin dialect with perfect fluency. We had the company with us; as in the old, old days, the squeak of the real pig was voted not to be so natural as the squeak of the sham pig. O Arcturus, the sham pig squeaks in our streets now to the applause of multitudes, and the real porker grunts unheeded in his sty!

I once talked for some little time with an amiable lady: it was for the first time; and I saw an expression of surprise on her kind face, which said as plainly as face could say, "Sir, do you know that up to this moment I have had a certain opinion of you, and that I begin to think I have been mistaken or misled?" I not only know that she had heard evil reports of me, but I know who told her—one of those acute fellows, my dear brethren, of whom we spoke in a previous sermon, who has found me out—found out actions which I never did, found out thoughts and sayings which I never spoke, and judged me accordingly. Ah, my lad! have I found *you* out? *O risum teneatis.* Perhaps the person I am accusing is no more guilty than I.

How comes it that the evil which men say spreads so widely and lasts so long, whilst our good, kind words don't seem somehow to take root and bear blossom? Is it that in the stony hearts of mankind these pretty flowers can't find a place to grow? Certain it is that scandal is good brisk talk, whereas praise of one's neighbour is by no means lively hearing. An acquaintance grilled, scored, devilled, and served with mustard and cayenne pepper, excites the appetite; whereas a slice of cold friend with currant jelly is but a sickly, unrelishing meat.

Now, such being the case, my dear worthy Mrs. Candour, in whom I know there are a hundred good and generous qualities; it being perfectly clear that the good things which we say of our neighbours don't fructify, but some-how perish in the ground where they are dropped, whilst the evil words are wafted by all the winds of scandal, take root in all soils, and flourish amazingly—seeing, I say, that this conversation does not give us a fair chance, sup-pose we give up censoriousness altogether, and decline ut-tering our opinions about Brown, Jones, and Robinson (and Mesdames B., J., and R.) at all? We may be mistaken about every one of them, as, please goodness, those anec-dote-mongers against whom I have uttered my meek pro-test have been mistaken about me. We need not go to the extent of saying that Mrs. Manning was an amiable creat-ure, much misunderstood; and Jack Thurtell a gallant, unfortunate fellow, not near so black as he was painted; but we will try and avoid personalities altogether in talk, won't we? We will range the fields of science, dear madam, and communicate to each other the pleasing re-sults of our studies. We will, if you please, examine the infinitesimal wonders of nature through the microscope. We will cultivate entomology. We will sit with our arms round each other's waists on the *pons asinorum*, and see the stream of mathematics flow beneath. We will take refuge in cards, and play at "beggar my neighbour," not abuse my neighbour. We will go to the Zoological Gar-dens and talk freely about the gorilla and his kindred, but not talk about people who can talk in their turn. Suppose we praise the High Church? we offend the Low Church. The Broad Church? High and Low are both offended. What do you think of Lord Derby as a politician? And what is your opinion of Lord Palmerston? If you please, will you play me those lovely variations of " In my cottage near a wood?" It is a charming air (you know it in French, I suppose? *Ah ! te dirai-je, maman !*) and was a favourite with poor Marie Antoinette. I say "poor" be-cause I have a right to speak with pity of a sovereign who was renowned for so much beauty and so much misfortune. But as for giving any opinion on her conduct, saying that she was good or bad, or indifferent, goodness forbid! We have agreed we will not be censorious.   Let us have a game at cards—at *écarté* if you please.   You deal.   I ask for cards.   I lead the deuce of clubs.   *   *   *

What? there is no deuce!   Deuce take it!   What? People *will* go on talking about their neighbours, and won't have their mouths stopped by cards, or ever so much micro-scopes and aquariums? Ah, my poor dear Mrs. Candour, I agree with you.   By the way, did you ever see anything like Lady Godiva Trotter's dress last night? People *will* go on chattering, although we hold our tongues; and, after all, my good soul, what will their scandal matter a hun-dred years hence?

SMALL-BEER CHRONICLE.

NOT long since, at a certain banquet, I had the good fortune to sit by Doctor Polymathesis, who knows everything, and who, about the time when the claret made its appearance, mentioned that old dictum of the grumbling Oxford Don, that "ALL CLARET *would be port if it could!*" Imbibing a bumper of one or the other not ungratefully, I thought to myself, "Here surely, Mr. Roundabout, is a good text for one of your reverence's sermons." Let us apply to the human race, dear brethren, what is here said of the vintages of Portugal and Gascony, and we shall have no difficulty in perceiving how many clarets aspire to be ports in their way; how most men and women of our acquaintance, how we ourselves, are Acquitainians giving ourselves Lusitanian airs; how we wish to have credit for being stronger, braver, more beautiful, more worthy than we really are.

Nay, the beginning of this hypocrisy—a desire to excel, a desire to be hearty, fruity, generous, strength-imparting —is a virtuous and noble ambition; and it is most difficult for a man in his own case, or his neighbour's, to say at what point this ambition transgresses the boundary of virtue, and becomes vanity, pretence, and self-seeking. You are a poor man, let us say, showing a bold face to adverse fortune, and wearing a confident aspect. Your purse is very narrow, but you owe no man a penny; your means are scanty, but your wife's gown is decent; your old coat well brushed; your children at a good school; you grumble to no one; ask favours of no one; truckle to no neighbours on account of their superior rank, or (a worse, and a meaner, and a more common crime still) envy none for their better fortune. To all outward appearances you are as well to do as your neighbours, who have thrice your income. There may be in this case some little mixture of pretension in your life and behaviour. You certainly *do* put on a smiling face whilst fortune is pinching you. Your wife and girls, so smart and neat at evening parties, are cutting, patching, and cobbling all day to make both ends of life's haberdashery meet. You give a friend a bottle of wine on occasion, but are content yourself with a glass of whisky and water. You avoid a cab, saying, that of all things you like to walk home after dinner (which you know, my good friend, is a fib). I grant you that in this scheme of life there does enter ever so little hypocrisy; that this claret is loaded, as it were; but your desire to *portify* yourself is amiable, is pardonable, is perhaps honourable: and were there no other hypocrisies than yours in the world we should be a set of worthy fellows; and sermonizers, moralizers, satirizers, would have to hold their tongues, and go to some other trade to get a living.

But you know you *will* step over that boundary line of virtue and modesty, into the district where humbug and vanity begin, and there the moralizer catches you and makes an example of you. For instance, in a certain novel in another place my friend Mr. Talbot Twysden is mentioned—a man whom you and I know to be a wretched ordinaire, but who persists in treating himself as if he was the finest '20 port. In our Britain there are hundreds of men like him; forever striving to swell beyond their natural size, to strain beyond their natural strength, to step beyond their natural stride. Search, search within your own waistcoats, dear brethren—*you* know in your hearts, which of your ordinaire qualities you would pass off, and fain consider as first-rate port? And why not you yourself, Mr. Preacher? says the congregation. Dearly beloved, neither in nor out of this pulpit do I profess to be bigger, or cleverer, or wiser, or better than any of you. A short while since, a certain Reviewer announced that I gave myself great pretensions as a philosopher. I a philosopher! I advance pretensions! My dear Saturday friend; and you? Don't you teach everything to everybody? and punish the naughty boys if they don't learn as you bid them? You teach politics to Lord John and Mr. Gladstone. You teach poets how to write; painters, how to paint; gentlemen, manners; and opera-dancers, how to pirouette. I was not a little amused of late by an instance of the modesty of our Saturday friend, who, more Athenian than the Athenians, and apropos of a Greek book by a Greek author, sate down and gravely showed the Greek gentleman how to write his own language.

No, I do not, as far as I know, try to be port at all; but offer in these presents, a sound genuine ordinaire, at 18*s.* per doz. let us say, grown on my own hill-side, and offered *de bon cœur* to those who will sit down under my *tonnelle*, and have a half-hour's drink and gossip. It is none of your hot porto, my friend. I know there is much better and stronger liquor elsewhere. Some pronounce it sour; some say it is thin; some that it has wofully lost its flavour. This may or may not be true. There are good and bad years; years that surprise everybody; years of which the produce is small and bad, or rich and plentiful. But if my tap is not genuine it is naught, and no man should give himself the trouble to drink it. I do not even say that I would be port if I could; knowing that port (by which I would imply much stronger, deeper, richer, and more durable liquor than my vineyard can furnish) is not relished by all palates, or suitable to all heads. We will assume then, dear brother, that you and I are tolerably modest people; and, ourselves being thus out of the question, proceed to show how pretentious our neighbours are, and how very many of them would be port if they could.

Have you never seen a small man from college placed amongst great folk, and giving himself the airs of a man of fashion? He goes back to his common room with fond reminiscences of Ermine Castle or Strawberry Hall. He writes to the dear countess, to say that dear Lord Lollypop is getting on very well at St. Boniface, and that the accident which he met with in a scuffle with an inebriated bargeman only showed his spirit and honour, and will not permanently disfigure his lordship's nose. He gets his clothes from dear Lollypop's London tailor, and wears a mauve or magenta tie when he rides out to see the hounds. A love of fashionable people is a weakness, I do not say of all, but of some tutors. Witness that Eton tutor t'other day, who intimated that in Cornhill we could not understand the perfect purity, delicacy, and refinement of those genteel families who sent their sons to Eton. O usher, *mon ami!* Old Sam Johnson, who, too, had been an usher in his early life, kept a little of that weakness always. Suppose Goldsmith had knocked him up at three in the morning and proposed a boat to Greenwich, as Topham Beauclerc and his friend did, would he have said, "What, my boy, are you for a frolic? I'm with you!" and gone and put on his clothes? Rather he would have pitched poor Goldsmith downstairs. He would have liked to be port if he could. Of course *we* wouldn't. Our opinion of the Portugal grape is known. It grows very high, and is very sour, and we don't go for that kind of grape at all.

"I was walking with Mr. Fox"—and sure this anecdote comes very pat after the grapes—"I was walking with Mr. Fox in the Louvre," says Benjamin West (*apud* some paper I have just been reading), "and I remarked how many people turned round to look at *me*. This shows the respect of the French for the fine arts." This is a curious instance of a very small claret indeed, which imagined itself to be port of the strongest body. There are not many instances of a faith so deep, so simple, so satisfactory as this. I have met many who would like to be port; but with few of the Gascon sort, who absolutely believe they *were* port. George III. believed in West's port, and thought Reynolds' overrated stuff. When I saw West's pictures at Philadelphia, I looked at them with astonishment and awe. Hide, blushing glory, hide your head under your old night-cap. O immortality! is this the end of you? Did any of you, my dear brethren, ever try and read Blackmore's Poems, or the Epics of Baour-Lormian, or the "Henriade," or— what shall we say?—Pollok's "Course of Time?" They were thought to be more lasting than brass by some people,

and where are they now? And *our* masterpieces of literature—*our* ports—that, if not immortal, at any rate are to
last their fifty, their hundred years—oh, sirs, don't you
think a very small cellar will hold them?

Those poor people in brass, on pedestals, hectoring about
Trafalgar Square and that neighbourhood, don't you think
many of them—apart even from the ridiculous execution
—cut rather a ridiculous figure, and that we are too eager
to set up our ordinaire heroism and talent for port? A
Duke of Wellington or two I will grant, though even of
these idols a moderate supply will be sufficient. Some
years ago a famous and witty French critic was in London,
with whom I walked the streets. I am ashamed to say
that I informed him (being in hopes that he was about to
write some papers regarding the manners and customs of
this country) that all the statues he saw represented the
Duke of Wellington. That on the arch opposite Apsley
House? the Duke in a cloak, and cocked hat, on horseback.
That behind Apsley House in an airy fig-leaf costume?
the Duke again. That in Cockspur Street? the Duke with
a pigtail—and so on. I showed him an army of Dukes.
There are many bronze heroes who after a few years look
already as foolish, awkward, and out of place as a man,
say at Shoolbred's or Swan and Edgar's. For example,
those three Grenadiers in Pall Mall, who have been up only
a few months, don't you pity those unhappy household
troops, who have to stand frowning and looking fierce
there; and think they would like to step down and go to
barracks? That they fought very bravely there is no
doubt; but so did the Russians fight very bravely; and the
French fight very bravely; and so did Colonel Jones and
the 99th, and Colonel Brown and the 100th; and I say
again that ordinaire should not give itself port airs, and
that an honest ordinaire would blush to be found swaggering so. I am sure if you could consult the Duke of York,
who is impaled on his column between the two clubs, and
ask his late Royal Highness whether he thought he ought
to remain there, he would say no. A brave, worthy man,

not a braggart or boaster, to be put upon that heroic perch must be painful to him. Lord George Bentinck, I suppose, being in the midst of the family park in Cavendish Square, may conceive that he has a right to remain in his place. But look at William of Cumberland, with his hat cocked over his eye, prancing behind Lord George on his Roman-nosed charger; he, depend on 'it, would be for getting off his horse if he had the permission. He did not hesitate about trifles, as we know; but he was a very truth-telling and honourable soldier: and as for heroic rank and stat-uesque dignity, I would wager a dozen of '20 port against a bottle of pure and sound Bordeaux, at 18*s.* per dozen (bottles included), that he never would think of claiming any such absurd distinction. They have got a statue of Thomas Moore at Dublin, I hear. Is he on horseback? Some men should have, say, a fifty years' lease of glory. After a while some gentlemen now in brass should go to the melting furnace, and reappear in some other gentle-man's shape. Lately I saw that Melville column rising over Edinburgh; come, good men and true, don't you feel a little awkward and uneasy when you walk under it? Who was this to stand in heroic places? and is yon the man whom Scotchmen most delight to honour? I must own deferentially that there is a tendency in North Britain to over-esteem its heroes. Scotch ale is very good and strong, but it is not stronger than all the other beer in the world, as some Scottish patriots would insist. When there has been a war, and stout old Sandy Sansculotte returns home from India or Crimea, what a bagpiping, shouting, hurray-ing, and self-glorification takes place round about him! You would fancy, to hear McOrator after dinner, that the Scotch had fought all the battles, killed all the Russians, Indian rebels, or what not. In Cupar-Fife, there's a little inn called the "Battle of Waterloo," and what do you think the sign is? (I sketch from memory, to be sure.) "The Battle of Waterloo" is one broad Scotchman laying about him with a broadsword. Yes, yes, my dear Mac, you are wise, you are good, you are clever, you are handsome, you

are brave, you are rich, &c.; but so is Jones over the bor-
der.   Scotch salmon is good, but there are other good fish
in the sea.   I once heard a Scotchman lecture on poetry in
London.   Of course the pieces he selected were chiefly by
Scottish authors, and Walter Scott was his favourite poet.
I whispered to my neighbour, who was a Scotchman (by
the way, the audience were almost all Scotch, and the room
was All-Mac's—I beg your pardon, but I couldn't help it,

I really couldn't help it)—"The professor has said the best
poet was a Scotchman: I wager that he will say the worst
poet was a Scotchman, too."   And sure enough that worst
poet, when he made his appearance, was a Northern Briton.
    And as we are talking of bragging, and I am on my
travels, can I forget one mighty republic—one—two mighty
republics, where people are notoriously fond of passing off
their claret for port?   I am very glad, for the sake of a
kind friend, that there is a great and influential party in
the United, and, I trust, in the Confederate States, who
believe that Catawba wine is better than the best Champagne.   Opposite that famous old White House at Washington, whereof I shall ever have a grateful memory, they

have set up an equestrian statue of General Jackson, by a self-taught American artist of no inconsiderable genius and skill. At an evening party a member of Congress seized me in a corner of the room, and asked me if I did not think this was *the finest equestrian statue in the world?* How was I to deal with this plain question, put to me in a corner? I was bound to reply, and accordingly said that I did *not* think it was the finest statue in the world. "Well, sir," says the member of Congress, "but you must remember that Mr. M—— had never seen a statue when he made this!" I suggested that to see other statues might do Mr. M—— no harm. Nor was any man more willing to own his defects, or more modest regarding his merits, than the sculptor himself, whom I met subsequently. But, oh! what a charming article there was in a Washington paper next day about the impertinence of criticism and offensive tone of arrogance which Englishmen adopted towards men and works of genius in America! "Who was this man, who, &c. &c." The Washington writer was angry because I would not accept this American claret as the finest port wine in the world. Ah me! It is about blood and not wine that the quarrel now is, and who shall foretell its end?

How much claret that would be port if it could is handed about in every society! In the House of Commons what small-beer orators try to pass for strong? Stay: have I a spite against any one? It is a fact that the wife of the member for Bungay has left off asking me and Mrs. Roundabout to her evening parties. Now is the time to have a slap at him. I will say that he was always overrated, and that now he is lamentably falling off even from what he has been. I will back the member for Stoke Pogis against him; and show that the dashing young member for Islington is a far sounder man than either. Have I any little literary animosities? Of course not. Men of letters never have. Otherwise, how I could serve out a competitor here, make a face over his works, and show that his would-be port is very meagre ordinaire indeed! Nonsense, man!

Why so squeamish? Do they spare *you !* Now you have the whip in your hand, won't you lay on? You used to be a pretty whip enough as a young man, and liked it too. Is there no enemy who would be the better for a little thonging? No. I have militated in former times, not without glory; but I grow peaceable as I grow old. And if I have a literary enemy, why, he will probably write a book ere long, and then it will be *his* turn, and my favourite review will be down upon him.

My brethren, these sermons are professedly short; for I have that opinion of my dear congregation, which leads me to think that were I to preach at great length they would yawn, stamp, make noises, and perhaps go straightway out of church; and yet with this text I protest I could go on for hours. What multitudes of men, what multitudes of women, my dears, pass off their ordinaire for port, their small beer for strong! In literature, in politics, in the army, the navy, the church, at the bar, in the world, what an immense quantity of cheap liquor is made to do service for better sorts! Ask Serjeant Rowland his opinion of Oliver, Q.C.? "Ordinaire, my good fellow, ordinaire, with a port-wine label!" Ask Oliver his opinion of Rowland. Never was a man so overrated by the world and by himself. Ask Tweedledumski his opinion of Tweedledeestein's performance, "A quack, my tear sir! an ignoramus, I geef you my vort? He gombose an opera! He is not fit to make dance a bear!" Ask Paddington and Buckmister, those two "swells" of fashion, what they think of each other? They are notorious ordinaire. You and I remember when they passed for very small wine, and now how high and mighty they have become? What do you say to Tomkins' sermons? Ordinaire, trying to go down as orthodox port, and very meagre ordinaire too! To Hopkins' historical works?—to Pumkins' poetry? Ordinaire, ordinaire again—thin, feeble, overrated; and so down the whole list. And when we have done discussing our men friends, have we not all the women? Do these not advance absurd pretensions? Do these never give themselves

G

airs? With feeble brains, don't they often set up to be
esprits forts? Don't they pretend to be women of fashion,
and cut their betters? Don't they try and pass off their
ordinary-looking girls as beauties of the first order? Every
man in his circle knows women who give themselves airs,
and to whom we can apply the port-wine simile.

Come, my friends. Here is enough of ordinaire and
port for to-day. My bottle has run out. Will anybody
have any more? Let us go upstairs, and get a cup of tea
from the ladies.

OGRES.

I DARESAY the reader has remarked that the upright and independent vowel, which stands in the vowel-list between E and O, has formed the subject of the main part of these essays. How does that vowel feel this morning?—fresh, good-humoured, and lively? The Roundabout lines, which fall from this pen, are correspondingly brisk and cheerful. Has anything, on the contrary, disagreed with the vowel? Has its rest been disturbed, or was yesterday's dinner too good, or yesterday's wine not good enough? Under such circumstances, a darkling, misanthropic tinge, no doubt, is cast upon the paper. The jokes, if attempted, are elaborate and dreary. The bitter temper breaks out. That sneering manner is adopted, which you know, and which exhibits itself so especially when the writer is speaking about women. A moody carelessness comes over him. He sees no good in any body or thing: and treats gentlemen, ladies, history, and things in general, with a like gloomy flippancy. Agreed. When the vowel in question is in that mood; if you like airy gaiety and tender gushing benevolence—if you want to be satisfied with yourself and the rest of your fellow-beings; I recommend you, my dear creature, to go to some other shop in Cornhill, or turn to some other article. There are moods in the mind of the vowel of which we are speaking, when it is ill-conditioned and captious. Who always keeps good health, and good humour? Do not philosophers grumble? Are not sages sometimes out of temper? and do not angel-women go off in tantrums? To-day my mood is dark. I scowl as I dip my pen in the inkstand.

Here is the day come round—for everything here is done with the utmost regularity:—intellectual labour, sixteen hours; meals, thirty-two minutes; exercise, a hundred and forty-eight minutes; conversation with the family, chiefly literary, and about the housekeeping, one hour and four minutes; sleep, three hours and fifteen minutes (at the end of the month, when the Magazine is complete, I own I take eight minutes more); and the rest for the toilette and the world. Well, I say, the "Roundabout Paper Day" being come, and the subject long since settled in my mind, an excellent subject—a most telling, lively, and popular subject—I go to breakfast determined to finish that meal in $9\frac{3}{4}$ minutes, as usual, and then retire to my desk and work, when—oh, provoking!—here in the paper is the very subject treated, on which I was going to write! Yesterday another paper which I saw treated it—and of course, as I need not tell you, spoiled it. Last Saturday, another paper had an article on the subject; perhaps you may guess what it was—but I won't tell you. Only this is true, my favourite subject, which was about to make the best paper we have had for a long time: my bird, my game that I was going to shoot and serve up with such a delicate sauce, has been found by other sportsmen; and pop, pop, pop, a half-dozen of guns have banged at it, mangled it, and brought it down.

"And can't you take some other text?" say you. All this is mighty well. But if you have set your heart on a certain dish for dinner, be it cold boiled veal, or what you will; and they bring you turtle and venison, don't you feel disappointed? During your walk you have been making up your mind that that cold meat, with moderation and a pickle, will be a very sufficient dinner: you have accustomed your thoughts to it; and here, in place of it, is a turkey, surrounded by coarse sausages, or a reeking pigeon-pie or a fulsome roast pig. I have known many a good and kind man made furiously angry by such a *contretemps*. I have known him lose his temper, call his wife and servants names, and a whole household made miserable. If, then, as is notoriously the case, it is too dangerous to baulk a man about his dinner, how much more about his article? I came to my meal with an ogre-like appetite and gusto. Fee, faw, fum! Wife, where is that tender little Prince-kin? Have you trussed him, and did you stuff him nicely, and have you taken care to baste him and do him, not too brown, as I told you? Quick! I am hungry! I begin to whet my knife, to roll my eyes about, and roar and clap my huge chest like a gorilla; and then my poor Ogrina has to tell me that the little princes have all run away, whilst she was in the kitchen, making the paste to bake them in! I pause in the description. I won't condescend to report the bad language, which you know must ensue, when an ogre, whose mind is ill-regulated, and whose habits of self-indulgence are notorious, finds himself disappointed of his greedy hopes. What treatment of his wife, what abuse and brutal behaviour to his children, who, though ogrillons, are children! My dears, you may fancy, and need not ask my delicate pen to describe, the language and behaviour of a vulgar, coarse, greedy, large man with an immense mouth and teeth, which are too frequently employed in the gobbling and crunching of raw man's meat.

And in this circuitous way you see I have reached my present subject, which is, Ogres. You fancy they are dead or only fictitious characters—mythical representatives of strength, cruelty, stupidity, and lust for blood? Though they had seven-leagued boots, you remember all sorts of little whipping-snapping Tom Thumbs used to elude and out-run them. They were so stupid that they gave into the most shallow ambuscades and artifices: witness that well-known ogre, who, because Jack cut open the hasty-pudding, instantly ripped open his own stupid waistcoat and interior. They were cruel, brutal, disgusting with their sharpened teeth, immense knives, and roaring voices: but they always ended by being overcome by little Tom Thumbkins, or some other smart little champion.

Yes; they were conquered in the end there is no doubt. They plunged headlong (and uttering the most frightful bad language) into some pit where Jack came with his smart *couteau de chasse* and whipped their brutal heads off. They would be going to devour maidens,

But ever when it seemed
　　Their need was at the sorest,
A knight, in armour bright,
　　Came riding through the forest.

And, down after a combat, would go the brutal persecutor
with a lance through his midriff.   Yes, I say, this is very
true and well.   But you remember that round the ogre's
cave, the ground was covered, for hundreds and hundreds
of yards, *with the bones of the victims* whom he had lured
into the castle.   Many knights and maids came to him
and perished under his knife and teeth.   Were dragons
the same as ogres? monsters dwelling in caverns, whence
they rushed, attired in plate armour, wielding pikes and
torches, and destroying stray passengers who passed by
their lair?   Monsters, brutes, rapacious tyrants, ruffians,
as they were, doubtless they ended by being overcome.
But, before they were destroyed, they did a deal of mis-
chief.   The bones round their caves were countless.   They
had sent many brave souls to Hades, before their own fled,
howling out of their rascal carcasses, to the same place of
gloom.

　　There is no greater mistake than to suppose that fairies,
champions, distressed damsels, and by consequence ogres,
have ceased to exist.   It may not be *ogreable* to them (pardon the horrible pleasantry, but, as I am writing in the
solitude of my chamber, I am grinding my teeth—yelling,
roaring, and cursing—brandishing my scissors and paper-
cutter, and, as it were, have become an ogre).   I say there
is no greater mistake than to suppose that ogres have ceased
to exist.   We all *know* ogres.   Their caverns are round us,
and about us.   There are the castles of several ogres within
a mile of the spot where I write.   I think some of them
suspect I am an ogre myself.   I am not: but I know they
are.   I visit them.   I don't mean to say that they take a
cold roast prince out of the cupboard, and have a cannibal
feast before *me*.   But I see the bones lying about the roads
to their houses, and in the areas and gardens.   Politeness,
of course, prevents me from making any remarks; but I

know them well enough. One of the ways to know 'em is to watch the scared looks of the ogres' wives and children. They lead an awful life. They are present at dreadful cruelties. In their excesses those ogres will stab about, and kill not only strangers who happen to call in and ask a night's lodging, but they will outrage, murder, and chop up their own kin. We all know ogres, I say, and have been in their dens often. It is not necessary that ogres who ask you to dine should offer their guests the *peculiar dish* which they like. They cannot always get a Tom Thumb family. They eat mutton and beef too; and I daresay even go out to tea, and invite you to drink it. But I tell you there are numbers of them going about in the world. And now you have my word for it, and this little hint, it is quite curious what an interest society may be made to have for you, by your determining to find out the ogres you meet there.

What does the man mean? says Mrs. Downright, to whom a joke is a very grave thing. I mean, madam, that in the company assembled in your genteel drawing-room, who bow here and there and smirk in white neckcloths, you receive men who elbow through life successfully enough, but who are ogres in private: men wicked, false, rapacious, flattering; cruel hectors at home; smiling courtiers abroad; causing wives, children, servants, parents, to tremble before them, and smiling and bowing as they bid strangers welcome into their castles. I say, there are men who have crunched the bones of victim after victim; in whose closets lie skeletons picked frightfully clean. When these ogres come out into the world, you don't suppose they show their knives, and their great teeth? A neat simple white neckcloth, a merry rather obsequious manner, a cadaverous look, perhaps, now and again, and a rather dreadful grin; but I know ogres very considerably respected: and when you hint to such and such a man, "My dear sir, Mr. Sharpus whom you appear to like, is, I assure you, a most dreadful cannibal;" the gentleman cries, "Oh, psha, nonsense! Daresay not so black as he is painted. Daresay not worse than his neighbours." We condone everything in this country—private treason, falsehood, flattery, cruelty at home, roguery, and double dealing—What? Do you mean to say in your acquaintance you don't know ogres guilty of countless crimes of fraud and force, and that knowing them you don't shake hands with them; dine with them at your table; and meet them at their own? Depend upon it, in the time when there were real live ogres in real caverns or castles, gobbling up real knights and virgins—when they went into the world—the neighbouring market-town, let us say, or earl's castle; though their nature and reputation were pretty well known, their notorious foibles were never alluded to. You would say, " What, Blunderbore, my boy! How do you do? How well and fresh you look! What's the receipt you have for keeping so young and rosy? " And your wife would softly ask after Mrs. Blunderbore and the dear children. Or it would be, " My dear Humguffin! try that pork. It is home-bred, home-fed, and, I promise you, tender. Tell me if you think it is as good as yours? John, a glass of Burgundy to Colonel Humguffin! " You don't suppose there would be any unpleasant allusions to disagreeable home-reports regarding Humguffin's manner of furnishing his larder? I say we all of us know ogres. We shake hands and dine with ogres. And if inconvenient moralists tell us we are cowards for our pains, we turn round with a *tu quoque*, or say that we don't meddle with other folk's affairs; that people are much less black than they are painted, and so on. What? Won't half the county go to Ogreham Castle? Won't some of the clergy say grace at dinner? Won't the mothers bring their daughters to dance with the young Rawheads? And if Lady Ogreham happens to die—I won't say to go the way of all flesh, that is too revolting—I say if Ogreham is a widower, do you aver, on your conscience and honour, that mothers will not be found to offer their young girls to supply the lamented lady's place? How stale this misanthropy is! Something must have disagreed with this cynic. Yes, my good woman. I daresay you would like to call another subject. Yes, my fine fellow; ogre at home, supple as a dancing-master abroad, and shaking in thy pumps, and wearing a horrible grin of sham gaiety to conceal thy terror, lest I should point thee out:—thou art prosperous and honoured, art thou? I say thou hast been a tyrant and a robber. Thou hast plundered the poor. Thou hast bullied the weak. Thou hast laid violent hands on the goods of the innocent and confiding. Thou hast made a prey of the meek and gentle who asked for thy protection. Thou hast been hard to thy kinsfolk, and cruel to thy family. Go, monster! Ah, when shall little Jack come and drill daylight through thy wicked cannibal carcass? I see the ogre pass on, bowing right and left to the company; and he gives a dreadful sidelong glance of suspicion as he is talking to my lord bishop in the corner there.

Ogres in our days need not be giants at all. In former times, and in children's books, where it is necessary to paint your moral in such large letters that there can be no mistake about it, ogres are made with that enormous mouth and *ratelier* which you know of, and with which they can swallow down a baby, almost without using that great knife which they always carry. They are too cunning nowa-days. They go about in society, slim, small, quietly dressed, and showing no especially great appetite. In my own young days there used to be play ogres—men who would devour a young fellow in one sitting, and leave him without a bit of flesh on his bones. They were quiet gentlemanlike-looking people. They got the young fellow into their cave. Champagne, paté de foie-gras, and numberless good things, were handed about; and then, having eaten, the young man was devoured in his turn. I believe these card and dice ogres have died away almost as entirely as the hasty-pudding giants whom Tom Thumb overcame. Now, there are ogres in City courts who lure you into their dens. About our Cornish mines I am told there are many most plausible ogres, who tempt you into their caverns and pick your bones there. In a certain newspaper there used to be lately a whole column of advertisements from ogres

who would put on the most plausible, nay, piteous appearance, in order to inveigle their victims.   You would read,
" A tradesman, established for seventy years in the City, and
known, and much respected by Messrs. N. M. Rothschild
and Baring Brothers, has pressing need for three pounds
until next Saturday.   He can give security for half a million, and forty thousand pounds will be given for the use
of the loan," and so on; or, "An influential body of capi-
talists are about to establish a company, of which the business will be enormous and the profits proportionately prodigious.   They will require A SECRETARY, of good address
and appearance, at a salary of two thousand per annum.
He need not be able to write, but address and manners are
absolutely necessary.   As a mark of confidence in the company, he will have to deposit," &c.; or, " A young widow
(of pleasing manners and appearance) who has a pressing
necessity for four pounds ten for three weeks, offers her
Erard's grand piano valued at three hundred guineas; a
diamond cross of eight hundred pounds; and board and
lodging in her elegant villa near Banbury Cross, with the
best references and society, in return for the loan."   I suspect these people are ogres.   There are ogres and ogres.
Polyphemus was a great, tall, one-eyed, notorious ogre,
fetching his victims out of a hole, and gobbling them one
after another.   There could be no mistake about him.   But
so were the Sirens ogres—pretty blue-eyed things, peeping
at you coaxingly from out of the water, and singing their
melodious wheedles.   And the bones round their caves
were more numerous than the ribs, skulls, and thigh bones
round the cavern of hulking Polypheme.

     To the castle-gates of some of these monsters up rides the
dapper champion of the pen; puffs boldly upon the horn
which hangs by the chain; enters the hall resolutely, and
challenges the big tyrant sulking within.   We defy him to
combat, the enormous roaring ruffian!   We give him a
meeting on the green plain before his castle.   Green?   No
wonder it should be green: it is manured with human bones.
After a few graceful wheels and curvets, we take our

ground. We stoop over our saddle. 'Tis but to kiss the locket of our lady-love's hair. And now the vizor is up: the lance is in rest (Gillott's iron is the point for me). A touch of the spur in the gallant sides of Pegasus, and we gallop at the great brute.

"Cut off his ugly head, Flibbertygibbet, my squire!" And who are these who pour out of the castle? the imprisoned maidens, the maltreated widows, the poor old hoary grandfathers, who have been locked up in the dungeons these scores and scores of years, writhing under the tyranny of that ruffian! Ah! ye knights of the pen! May honour be your shield and truth tip your lances! Be gentle to all gentle people. Be modest to women. Be tender to children. And as for the Ogre Humbug, out sword, and have at him.

ON TWO ROUNDABOUT PAPERS WHICH
I INTENDED TO WRITE.

WE have all heard of a place paved with good intentions:
—a place which I take to be a very dismal, useless and unsatisfactory terminus for many pleasant thoughts, kindly
fancies, gentle wishes, merry little quips and pranks, harmless jokes which die as it were the moment of their birth.
Poor little children of the brain! He was a dreary theo-
logian who huddled you under such a melancholy cenotaph,
and laid you in the vaults under the flagstones of Hades! I
trust that some of the best actions we have all of us committed in our lives have been committed in fancy. It is
not all wickedness we are thinking, *que diable!* Some of
our thoughts are bad enough I grant you. Many a one you
and I have had here below. Ah mercy, what a monster!
what crooked horns! what leering eyes! what a flaming
mouth! what cloven feet, and what a hideous writhing tail!
Oh, let us fall down on our knees, repeat our most potent
exorcisms, and overcome the brute. Spread your black
pinions, fly—fly to the dusky realms of Eblis and bury
thyself under the paving stones of his hall, dark genie!
But *all* thoughts are not so. No—no. There are the pure:
there are the kind: there are the gentle. There are sweet
unspoken thanks before a fair scene of nature: at a sun-
setting below a glorious sea; or a moon and a host of stars
shining over it: at a bunch of children playing in the
street, or a group of flowers by the hedge-side, or a bird
singing there. At a hundred moments or occurrences of
the day good thoughts pass through the mind, let us trust,
which never are spoken; prayers are made which never are
said; and Te Deum is sung without church, clerk, choristers, parson, or organ. Why, there's my enemy: who got
the place I wanted; who maligned me to the woman I
wanted to be well with; who supplanted me in the good

graces of my patron. I don't say anything about the matter: but, my poor old enemy, in my secret mind I have movements of as tender charity towards you, you old scoundrel, as ever I had when we were boys together at school. You ruffian! do you fancy I forget that we were fond of each other? We are still. We share our toffy; go halves at the tuck-shop; do each other's exercises; prompt each other with the word in construing or repetition; and tell the most frightful fibs to prevent each other from being found out. We meet each other in public. Ware a fight! Get them into different parts of the room! Our friends hustle round us. Capulet and Montague are not more at odds than the houses of Roundabout and Wrightabout, let us say. It is, "My dear Mrs. Buffer, do kindly put yourself in the chair between those two men!" Or, "My dear Wrightabout, will you take that charming Lady Blanc-mange down to supper? She adores your poems; and gave five shillings for your autograph at the fancy fair." In like manner the peace-makers gather round Roundabout on his part: he is carried to a distant corner, and coaxed out of the way of the enemy with whom he is at feud.

When we meet in the Square at Verona, out flash rapiers, and we fall to. But in his private mind Tybalt owns that Mercutio has a rare wit, and Mercutio is sure that his adversary is a gallant gentleman. Look at the amphitheatre yonder. You do not suppose those gladiators who fought and perished, as hundreds of spectators in that grim Circus held thumbs down, and cried "Kill, kill!"—you do not suppose the combatants of necessity hated each other? No more than the celebrated trained bands of literary sword-and-buckler men hate the adversaries whom they meet in the arena. They engage at the given signal; feint and parry; slash, poke, rip each other open, dismember limbs, and hew off noses: but in the way of business, and, I trust, with mutual private esteem. For instance, I salute the warriors of the Superfine Company with the honours due among warriors. Here's at you, Spartacus, my lad. A hit I acknowledge. A palpable hit! Ha! how do you like that poke in the eye in return? When the trumpets sing truce, or the spectators are tired, we bow to the noble company; withdraw; and get a cool glass of wine in our *rendezvous des braves gladiateurs.*

By the way, I saw that amphitheatre of Verona under the strange light of a lurid eclipse some years ago: and I have been there in spirit for these twenty lines past, under a vast gusty awning, now with twenty thousand fellow-citizens looking on from the benches, now in the circus itself a grim gladiator with sword and net, or a meek martyr —was I?—brought out to be gobbled up by the lions? or a huge shaggy, tawny lion myself, on whom the dogs were going to be set? What a day of excitement I have had to be sure! But I must get away from Verona, or who knows how much farther the Roundabout Pegasus may carry me?

We were saying, my Muse, before we dropped and perched on earth for a couple of sentences, that our unsaid words were in some limbo or other, as real as those we have uttered; that the thoughts which have passed through our brains are as actual as any to which our tongues and pens have given currency. For instance, besides what is here hinted at, I have thought ever so much more about Verona: about an early Christian church I saw there: about a great dish of rice we had at the inn: about the bugs there; about ever so many more details of that day's journey from Milan to Venice: about lake Garda, which lay on the way from Milan, and so forth. I say what fine things we have thought of, haven't we, all of us? Ah, what a fine tragedy that was I thought of, and never wrote! On the day of the dinner of the Oystermongers' Company, what a noble speech I thought of in the cab, and broke down—I don't mean the cab, but the speech. Ah, if you could but read some of the unwritten Roundabout Papers—how you would be amused! Aha! my friend, I catch you saying, "Well, then, I wish *this* was unwritten, with all my heart." Very good. I owe you one. I do confess a hit, a palpable hit.

One day in the past month, as I was reclining on the bench of thought, with that ocean the *Times* newspaper spread before me, the ocean cast up on the shore at my feet two famous subjects for Roundabout Papers, and I picked up those waifs, and treasured them away until I could polish them and bring them to market. That scheme is not to be carried out. I can't write about those subjects. And though I cannot write about them, I may surely tell what are the subjects I am going *not* to write about.

The first was that Northumberland Street encounter, which all the papers have narrated. Have any novelists of our days a scene and catastrophe more strange and terrible than this which occurs at noonday within a few yards of the greatest thoroughfare in Europe? At the theatres they have a new name for their melodramatic pieces, and call them "Sensation Dramas." What a sensation drama this is! What have people been flocking to see at the Adelphi Theatre for the last hundred and fifty nights? A woman pitched overboard out of a boat, and a certain Miles taking a tremendous "header," and bringing her to shore? Bagatelle! What is this compared to the real life drama, of which a midday representation takes place just opposite the Adelphi in Northumberland Street? The brave Dumas, the intrepid Ainsworth, the terrible Eugene Sue, the cold-shudder-inspiring "Woman in White," the astounding author of the "Mysteries of the Court of London," never invented anything more tremendous than this. It might have happened to you and me. We want to borrow a little money. We are directed to an agent. We propose a pecuniary transaction at a short date. He goes into the next room, as we fancy, to get the bank-notes, and returns with "two very pretty, delicate little ivory-handled pistols," and blows a portion of our heads off. After this, what is the use of being squeamish about the probabilities and possibilities in the writing of fiction? Years ago I remember making merry over a play of Dumas, called "Kean," in which the Coal-Hole Tavern was represented on the Thames with a fleet of pirate-ships moored alongside. Pirate ships? Why not? What a cavern of terror was this in Northumberland Street, with its splendid furniture covered with dust, its empty bottles, in the midst of which sits a grim "agent," amusing himself by firing pistols, aiming at the unconscious mantelpiece, or at the heads of his customers!

After this, what is not possible? It is possible Hungerford Market is mined, and will explode some day. Mind how you go in for a penny ice unawares. "Pray, step this way," says a quiet person at the door. You enter—into a back room:—a quiet room; rather a dark room. "Pray, take your place in a chair." And she goes to fetch the penny ice. *Malheureux!* The chair sinks down with you —sinks, and sinks, and sinks—a large wet flannel suddenly envelopes your face and throttles you. Need we say any more? After Northumberland Street, what is improbable? Surely there is no difficulty in crediting Bluebeard. I withdraw my last month's opinions about ogres. Ogres? Why not? I protest I have seldom contemplated anything more terribly ludicrous than this "agent" in the dingy splendour of his den, surrounded by dusty ormolu and piles of empty bottles, firing pistols for his diversion at the mantelpiece until his clients come in! Is pistol practice so common in Northumberland Street, that it passes without notice in the lodging-houses there?

We spake anon of good thoughts. About bad thoughts? Is there some Northumberland Street chamber in your heart and mine, friend: close to the every-day street of life: visited by daily friends; visited by people on business; in which affairs are transacted; jokes are uttered; wine is drunk; through which people come and go; wives and children pass; and in which murder sits unseen until the terrible moment when he rises up and kills? A farmer, say, has a gun over the mantelpiece in his room where he sits at his daily meals and rest; caressing his children, joking with his friends, smoking his pipe in his calm. One night the gun is taken down: the farmer goes out: and it is a murderer who comes back and puts the piece up and drinks by that fireside. Was he a murderer yesterday when he was tossing the baby on his knee, and when his hands were playing with his little girl's yellow hair? Yesterday there was no blood on them at all: they were shaken by honest men: have done many a kind act in their time very likely. He leans his head on one of them, the wife comes in with her anxious looks of welcome, the children are prattling as they did yesterday round the father's knee at the fire, and Cain is sitting by the embers and Abel lies dead on the moor. Think of the gulph between now and yesterday. Oh, yesterday! Oh, the days when those two loved each other and said their prayer side by side! He goes to sleep, perhaps, and dreams that his brother is alive. Be true, O dream! Let him live in dreams, and wake no more. Be undone, O crime, O crime! But the sun rises: and the officers of conscience come: and yonder lies the body on the moor. I happened to pass, and looked at the Northumberland Street house the other day. A few loiterers were gazing up at the dingy windows. A plain, ordinary face of a house enough—and in a chamber in it one man suddenly rose up, pistol in hand, to slaughter another. Have you ever killed any one in your thoughts? Has your heart compassed any man's death? In your mind, have you ever taken a brand from the altar, and slain your brother? How many plain, ordinary faces of men do we look at, unknowing of murder behind those eyes? Lucky for you and me, brother, that we have good thoughts unspoken. But the bad ones? I tell you that the sight of those blank windows in Northumberland Street—through which, as it were, my mind could picture the awful tragedy glimmering behind—set me thinking, "Mr. Street-Preacher, here is a text for one of your pavement sermons. But it is too glum and serious. You eschew dark thoughts; and desire to be cheerful and merry in the main." And, such being the case, you see we must have no Roundabout Essay on this subject.

Well, I had another arrow in my quiver. (So, you know, had William Tell a bolt for his son, the apple of his eye: and a shaft for Gessler, in case William came to any trouble with the first poor little target.) And this, I must tell you, was to have been a rare Roundabout performance

—one of the very best that has ever appeared in this series. It was to have contained all the deep pathos of Addison; the logical precision of Rabelais; the childlike playfulness of Swift; the manly stoicism of Sterne; the metaphysical depth of Goldsmith; the blushing modesty of Fielding; the epigrammatic terseness of Walter Scott; the uproarious humour of Sam Richardson; and the gay simplicity of Sam Johnson;—it was to have combined all these qualities, with some excellencies of modern writers whom I could name:—but circumstances have occurred which have rendered this Roundabout Essay also impossible.

I have not the least objection to tell you what was to have been the subject of that other admirable Roundabout Paper. Gracious powers! the Dean of St. Patrick's never had a better theme. The paper was to have been on the Gorillas, to be sure. I was going to imagine myself to be a young surgeon-apprentice from Charleston, in South Carolina, who ran away to Cuba on account of unhappy family circumstances, with which nobody has the least concern; who sailed thence to Africa in a large, roomy schooner with an extraordinary vacant space between decks. I was subject to dreadful ill-treatment from the first mate of the ship, who, when I found she was a slaver, altogether declined to put me on shore. I was chased—we were chased —by three British frigates and a seventy-four, which we engaged and captured; but were obliged to scuttle and sink, as we could sell them in no African port: and I never shall forget the look of manly resignation, combined with considerable disgust, of the British Admiral as he walked the plank, after cutting off his pigtail, which he handed to me, and which I still have in charge for his family at Boston, Lincolnshire, England.

We made the port of Bpoopoo, at the confluence of the Bungo and Sgglolo rivers (which you may see in Swammerdahl's map) on the 31st April last year. Our passage had been so extraordinarily rapid, owing to the continued drunkenness of the captain and chief officers, by which I was obliged to work the ship and take her in command, that we reached Bpoopoo six weeks before we were expected, and five before the coffers from the interior and from the great slave depôt at Zbabblo were expected. Their delay caused us not a little discomfort, because, though we had taken the six English ships, we knew that Sir Byam Martin's iron-cased squadron, with the *Warrior*, the *Impregnable*, the *Sanconiathon*, and the *Berosus*, were cruising in the neighbourhood, and might prove too much for us.

It not only became necessary to quit Bpoopoo before the arrival of the British fleet or the rainy season, but to get our people on board as soon as might be. While the chief mate, with a detachment of seamen, hurried forward to the Pgogo lake, where we expected a considerable part of our cargo, the second mate, with six men, four chiefs, king Fbumbo, an Obi man, and myself, went N.W. by W., towards King Mtoby's-town, where we knew many hundreds of our between-deck passengers were to be got together. We went down the Pdodo river, shooting snipes, ostriches, and rhinoceros in plenty, and I think a few elephants, until, by the advice of a guide, who I now believe was treacherous, we were induced to leave the Pdodo, and march N.E. by N.N. Here Lieutenant Larkins, who had persisted in drinking rum from morning to night, and thrashing me in his sober moments during the whole journey, died, and I have too good reason to know was eaten with much relish by the natives. At Mgoo, where there are barracoons and a depôt for our cargo, we had no news of our expected freight; accordingly, as time pressed exceedingly, parties were despatched in advance towards the great Washaboo lake, by which the caravans usually come towards the coast. Here we found no caravan, but only four negroes down with the ague, whom I treated, I am bound to say, unsuccessfully, whilst we waited for our friends. We used to take watch and watch in front of the place, both to guard ourselves from attack, and get early news of the approaching caravan.

At last, on the 23rd September, as I was in advance with

Charles Rogers, second mate, and two natives with bows and arrows, we were crossing a great plain skirted by a forest, when we saw emerging from a ravine what I took to be three negroes—a very tall one, one of a moderate size, and one quite little.

Our native guides shrieked out some words in their language, of which Charles Rogers knew something. I thought it was the advance of the negroes whom we expected. "No!" said Rogers (who swore dreadfully in conversation), "it is the Gorillas!" And he fired both barrels of his gun, bringing down the little one first, and the female afterwards.

The male, who was untouched, gave a howl that you might have heard a league off; advanced towards us as if he would attack us, and turned and ran away with inconceivable celerity towards the wood.

We went up towards the fallen brutes. The little one by the female appeared to be about two years old. It lay bleating and moaning on the ground, stretching out its little hands, with movements and looks so strangely resembling human, that my heart sickened with pity. The female, who had been shot through both legs, could not move. She howled most hideously when I approached the little one.

"We must be off," said Rogers, "or the whole Gorilla race may be down upon us. The little one is only shot in the leg, I said. I'll bind the limb up, and we will carry the beast with us on board."

The poor little wretch held up its leg to show it was wounded, and looked to me with appealing eyes. It lay quite still whilst I looked for and found the bullet, and, tearing off a piece of my shirt, bandaged up the wound. I was so occupied in this business, that I hardly heard Rogers cry, "Run! run!" and when I looked up ——

When I looked up, with a roar the most horrible I ever heard—a roar? ten thousand roars—a whirling army of dark beings rushed by me. Rogers, who had bullied me so frightfully during the voyage, and who had encouraged my fatal passion for play, so that I own I owed him 1,500 dollars, was overtaken, felled, brained, and torn into ten thousand pieces; and I daresay the same fate would have fallen on me, but that the little Gorilla, whose wound I had dressed, flung its arms round my neck (their arms, you know, are much longer than ours). And when an immense grey Gorilla, with hardly any teeth, brandishing the trunk of a gollybosh tree about sixteen feet long, came up to me roaring, the little one squeaked out something plaintive, which, of course, I could not understand; on which suddenly the monster flung down his tree, squatted down on his huge hams by the side of the little patient, and began to bellow and weep.

And now, do you see whom I had rescued? I had rescued the young Prince of the Gorillas, who was out walking with his nurse and footman. The footman had run off to alarm his master, and certainly I never saw a footman run quicker. The whole army of Gorillas rushed forward to rescue their prince, and punish his enemies. If the King Gorilla's emotion was great, fancy what the queen's must have been when *she* came up! She arrived on a litter, neatly enough made with wattled branches, on which she lay, with her youngest child, a prince of three weeks old.

My little *protégé*, with the wounded leg, still persisted in hugging me with its arms (I think I mentioned that they are longer than those of men in general) and as the poor little brute was immensely heavy, and the Gorillas go at a prodigious pace, a litter was made for us likewise; and my thirst much refreshed by a footman (the same domestic who had given the alarm) running hand over hand up a cocoanut-tree, tearing the rinds off, breaking the shell on his head, and handing me the fresh milk in its cup. My little patient partook of a little, stretching out its dear little unwounded foot, with which, or with its hand, a Gorilla can help itself indiscriminately. Relays of large Gorillas relieved each other at the litters at intervals of twenty minutes, as I calculated by my watch, one of Jones and

Bates', of Boston, Mass., though I have been unable to this day to ascertain how these animals calculate time with such surprising accuracy. We slept for that night under——

And now you see we arrive at really the most interesting part of my travels in the country which I intended to visit, viz., the manners and habits of the Gorillas *chez eux.* I give the heads of this narrative only, the full account being suppressed for a reason which shall presently be given. The heads, then, of the chapters, are briefly as follows:—

The author's arrival in the Gorilla country. Its geographical position. Lodgings assigned to him up a gum-tree. Constant attachment of the little prince. His royal highness's gratitude. Anecdotes of his wit, playfulness, and extraordinary precocity. Am offered a portion of poor Larkins for my supper, but decline with horror. Footman brings me a young crocodile, fishy but very palatable. Old crocodiles too tough: ditto rhinoceros. Visit the queen mother—an enormous old Gorilla, quite white. Prescribe for her majesty. Meeting of Gorillas at what appears a parliament amongst them: presided over by old Gorilla in cocoa-nut-fibre wig. Their sports. Their customs. A privileged class amongst them. Extraordinary likeness of Gorillas to people at home, both at Charleston, S. C., my native place; and London, England, which I have visited. Flat-nosed Gorillas and blue-nosed Gorillas; their hatred, and wars between them. In a part of the country (its geographical position described) I see several negroes under Gorilla domination. Well treated by their masters. Frog-eating Gorillas across the Salt Lake. Bull-headed Gorillas—their mutual hostility. Green Island Gorillas. More quarrelsome than the Bullheads, and howl much louder. I am called to attend one of the princesses. Evident partiality of H. R. H. for me. Jealousy and rage of large red-headed Gorilla. How shall I escape!

Ay, how indeed? Do you wish to know? Is your curiosity excited? Well, I *do* know how I escaped. I could tell the most extraordinary adventures that happened to me. I could show you resemblances to people at home, that would make them blue with rage and you crack your sides with laughter. * * * And what is the reason I cannot write this paper, having all the facts before me? The reason is, that walking down St. James Street yesterday, I met a friend who says to me, "Roundabout, my boy, have you seen your picture? Here it is!" And he pulls out a portrait, executed in photography, of your humble servant, as an immense and most unpleasant-featured baboon, with long hairy hands, and called by the waggish artist "A Literary Gorilla." O horror! And now you see why I can't play off this joke myself, and moralize on the fable, as it has been narrated already *de me*.

A MISSISSIPPI BUBBLE.

THIS initial group of dusky children of the captivity is
copied out of a little sketch-book which I carried in many
a roundabout journey, and will point a moral or adorn a
T as well as any other sketch in the volume.   The draw-

ing was made in a country where there was such hospitality, friendship, kindness shown to the humble designer,
that his eyes do not care to look out for faults, or his pen
to note them.   How they sang; how they laughed and
grinned; how they scraped, bowed, and complimented you
and each other, those negroes of the cities of the southern
parts of the then United States!   My business kept me in

the towns; I was but in one negro plantation-village, and there were only women and little children, the men being out a-field. But there was plenty of cheerfulness in the huts, under the great trees—I speak of what I saw—and amidst the dusky bondsmen of the cities. I witnessed a curious gaiety; heard amongst the black folk endless singing, shouting, and laughter; and saw on holydays black gentlemen and ladies arrayed in such splendour and comfort as freeborn workmen in our towns seldom exhibit. What a grin and bow that dark gentleman performed, who was the porter at the colonel's, when he said, "You write your name, mas'r, else I will forgot." I am not going into the slavery question, I am not an advocate for "the institution," as I know, madam, by that angry toss of your head, you are about to declare me to be. For domestic purposes, my dear lady, it seemed to me about the dearest institution that can be devised. In a house in a Southern city you will find fifteen negroes doing the work which John, the cook, the housemaid, and the help, do perfectly in your own comfortable London house. And these fifteen negroes are the pick of a family of some eighty or ninety. Twenty are too sick, or too old for work, let us say: twenty too clumsy: twenty are too young, and have to be nursed and watched by ten more.* And master has to maintain the immense crew to do the work of half-a-dozen willing hands. No, no; let Mitchel, the exile from poor dear enslaved Ireland, wish for a gang of "fat niggers;" I would as soon you should make me a present of a score of Bengal elephants, when I need but a single stout horse to pull my brougham.

How hospitable they were, those Southern men! In the North itself the welcome was not kinder, as I, who have eaten Northern and Southern salt, can testify. As for New Orleans, in spring-time,—just when the orchards

---

* This was an account given by a gentleman at Richmond of his establishment. Six European servants would have kept his house and stables well. "His farm," he said, "barely sufficed to maintain the negroes residing on it."

were flushing over with peach-blossoms, and the sweet herbs came to flavour the juleps—it seemed to me the city of the world where you can eat and drink the most and suffer the least. At Bordeaux itself, claret is not better to drink than at New Orleans. It was all good—believe an expert Robert—from the half-dollar Médoc of the public hotel table, to the private gentleman's choicest wine. Claret is, somehow, good in that gifted place at dinner, at supper, and at breakfast in the morning. It is good: it is superabundant—and there is nothing to pay. Find me speaking ill of such a country! When I do, *pone me pigris campis:* smother me in a desert, or let Mississippi or Garonne drown me! At that comfortable tavern on Pontchartrain we had a *bouillabaisse* than which a better was never eaten at Marseilles: and not the least headache in the morning, I give you my word: on the contrary, you only wake with a sweet refreshing thirst for claret and water. They say there is fever there in the autumn: but not in the spring-time, when the peach-blossoms blush over the orchards, and the sweet herbs come to flavour the juleps.

I was bound from New Orleans to Saint Louis; and our walk was constantly on the Levee, whence we could see a hundred of those huge white Mississippi steamers at their moorings in the river: "Look," said my friend Lochlomond to me, as we stood one day on the quay—"look at that post! Look at that coffee-house behind it! Sir, last year a steamer blew up in the river yonder, just where you see those men pulling off in the boat. By that post where you are standing a mule was cut in two by a fragment of the burst machinery, and a bit of the chimney stove in that first-floor window of the coffee-house, killed a negro who was cleaning knives in the top-room!" I looked at the post, at the coffee-house window, at the steamer in which I was going to embark, at my friend, with a pleasing interest not divested of melancholy. Yesterday, it was the donkey, thinks I, who was cut in two: it may be *cras mihi.* Why, in the same little sketch-book, there is a drawing of an Alabama river steamer which blew up on the very next voyage after that in which your humble servant was on board! Had I but waited another week, I might have * * * These incidents give a queer zest to the voyage down the life stream in America. When our huge, tall, white, pasteboard castle of a steamer began to work up stream, every limb in her creaked, and groaned, and quivered, so that you might fancy she would burst right off. Would she hold together, or would she split into ten million of shivers? O my home and children! Would your humble servant's body be cut in two across yonder chain on the Levee, or be precipitated into yonder first-floor, so as to damage the chest of a black man cleaning boots at the window? The black man is safe for me, thank goodness. But you see the little accident *might* have happened. It has happened; and if to a mule, why not to a more docile animal? On our journey up the Mississippi, I give you my honour we were on fire three times, and burned our cook-room down. The deck at night was a great fire-work —the chimney spouted myriads of stars, which fell blackening on our garments, sparkling on to the deck, or gleaming into the mighty stream through which we laboured— the mighty yellow stream with all its snags.

How I kept up my courage through these dangers shall now be narrated. The excellent landlord of the Saint Charles Hotel, when I was going away, begged me to accept two bottles of the very finest Cognac, with his compliments; and I found them in my state-room with my luggage. Lochlomond came to see me off, and as he squeezed my hand at parting, "Roundabout," says he, "the wine mayn't be very good on board, so I have brought a dozen-case of the Médoc which you liked;" and we grasped together the hands of friendship and farewell. Whose boat is this pulling up to the ship? It is our friend Glenlivat, who gave us the dinner on Lake Pontchartrain. "Roundabout," says he, "we have tried to do what we could for you, my boy; and it has been done *de bon cœur*" (I detect a kind tremulousness in the good fellow's voice as he speaks). "I say—hem!—the a—the wine isn't too good on board, so I've brought you a dozen of Médoc for your voyage, you know. And God bless you; and when I come to London in May I shall come and see you. Hallo! here's Johnson come to see you off, too!"

As I am a miserable sinner, when Johnson grasped my hand, he said, "Mr. Roundabout, you can't be sure of the wine on board these steamers, so I thought I would bring you a little case of that light claret which you liked at my house." *Et de trois!* No wonder I could face the Mississippi with so much courage supplied to me! Where are you, honest friends, who gave me of your kindness and your cheer? May I be considerably boiled, blown up, and snagged, if I speak hard words of you. May claret turn sour ere I do!

Mounting the stream it chanced that we had very few passengers. How far is the famous city of Memphis from New Orleans? I do not mean the Egyptian Memphis, but the American Memphis, from which to the American Cairo we slowly toiled up the river—to the American Cairo at the confluence of the Ohio and Mississippi rivers. And at Cairo we parted company from the boat, and from some famous and gifted fellow-passengers who joined us at Memphis, and whose pictures we had seen in many cities of the South. I do not give the names of these remarkable people, unless, by some wondrous chance, in inventing a name I should light upon that real one which some of them bore; but if you please I will say that our fellow-passengers whom we took in at Memphis were no less personages than the Vermont Giant and the famous Bearded Lady of Kentucky and her son. Their pictures I had seen in many cities through which I travelled with my own little performance. I think the Vermont Giant was a trifle taller in his pictures than he was in life (being represented in the former as, at least, some two stories high): but the lady's prodigious beard received no more than justice at the hands of the painter; that portion of it which I saw being really most black, rich, and curly—I say the portion of beard, for this modest or prudent woman kept I don't know how much of the beard covered up with a red handkerchief, from which I suppose it only emerged when she went to bed, or when she exhibited it professionally.

The Giant, I must think, was an overrated giant. I have known gentlemen, not in the profession, better made, and I should say taller, than the Vermont gentleman. A strange feeling I used to have at meals; when, on looking round our little society, I saw the Giant, the Bearded Lady of Kentucky, the little Bearded Boy of three years old, the Captain (this I *think*; but at this distance of time I would not like to make the statement on affidavit), and the three other passengers, all with their knives in their mouths making play at the dinner—a strange feeling I say it was, and as though I was in a castle of ogres. But, after all, why so squeamish? A few scores of years back, the finest gentlemen and ladies of Europe did the like. Belinda ate with her knife; and Saccharissa had only that weapon, or a two-pronged fork, or a spoon, for her pease. Have you ever looked at Gilray's print of the Prince of Wales, a languid voluptuary, retiring after his meal, and noted the toothpick which he uses? * * * You are right, madam, I own that the subject is revolting and terrible. I will not pursue it. Only—allow that a gentleman, in a shaky steamboat, on a dangerous river, in a far-off country, which caught fire three times during the voyage—(of course I mean the steamboat, not the country), seeing a giant, a voracious supercargo, a bearded lady, and a little boy, not three years of age, with a chin already quite black and curly, all plying their victuals down their throats with their knives—allow, madam, that in such a company a man had a right to feel a little nervous. I don't know whether you have ever remarked the Indian jugglers swallowing their knives, or seen, as I have, a whole table of people performing the same trick, but if you look at their eyes when they do it, I assure you there is a roll in them which is dreadful.

Apart from this usage which they practise in common with many thousand most estimable citizens, the Vermont gentleman, and the Kentucky whiskered lady—or did I say the reverse?—whichever you like, my dear sir—were quite quiet, modest, unassuming people. She sate working with her needle, if I remember right. He, I suppose, slept in the great cabin, which was seventy feet long at the least, nor, I am bound to say, did I hear in the night any snores or roars, such as you would fancy ought to accompany the sleep of ogres. Nay, this giant had quite a small appetite, (unless, to be sure, he went forward and ate a sheep or two in private with his horrid knife—oh, the dreadful thought!—but *in public,* I say, he had quite a delicate appetite,) and was also a tea-totaller. I don't remember to have heard the lady's voice, though I might, not unnaturally, have been curious to hear it. Was her voice a deep, rich, magnificent bass; or was it soft, fluty, and mild? I shall never know now. Even if she comes to this country, I shall never go and see her. I *have* seen her, and for nothing.

You would have fancied that, as after all we were only some half-dozen on board, she might have dispensed with her red handkerchief, and talked, and eaten her dinner in comfort: but in covering her chin there was a kind of modesty. That beard was her profession: that beard brought the public to see her: out of her business she wished to put that beard aside as it were: as a barrister would wish to put off his wig. I know some who carry theirs into private life, and who mistake you and me for jury-boxes when they address us: but these are not your modest barristers, not your true gentlemen.

Well, I own I respected the lady for the modesty with which, her public business over, she retired into private life. She respected her life, and her beard. That beard having done its day's work, she puts it away in a handkerchief; and becomes, as far as in her lies, a private ordinary person. All public men and women of good sense, I should think, have this modesty. When, for instance, in my small way, poor Mrs. Brown comes simpering up to me, with her album in one hand, a pen in the other, and says,

"Ho, ho, dear Mr. Roundabout, write us one of your amusing, &c. &c." my beard drops behind my handkerchief instantly. Why am I to wag my chin and grin for Mrs. Brown's good pleasure? My dear madam, I have been making faces all day. It is my profession. I do my comic business with the greatest pains, seriousness, and trouble: and with it make, I hope, a not dishonest livelihood. If you ask Mons. Blondin to tea, you don't have a rope stretched from your garret window to the opposite side of the square, and request Monsieur to take his tea out on the centre of the rope? I lay my hand on this waistcoat, and declare that not once in the course of our voyage together did I allow the Kentucky Giant to suppose I was speculating on his stature, or the Bearded Lady to surmise that I wished to peep under the handkerchief which muffled the lower part of her face.

And the more fool you, says some cynic. (Faugh, those cynics, I hate 'em!) Don't you know, sir, that a man of genius is pleased to have his genius recognized; that a beauty likes to be admired; that an actor likes to be applauded; that stout old Wellington himself was pleased, and smiled when the people cheered him as he passed? Suppose you had paid some respectful elegant compliment to that lady? Suppose you had asked that giant, if, for once, he would take anything at the liquor-bar? you might have learned a great deal of curious knowledge regarding giants and bearded ladies, about whom you evidently now know very little. There was that little boy of three years old, with a fine beard already, and his little legs and arms, as seen out of his little frock, covered with a dark down. What a queer little capering satyr! He was quite good-natured, childish, rather solemn. He had a little Norval dress, I remember: the drollest little Norval.

I have said the B. L. had another child. Now this was a little girl of some six years old, as fair and as smooth of skin, dear madam, as your own darling cherubs. She wandered about the great cabin quite melancholy. No one seemed to care for her. All the family affections were centred on Master Esau yonder. His little beard was beginning to be a little fortune already, whereas Miss Rosalba was of no good to the family. No one would pay a cent to see *her* little fair face. No wonder the poor little maid was melancholy. As I looked at her, I seemed to walk more and more in a fairy tale, and more and more in a cavern of ogres. Was this a little fondling whom they had picked up in some forest, where lie the picked bones of the queen, her tender mother, and the tough old defunct monarch, her father? No. Doubtless they were quite good-natured people, these. I don't believe they were unkind to the little girl without the mustachios. It may have been only my fancy that she repined because she had a cheek no more bearded than a rose's.

Would you wish your own daughter, madam, to have a smooth cheek, a modest air, and a gentle feminine behaviour, or to be—I won't say a whiskered prodigy, like this Bearded Lady of Kentucky—but a masculine wonder, a virago, a female personage of more than female strength, courage, wisdom? Some authors, who shall be nameless, are, I know, accused of depicting the most feeble, brainless, namby-pamby heroines, forever whimpering tears and prattling commonplaces. *You* would have the heroine of your novel so beautiful that she should charm the captain (or hero, whoever he may be) with her appearance; surprise and confound the bishop with her learning; outride the squire, and get the brush, and, when he fell from his horse, whip out a lancet and bleed him; rescue from fever and death the poor cottager's family whom the doctor had given up; make 21 at the butts with the rifle, when the poor captain only scored 18; give him twenty in fifty at billiards and beat him; and draw tears from the professional Italian people by her exquisite performance (of voice and violoncello) in the evening;—I say, if a novelist would be popular with ladies—the great novel readers of the world—this is the sort of heroine who would carry him through half-a-dozen editions. Suppose I had asked that Bearded Lady to sing? Confess, now, miss, you would not have been displeased if I had told you that she had a voice like Lablache, only ever so much lower.

My dear, you would like to be a heroine? You would like to travel in triumphal caravans; to see your effigy placarded on city walls; to have your levées attended by admiring crowds, all crying out, "Was there ever such a wonder of a woman?" You would like admiration? Consider the tax you pay for it. You would be alone were you eminent. Were you so distinguished from your neighbours —I will not say beard and whiskers, that were odious—but by a great and remarkable intellectual superiority—would you, do you think, be any the happier? Consider envy. Consider solitude. Consider the jealousy and torture of mind which this Kentucky lady must feel, suppose she is to hear that there is, let us say, a Missouri prodigy, with a beard larger than hers? Consider how she is separated from her kind by the possession of that wonder of a beard? When that beard grows grey, how lonely she will be, the poor old thing! If it falls off, the public admiration falls off too; and how she will miss it—the compliments of the trumpeters, the admiration of the crowd, the gilded progress of the car. I see an old woman alone in a decrepit old caravan, with cobwebs on the knocker, with a blistered ensign flapping idly over the door. Would you like to be that deserted person? Ah, Chloe! To be good, to be simple, to be modest, to be loved, be thy lot. Be thankful thou art not taller, nor stronger, nor richer, nor wiser than the rest of the world!

ON LETTS'S DIARY.

MINE is one of your No. 12 diaries, three shillings cloth boards; silk limp, gilt edges, three-and-six; French morocco, tuck ditto, four-and-six. It has two pages, ruled with faint lines for memoranda, for every week, and a ruled account at the end, for the twelve months from January to December, where you may set down your incomings and your expenses. I hope yours, my respected reader, are large; that there are many fine round sums of figures on each side of the page: liberal on the expenditure side, greater still on the receipt. I hope, sir, you will be "a better man," as they say, in '62 than in this moribund '61, whose career of life is just coming to its terminus. A better man in purse? in body? in soul's health? Amen, good sir, in all. Who is there so good in mind, body or estate, but bettering won't still be good for him? O unknown fate, presiding over next year, if you will give me better health, a better appetite, a better digestion, a better income, a better temper in '62 than you have bestowed in '61, I think your servant will be the better for the changes. For instance, I should be the better for a new coat. This one, I acknowledge, is very old. The family says so. My good friend, who amongst us would not be the better if he would give up some old habits? Yes, yes. You agree with me. You take the allegory? Alas! at our time of life we don't like to give up those old habits, do we? It is ill to change. There is the good old loose, easy, slovenly bedgown, laziness, for example. What man of sense likes to fling it off and put on a tight *guindé* prim dress coat that pinches him? There is the cozy wrap-rascal self-indulgence—how easy it is! How warm! How it always seems to fit! You can walk out in it; you can go down to dinner in it. You can say of such what Tully says of his books: *Pernoctat nobiscum, peregrinatur, rusticatur.* It is a little slatternly—it is a good deal stained—it isn't becoming—it smells of cigar smoke; but, *allons donc!* let the world call me idle and sloven. I love my ease better than my neighbour's opinion. I live to please myself; not **you,** Mr. Dandy, with your supercilious airs. I am a **philosopher.** Perhaps I live in my tub, and don't make any other use of it—— We won't pursue further this unsavoury metaphor; but, with regard to some of your old habits, let us say—

1. The habit of being censorious, and speaking ill of your neighbours.

2. The habit of getting into a passion with your man-servant, your maid-servant, your daughter, wife, &c.

3. The habit of indulging too much at table.

4. The habit of smoking in the dining-room after dinner.

5. The habit of spending insane sums of money in *bric à brac*, tall copies, binding, Elzevirs, &c.; '20 Port, outrageously fine horses, ostentatious entertainments, and what not; or,

6. The habit of screwing meanly, when rich, and chuckling over the saving of half-a-crown, whilst you are poisoning your friends and family with bad wine.

7. The habit of going to sleep immediately after dinner, instead of cheerfully entertaining Mrs. Jones and the family; or,

8. LADIES! The habit of running up bills with the milliners, and swindling paterfamilias on the house bills.

9. The habit of keeping him waiting for breakfast.

10. The habit of sneering at Mrs. Brown and the Miss Browns, because they are not quite *du monde,* or quite so genteel as Lady Smith.

11. The habit of keeping your wretched father up at balls till five o'clock in the morning, when he has to be at his office at eleven.

12. The habit of fighting with each other, dear Louisa, Jane, Arabella, Amelia.

13. The habit of *always* ordering John Coachman three-quarters of an hour before you want him.

Such habits, I say, sir or madam, if you have had to note in your diary of '61, I have not the slightest doubt you will enter in your pocket-book of '62. There are habits, Nos. 4 and 7, for example. I am morally sure that some of us will not give up those bad customs, though the women cry out and grumble, and scold ever so justly. There are habits, Nos. 9 and 13. I feel perfectly certain, my dear young ladies, that you will continue to keep John Coachman waiting; that you will continue to give the most satisfactory reasons for keeping him waiting: and as for (9), you will show that you once (on the 1st of April last, let us say) came to breakfast first, and that you are *always* first in consequence.

Yes; in our '62 diaries, I fear we may all of us make some of the '61 entries. There is my friend Freehand, for instance. (Aha! Master Freehand, how you will laugh to find yourself here!) F. is in the habit of spending a little, ever so little, more than his income. He shows you how Mrs. Freehand works, and works (and indeed, Jack Freehand, if you say she is an angel, you don't say too much of her); how they toil, and how they mend, and patch, and pinch; and how they *can't* live on their means. And I very much fear, nay, I will bet him half a bottle of Gladstone 14*s.* per dozen claret, that the account which is a little on the wrong side this year, will be a little on the wrong side in the next ensuing year of grace.

A diary. Dies To die. How queer to read are some of the entries in the journal! Here are the records of dinners eaten, and gone the way of flesh. The lights burn blue somehow, and we sit before the ghosts of victuals. Hark at the dead jokes resurging! Memory greets them with a ghost of a smile. Here are the lists of the individuals who have dined at your own humble table. The agonies endured before and during those entertainments are renewed and smart again. What a failure that special grand dinner was! How those dreadful occasional waiters did break the old china! What a dismal hash poor Mary, the cook, made of the French dish which she *would* try out of *Fran-*

catelli! How angry Mrs. Pope was at not going down to dinner before Mrs. Bishop! How Trimalchio sneered at your absurd attempt to give a feast; and Harpagon cried out at your extravagance and ostentation! How Lady Almack bullied the other ladies in the drawing-room (when no gentlemen were present): never asked you back to dinner again: left her card by her footman: and took not the slightest notice of your wife and daughters at Lady Hustleby's assembly! On the other hand how easy, cozy, merry, comfortable, those little dinners were; got up at one or two days' notice; when everybody was contented; the soup as clear as amber; the wine as good as Trimalchio's own; and the people kept their carriages waiting, and would not go away till midnight!

Along with the catalogue of bygone pleasures, balls, banquets, and the like which the pages record, comes a list of much more important occurrences and remembrances of graver import. On two days of Dives' diary are printed notices that "Dividends are due at the Bank." Let us hope, dear sir, that this announcement considerably interests you; in which case, probably, you have no need of the almanac-maker's printed reminder. If you look over poor Jack Reckless's note-book, amongst his memoranda of racing odds given and taken, perhaps you may read:—"Nabbam's bill, due 29th September, 142*l*. 15*s*. 6*d*." Let us trust, as the day has passed, that the little transaction here noted has been satisfactorily terminated. If you are paterfamilias, and a worthy kind gentleman, no doubt you have marked down on your register, 17th December (say), "Boys come home." Ah, how carefully that blessed day is marked in *their* little calendars! In my time it used to be, Wednesday, 13th November, "*5 weeks from the holidays;*" Wednesday, 20th November, "*4 weeks from the holidays;*" until sluggish time sped on, and we came to WEDNESDAY, 18TH DECEMBER. O rapture! Do you remember peashooters? I think we only had them on going home for holidays from private schools,—at public schools, men are too dignified. And then came that glorious announcement,

Wednesday, 27th, "Papa took us to the Pantomime;" or if not papa, perhaps you condescended to go to the pit, under charge of the footman.

That was near the end of the year—and mamma gave you a new pocket-book, perhaps, with a little coin, God bless her, in the pocket. And that pocket-book was for next year, you know; and, in that pocket-book, you had to write down that sad day, Wednesday, January 24th, eighteen hundred and never mind what,—when Dr. Birch's young friends were expected to re-assemble.

Ah me! Every person who turns this page over has his own little diary in paper or ruled in his memory tablets, and in which are set down the transactions of the now dying year. Boys and men, we have our calendar, mothers and maidens. For example, in your calendar pocket-book, my good Eliza, what a sad, sad day that is; how fondly and bitterly remembered; when your boy went off to his regiment, to India, to danger, to battle, perhaps. What a day was that last day at home, when the tall brother sat yet amongst the family, the little ones round about him wondering at saddle-boxes, uniforms, sword-cases, gun-cases, and other wondrous apparatus of war and travel which poured in and filled the hall; the new dressing-case for the beard not yet grown; the great sword-case at which little brother Tom looks so admiringly! What a dinner that was, that last dinner, when little and grown children assembled together, and all tried to be cheerful! What a night was that last night, when the young ones were at roost for the last time together under the same roof, and the mother lay alone in her chamber counting the fatal hours as they tolled one after another, amidst her tears, her watching, her fond prayers. What a night that was, and yet how quickly the melancholy dawn came! Only too soon the sun rose over the houses. And now in a moment more the city seemed to wake. The house began to stir. The family gathers together for the last meal. For the last time in the midst of them the widow kneels amongst her kneeling children, and falters a prayer in which she commits her dearest, her eldest born, to the care of the Father of all. O night, what tears you hide—what prayers you hear! And so the nights pass and the days succeed, until that one comes when tears and parting shall be no more.

In your diary, as in mine, there are days marked with sadness, not for this year only, but for all. On a certain day, and the sun, perhaps, shining ever so brightly, the house-mother comes down to her family with a sad face, which scares the children round about in the midst of their laughter and prattle. They may have forgotten—but she has not—a day which came, twenty years ago it may be, and which she remembers only too well; the long night watch; the dreadful dawning and the rain beating at the pane; the infant speechless, but moaning in its little crib; and then the awful calm, the awful smile on the sweet cherub face, when the cries have ceased, and the little suffering breast heaves no more. Then the children, as they see their mother's face, remember this was the day on which their little brother died. It was before they were born; but she remembers it. And as they pray together, it seems almost as if the spirit of the little lost one was hovering round the group. So they pass away: friends, kindred, the dearest-loved, grown people, aged, infants. As we go on the down-hill journey, the mile-stones are grave-stones, and on each more and more names are written; unless haply you live beyond man's common age, when friends have dropped off, and, tottering, and feeble, and unpitied, you reach the terminus alone.

In this past year's diary is there any precious day noted on which you have made a new friend? This is a piece of good fortune bestowed but grudgingly on the old. After a certain age a new friend is a wonder, like Sarah's child. Aged persons are seldom capable of bearing friendships. Do you remember how warmly you loved Jack and Tom when you were at school; what a passionate regard you had for Ned when you were at college, and the immense letters you wrote to each other? How often do you write,

now that postage costs nothing? There is the age of blos-
soms and sweet budding green : the age of generous summer; the autumn when the leaves drop; and then winter,
shivering and bare. Quick, children, and sit at my feet:
for they are cold, very cold: and it seems as if neither
wine nor worsted will warm 'em.

In this past year's diary is there any dismal day noted
in which you have lost a friend? In mine there is. I do
not mean by death. Those who are gone, you have. Those
who departed loving you, love you still; and you love them
always. They are not really gone, those dear hearts and
true; they are only gone into the next room: and you will
presently get up and follow them, and yonder door will
close upon *you*, and you will be no more seen. As I am in
this cheerful mood, I will tell you a fine and touching story
of a doctor which I heard lately. About two years since
there was, in our or some other city, a famous doctor, into
whose consulting room crowds come daily, so that they
might be healed. Now this doctor had a suspicion that
there was something vitally wrong with himself, and he
went to consult another famous physician at Dublin, or it
may be at Edinburgh. And he of Edinburgh punched his
comrade's sides; and listened at his heart and lungs; and
felt his pulse, I suppose; and looked at his tongue; and
when he had done, Doctor London said to Doctor Edinburgh, "Doctor, how long have I to live?" And Doctor
Edinburgh said to Doctor London, "Doctor, you may last
a year."

Then Doctor London came home, knowing that what
Doctor Edinburgh said was true. And he made up his accounts, with man and heaven, I trust. And he visited his
patients as usual. And he went about healing, and cheering, and soothing and doctoring; and thousands of sick
people were benefited by him. And he said not a word to
his family at home; but lived amongst them cheerful and
tender, and calm, and loving ; though he knew the night
was at hand when he should see them and work no more.

And it was winter time, and they came and told him

that some man at a distance—very sick, but very rich—
wanted him; and, though Doctor London knew that he was
himself at death's door, he went to the sick man; for he
knew the large fee would be good for his children after
him. And he died; and his family never knew until he
was gone, that he had been long aware of the inevitable
doom.

This is a cheerful carol for Christmas, is it not? You
see, in regard to these Roundabout discourses, I never know
whether they are to be merry or dismal. My hobby has
the bit in his mouth; goes his own way; and sometimes
trots through a park, and sometimes paces by a cemetery.
Two days since came the printer's little emissary, with a
note saying, "We are waiting for the Roundabout Paper!"
A Roundabout Paper about what or whom? How stale it
has become, that printed jollity about Christmas! Carols,
and wassail bowls, and holly, and mistletoe, and yule logs
de commande—what heaps of these have we not had for
years past! Well, year after year the season comes. Come
frost, come thaw, come snow, come rain, year after year
my neighbour the parson has to make his sermon. They
are getting together the bonbons, iced cakes, Christmas
trees at Fortnum's and Mason's now. The genii of the
theatres are composing the Christmas pantomime, which
our young folks will see and note anon in their little
diaries.

And now, brethren, may I conclude this discourse with
an extract out of that great diary, the newspaper? I read
it but yesterday, and it has mingled with all my thoughts
since then. Here are the two paragraphs, which appeared
following each other :—

"Mr. R., the Advocate-General of Calcutta, has been
appointed to the post of Legislative Member of the Council
of the Governor-General."

"Sir R. S., agent to the Governor-General for Central
India, died on the 29th of October, of bronchitis."

These two men, whose different fates are recorded in two
paragraphs and half-a-dozen lines of the same newspaper,

were sisters' sons. In one of the stories by the present writer, a man is described tottering "up the steps of the ghaut," having just parted with his child, whom he is despatching to England from India. I wrote this, remembering in long, long distant days, such a ghaut, or river-stair, at Calcutta; and a day when, down those steps, to a boat which was in waiting, came two children, whose mothers remained on the shore. One of those ladies was never to see her boy more; and he, too, is just dead in India, "of bronchitis, on the 29th October." We were first cousins; had been little playmates and friends from the time of our birth; and the first house in London to which I was taken, was that of our aunt, the mother of his Honour the Member of Council. His Honour was even then a gentleman of the long robe, being, in truth, a baby in arms. We Indian children were consigned to a school of which our deluded parents had heard a favourable report, but which was governed by a horrible little tyrant, who made our young lives so miserable that I remember kneeling by my little bed of a night, and saying, "Pray God, I may dream of my mother!" Thence we went to a public school; and my cousin to Addiscombe and to India.

"For thirty-two years," the paper says, "Sir Richmond Shakespear faithfully and devotedly served the Government of India, and during that period but once visited England, for a few months and on public duty. In his military capacity he saw much service, was present in eight general engagements, and was badly wounded in the last. In 1840, when a young lieutenant, he had the rare good fortune to be the means of rescuing from almost hopeless slavery in Khiva 416 subjects of the Emperor of Russia; and, but two years later, greatly contributed to the happy recovery of our own prisoners from a similar fate in Cabul. Throughout his career this officer was ever ready and zealous for the public service, and freely risked life and liberty in the discharge of his duties. Lord Canning, to mark his high sense of Sir Richmond Shakespear's public services, had lately offered him the Chief Commissionership of the

Mysore, which he had accepted, and was about to undertake, when death terminated his career."

When he came to London the cousins and playfellows of early Indian days met once again, and shook hands. "Can I do anything for you?" I remember the kind fellow asking. He was always asking that question: of all kinsmen; of all widows and orphans; of all the poor; of young men who might need his purse or his service. I saw a young officer yesterday to whom the first words Sir Richmond Shakespear wrote on his arrival in India were, "Can I do anything for you?" His purse was at the command of all. His kind hand was always open. It was a gracious fate which sent him to rescue widows and captives. Where could they have a champion more chivalrous, or protector more loving and tender?

I write down his name in my little book, among those of others dearly loved, who, too, have been summoned hence. And so we meet and part; we struggle and succeed; or we fail and drop unknown on the way. As we leave the fond mother's knee, the rough trials of childhood and boyhood begin; and then manhood is upon us, and the battle of life, with its chances, perils, wounds, defeats, distinctions. And Fort William guns are saluting in one man's honour,* while the troops are firing the last volleys over the other's grave—over the grave of the brave, the gentle, the faithful Christian soldier.

* W. R. obiit March 22, 1862.

NOTES OF A WEEK'S HOLIDAY.

MOST of us tell old stories in our families. The wife and children laugh for the hundredth time at the joke. The old servants (though old servants are fewer every day) nod and smile a recognition at the well-known anecdote. "Don't tell that story of Grouse in the gun-room," says Diggory to Mr. Hardcastle in the play, "or I must laugh." As we twaddle, and grow old and forgetful, we may tell an old story; or, out of mere benevolence, and a wish to amuse a friend when conversation is flagging, disinter a Joe Miller now and then; but the practice is not quite honest, and entails a certain necessity of hypocrisy on story hearers and tellers. It is a sad thing, to think that a man with what you call a fund of anecdote is a humbug, more or less amiable and pleasant. What right have I to tell my "Grouse and the gun-room" over and over in the presence of my wife, mother, mother-in-law, sons, daughters, old footman or parlour-maid, confidential clerk, curate, or what not? I smirk and go through the history, giving my admirable imitations of the characters introduced: I mimic Jones's grin, Hobbs's squint, Brown's stammer, Grady's brogue, Sandy's Scotch accent, to the best of my power: and the family part of my audience laughs good-humouredly. Perhaps the stranger, for whose amusement the performance is given, is amused by it, and laughs too. But this practice continued is not moral. Self-indulgence on your part, my dear Paterfamilias, is weak, vain—not to say culpable. I can imagine many a worthy man, who begins unguardedly to read this page, and comes to the present sentence, lying back in his chair, thinking of that story which he has told innocently for fifty years, and rather piteously owning to himself, "Well, well, it *is* wrong; I have no right to call on my poor wife to laugh, my daughters to affect to be amused, by that old, old jest of mine. And

they would have gone on laughing, and they would have
pretended to be amused, to their dying day, if this man
had not flung his damper over our hilarity." * * * I
lay down the pen, and think, "Are there any old stories
which I still tell myself in the bosom of my family? Have
I any ' Grouse in my gun-room? ' " If there are such, it is
because my memory fails; not because I want applause,
and wantonly repeat myself. You see, men with the so-
called fund of anecdote will not repeat the same story to
the same individual; but they do think that, on a new
party, the repetition of a joke ever so old may be honourably tried. I meet men walking the London street, bearing
the best reputation, men of anecdotical powers:—I know
such, who very likely will read this, and say, "Hang the
fellow, he means *me!*" And so I do. No—no man ought
to tell an anecdote more than thrice, let us say, unless he
is sure he is speaking only to give pleasure to his hearers—
unless he feels that it is not a mere desire for praise which
makes him open his jaws.

And is it not with writers as with *raconteurs?* Ought
they not to have their ingenuous modesty? May authors
tell old stories, and how many times over? When I come
to look at a place which I have visited any time these
twenty or thirty years, I recall not the place merely, but
the sensations I had at first seeing it, and which are quite
different to my feelings to-day. That first day at Calais;
the voices of the women crying out at night, as the vessel
came alongside the pier; the supper at Quillacq's and the
flavour of the cutlets and wine; the red-calico canopy under
which I slept; the tiled floor, and the fresh smell of the
sheets; the wonderful postilion in his jackboots and pigtail;—all return with perfect clearness to my mind, and I
am seeing them, and not the objects which are actually
under my eyes. Here is Calais. Yonder is that commissioner I have known this score of years. Here are the
women screaming and bustling over the baggage; the people at the passport-barrier who take your papers. My
good people, I hardly see you. You no more interest me

than a dozen orange women in Covent Garden, or a shop book-keeper in Oxford Street. But you make me think of a time when you were indeed wonderful to behold—when the little French soldiers wore white cockades in their shakos—when the diligence was forty hours going to Paris; and the great-booted postilion, as surveyed by youthful eyes from the coupé, with his *jurons,* his ends of rope for the harness, and his clubbed pigtail, was a wonderful being, and productive of endless amusement. You young folks don't remember the apple-girls who used to follow the diligence up the hill beyond Boulogne, and the delights of the jolly road? In making continental journeys with young folks, an oldster may be very quiet, and, to outward appearance melancholy; but really he has gone back to the days of his youth, and he is seventeen or eighteen years of age (as the case may be), and is amusing himself with all his might. He is noting the horses as they come squealing out of the post-house yard at midnight; he is enjoying the delicious meals at Beauvais and Amiens, and quaffing *ad libitum* the rich table-d'hôte wine; he is hail-fellow with the conductor, and alive to all the incidents of the road. A man can be alive in 1860 and 1830 at the same time, don't you see? Bodily, I may be in 1860, inert, silent, torpid; but in the spirit I am walking about in 1828, let us say;—in a blue dress coat and brass buttons, a sweet figured silk waistcoat (which I button round a slim waist with perfect ease), looking at beautiful beings with gigot sleeves and tea-tray hats under the golden chestnuts of the Tuileries, or round the Place Vendôme, where the *drapeau blanc* is floating from the statueless column. Shall we go and dine at Bombarda's, near the Hôtel Breteuil, or at the Café Virginie?—Away! Bombarda's and the Hôtel Breteuil have been pulled down ever so long. They knocked down the poor old Virginia Coffee-house last year. My spirit goes and dines there. My body, perhaps, is seated with ever so many people in a railway carriage, and no wonder my companions find me dull and silent. Have you read Mr. Dale Owens' "Footsteps on the Confines of

Another World?"—(My dear sir, it will make your hair
stand quite refreshingly on end.) In that work you will
read that when gentlemen's or ladies' spirits travel off a
few score or thousand miles to visit a friend, their bodies
lie quiet and in a torpid state in their beds or in their arm-
chairs at home. So in this way, I am absent. My soul
whisks away thirty years back into the past. I am looking out anxiously for a beard. I am getting past the age
of loving Byron's poems, and pretend that I like Words-
worth and Shelley much better. Nothing I eat or drink
(in reason) disagrees with me; and I know whom I think
to be the most lovely creature in the world. Ah, dear
maid (of that remote but well-remembered period), are you
a wife or widow now?—are you dead?—are you thin and
withered and old?—or are you grown much stouter, with a
false front? and so forth.

O Eliza, Eliza!—Stay, *was* she Eliza? Well, I protest
I have forgotten what your Christian name was. You
know I only met you for two days, but your sweet face is
before me now, and the roses blooming on it are as fresh as
in that time of May. Ah, dear Miss X——, my timid
youth and ingenuous modesty would never have allowed
me, even in my private thoughts, to address you otherwise
than by your paternal name, but *that* (though I conceal it)
I remember perfectly well, and that your dear and respected
father was a brewer.

CARILLON.—I was awakened this morning with the chime
which Antwerp cathedral clock plays at half-hours. The
tune has been haunting me ever since, as tunes will. You
dress, eat, drink, walk, and talk to yourself to their tune:
their inaudible jingle accompanies you all day: you read
the sentences of the paper to their rhythm. I tried un-
couthly to imitate the tune to the ladies of the family at
breakfast, and they say it is "the shadow dance of 'Dinorah.'" It may be so. I dimly remember that my body
was once present during the performance of that opera,
whilst my eyes were closed, and my intellectual faculties

dormant at the back of the box; howbeit, I have learned that shadow dance from hearing it pealing up ever so high in the air, at night, morn, noon.

How pleasant to lie awake and listen to the cheery peal! whilst the old city is asleep at midnight, or waking up rosy at sunrise, or basking in noon, or swept by the scudding rain which drives in gusts over the broad places, and the great shining river; or sparkling in snow which dresses up a hundred thousand masts, peaks, and towers; or wrapt round with thunder-cloud canopies, before which the white gables shine whiter; day and night the kind little carillon plays its fantastic melodies overhead. The bells go on ringing. *Quot vivos vocant, mortuos plangunt, fulgura frangunt;* so on to the past and future tenses, and for how many nights, days, and years! Whilst the French were pitching their *fulgura* into Chassé's citadel, the bells went on ringing quite cheerfully. Whilst the scaffolds were up and guarded by Alva's soldiery, and regiments of penitents, blue, black, and grey, poured out of churches and convents, droning their dirges, and marching to the place of the Hôtel de Ville, where heretics and rebels were to meet their doom, the bells up yonder were chanting at their appointed half-hours and quarters, and rang the *mauvais quart d'heure* for many a poor soul. This bell can see as far away as the towers and dykes of Rotterdam. That one can call a greeting to St. Ursula's at Brussels, and toss a recognition to that one at the town-hall of Oudenarde, and remember how after a great struggle there a hundred and fifty years ago the whole plain was covered with the flying French chivalry—Burgundy, and Berri, and the Chevalier of St. George flying like the rest. "What is your clamour about Oudenarde?" says another bell (Bob Major *this* one must be). "Be still, thou querulous old clapper! *I* can see over to Hougoumont and St. John. And about forty-five years since, I rang all through one Sunday in June, when there was such a battle going on in the corn-fields there, as none of you others ever heard tolled of. Yes, from morning service until after vespers, the French and

English were all at it, ding-dong." And then calls of business intervening, the bells have to give up their private jangle, resume their professional duty, and sing their hourly chorus out of "Dinorah."

What a prodigious distance those bells can be heard! I was awakened this morning to their tune, I say. I have been hearing it constantly ever since. And this house whence I write, Murray says, is two hundred and ten miles from Antwerp. And it is a week off; and there is the bell still jangling its shadow dance out of "Dinorah." An audible shadow you understand, and an invisible sound, but quite distinct; and a plague take the tune!

UNDER THE BELLS.—Who has not seen the church under the bell? Those lofty aisles, those twilight chapels, that cumbersome pulpit with its huge carvings, that wide grey pavement flecked with various light from the jewelled windows, those famous pictures between the voluminous columns over the altars which twinkle with their ornaments, their votive little silver hearts, legs, limbs, their little guttering tapers, cups of sham roses, and what not? I saw two regiments of little scholars creeping in and forming square, each in its appointed place, under the vast roof; and teachers presently coming to them. A stream of light from the jewelled windows beams slanting down upon each little squad of children, and the tall background of the church retires into a greyer gloom. Pattering little feet of laggards arriving echo through the great nave. They trot in and join their regiments, gathered under the slanting sunbeams. What are they learning? Is it truth? Those two grey ladies with their books in their hands in the midst of these little people have no doubt of the truth of every word they have printed under their eyes. Look, through the windows jewelled all over with saints, the light comes streaming down from the sky, and heaven's own illuminations paint the book! A sweet, touching picture indeed it is, that of the little children assembled in this immense temple, which has endured for ages, and grave teachers

I

bending over them.   Yes, the picture is very pretty of the
children and their teachers, and their book—but the text?
Is it the truth, the only truth, nothing but the truth?   If
I thought so, I would go and sit down on the form
cum parvulis, and learn the precious lesson with all my
heart.

BEADLE.—But I submit, an obstacle to conversions is
the intrusion and impertinence of that Swiss fellow with
the baldric—the officer who answers to the beadle of the
British Islands—and is pacing about the church with an
eye on the congregation.   Now the boast of Catholics is
that their churches are open to all; but in certain places
and churches there are exceptions.   At Rome I have been
into St. Peter's at all hours: the doors are always open,
the lamps are always burning, the faithful are forever
kneeling at one shrine or the other.   But at Antwerp not
so.   In the afternoon you can go to the church, and be
civilly treated; but you must pay a franc at the side gate.
In the forenoon the doors are open, to be sure, and there is
no one to levy an entrance fee.   I was standing ever so
still, looking through the great gates of the choir at the
twinkling lights, and listening to the distant chants of the
priests performing the service, when a sweet chorus from
the organ loft broke out behind me overhead, and I turned
round.   My friend the drum-major ecclesiastic was down
upon me in a moment.   "Do not turn your back to the
altar during divine service," says he, in very intelligible
English.   I take the rebuke, and turn a soft right-about
face, and listen awhile as the service continues.   See it I
cannot, nor the altar and its ministrants.   We are separated from these by a great screen and closed gates of iron,
through which the lamps glitter and the chant comes by
gusts only.   Seeing a score of children trotting down a side
aisle, I think I may follow them.   I am tired of looking at
that hideous old pulpit with its grotesque monsters and
decorations.   I slip off to the side aisle; but my friend the
drum-major is instantly after me—almost I thought he was

going to lay hands on me. "You mustn't go there," says he; "you mustn't disturb the service." I was moving as quietly as might be, and ten paces off there were twenty children kicking and clattering at their ease. I point them out to the Swiss. "They come to pray," says he. "*You* don't come to pray, you——" "When I come to pay," says I, "I am welcome," and with this withering sarcasm, I walk out of church in a huff. I don't envy the feelings of that beadle after receiving point blank such a stroke of wit.

LEO BELGICUS.—Perhaps you will say after this I am a prejudiced critic. I see the pictures in the cathedral fuming under the rudeness of that beadle, or, at the lawful hours and prices, pestered by a swarm of shabby touters, who come behind me chattering in bad English, and who would have me see the sights through their mean, greedy eyes. Better see Rubens anywhere than in a church. At the Academy, for example, where you may study him at your leisure. But at church?—I would as soon ask Alexandre Dumas for a sermon. Either would paint you a martyrdom very fiercely and picturesquely—writhing muscles, flaming coals, scowling captains and executioners, swarming groups, and light, shade, colour, most dexterously brilliant or dark; but in Rubens I am admiring the performer rather than the piece. With what astonishing rapidity he travels over his canvas; how tellingly the cool lights and warm shadows are made to contrast and relieve each other; how that blazing, blowsy penitent in yellow satin and glittering hair carries down the stream of light across the picture! This is the way to work, my boys, and earn a hundred florins a day. See! I am sure of my line as a skater of making his figure of eight! and down with a sweep goes a brawny arm or a flowing curl of drapery. The figures arrange themselves as if by magic. The paint-pots are exhausted in furnishing brown shadows. The pupils look wondering on, as the master careers over the canvas. Isabel or Helena, wife No. 1 or No. 2, are sitting by, buxom, exuberant, ready to be painted; and the children are boxing in the corner, waiting till they are wanted to figure as cherubs in the picture. Grave burghers and gentlefolks come in on a visit. There are oysters and Rhenish always ready on yonder table. Was there ever such a painter? He has been an ambassador, an actual Excellency, and what better man could be chosen? He speaks all the languages. He earns a hundred florins a day. Prodigious! Thirty-six thousand five hundred florins a year. Enormous! He rides out to his castle with a score of gentlemen after him, like the Governor. That is his own portrait as St. George. You know he is an English knight? Those are his two wives as the two Maries. He chooses the handsomest wives. He rides the handsomest horses. He paints the handsomest pictures. He gets the handsomest prices for them. That slim young Van Dyck, who was his pupil, has genius too, and is painting all the noble ladies in England, and turning the heads of some of them. And Jordaens—what a droll dog and clever fellow! Have you seen his fat Silenus? The master himself could not paint better. And his altar-piece at St. Bavon's? He can paint you anything, that Jordaens can—a drunken jollification of boors and doxies, or a martyr howling with half his skin off. What a knowledge of anatomy! But there is nothing like the master—nothing. He can paint you his thirty-six thousand five hundred florins' worth a year. Have you heard of what he has done for the French Court? Prodigious! I can't look at Rubens' pictures without fancying I see that handsome figure swaggering before the canvas. And Hans Hemmelinck at Bruges? Have you never seen that dear old hospital of St. John, on passing the gate of which you enter into the fifteenth century? I see the wounded soldier still lingering in the house, and tended by the kind grey sisters. His little panel on its easel is placed at the light. He covers his board with the most wondrous, beautiful little figures, in robes as bright as rubies and amethysts. I think he must have a magic glass, in which he catches the reflection of little cherubs with many-coloured wings, very little and bright. Angels, in long crisp robes of white, surrounded with haloes of gold, come and flutter across the mirror, and he draws them. He hears mass every day. He fasts through Lent. No monk is more austere and holy than Hans. Which do you love best to behold, the lamb or the lion? the eagle rushing through the storm, and pouncing mayhap on carrion; or the linnet warbling on the spray?

By much the most delightful of the *Christopher* set of Rubens to my mind (and *ego* is introduced on these occasions, so that the opinion may pass only for my own, at the reader's humble service to be received or declined) is the "Presentation in the Temple:" splendid in colour, in sentiment sweet and tender, finely conveying the story. To be sure, all the others tell their tale unmistakably— witness that coarse "Salutation," that magnificent "Adoration of the Kings" (at the Museum), by the same strong downright hands; that wonderful "Communion of St. Francis," which, I think, gives the key to the artist's *faire* better than any of his performances. I have passed hours before that picture in my time, trying and sometimes fancying I could understand by what masses and contrasts the artist arrived at his effect. In many others of the pictures parts of this method are painfully obvious, and you see how grief and agony are produced by blue lips, and eyes rolling blood-shot with dabs of vermilion. There is something simple in the practice. Contort the eyebrow sufficiently, and place the eyeball near it,—by a few lines you have anger or fierceness depicted. Give me a mouth with no special expression, and pop a dab of carmine at each extremity—and there are the lips smiling. This is art if you will, but a very naïve kind of art: and now you know the trick, don't you see how easy it is?

Tu Quoque.—Now you know the trick, suppose you take a canvas and see whether *you* can do it? There are brushes, palettes, and gallipots full of paint and varnish. Have you tried, my dear sir—you, who set up to be a connoisseur? Have you tried? I have—and many a day. And the end of the day's labour? O dismal conclusion! Is this puerile niggling, this feeble scrawl, this impotent rubbish, all you can produce—you, who but now found Rubens commonplace and vulgar, and were pointing out the tricks of his mystery? Pardon, O great chief, magnificent master and poet! You can *do*. We critics, who sneer and are wise, can but pry, and measure, and doubt, and carp. Look at the lion. Did you ever see such a gross, shaggy, mangy, roaring brute? Look at him eating lumps of raw meat—positively bleeding, and raw, and tough—till, faugh! it turns one's stomach to see him—O the coarse wretch! Yes, but he is a lion. Rubens has lifted his great hand, and the mark he has made has endured for two centuries, and we still continue wondering at him, and admiring him. What a strength in that arm! What splendour of will hidden behind that tawny beard, and those honest eyes! Sharpen your pen, my good critic. Shoot a feather into him; hit him, and make him wince. Yes, you may hit him fair, and make him bleed, too; but, for all that, he is a lion—a mighty, conquering, generous, rampagious Leo Belgicus—monarch of his wood. And he is not dead yet, and I will not kick at him.

Sir Antony.—In that "Pietà" of Van Dyck, in the Museum, have you ever looked at the yellow-robed angel, with the black scarf thrown over her wings and robe? What a charming figure of grief and beauty! What a pretty compassion it inspires! It soothes and pleases me like a sweet rhythmic chant. See how delicately the yellow robe contrasts with the blue sky behind, and the scarf binds the two! If Rubens lacked grace, Van Dyck abounded in it. What a consummate elegance! What a perfect cavalier! No wonder the fine ladies in England admired Sir Antony. Look at——

Here the clock strikes three, and the three gendarmes who keep the Musée cry out, "*Allons! Sortons! Il est trois heures! Allez! Sortez!*" and they skip out of the gallery as happy as boys running from school. And we must go too, for though many stay behind—many Britons with Murray's handbooks in their handsome hands; they have paid a franc for entrance-fee, you see—and we knew nothing about the franc for entrance until those gendarmes with sheathed sabres had driven us out of this Paradise.

But it was good to go and drive on the great quays, and see the ships unlading, and by the citadel, and wonder howabouts and whereabouts it was so strong. We expect a citadel to look like Gibraltar or Ehrenbreitstein at least. But in this one there is nothing to see but a flat plain and some ditches, and some trees, and mounds of uninteresting green. And then I remember how there was a boy at school, a little dumpy fellow of no personal appearance whatever, who couldn't be overcome except by a much bigger champion, and the immensest quantity of thrashing. A perfect citadel of a boy, with a General Chassé sitting in that bomb-proof casemate, his heart, letting blow after blow come thumping about his head, and never thinking of giving in.

And we go home, and we dine in the company of Britons, at the comfortable Hôtel du Parc, and we have bought a novel apiece for a shilling, and every half-hour the sweet carillon plays the waltz from "Dinorah" in the air. And we have been happy; and it seems about a month since we left London yesterday; and nobody knows where we are, and we defy care and the postman.

Spoorweg.—Vast green flats, speckled by spotted cows, and bound by a grey frontier of windmills; shining canals stretching through the green; odours like those exhaled from the Thames in the dog-days, and a fine pervading smell of cheese; little trim houses, with tall roofs, and great windows of many panes; gazebos, or summer-houses, hanging over pea-green canals; kind-looking, dumpling-faced farmers' women, with laced caps and golden frontlets and earrings; about the houses and towns which we pass a

great air of comfort and neatness; a queer feeling of wonder that you can't understand what your fellow-passengers
are saying, the tone of whose voices, and a certain comfortable dowdiness of dress, are so like our own;—whilst
we are remarking on these sights, sounds, smells, the little
railway journey from Rotterdam to the Hague comes to an
end. I speak to the railway porters and hackney coach-
men in English, and they reply in their own language, and
it seems somehow as if we understood each other perfectly.
The carriage drives to the handsome, comfortable, cheerful hotel. We sit down a score at the table; and there is
one foreigner and his wife,—I mean every other man and
woman at dinner are English. As we are close to the sea,
and in the midst of endless canals, we have no fish. We
are reminded of dear England by the noble prices which
we pay for wines. I confess I lost my temper yesterday
at Rotterdam, where I had to pay a florin for a bottle of
ale (the water not being drinkable, and country or Bavarian
beer not being genteel enough for the hotel);—I confess, I
say, that my fine temper was ruffled, when the bottle of
pale ale turned out to be a pint bottle; and I meekly told
the waiter that I had bought beer at Jerusalem at a less
price. But then Rotterdam is eighteen hours from London, and the steamer with the passengers and beer comes
up to the hotel window; whilst to Jerusalem they have to
carry the ale on camels' backs from Beyrout or Jaffa, and
through hordes of marauding Arabs, who evidently don't
care for pale ale, though I am told it is not forbidden in
the Koran. Mine would have been very good, but I choked
with rage whilst drinking it. A florin for a bottle, and
that bottle having the words "imperial pint," in bold relief,
on the surface! It was too much. I intended not to say
anything about it; but I *must* speak. A florin a bottle,
and that bottle a pint! Oh, for shame! for shame! I
can't cork down my indignation; I froth up with fury; I
am pale with wrath, and bitter with scorn.

As we drove through the old city at night, how it
swarmed and hummed with life! What a special clatter,

crowd, and outcry there was in the Jewish quarter, where myriads of young ones were trotting about the fishy street! Why don't they have lamps? We passed by canals seeming so full that a pailful of water more would overflow the place. The *laquais de place* calls out the names of the buildings: the town-hall, the cathedral, the arsenal, the synagogue, the statue of Erasmus. Get along! *We* know the statue of Erasmus well enough. We pass over drawbridges by canals where thousand of barges are at roost. At roost—at rest! Shall *we* have rest in those bedrooms, those ancient lofty bedrooms, in that inn where we have to pay a florin for a pint of pa—psha! at the New Bath Hotel on the Boompjes? If this dreary edifice is the New Bath, what must the Old Bath be like? As I feared to go to bed, I sat in the coffee-room as long as I might; but three young men were imparting their private adventures to each other with such freedom and liveliness that I felt I ought not to listen to their artless prattle. As I put the light out, and felt the bed-clothes and darkness overwhelm me, it was with an awful sense of terror—that sort of sensation which I should think going down in a diving-bell would give. Suppose the apparatus goes wrong, and they don't understand your signal to mount? Suppose your matches miss fire when you wake; when you *want* them, when you will have to rise in half-an-hour, and do battle with the horrid enemy who crawls on you in the darkness? I protest I never was more surprised than when I woke and beheld the light of dawn. Indian birds and strange trees were visible on the ancient gilt hangings of the lofty chamber, and through the windows the Boompjes and the ships along the quay. We have all read of deserters being brought out, and made to kneel, with their eyes bandaged, and hearing the word to "Fire" given! I declare I underwent all the terrors of execution that night, and wonder how I ever escaped unwounded.

But if ever I go to the Bath Hotel, Rotterdam, again, I am a Dutchman. A guilder for a bottle of pale ale, and that bottle a pint! Ah! for shame—for shame!

MINE EASE IN MINE INN.—Do you object to talk about inns? It always seems to me to be very good talk. Walter Scott is full of inns. In "Don Quixote" and "Gil Blas" there is plenty of inn-talk. Sterne, Fielding, and Smollett constantly speak about them; and, in their travels, the last two tot up the bill, and describe the dinner quite honestly; whilst Mr. Sterne becomes sentimental over a cab, and weeps generous tears over a donkey.

How I admire and wonder at the information in Murray's Handbooks—wonder how it is got, and admire the travellers who get it. For instance, you read: Amiens (please select your towns), 60,000 inhabitants. Hotels, &c.—Lion d'Or, good and clean. Le Lion d'Argent, so so. Le Lion Noir, bad, dirty, and dear. Now say, there are three travellers—three inn-inspectors, who are sent forth by Mr. Murray on a great commission, and who stop at every inn in the world. The eldest goes to the Lion d'Or —capital house, good table d'hôte, excellent wine, moderate charges. The second commissioner tries the Silver Lion—tolerable house, bed, dinner, bill, and so forth. But fancy Commissioner No. 3—the poor fag, doubtless, and boots of the party. He has to go to the Lion Noir. He knows he is to have a bad dinner—he eats it uncomplainingly. He is to have bad wine. He swallows it, grinding his wretched teeth, and aware that he will be unwell in consequence. He knows he is to have a dirty bed, and what he is to expect there. He pops out the candle. He sinks into those dingy sheets. He delivers over his body to the nightly tormentors, he pays an exorbitant bill, and he writes down, "Lion Noir, bad, dirty, dear." Next day the commission sets out for Arras, we will say, and they begin again: Le Cochon d'Or, Le Cochon d'Argent, Le Cochon Noir—and that is poor Boots's inn, of course. What a life that poor man must lead! What horrors of dinners he has to go through! What a hide he must have! And yet not impervious; for unless he is bitten, how is he to be able to warn others? No; on second thoughts, you will perceive that he ought to have a very delicate skin. The monsters

ought to troop to him eagerly, and bite him instantaneously
and freely, so that he may be able to warn all future handbook buyers of their danger. I fanc, his man devoting
himself to danger, to dirt, to bad d.n.er3, to sour wine, to
damp beds, to midnig' t agonie., to extortionate bills. I
admire him, I thank him. Think of this champion, who
devotes his body for us—this dauntless gladiator going to
do battle alone in the darkness, with no other armour than
a light helmet of cotton, and a *lorica* of calico. I pity and
honour him. Go, Spartacus! Go, devoted man—to bleed,
to groan, to suffer—and smile in silence as the wild beasts
assail thee!

How did I come into this talk? I protest it was the
word inn set me off—and here is one, the Hôtel de Belle
Vue, at the Hague, as comfortable, as handsome, as cheerful, as any T ever took mine case in. And the Bavarian
beer, my dear friend, how good and bris' and light it is!
Take another glass—it refreshes and does not stupefy—
and then we will sally out, and see the town and the park
and the pictures.

The prettiest little brick city, the pleasantest little park
to ride in, the neatest comfortable people walking about,
the canals not unsweet, and busy and picturesque with old-
world life. Rows upon rows of houses, built with the
neatest little bricks, with windows fresh painted, and tall
doors polished and carved to a nicety. What a pleasant
spacious garden our inn has, all sparkling with autumn
flowers, and bedizened with statues! At the end is a row
of trees, and a summer-house, over the canal, where you
might go and smoke a pipe with Mynheer Van Dunck, and
quite cheerfully catch the ague. Yesterday, as we passed,
they were making hay, and stacking it in a barge which
was lying by the meadow, handy. Round about Kensington Palace there are houses, roofs, chimneys, and bricks
like these. I feel that a Dutchman is a man and a
brother. It is very funny to read the newspaper, one can
understand it somehow. Sure it is the neatest, gayest
little city—scores and hundreds of mansions looking like

Cheyne Walk, or the ladies' schools about Chiswick and Hackney.

LE GROS LOT.—To a few lucky men the chance befals of reaching fame at once, and (if it is of any profit *morituro*) retaining the admiration of the world. Did poor Oliver, when he was at Leyden yonder, ever think that he should paint a little picture which should secure him the applause and pity of all Europe for a century after? He and Sterne drew the twenty thousand prize of fame. The latter had splendid instalments during his lifetime. The ladies pressed round him; the wits admired him, the fashion hailed the successor of Rabelais. Goldsmith's little gem was hardly so valued until later days. Their works still form the wonder and delight of the lovers of English art; and the pictures of the Vicar and Uncle Toby are among the masterpieces of our English school. Here in the Hague Gallery is Paul Potter's pale, eager face, and yonder is the magnificent work by which the young fellow achieved his fame. How did you, so young, come to paint so well? What hidden power lay in that weakly lad that enabled him to achieve such a wonderful victory? Could little Mozart, when he was five years old, tell you how he came to play those wonderful sonatas? Potter was gone out of the world before he was thirty, but left this prodigy (and I know not how many more specimens of his genius and skill) behind him. The details of this admirable picture are as curious as the effect is admirable and complete. The weather being unsettled, and clouds and sunshine in the gusty sky, we saw in our little tour numberless Paul Potters—the meadows streaked with sunshine and spotted with the cattle, the city twinkling in the distance, the thunderclouds glooming overhead. Napoleon carried off the picture (*vide* Murray) amongst the spoils of his bow and spear to decorate his triumph of the Louvre. If I were a conquering prince, I would have this picture certainly, and the Raphael "Madonna" from Dresden, and the Titian "Assumption" from Venice, and that matchless

Rembrandt of the "Dissection." The prostrate nations
would howl with rage as my gendarmes took off the pictures, nicely packed and addressed, to "Mr. the Director
of my Imperial Palace of the Louvre, at Paris. This side
uppermost." The Austrians, Prussians, Saxons, Italians,
&c., should be free to come and visit my capital, and bleat
with tears before the pictures torn from their native cities.
Their ambassadors would meekly remonstrate, and with
faded grins make allusions to the feeling of despair occasioned by the absence of the beloved works of art. Bah!
I would offer them a pinch of snuff out of my box as I
walked along my gallery, with their Excellencies cringing
after me. Zenobia was a fine woman and a queen, but she
had to walk in Aurelian's triumph. The *procédé was peu
délicat? En usez vous, mon cher monsieur?* (The marquis
says the Macaba is delicious.) What a splendour of colour
there is in that cloud! What a richness, what a freedom
of handling, and what a marvellous precision! I trod upon
your Excellency's corn?—a thousand pardons. His Excellency grins and declares that he rather likes to have his
corns trodden on. Were you ever very angry with Soult
—about that Murillo which we have bought? The veteran
loved that picture because it saved the life of a fellow-
creature—the fellow-creature who hid it, and whom the
Duke intended to hang unless the picture was forthcoming.

We gave several thousand pounds for it—how many
thousand? About its merit is a question of taste which
we will not here argue. If you choose to place Murillo in
the first class of painters, founding his claim upon these
Virgin altar-pieces, I am your humble servant. Tom Moore
painted altar-pieces as well as Milton, and warbled Sacred
Songs and Loves of the Angels after his fashion. I wonder did Watteau ever try historical subjects? And as for
Greuze, you know that his heads will fetch 1,000*l.*, 1,500*l.*,
2,000*l.*,—as much as a Sèvres cabaret of Rose du Barri. If
cost price is to be your criterion of worth, what shall we
say to that little receipt for 10*l.* for the copyright of "Paradise Lost," which used to hang in old Mr. Rogers' room?

When living painters, as frequently happens in our days, see their pictures sold at auctions for four or five times the sums which they originally received, are they enraged or elated? A hundred years ago the state of the picture-market was different: that dreary old Italian stock was much higher than at present; Rembrandt himself, a close man, was known to be in difficulties. If ghosts are fond of money still, what a wrath his must be at the present value of his works!

The Hague Rembrandt is the greatest and grandest of all his pieces to my mind. Some of the heads are as sweetly and lightly painted as Gainsborough; the faces not ugly, but delicate and high-bred; the exquisite grey tones are charming to mark and study; the heads not plastered, but painted with a free, liquid brush: the result, one of the great victories won by this consummate chief, and left for the wonder and delight of succeeding ages.

The humblest volunteer in the ranks of art, who has served a campaign or two ever so ingloriously, has at least this good fortune of understanding, or fancying he is able to understand, how the battle has been fought, and how the engaged general won it. This is the Rhinelander's most brilliant achievement—victory along the whole line. The "Night-watch" at Amsterdam is magnificent in parts, but on the side to the spectator's right, smoky and dim. The "Five Masters of the Drapers" is wonderful for depth, strength, brightness, massive power. What words are these to express a picture! to describe a description! I once saw a moon riding in the sky serenely, attended by her sparkling maids of honour, and a little lady said, with an air of great satisfaction, "*I must sketch it.*" Ah, my dear lady, if with an H.B., a Bristol board, and a bit of india-rubber, you can sketch the starry firmament on high, and the moon in her glory, I make you my compliment! I can't sketch "The Five Drapers" with any ink or pen at present at command—but can look with all my eyes, and be thankful to have seen such a masterpiece.

They say he was a moody, ill-conditioned man, the old

tenant of the mill. What does he think of the Vander Helst which hangs opposite his "Night-watch," and which is one of the great pictures of the world? It is not painted by so great a man as Rembrandt; but there it is—to see it is an event of your life. Having beheld it you have lived in the year 1648, and celebrated the treaty of Munster. You have shaken the hands of the Dutch Guardsmen, eaten from their platters, drunk their Rhenish, heard their jokes as they wagged their jolly beards. The Amsterdam Catalogue discourses thus about it:—a model catalogue: it gives you the prices paid, the signatures of the painters, a succinct description of the work.

"This masterpiece represents a banquet of the civic guard, which took place on the 18th June, 1648, in the great hall of the St. Joris Doele, on the Singel at Amsterdam, to celebrate the conclusion of the Peace at Munster. The thirty-five figures composing the picture are all portraits.

"The Captain Witse is placed at the head of the table, and attracts our attention first. He is dressed in black velvet, his breast covered with a cuirass, on his head a broad-brimmed black hat with white plumes. He is comfortably seated on a chair of black oak, with a velvet cushion, and holds in his left hand, supported on his knee, a magnificent drinking-horn, surrounded by a St. George destroying the dragon, and ornamented with olive-leaves. The captain's features express cordiality and good-humour; he is grasping the hand of Lieutenant Van Waveren seated near him, in a habit of dark grey, with lace and buttons of gold, lace-collar and wrist-bands, his feet crossed, with boots of yellow leather, with large tops, and gold spurs, on his head a black hat and dark-brown plumes. Behind him, at the centre of the picture, is the standard-bearer, Jacob Banning, in an easy martial attitude, hat in hand, his right hand on his chair, his right leg on his left knee. He holds the flag of blue silk, in which the Virgin is embroidered, (such a silk! such a flag! such a piece of painting!) emblematic of the town of Amsterdam. The banner covers his shoulder, and he looks towards the spectator frankly and complacently.

"The man behind him is probably one of the sergeants. His head is bare. He wears a cuirass, and yellow gloves, grey stockings, and boots with large tops, and kneecaps of cloth. He has a napkin on his knees, and in his hand a piece of ham, a slice of bread, and a knife. The old man behind is probably William the Drummer. He has his hat in his right hand, and in his left a gold-footed wineglass, filled with white wine. He wears a red scarf, and a black satin doublet, with little slashes of yellow silk. Behind the drummer, two matchlock men are seated at the end of the table. One in a large black habit, a napkin on his knee, a *hausse-col* of iron, and a linen scarf and collar. He is eating with his knife. The other holds a long glass of white wine. Four musketeers, with different shaped hats, are behind these, one holding a glass, the three others with their guns on their shoulders. Other guests are placed between the personage who is giving the toast and the standard-bearer. One with his hat off, and his hand uplifted, is talking to another. The second is carving a fowl. A third holds a silver plate; and another, in the background, a silver flagon, from which he fills a cup. The corner behind the captain is filled by two seated personages, one of whom is peeling an orange. Two others are standing, armed with halberts, of whom one holds a plumed hat. Behind him are other three individuals, one of them holding a pewter pot, on which the name Poock, the landlord of the Hotel Doele, is engraved. At the back, a maidservant is coming in with a pasty, crowned with a turkey. Most of the guests are listening to the captain. From an open window in the distance, the façades of two houses are seen, surmounted by stone figures of sheep."

There, now you know all about it: now you can go home and paint just such another. If you do, do pray remember to paint the hands of the figures as they are here depicted; they are as wonderful portraits as the faces. None of your slim Vandyck elegancies, which have done duty at the cuffs of so many doublets; but each man with a hand for himself, as with a face for himself. I blushed for the coarseness of one of the chiefs in this great company, that fellow behind William the Drummer, splendidly attired, sitting full in the face of the public; and holding a pork-bone in his hand. Suppose the *Saturday Review* critic were to come suddenly on this picture? Ah! what a shock it would give that noble nature! Why is that knuckle of pork not painted out? at any rate, why is not a little fringe of lace painted round it? or a cut pink paper? or couldn't a smelling-bottle be painted in instead, with a crest and a gold top, or a cambric pocket-handkerchief, in lieu of the horrid pig, with a pink coronet in the corner? or suppose you covered the man's hand (which is very coarse and strong) and gave him the decency of a kid glove? But a piece of pork in a naked hand? O nerves and eau de Cologne, hide it, hide it!

In spite of this lamentable coarseness, my noble sergeant, give me thy hand as nature made it! A great, and famous, and noble handiwork I have seen here. Not the greatest picture in the world—not a work of the highest genius—but a performance so great, various, and admirable, so shrewd of humour, so wise of observation, so honest and complete of expression, that to have seen it has been a delight, and to remember it will be a pleasure for days to come. Well done, Bartholomeus Vander Helst! Brave, meritorious, victorious, happy Bartholomew, to whom it has been given to produce a master-piece!

May I take off my hat and pay a respectful compliment to Jan Steen, Esq.? He is a glorious composer. His humour is as frank as Fielding's. Look at his own figure sitting in the window-sill yonder, and roaring with laughter. What a twinkle in the eyes! what a mouth it is for a song, or a joke, or a noggin! I think the composition in some of Jan's pictures amounts to the sublime, and look at them with the same delight and admiration which I have felt before works of the very highest style. This gallery is admirable—and the city in which the gallery is, is perhaps even more wonderful and curious to behold than the gallery.

The first landing at Calais (or, I suppose, on any foreign shore)—the first sight of an Eastern city—the first view of Venice—and this of Amsterdam, are among the delightful shocks which I have had as a traveller. Amsterdam is as good as Venice, with a superadded humour and grotesqueness, which gives the sight-seer the most singular zest and pleasure. A run through Pekin I could hardly fancy to be more odd, strange, and yet familiar. This rush, and crowd, and prodigious vitality; this immense swarm of life; these busy waters, crowding barges, swinging drawbridges, piled ancient gables, spacious markets teeming with people; that ever-wonderful Jews' quarter; that dear old world of painting and the past, yet alive, and throbbing, and palpable—actual, and yet passing before you swiftly and strangely as a dream! Of the many journeys of this Roundabout life, that drive through Amsterdam is to be specially and gratefully remembered. You have never seen the palace of Amsterdam, my dear sir? Why, there's a marble hall in that palace that will frighten you as much as any hall in "Vathek," or a nightmare. At one end of that old, cold, glassy, glittering, ghostly marble hall there stands a throne, on which a white marble king ought to sit with his white legs gleaming down into the white marble below, and his white eyes looking at a great white marble Atlas, who bears on his icy shoulders a blue globe as big as the full moon. If he were not a genie, and enchanted, and with a strength altogether hyperatlantean, he would drop the moon with a shriek on to the white marble floor, and it would splitter into perdition. And the palace would rock, and heave, and tumble; and the waters would rise, rise, rise; and the gables sink, sink, sink; and the barges would rise up to the chimneys; and the watersouchee fishes would flap over the Boompjes, where the pigeons and storks used to perch; and the Amster, and the Rotter, and the Saar, and the Op, and all the dams of Holland would burst, and the Zuyder Zee roll over the dykes;

and you would wake out of your dream, and find yourself sitting in your arm-chair.

Was it a dream? it seems like one. Have we been to Holland? have we heard the chimes at midnight at Antwerp? Were we really away for a week, or have I been sitting up in the room dozing, before this stale old desk? Here's the desk; yes. But, if it has been a dream, how could I have learned to hum that tune out of "Dinorah?" Ah, is it that tune, or myself that I am humming? If it was a dream, how comes this yellow NOTICE DES TABLEAUX DU MUSÉE D'AMSTERDAM AVEC FACSIMILE DES MONOGRAMMES before me, and this signature of the gallant

Bartholomeus van der Helst fecit A.º 1648.

Yes, indeed, it was a delightful little holiday; it lasted a whole week. With the exception of that little pint of *amari aliquid* at Rotterdam, we were all very happy. We might have gone on being happy for whoever knows how many days more? a week more, ten days more: who knows how long that dear tetotum happiness can be made to spin without toppling over?

But one of the party had desired letters to be sent *poste restante*, Amsterdam. The post-office is hard by that awful palace where the Atlas is, and which we really saw.

There was only one letter, you see. Only one chance of finding us. There it was. "The post has only this moment come in," says the smirking commissioner. And he hands over the paper, thinking he has done something clever.

Before the letter had been opened, I could read, COME BACK as clearly as if it had been painted on the wall. It was all over. The spell was broken. The sprightly little holiday fairy that had frisked and gambolled so kindly beside us for eight days of sunshine—or rain which was as cheerful as sunshine—gave a parting piteous look, and whisked away and vanished. And yonder scuds the postman, and here is the old desk.

NIL NISI BONUM.

ALMOST the last words which Sir Walter spoke to Lock-
hart, his biographer, were, "Be a good man, my dear!"
and with the last flicker of breath on his dying lips, he
sighed a farewell to his family, and passed away blessing
them.

Two men, famous, admired, beloved, have just left us,
the Goldsmith and the Gibbon of our time.* Ere a few
weeks are over, many a critic's pen will be at work, review-
ing their lives, and passing judgment on their works. This
is no review, or history, or criticism: only a word in testimony of respect and regard from a man of letters, who owes
to his own professional labour the honour of becoming acquainted with these two eminent literary men. One was
the first ambassador whom the New World of Letters sent
to the Old. He was born almost with the republic; the
pater patriæ had laid his hand on the child's head. He
bore Washington's name: he came amongst us bringing the
kindest sympathy, the most artless, smiling goodwill. His
new country (which some people here might be disposed to
regard rather superciliously) could send us, as he showed
in his own person, a gentleman, who, though himself born
in no very high sphere, was most finished, polished, easy,
witty, quiet; and, socially, the equal of the most refined
Europeans. If Irving's welcome in England was a kind
one, was it not also gratefully remembered? If he ate our
salt, did he not pay us with a thankful heart? Who can
calculate the amount of friendliness and good feeling for
our country which this writer's generous and untiring regard for us disseminated in his own? His books are read

* Washington Irving died, November 28, 1859; Lord Macaulay
died, December 28, 1859.

by millions of his countrymen, whom he has taught to love England, and why to love her. It would have been easy to speak otherwise than he did: to inflame national rancours, which, at the time when he first became known as a public writer, war had just renewed: to cry down the old civilization at the expense of the new: to point out our faults, arrogance, short-comings, and give the republic to infer how much she was the parent state's superior. There are writers enough in the United States, honest and otherwise, who preach that kind of doctrine. But the good Irving, the peaceful, the friendly, had no place for bitterness in his heart, and no scheme but kindness. Received in England with extraordinary tenderness and friendship (Scott, Southey, Byron, a hundred others have borne witness to their liking for him), he was a messenger of goodwill and peace between his country and ours. "See, friends!" he seems to say, "these English are not so wicked, rapacious, callous, proud, as you have been taught to believe them. I went amongst them a humble man; won my way by my pen; and, when known, found every hand held out to me with kindliness and welcome. Scott is a great man, you acknowledge. Did not Scott's king of England give a gold medal to him, and another to me, your countryman, and a stranger?"

Tradition in the United States still fondly retains the history of the feasts and rejoicings which awaited Irving on his return to his native country from Europe. He had a national welcome; he stammered in his speeches, hid himself in confusion, and the people loved him all the better. He had worthily represented America in Europe. In that young community a man who brings home with him abundant European testimonials is still treated with respect (I have found American writers, of wide-world reputation, strangely solicitous about the opinions of quite obscure British critics, and elated or depressed by their judgments); and Irving went home medalled by the king, diplomatized

* See his "Life" in the most remarkable "Dictionary of Authors," published lately at Philadelphia, by Mr. Alibone.

by the university, crowned and honoured and admired. He had not in any way intrigued for his honours, he had fairly won them; and, in Irving's instance, as in others, the old country was glad and eager to pay them.

In America the love and regard for Irving was a national sentiment. Party wars are perpetually raging there, and are carried on by the press with a rancour and fierceness against individuals which exceed British, almost Irish, virulence. It seemed to me, during a year's travel in the country, as if no one ever aimed a blow at Irving. All men held their hand from that harmless, friendly peacemaker. I had the good fortune to see him at New York, Philadelphia, Baltimore and Washington,* and remarked how in every place he was honoured and welcome. Every large city has its "Irving House." The country takes pride in the fame of its men of letters. The gate of his own charming little domain on the beautiful Hudson River was forever swinging before visitors who came to him. He shut out no one.† I had seen many pictures of his house, and read descriptions of it, in both of which it was treated with a not unusual American exaggeration. It was but a pretty little cabin of a place; the gentleman of the press who took notes of the place, whilst his kind old host was sleeping, might have visited the whole house in a couple of minutes.

* At Washington, Mr. Irving came to a lecture given by the writer, which Mr. Filmore and General Pierce, the president and president elect, were also kind enough to attend together. "Two kings of Brentford smelling at one rose," says Irving, looking up with his good-humoured smile.

† Mr. Irving described to me, with that humour and good humour which he always kept, how, amongst other visitors, a member of the British press who had carried his distinguished pen to America (where he employed it in vilifying his own country) came to Sunnyside, introduced himself to Irving, partook of his wine and luncheon, and in two days described Mr. Irving, his house, his nieces, his meal, and his manner of dozing afterwards, in a New York paper. On another occasion, Irving said, laughing, "Two persons came to me, and one held me in conversation whilst the other miscreant took my portrait!"

And how came it that this house was so small, when Mr. Irving's books were sold by hundreds of thousands, nay, millions, when his profits were known to be large, and the habits of life of the good old bachelor were notoriously modest and simple? He had loved once in his life. The lady he loved died; and he, whom all the world loved, never sought to replace her. I can't say how much the thought of that fidelity has touched me. Does not the very cheerfulness of his after life add to the pathos of that untold story? To grieve always was not in his nature; or, when he had his sorrow, to bring all the world in to condole with him and bemoan it. Deep and quiet he lays the love of his heart, and buries it; and grass and flowers grow over the scarred ground in due time.

Irving had such a small house and such narrow rooms, because there was a great number of people to occupy them. He could only afford to keep one old horse (which, lazy and aged as it was, managed once or twice to run away with that careless old horseman). He could only afford to give plain sherry to that amiable British paragraph-monger from New York, who saw the patriarch asleep over his modest, blameless cup, and fetched the public into his private chamber to look at him. Irving could only live very modestly, because the wifeless, childless man had a number of children to whom he was as a father. He had as many as nine nieces, I am told—I saw two of these ladies at his house—with all of whom the dear old man had shared the produce of his labour and genius.

"*Be a good man, my dear.*" One can't but think of these last words of the veteran Chief of Letters, who had tasted and tested the value of worldly success, admiration, prosperity. Was Irving not good, and, of his works, was not his life the best part? In his family, gentle, generous, good-humoured, affectionate, self-denying: in society, a delightful example of complete gentlemanhood; quite unspoiled by prosperity; never obsequious to the great (or, worse still, to the base and mean, as some public men are forced to be in his and other countries); eager to acknowledge every contemporary's merit; always kind and affable with the young members of his calling; in his professional bargains and mercantile dealings delicately honest and grateful; one of the most charming masters of our lighter language; the constant friend to us and our nation; to men of letters doubly dear, not for his wit and genius merely, but as an examplar of goodness, probity, and pure life:—I don't know what sort of testimonial will be raised to him in his own country, where generous and enthusiastic acknowledgment of American merit is never wanting: but Irving was in our service as well as theirs; and as they have placed a stone at Greenwich yonder in memory of that gallant young Bellot, who shared the perils and fate of some of our Arctic seamen, I would like to hear of some memorial raised by English writers and friends of letters in affectionate remembrance of the dear and good Washington Irving.

As for the other writer, whose departure many friends, some few most dearly-loved relatives, and multitudes of admiring readers deplore, our republic has already decreed his statue, and he must have known that he had earned this posthumous honour. He is not a poet and man of letters merely, but citizen, statesman, a great British worthy. Almost from the first moment when he appears, amongst boys, amongst college students, amongst men, he is marked, and takes rank as a great Englishman.   All sorts of successes are easy to him: as a lad he goes down into the arena with others, and wins all the prizes to which he has a mind.   A place in the senate is straightway offered to the young man.   He takes his seat there; he speaks, when so minded, without party anger or intrigue, but not without party faith and a sort of heroic enthusiasm for his cause. Still he is poet and philosopher even more than orator. That he may have leisure and means to pursue his darling studies, he absents himself for a while, and accepts a richly-remunerative post in the East.   As learned a man may live in a cottage or a college common-room; but it always seemed to me that ample means and recognized rank were

Macaulay's as of right. Years ago there was a wretched outcry raised because Mr. Macaulay dated a letter from Windsor Castle, where he was staying. Immortal gods! Was this man not a fit guest for any palace in the world? or a fit companion for any man or woman in it? I daresay, after Austerlitz, the old K. K. court officials and footmen sneered at Napoleon for dating from Schönbrunn. But that miserable "Windsor Castle" outcry is an echo out of fast-retreating old-world remembrances. The place of such a natural chief was amongst the first of the land; and that country is best, according to our British notion, at least, where the man of eminence has the best chance of investing his genius and intellect.

If a company of giants were got together, very likely one or two of the mere six-feet-six people might be angry at the incontestable superiority of the very tallest of the party: and so I have heard some London wits, rather peevish at Macaulay's superiority, complain that he occupied too much of the talk, and so forth. Now that wonderful tongue is to speak no more, will not many a man grieve that he no longer has the chance to listen? To remember the talk is to wonder: to think not only of the treasures he had in his memory, but of the trifles he had stored there, and could produce with equal readiness. Almost on the last day I had the fortune to see him, a conversation happened suddenly to spring up about senior wranglers, and what they had done in after life. To the almost terror of the persons present, Macaulay began with the senior wrangler of 1801-2-3-4, and so on, giving the name of each, and relating his subsequent career and rise. Every man who has known him has his story regarding that astonishing memory. It may be that he was not ill-pleased that you should recognize it; but to those prodigious intellectual feats, which were so easy to him, who would grudge his tribute of homage? His talk was, in a word, admirable, and we admired it.

Of the notices which have appeared regarding Lord Macaulay, up to the day when the present lines are written

J

(the 9th of January), the reader should not deny himself the pleasure of looking especially at two.. It is a good sign of the times when such articles as these (I mean the articles in the *Times* and *Saturday Review*) appear in our public prints about our public men. They educate us, as it were, to admire rightly. An uninstructed person in a museum or at a concert may pass by without recognizing a picture or a passage of music, which the connoisseur by his side may show him is a masterpiece of harmony, or a wonder of artistic skill. After reading these papers you like and respect more the person you have admired so much already. And so with regard to Macaulay's style there may be faults of course—what critic can't point them out? But for the nonce we are not talking about faults: we want to say *nil nisi bonum*. Well—take at hazard any three pages of the "Essays" or "History"—and, glimmering below the stream of the narrative, as it were, you, an average reader, see one, two, three, a half-score of allusions to other historic facts, characters, literature, poetry, with which you are acquainted. Why is this epithet used? Whence is that simile drawn? How does he manage, in two or three words, to paint an individual, or to indicate a landscape? Your neighbour, who has *his* reading, and his little stock of literature stowed away in his mind, shall detect more points, allusions, happy touches, indicating not only the prodigious memory and vast learning of this master, but the wonderful industry, the honest, humble previous toil of this great scholar. He reads twenty books to write a sentence; he travels a hundred miles to make a line of description.

Many Londoners— not all—have seen the British Museum Library. I speak *à cœur ouvert*, and pray the kindly reader to bear with me. I have seen all sorts of domes of Peters and Pauls, Sophia, Pantheon,—what not?—and have been struck by none of them so much as by that catholic dome in Bloomsbury, under which our million volumes are housed. What peace, what love, what truth, what beauty, what happiness for all, what generous kindness **for** you and me, are here spread out! It seems to me one cannot sit down in that place without a heart full of grateful reverence. I own to have said my grace at the table, and to have thanked heaven for this my English birthright, freely to partake of these bountiful books, and to speak the truth I find there. Under the dome which held Macaulay's brain, and from which his solemn eyes looked out on the world but a fortnight since, what a vast, brilliant, and wonderful store of learning was ranged! what strange lore would he not fetch for you at your bidding! A volume of law, or history, or book of poetry familiar or forgotten (except by himself who forgot nothing), a novel ever so old, and he had it at hand. I spoke to him once about "Clarissa." "Not read 'Clarissa!'" he cried out. "If you have once thoroughly entered on 'Clarissa,' and are infected by it, you can't leave it. When I was in India I passed one hot season at the hills, and there were the governor-general, and the secretary of government, and the commander-in-chief, and their wives. I had 'Clarissa' with me: and, as soon as they began to read, the whole station was in a passion of excitement about Miss Harlowe and her misfortunes, and her scoundrelly Lovelace! The governor's wife seized the book, and the secretary waited for it, and the chief justice could not read it for tears!" He acted the whole scene: he paced up and down the Athenæum library: I daresay he could have spoken pages of the book—of that book, and of what countless piles of others!

In this little paper let us keep to the text of *nil nisi bonum*. One paper I have read regarding Lord Macaulay says "he had no heart." Why, a man's books may not always speak the truth, but they speak his mind in spite of himself: and it seems to me this man's heart is beating through every page he penned. He is always in a storm of revolt and indignation against wrong, craft, tyranny. How he cheers heroic resistance; how he backs and applauds freedom struggling for its own; how he hates scoundrels, ever so victorious and successful; how he recognizes genius, though selfish villains possess it! The critic who says Macaulay had no heart, might say that Johnson had none: and two men more generous, and more loving, and more hating, and more partial, and more noble, do not live in our history. Those who knew Lord Macaulay knew how admirably tender, and generous,* and affectionate he was. It was not his business to bring his family before the theatre footlights, and call for bouquets from the gallery as he wept over them.

If any young man of letters reads this little sermon—and to him, indeed, it is addressed—I would say to him, " Bear Scott's words in your mind, and ' *be good, my dear*.' " Here are two literary men gone to their account, and, *laus Deo*, as far as we know, it is fair, and open, and clean. Here is no need of apologies for shortcomings, or explanations of vices which would have been virtues but for unavoidable, &c. Here are two examples of men most differently gifted: each pursuing his calling; each speaking his truth as God bade him; each honest in his life; just and irreproachable in his dealings; dear to his friends; honoured by his country; beloved at his fireside. It has been the fortunate lot of both to give incalculable happiness and delight to the world, which thanks them in return with an immense kindliness, respect, affection. It may not be our chance, brother scribe, to be endowed with such merit, or rewarded with such fame. But the rewards of these men are rewards paid to *our service*. We may not win the baton or epaulettes; but God give us strength to guard the honour of the flag!

---

* Since the above was written, I have been informed that it has been found, on examining Lord Macaulay's papers, that he was in the habit of giving away *more than a fourth part* of his annual income.

ON HALF A LOAF.

A LETTER TO MESSRS. BROADWAY, BATTERY AND CO., OF NEW YORK, BANKERS.

Is it all over? May we lock up the case of instruments? Have we signed our wills; settled up our affairs; pretended to talk and rattle quite cheerfully to the women at dinner, so that they should not be alarmed; sneaked away under some pretext, and looked at the children sleeping in their beds with their little unconscious thumbs in their mouths, and a flush on the soft-pillowed cheek; made every arrangement with Colonel MacTurk, who acts as our second, and knows the other principal a great deal too well to think he will ever give in; invented a monstrous figment about going to shoot pheasants with Mac in the morning, so as to soothe the anxious fears of the dear mistress of the house; early as the hour appointed for the—the little affair—was, have we been awake hours and hours sooner; risen before daylight, with a faint hope, perhaps, that MacTurk might have come to some arrangement with the other side; at seven o'clock (confound his punctuality!) heard his cab-wheel at the door, and let him in looking perfectly trim, fresh, jolly, and well shaved; driven off with him in the cold morning, after a very unsatisfactory breakfast of coffee and stale bread-and-butter (which choke, somehow, in the swallowing); driven off to Wormwood Scrubs in the cold, muddy, misty, moonshiny morning; stepped out of the cab, where Mac has bid the man to halt on a retired spot in the common; in one minute more, seen another cab arrive, from which descend two gentlemen, one of whom has a case like MacTurk's under his arm;—looked round and round the solitude, and seen not one single sign of a police-man—no, no more than in a row in London;—deprecated the horrible necessity which drives civilized men to the use of powder and bullet;—taken ground as firmly as may be, and looked on whilst Mac is neatly loading his weapons; and when all ready, and one looked for the decisive One, Two, Three—have we even heard Captain O'Toole (the second of the other principal) walk up, and say: "Colonel MacTurk, I am desired by my principal to declare at this eleventh—this twelfth hour, that he is willing to own that he sees HE HAS BEEN WRONG in the dispute which has arisen between him and your friend; that he apologizes for offensive expressions which he has used in the heat of the quarrel; and regrets the course he has taken?" If something like this has happened to you, however great your courage, you have been glad not to fight;—however accurate your aim, you have been pleased not to fire.

On the sixth day of January in this year sixty-two, what hundreds of thousands—I may say, what millions of Englishmen, were in the position of the personage here sketched —Christian men, I hope, shocked at the dreadful necessity of battle; aware of the horrors which the conflict must produce, and yet feeling that the moment was come, and that there was no arbitrament left but that of steel and cannon! My reader, perhaps, has been in America. If he has, he knows what good people are to be found there; how polished, how generous, how gentle, how courteous. But it is not the voices of these you hear in the roar of hate, defiance, folly, falsehood, which comes to us across the Atlantic. You can't hear gentle voices; very many who could speak are afraid. Men must go forward, or be crushed by the maddened crowd behind them. I suppose after the perpetration of that act of—what shall we call it?—of sudden war, which Wilkes did, and Everett approved, most of us believed that battle was inevitable. Who has not read the American papers for six weeks past? Did you ever think the United States Government would give up those Commissioners? I never did, for my part. It seems to me the United States Government have done the most courageous act of the war. Before that act was done, what an excitement prevailed in London! In every Club there was a parliament sitting in permanence: in every domestic gathering this subject was sure to form a main part of the talk. Of course I have seen many people who have travelled in America, and heard them on this matter—friends of the South, friends of the North, friends of peace, and American stockholders in plenty.—"They will never give up the men, sir," that was the opinion on all sides; and, if they would not, we knew what was to happen.

For weeks past this nightmare of war has been riding us. The City was already gloomy enough. When a great domestic grief and misfortune visits the chief person of the State, the heart of the people, too, is sad and awe-stricken. It might be this sorrow and trial were but presages of greater trials and sorrow to come. What if the sorrow of war is to be added to the other calamity? Such forebodings have formed the theme of many a man's talk, and darkened many a fireside. Then came the rapid orders for ships to arm and troops to depart. How many of us have had to say farewell to friends whom duty called away with their regiments; on whom we strove to look cheerfully, as we shook their hands, it might be for the last time; and whom our thoughts depicted, treading the snows of the immense Canadian frontier, where their intrepid little band might have to face the assaults of other enemies than winter and rough weather! I went to a play one night, and protest I hardly know what was the entertainment which passed before my eyes. In the next stall was an American gentleman, who knew me. "Good heavens, sir," I thought, "is it decreed that you and I are to be authorized to murder each other next week; that my people shall be bombarding your cities, destroying your navies, making a hideous desolation of your coast; that our peaceful frontiers shall be subject to fire, rapine, and murder?" "They will never give up the men," said the Englishmen. "They will never give up the men," said the American. And the Christmas piece which the actors were playing proceeded like a piece in a dream. To make the grand comic performance doubly comic, my neighbour presently informed

me how one of the best friends I had in America—the
most hospitable, kindly, amiable of men, from whom I had
twice received the warmest welcome and the most delightful hospitality—was a prisoner in Fort Warren, on charges
by which his life perhaps might be risked. I think that
was the most dismal Christmas fun which these eyes ever
looked on.

Carry out that notion a little farther, and depict ten
thousand, a hundred thousand homes in England saddened
by the thought of the coming calamity, and oppressed by
the pervading gloom. My next-door neighbour perhaps
has parted with her son. Now the ship in which he is,
with a thousand brave comrades, is ploughing through the
stormy midnight ocean. Presently (under the flag we
know of) the thin red line in which her boy forms a speck,
is winding its way through the vast Canadian snows.
Another neighbour's boy is not gone, but is expecting orders to sail; and some one else, besides the circle at home
maybe, is in prayer and terror, thinking of the summons
which calls the young sailor away. By firesides modest
and splendid, all over the three kingdoms, that sorrow is
keeping watch, and myriads of hearts beating with that
thought, " Will they give up the men? "

I don't know how, on the first day after the capture of
the Southern Commissioners was announced, a rumour got
abroad in London that the taking of the men was an act
according to law, of which our nation could take no notice.
It was said that the law authorities had so declared, and a
very noble testimony to the *loyalty* of Englishmen, I think,
was shown by the instant submission of high-spirited gentlemen, most keenly feeling that the nation had been subject to a coarse outrage, who were silent when told that the
law was with the aggressor. The relief which presently
came, when, after a pause of a day, we found that law was
on our side, was indescribable. The nation *might* then
take notice of this insult to its honour. Never were people more eager than ours when they found they had a right
to reparation.

I have talked during the last week with many English holders of American securities, who, of course, have been aware of the threat held over them. "England," says the *New York Herald*, "cannot afford to go to war with us, for six hundred millions' worth of American stock is owned by British subjects, which, in event of hostilities, would be confiscated; and we now call upon the Companies not to take it off their hands on any terms. *Let its forfeiture be held over England as a weapon in terrorem.* British subjects have two or three hundred millions of dollars invested in shipping and other property in the United States. All this property, together with the stocks, would be seized, amounting to nine hundred millions of dollars. Will England incur this tremendous loss for a mere abstraction?"

Whether "a mere abstraction" here means the abstraction of the two Southern Commissioners from under our flag, or the abstract idea of injured honour, which seems ridiculous to the *Herald*, it is needless to ask. I have spoken with many men who have money invested in the States, but I declare I have not met one English gentleman whom the publication of this threat has influenced for a moment. Our people have nine hundred millions of dollars invested in the United States, have they? And the *Herald* "calls upon the Companies" not to take any of this debt off our hands. Let us, on our side, entreat the English press to give this announcement every publicity. Let us do everything in our power to make this "call upon the Americans" well known in England. I hope English newspaper editors will print it, and print it again and again. It is not we who say this of American citizens, but American citizens who say this of themselves. "Bull is odious. We can't bear Bull. He is haughty, arrogant, a braggart, and a blusterer; and we can't bear brag and bluster in our modest and decorous country. We hate Bull, and if he quarrels with us on a point in which we are in the wrong, we have goods of his in our custody, and we will rob him!" Suppose your London banker saying to you, "Sir, I have ways thought your manners disgusting, and your arrogance insupportable. You dare to complain of my conduct because I have wrongfully imprisoned Jones? My answer to your vulgar interference is, that I confiscate your balance!"

What would be an English merchant's character after a few such transactions? It is not improbable that the moralists of the *Herald* would call him a rascal. Why have the United States been paying seven, eight, ten per cent. for money for years past, when the same commodity can be got elsewhere at half that rate of interest? Why, because though among the richest proprietors in the world, creditors were not sure of them. So the States have had to pay eighty millions yearly for the use of money which would cost other borrowers but thirty. Add up this item of extra interest alone for a dozen years, and see what a prodigious penalty the States have been paying for repudiation here and there, for sharp practice, for doubtful credit. Suppose the peace is kept between us, the remembrance of this last threat alone will cost the States millions and millions more. If they must have money, we must have a greater interest to insure our jeopardized capital. Do American Companies want to borrow money—as want to borrow they will? Mr. Brown, show the gentlemen that extract from the *New York Herald*, which declares that the United States will confiscate private property in event of a war. As the country newspapers say, "Please, country papers, copy this paragraph." And, gentlemen in America, when the honour of *your* nation is called in question, please to remember that it is the American press which glories in announcing that you are prepared to be rogues.

And when this war has drained uncounted hundreds of millions more out of the United States exchequer, will they be richer or more inclined to pay debts, or less willing to evade them, or more popular with their creditors, or more likely to get money from men whom they deliberately announce that they will cheat? I have not followed the *Herald* on the "stone-ship" question—that great naval victory appears to me not less horrible and wicked than suicidal. Block the harbours forever; destroy the inlets of the commerce of the world; perish cities,—so that we may wreak an injury on them. It is the talk of madmen, but not the less wicked. The act injures the whole Republic: but it is perpetrated. It is to deal harm to ages hence; but it is done. The Indians of old used to burn women and their unborn children. This stone-ship business is Indian warfare. And it is performed by men who tell us every week that they are at the head of civilization, and that the Old World is decrepit, and cruel, and barbarous as compared to theirs.

The same politicians who throttle commerce at its neck, and threaten to confiscate trust-money, say that when the war is over and the South is subdued, then the turn of the old country will come, and a direful retribution shall be taken for our conduct. This has been the cry all through the war. "We should have conquered the South," says an American paper which I read this very day, "but for England." Was there ever such puling heard from men who have an army of a million, and who turn and revile a people who have stood as aloof from their contest as we have from the war of Troy? Or is it an outcry made with malice prepense? And is the song of the *New York Times* a variation of the *Herald* tune?—"The conduct of the British, in folding their arms and taking no part in the fight, has been so base that it has caused the prolongation of the war, and occasioned a prodigious expense on our part. Therefore, as we have British property in our hands, we &c. &c." The lamb troubled the water dreadfully, and the wolf in a righteous indignation "confiscated" him. Of course we have heard that at an undisturbed time Great Britain would never have dared to press its claim for redress. Did the United States wait until we were at peace with France before they went to war with us last? Did Mr. Seward yield the claim which he confesses to be just, until he himself was menaced with war? How long were the Southern gentlemen kept in prison? What caused them to be set free? and did the Cabinet of Washington see its error before or after the demand for redress? * The captor was feasted at Boston, and the captives in prison hard by. If the wrong-doer was to be punished, it was Captain Wilkes who ought to have gone into limbo. At any rate, as "the Cabinet of Washington could not give its approbation to the commander of the *San Jacinto*," why were the men not sooner set free? To sit at the Tremont House, and hear the captain after dinner give his opinion on international law, would have been better sport for the prisoners than the grim *salle à manger* at Fort Warren.

I read in the commercial news brought by the *Teutonia*, and published in London on the present 13th January, that the pork market was generally quiet on the 29th December last; that lard, though with more activity, was heavy and decidedly lower; and at Philadelphia, whisky is steady and stocks firm. Stocks are firm: that is a comfort for the English holders, and the confiscating process recommended by the *Herald* is at least deferred. But presently comes an announcement which is not quite so cheering:—"The Saginaw Central Railway Company (let us call it) has postponed its January dividend on account of the disturbed condition of public affairs."

A la bonne heure. The bond and share holders of the

---

* "At the beginning of December the British fleet on the West Indian station mounted 850 guns, and comprised five liners, ten first-class frigates, and seventeen powerful corvettes. * * * In little more than a month the fleet available for operations on the American shore had been more than doubled. The reinforcements prepared at the various dockyards included two line-of-battle ships, twenty-nine magnificent frigates—such as the *Shannon*, the *Sutlej*, the *Euryalus*, the *Orlando*, the *Galatea;* eight corvettes, armed like the frigates in part, with 100- and 40-pounder Armstrong guns; and the two tremendous iron-cased ships, the *Warrior* and the *Black Prince;* and their smaller sisters, the *Resistance* and the *Defence.* There was work to be done which might have delayed the commission of a few of these ships for some weeks longer; but if the United States had chosen war instead of peace, the blockade of their coasts would have been supported by a steam fleet of more than sixty splendid ships, armed with 1,800 guns, many of them of the heaviest and most effective kind."—*Saturday Review:* Jan. 11.

Saginaw must look for loss and depression in times of war. This is one of war's dreadful taxes and necessities; and all sorts of innocent people must suffer by the misfortune. The corn was high at Waterloo when a hundred and fifty thousand men came and trampled it down on a Sabbath morning. There was no help for that calamity, and the Belgian farmers lost their crops for the year. Perhaps I am a farmer myself—an innocent *colonus*, and instead of being able to get to church with my family, have to see squadrons of French dragoons thundering upon my barley, and squares of English infantry forming and trampling all over my oats. (By the way, in writing of "Panics," an ingenious writer in the *Atlantic Magazine* says that the British panics at Waterloo were frequent and notorious.) Well, I am a Belgian peasant, and I see the British running away and the French cutting the fugitives down. What have I done that these men should be kicking down my peaceful harvest for me, on which I counted to pay my rent, to feed my horses, my household, my children? It is hard. But it is the fortune of war. But suppose the battle over; the Frenchman says, "You scoundrel! why did you not take a part with me? and why did you stand like a double-faced traitor looking on? I should have won the battle but for you. And I hereby confiscate the farm you stand on, and you and your family may go to the workhouse."

The New York press holds this argument over English people *in terrorem*. "We Americans may be ever so wrong in the matter in dispute, but if you push us to a war, we will confiscate your English property." Very good. It is peace now. Confidence of course is restored between us. Our eighteen hundred peace commissioners have no occasion to open their mouths; and the little question of confiscation is postponed. Messrs. Battery, Broadway and Co., of New York, have the kindness to sell my Saginaws for what they will fetch. I shall lose half my loaf very likely; but for the sake of a quiet life, let us give up a certain quantity of farinaceous food; and half a loaf, you know, is better than no bread at all.

THE NOTCH ON THE AXE.

A STORY À LA MODE.

PART I.

EVERY one remembers in the Fourth Book of the immortal poem of your Blind Bard, (to whose sightless orbs no doubt Glorious Shapes were apparent, and Visions Celestial,) how Adam discourses to Eve of the Bright Visitors who hovered round their Eden—

> "Millions of spiritual creatures walk the earth,
> Unseen both when we wake and when we sleep."

"'How often,' says Father Adam, 'from the steep of echoing hill or thicket, have we heard celestial voices to the midnight air, sole, or responsive to each other's notes, singing!' After the Act of Disobedience, when the erring pair from Eden took their solitary way, and went forth to toil and trouble on common earth—though the Glorious Ones no longer were visible, you cannot say they were gone? It was not that the Bright Ones were absent, but that the dim eyes of rebel man no longer could see them. In your chamber hangs a picture of one whom you never knew, but whom you have long held in tenderest regard, and who was painted for you by a friend of mine, the Knight of Plympton. She communes with you. She smiles on you. When your spirits are low, her bright eyes shine on you and cheer you. Her innocent sweet smile is a caress to you. She never fails to soothe you with her speechless prattle. You love her. She is alive with you. As you extinguish your candle and turn to sleep, though your eyes see her not, is she not there still smiling? As you lie in the night awake, and thinking of your duties, and the morrow's inevitable toil oppressing the busy,

weary, wakeful brain as with a remorse, the crackling fire
flashes up for a moment in the grate, and she is there, your
little Beauteous Maiden, smiling with her sweet eyes!
When moon is down, when fire is out, when curtains are
drawn, when lids are closed, is she not there, the little
Beautiful One, though invisible, present and smiling still?
Friend, the Unseen Ones are round about us. Does it not
seem as if the time were drawing near when it shall be
given to men to behold them?"

The print of which my friend spoke, and which, indeed,
hangs in my room, though he has never been there, is that
charming little winter piece of Sir Joshua, representing the
little Lady Caroline Montagu, afterwards Duchess of Buc-
cleuch. She is represented as standing in the midst of a
winter landscape, wrapped in muff and cloak; and she
looks out of her picture with a smile so exquisite that a
Herod could not see her without being charmed.

"I beg your pardon, Mr. Pinto," I said to the person
with whom I was conversing. (I wonder, by the way, that
I was not surprised at his knowing how fond I am of this
print.) "You spoke of the Knight of Plympton. Sir
Joshua died, 1792: and you say he was your dear friend?"

As I spoke I chanced to look at Mr. Pinto; and then it
suddenly struck me: Gracious powers! Perhaps you *are*
a hundred years old, now I think of it. You look more
than a hundred. Yes, you may be a thousand years old
for what I know. Your teeth are false. One eye is evidently false. Can I say that the other is not? If a man's
age may be calculated by the rings round his eyes, this
man may be as old as Methusaleh. He has no beard. He
wears a large curly glossy brown wig, and his eyebrows are
painted a deep olive-green. It was odd to hear this man,
this walking mummy, talking sentiment, in these queer old
chambers in Shepherd's Inn.

Pinto passed a yellow bandanna handkerchief over his
awful white teeth, and kept his glass eye steadily fixed on
me. "Sir Joshua's friend?" said he (you perceive, elud-
ing my direct question). "Is not every one that knows his

pictures Reynolds's friend? Suppose I tell you that I have been in his painting room scores of times, and that his sister Thé has made me tea, and his sister Toffy has made coffee for me? You will only say I am an old ombog." (Mr. Pinto, I remarked, spoke all languages with an accent equally foreign.) "Suppose I tell you that I knew Mr. Sam Johnson, and did not like him? that I was at that very ball at Madame Cornelis', which you have mentioned in one of your little—what do you call them?—bah! my memory begins to fail me—in one of your little Whirligig Papers? Suppose I tell you that Sir Joshua has been here, in this very room?"

"Have you, then, had these apartments for—more—than—seventy years?" I asked.

"They look as if they had not been swept for that time —don't they? Hey? I did not say that I had them for seventy years, but that Sir Joshua has visited me here."

"When?" I asked, eyeing the man sternly, for I began to think he was an impostor.

He answered me with a glance still more stern: "Sir Joshua Reynolds was here this very morning, with Angelica Kaufmann, and Mr. Oliver Goldschmidt. He is still very much attached to Angelica, who still does not care for him. Because he is dead (and I was in the fourth mourning coach at his funeral) is that any reason why he should not come back to earth again? My good sir, you are laughing at me. He has sat many a time on that very chair which you are occupying. There are several spirits in the room now, whom you cannot see. Excuse me." Here he turned round as if he was addressing somebody, and began rapidly speaking a language unknown to me. "It is Arabic," he said; "a bad patois, I own. I learned it in Barbary, when I was a prisoner amongst the Moors. In anno 1609, bin ick aldus ghekledt gheghaen. Ha! you doubt me: look at me well. At least I am like——"

Perhaps some of my readers remember a paper of which the figure of a man carrying a barrel formed the initial letter, and which I copied from an old spoon now in my possession. As I looked at Mr. Pinto I do declare he looked so like the figure on that old piece of plate that I started and felt very uneasy. "Ha!" said he, laughing through his false teeth (I declare they were false—I could see utterly toothless gums working up and down behind the pink coral), "you see I wore a beard den; I am shafed now; perhaps you tink I am *a spoon*. Ha, ha!" And as he laughed he gave a cough which I thought would have coughed his teeth out, his glass eye out, his wig off, his very head off, but he stopped this convulsion by stumping across the room and seizing a little bottle of bright pink medicine, which, being opened, spread a singular acrid aromatic odour through the apartment; and I thought I saw— but of this I cannot take an affirmation—a light green and violet flame flickering round the neck of the phial as he opened it. By the way, from the peculiar stumping noise which he made in crossing the bare-boarded apartment, I knew at once that my strange entertainer had a wooden leg. Over the dust which lay quite thick on the boards, you could see the mark of one foot very neat and pretty, and then a round O, which was naturally the impression made by the wooden stump. I own I had a queer thrill as I saw that mark, and felt a secret comfort that it was not *cloven*.

In this desolate apartment in which Mr. Pinto had invited me to see him, there were three chairs, one bottomless, a little table on which you might put a breakfast-tray, and not a single other article of furniture. In the next room, the door of which was open, I could see a magnificent gilt dressing-case, with some splendid diamond and ruby shirt-studs lying by it, and a chest of drawers, and a cupboard apparently full of clothes.

Remembering him in Baden Baden in great magnificence, I wondered at his present denuded state. "You have a house elsewhere, Mr. Pinto?" I said.

"Many," says he. "I have apartments in many cities. I lock dem up, and do not carry mosh logish."

I then remembered that his apartment at Baden, where I first met him, was bare, and had no bed in it.

"There is, then, a sleeping-room beyond?"

"This is the sleeping-room." (He pronounces it *dis*). Can this, by the way, give any clue to the nationality of this singular man?)

"If you sleep on these two old chairs you have a rickety couch; if on the floor, a dusty one."

"Suppose I sleep up dere?" said this strange man, and he actually pointed up to the ceiling. I thought him mad, or what he himself called an ombog. "I know. You do not believe me; for why should I deceive you? I came but to propose a matter of business to you. I told you I could give you the clue to the mystery of the Two Children in Black, whom we met at Baden, and you came to see me. If I told you you would not believe me. What for try and convinz you? Ha hey?" And he shook his hand once, twice, thrice, at me, and glared at me out of his eye in a peculiar way.

Of what happened now I protest I cannot give an accurate account. It seemed to me that there shot a flame from his eye into my brain, whilst behind his *glass* eye there was a green illumination as if a candle had been lit in it. It seemed to me that from his long fingers two quivering flames issued, sputtering, as it were, which penetrated me, and forced me back into one of the chairs—the broken one—out of which I had much difficulty in scrambling, when the strange glamour was ended. It seemed to me that, when I was so fixed, so transfixed in the broken chair, the man floated up to the ceiling, crossed his legs, folded his arms as if he was lying on a sofa, and grinned down at me. When I came to myself he was down from the ceiling, and, taking me out of the broken cane-bottomed chair, kindly enough—"Bah!" said he, "it is the smell of my medicine. It often gives the vertigo. I thought you would have had a little fit. Come into the open air." And we went down the steps, and into Shepherd's Inn, where the setting sun was just shining on the statue of Shepherd; the laundresses were trapesing about; the porters were leaning against the railings; and the

clerks were playing at marbles, to my inexpressible consolation.

"You said you were going to dine at the Gray's-inn
Coffee-house," he said. I was. I often dine there. There
is excellent wine at the Gray's-inn Coffee-house; but I declare I NEVER SAID SO. I was not astonished at his remark; no more astonished than if I was in a dream. Perhaps I *was* in a dream. Is life a dream? Are dreams
facts? Is sleeping being really awake? I don't know. I
tell you I am puzzled. I have read "The Woman in
White," "The Strange Story"—not to mention that story
stranger than fiction in the *Cornhill Magazine*—that story
for which THREE credible witnesses are ready to vouch. I
have read that Article in the *Times* about Mr. Foster. I
have had messages from the dead; and not only from the
dead, but from people who never existed at all. I own I
am in a state of much bewilderment: but, if you please,
will proceed with my simple, my artless story.

Well, then. We passed from Shepherd's Inn into Holborn, and looked for a while at Woodgate's bric-à-brac
shop, which I never can pass without delaying at the windows—indeed, if I were going to be hung, I would beg the
cart to stop, and let me have one look more at that delightful *omnium gatherum*. And passing Woodgate's, we come
to Gale's little shop, No. 47, which is also a favourite
haunt of mine.

Mr. Gale happened to be at his door, and as we exchanged salutations, "Mr. Pinto," I said, "will you like
to see a real curiosity in this curiosity shop? Step into
Mr. Gale's little back room."

In that little back parlour there are Chinese gongs; there
are old Saxe and Sèvres plates; there is Fürstenberg, Carl.
Theodor, Worcester, Amstel, Nankin and other jimcrock-
ery. And in the corner what do you think there is?
There is an actual GUILLOTINE. If you doubt me, go
and see—Gale, High Holborn, No. 47. It is a slim instrument, much slighter than those which they make now;—
some nine feet high, narrow, a pretty piece of upholstery

enough. There is the hook over which the rope used to play which unloosened the dreadful axe above; and look! dropped into the orifice where the head used to go—there is THE AXE itself, all rusty, with A GREAT NOTCH IN THE BLADE.

As Pinto looked at it—Mr. Gale was not in the room, I recollect—happening to have been just called out by a customer who offered him three pound fourteen and sixpence for a blue Shepherd in *pâte tendre*,—Mr. Pinto gave a little start, and seemed *crispé* for a moment. Then he looked steadily towards one of those great porcelain stools which you see in gardens—and—it seemed to me—I tell you I won't take my affidavit—I may have been maddened by the six glasses I took of that pink elixir—I may have been sleep-walking: perhaps am as I write now—I may have been under the influence of that astounding MEDIUM into whose hands I had fallen—but I vow I heard Pinto say, with rather a ghastly grin at the porcelain stool,

> "Nay, nefer shague your gory locks at me,
> Dou canst not say I did it."

(He pronounced it, by the way, I *dit* it, by which I *know* that Pinto was a German.)

I heard Pinto say those very words, and sitting on the porcelain stool I saw, dimly at first, then with an awful distinctness—a ghost—an *eidolon*—a form—A HEADLESS MAN seated, with his head in his lap, which wore an expression of piteous surprise.

At this minute, Mr. Gale entered from the front shop to show a customer some delf plates; and he did not see—but *we did*—the figure rise up from the porcelain stool, shake its head, which it held in its hand, and which kept its eyes fixed sadly on us, and disappear behind the guillotine.

" Come to the Gray's-inn Coffee-house," Pinto said, "and I will tell you how *the notch came to the axe*." And we walked down Holborn at about thirty-seven minutes past six o'clock.

If there is anything in the above statement which astonishes the reader, I promise him that in the next chapter of this little story he will be astonished still more.

PART II.

" You will excuse me," I said to my companion, " for remarking, that when you addressed the—the individual sitting on the porcelain stool, with his head in his lap, your ordinarily benevolent features "—(this I confess was a bouncer, for between ourselves a more sinister and ill-looking rascal than Mons. P. I have seldom set eyes on)—" your ordinarily handsome face wore an expression that was by no means pleasing. You grinned at the individual just as you did at me when you went up to the cei——, pardon me, as I *thought* you did, when I fell down in a fit in your chambers ; " and I qualified my words in a great flutter and tremble ; I did not care to offend the man—I did not *dare* to offend the man. I thought once or twice of jumping into a cab, and flying ; of taking refuge in Day and Martin's Blacking Warehouse ; of speaking to a policeman, but not one would come. I was this man's slave. I followed him like his dog. I *could* not get away from him. So, you see, I went on meanly conversing with him, and affecting a simpering confidence. I remember, when I was a little boy at school, going up fawning and smiling in this way to some great hulking bully of a sixth-form boy. So I said in a word, " Your ordinarily handsome face wore a disagreeable expression," &c.

"It is ordinarily *very* handsome," said he, with such a leer at a couple of passers-by, that one of them cried, "Oh crikey, here's a precious guy !" and a child, in its nurse's arms, screamed itself into convulsions. " *Oh, oui, che suis très choli garçon, bien peau, cerdainement,*" continued Mr. Pinto ; " but you were right. That—that person was not very well pleased, when he saw me. There was no love lost between us, as you say ; and the world never knew a more worthless miscreant. I hate him, *voyez-vous?* I

hated him alife; I hate him dead. I hate him man; I
hate him ghost: and he know it, and tremble before me.
If I see him twenty tausend years hence—and why not?
—I shall hate him still. You remarked how he was
dressed?"

"In black satin breeches and striped stockings; a white
piqué waistcoat, a grey coat, with large metal buttons, and
his hair in powder. He must have worn a pigtail—
only——"

"Only it was *cut off!* Ha, ha, ha!" Mr. Pinto cried,
yelling a laugh, which, I observed, made the policemen
stare very much. "Yes. It was cut off by the same blow
which took off the scoundrel's head—ho, ho, ho!" And
he made a circle with his hook-nailed finger round his own
yellow neck, and grinned with a horrible triumph. "I
promise you that fellow was surprised when he found his
head in the pannier. Ha! ha! Do you ever cease to hate
those whom you hate?"—fire flashed terrifically from his
glass eye, as he spoke—"or to love dose whom you once
loved? Oh, never, never!" And here his natural eye was
bedewed with tears. "But here we are at the Gray's-inn
Coffee-house. James, what is the joint?"

That very respectful and efficient waiter brought in the
bill of fare, and I, for my part, chose boiled leg of pork
and pease-pudding, which my acquaintance said would do
as well as anything else; though I remarked he only trifled
with the pease-pudding, and left all the pork on the plate.
In fact, he scarcely ate anything. But he drank a prodigious quantity of wine; and I must say that my friend Mr.
Hart's port wine is so good that I myself took—well, I
should think I took three glasses. Yes, three, certainly.
He—I mean Mr. P.—the old rogue, was insatiable: for we
had to call for a second bottle in no time. When that was
gone, my companion wanted another. A little red mounted
up to his yellow cheeks as he drank the wine, and he
winked at it in a strange manner. "I remember," said he
musing, "when port wine was scarcely drunk in this country—though the Queen liked it, and so did Harley; but

Bolingbroke didn't—he drank Florence and champagne.
Dr. Swift put water to his wine. 'Jonathan,' I once said
to him—but bah! *autres temps, autres mœurs.* Another
magnum, James."

This was all very well. "My good sir," I said, "it may
suit *you* to order bottles of '20 port, at a guinea a bottle;
but that kind of price does not suit me. I only happen to
have thirty-four and sixpence in my pocket, of which I
want a shilling for the waiter, and eighteen-pence for my
cab. You rich foreigners and *swells* may spend what you
like" (I had him there: for my friend's dress was as
shabby as an old-clothes-man's); "but a man with a family, Mr. What-d'you-call'im, cannot afford to spend seven
or eight hundred a year on his dinner alone."

"Bah!" he said. "Nunkey pays for all, as you say.
I will what you call stant the dinner, if you are *so poor!*"
and again he gave that disagreeable grin, and placed an
odious crooked-nailed, and by no means clean finger to his
nose. But I was not so afraid of him now, for we were in
a public place; and the two half glasses of port wine had,
you see, given me courage.

"What a pretty snuff-box!" he remarked, as I handed
him mine, which I am still old-fashioned enough to carry.
It is a pretty old gold box enough, but valuable to me especially as a relic of an old, old relative, whom I can just
remember as a child, when she was very kind to me.
"Yes; a pretty box. I can remember when many ladies—
most ladies, carried a box—nay, two boxes—*tabatière* and
bonbonnière. What lady carries snuff-box now, hey? Suppose your astonishment if a lady in an assembly were to
offer you a *prise?* I can remember a lady with such a box
as this, with a *tour*, as we used to call it then; with *paniers*,
with a tortoise-shell cane, with the prettiest little high-
heeled velvet shoes in the world!—ah! that was a time,
that was a time! Ah, Eliza, Eliza, I have thee now in my
mind's eye! At Bungay on the Waveney, did I not walk
with thee, Eliza? Aha, did I not love thee? Did I not
walk with thee then? Do I not see thee still?"

This was passing strange.   My ancestress—but there is no need to publish her revered name—did indeed live at Bungay Saint Mary's, where she lies buried.   She used to walk with a tortoise-shell cane.   She used to wear little black velvet shoes, with the prettiest high heels in the world.

"Did you—did you—know, then, my great gr-ndm-ther?" I said.

He pulled up his coat-sleeve—"Is that her name?" he said.

"Eliza ——"

There, I declare, was the very name of the kind old creature written in red on his arm.

"*You* knew her old," he said, divining my thoughts (with his strange knack); "*I* knew her young and lovely. I danced with her at the Bury ball.   Did I not, dear, dear Miss ——?

As I live, he here mentioned dear gr-nny's *maiden* name. Her *maiden* name was ——   Her honoured married name was ——

"She married your great gr-ndf-th-r the year Poseidon won the Newmarket Plate," Mr. Pinto drily remarked.

Merciful powers! I remember, over the old shagreen knife and spoon case on the sideboard in my gr-nny's parlour, a print by Stubbs of that very horse.   My grandsire, in a red coat and his fair hair flowing over his shoulders, was over the mantelpiece, and Poseidon won the Newmarket Cup in the year 1783!

"Yes; you are right.   I danced a minuet with her at Bury that very night, before I lost my poor leg.   And I quarrelled with your grandf——, ha!"

As he said "Ha!" there came three quiet little taps on the table—it is the middle table in the Gray's-inn Coffeehouse, under the bust of the late Duke of W-ll-ngt-n.

"I fired in the air," he continued, "did I not?"   (Tap, tap, tap.)   "Your grandfather hit me in the leg.   He married three months afterwards.   'Captain Brown,' I said, 'who could see Miss Sm-th without loving her?'   She is there! She is there!" (Tap, tap, tap.) "Yes, my first love——"

But here there came tap, tap, which everybody knows means "No."

"I forgot," he said, with a faint blush stealing over his wan features, "she was not my first love. In Germ——in my own country—there *was* a young woman——"

Tap, tap, tap. There was here quite a lively little treble knock; and when the old man said, "But I loved thee better than all the world, Eliza," the affirmative signal was briskly repeated.

And this I declare UPON MY HONOUR. There was, I have said, a bottle of port wine before us—I should say a decanter. That decanter was LIFTED UP, and out of it into our respective glasses two bumpers of wine were poured. I appeal to Mr. Hart, the landlord—I appeal to James, the respectful and intelligent waiter, if this statement is not true? And when we had finished that magnum, and I said—for I did not now in the least doubt of her presence—"Dear gr-nny, may we have another magnum?"—the table *distinctly* rapped "No."

"Now, my good sir," Mr. Pinto said, who really began to be affected by the wine, "you understand the interest I have taken in you. I loved Eliza ——" (of course I don't mention family names). "I knew you had that box which belonged to her—I will give you what you like for that box. Name your price at once, and I pay you on the spot."

"Why, when we came out, you said you had not sixpence in your pocket."

"Bah! give you anything you like—fifty—a hundred—a tausend pound."

"Come, come," said I, "the gold of the box may be worth nine guineas, and the *façon* we will put at six more."

"One tausend guineas!" he screeched. "One tausend and fifty pound, dere!" and he sank back in his chair—no, by the way, on his bench, for he was sitting with his back to one of the partitions of the boxes, as I daresay James remembers.

K

"*Don't* go on in this way," I continued, rather weakly, for I did not know whether I was in a dream. "If you offer me a thousand guineas for this box I *must* take it. Mustn't I, dear gr-nny?"

The table most distinctly said, "Yes;" and putting out his claws to seize the box, Mr. Pinto plunged his hooked nose into it and eagerly inhaled some of my 47 with a dash of Hardman.

"But stay, you old harpy!" I exclaimed, being now in a sort of rage, and quite familiar with him. "Where is the money. Where is the check?"

"James, a piece of note-paper and a receipt stamp!"

"This is all mighty well, sir," I said, "but I don't know you; I never saw you before. I will trouble you to hand me that box back again, or give me a check with some known signature."

"Whose? Ha, HA, HA!"

The room happened to be very dark. Indeed, all the waiters were gone to supper, and there were only two gentlemen snoring in their respective boxes. I saw a hand come quivering down from the ceiling—a very pretty hand, on which was a ring with a coronet, with a lion rampant gules for a crest. *I saw that hand take a dip of ink and write across the paper.* Mr. Pinto then, taking a grey receipt stamp out of his blue leather pocket-book, fastened it on to the paper by the usual process; and the hand then wrote across the receipt stamp, went across the table and shook hands with Pinto, and then, as if waving him an adieu, vanished in the direction of the ceiling.

There was the paper before me, wet with the ink. There was the pen which THE HAND had used. Does anybody doubt me? *I have that pen now.* A cedar stick of a not uncommon sort, and holding one of Gillott's pens. It is in my inkstand now, I tell you. Anybody may see it. The handwriting on the cheque, for such the document was, was the writing of a female. It ran thus:—"London, midnight, March 31, 1862. Pay the bearer one thousand

and fifty pounds. Rachel Sidonia. To Messrs. Sidonia, Pozzosanto, and Co., London."

"Noblest and best of women!" said Pinto, kissing the sheet of paper with much reverence; "my good Mr. Roundabout, I suppose you do not question *that* signature?"

Indeed, the house of Sidonia, Pozzosanto, and Co. is known to be one of the richest in Europe, and as for the Countess Rachel, she was known to be the chief manager of that enormously wealthy establishment. There was only one little difficulty, *the Countess Rachel died last October*.

I pointed out this circumstance, and tossed over the paper to Pinto with a sneer.

" *C'est à brendre ou à laisser*," he said with some heat. "You literary men are all imbrudent; but I did not tink you such a fool *wie* dis. Your box is not worthy twenty pound, and I offer you a tausend because I know you want money to pay dat rascal Tom's college bills."   (This strange man actually knew that my scapegrace Tom has been a source of great expense and annoyance to me.)   "You see money costs me nothing, and you refuse to take it! Once, twice; will you take this cheque in exchange for your trumpery snuff-box?"

What could I do? My poor granny's legacy was valuable and dear to me, but after all a thousand guineas are not to be had every day. "Be it a bargain," said I. "Shall we have a glass of wine on it?" says Pinto; and to this proposal I also unwillingly acceded, reminding him, by the way, that he had not yet told me the story of the headless man.

"Your poor gr-ndm-ther was right just now, when she said she was not my first love. 'Twas one those *banales* expressions" (here Mr. P. blushed once more) "which we use to women. We tell each she is our first passion. They reply with a similar illusory formula. No man is any woman's first love; no woman any man's. We are in love in our nurses' arms, and women coquette with their eyes before their tongue can form a word. How could your

lovely relative love me? I was far, far too old for her. I
am older than I look. I am so old that you would not believe my age were I to tell you. I have loved many and
many a woman before your relative. It has not always
been fortunate for them to love me. Ah, Sophronia!
Round the dreadful circus where you fell, and whence I
was dragged corpse-like by the heels, there sate multitudes
more savage than the lions which mangled your sweet form!
Ah, tenez! when we marched to the terrible stake together
at Valladolid—the Protestant and the J———. But away
with memory! Boy! it was happy for thy grandam that
she loved me not.

"During that strange period," he went on, "when the
teeming Time was great with the revolution that was
speedily to be born, I was on a mission in Paris with my
excellent, my maligned friend, Cagliostro. Mesmer was
one of our band. · I seemed to occupy but an obscure rank
in it: though, as you know, in secret societies the humble
man may be a chief and director—the ostensible leader but
a puppet moved by unseen hands. Never mind who was
chief, or who was second. Never mind my age. It boots
not to tell it: why shall I expose myself to your scornful
incredulity—or reply to your questions in words that are
familiar to you, but which yet you cannot understand?
Words are symbols of things which you know, or of things
which you don't know. If you don't know them, to speak
is idle." (Here I confess Mr. P. spoke for exactly thirty-
eight minutes, about physics, metaphysics, language, the
origin and destiny of man, during which time I was rather
bored, and, to relieve my *ennui*, drank a half glass or so
of wine.) "LOVE, friend, is the fountain of youth! It
may not happen to me once—once in an age: but when I
love, then I am young. I loved when I was in Paris.
Bathilde, Bathilde, I loved thee—ah, how fondly! Wine,
I say, more wine! Love is ever young. I was a boy at
the little feet of Bathilde de Béchamel—the fair, the fond,
the fickle, ah, the false!" The strange old man's agony
was here really terrific, and he showed himself much more

agitated than he had been when speaking about my gr-nd-m-th-r.

"I thought Blanche might love me. I could speak to her in the language of all countries, and tell her the lore of all ages. I could trace the nursery legends which she loved up to their Sanscrit source, and whisper to her the darkling mysteries of Egyptian Magi. I could chant for her the wild chorus that rang in the dishevelled Eleusinian revel: I could tell her, and I would, the watchword never known but to one woman, the Saban queen, which Hiram breathed in the abysmal ear of Solomon.—You don't attend. Psha! you have drunk too much wine!" Perhaps I may as well own that I was *not* attending, for he had been carrying on for about fifty-seven minutes; and I don't like a man to have *all* the talk to himself.

"Blanche de Béchamel was wild, then, about this secret of Masonry. In early, early days I loved, I married a girl fair as Blanche, who, too, was tormented by curiosity, who, too, would peep into my closet—into the only secret I guarded from her. A dreadful fate befel poor Fatima. An *accident* shortened her life. Poor thing! she had a foolish sister who urged her on. I always told her to beware of Ann. She died. They said her brothers killed her. A gross falsehood. *Am* I dead? If I were, could I pledge you in this wine?"

"Was your name," I asked, quite bewildered, "was your name, pray, then, ever Blueb——"

"Hush! the waiter will overhear you. Methought we were speaking of Blanche de Béchamel. I loved her, young man. My pearls, and diamonds, and treasure, my wit, my wisdom, my passion, I flung them all into the child's lap. I was a fool! Was strong Sampson not as weak as I? Was Solomon the Wise much better when Balkis wheedled him? I said to the king—— But enough of that, I spake of Blanche de Béchamel.

"Curiosity was the poor child's foible. I could see, as I talked to her, that her thoughts were elsewhere (as yours, my friend, have been absent once or twice to-night). To know the secret of Masonry was the wretched child's mad desire. With a thousand wiles, smiles, caresses, she strove to coax it from me—from *me*—ha! ha!

"I had an apprentice—the son of a dear friend, who died by my side at Rossbach, when Soubise, with whose army I happened to be, suffered a dreadful defeat for neglecting my advice. The young Chevalier Goby de Mouchy was glad enough to serve as my clerk, and help in some chemical experiments in which I was engaged with my friend Dr. Mesmer. Bathilde saw this young man. Since women were, has it not been their business to smile and deceive, to fondle and lure? Away! From the very first it has been so!" And as my companion spoke, he looked as wicked as the serpent that coiled round the tree, and hissed a poisoned counsel to the first woman.

"One evening I went, as was my wont, to see Blanche. She was radiant: she was wild with spirits: a saucy triumph blazed in her blue eyes. She talked, she rattled in her childish way. She uttered, in the course of her rhapsody, a hint—an intimation—so terrible that the truth flashed across me in a moment. Did I ask her? She would lie to me. But I know how to make falsehood impossible. And I *ordered her to go to sleep.*"

At this moment the clock (after its previous convulsions) sounded TWELVE. And as the new Editor of the *Cornhill Magazine*—and *he*, I promise you, won't stand any nonsense—will only allow seven pages, I am obliged to leave off at THE VERY MOST INTERESTING POINT OF THE STORY.

PART III.

"ARE you of our fraternity? I see you are not. The secret which Mademoiselle de Béchamel confided to me in her mad triumph and wild hoyden spirits—she was but a child, poor thing, poor thing, scarce fifteen :—but I love them young—a folly not unusual with the old!" (Here Mr. Pinto thrust his knuckles into his hollow eyes; and, I am sorry to say, so little regardful was he of personal cleanliness, that his tears made streaks of white over his gnarled dark hands). "Ah, at fifteen, poor child, thy fate was terrible! Go to! It is not good to love me, friend. They prosper not who do. I divine you. You need not say what you are thinking——"

In truth, I was thinking, if girls fall in love with this sallow, hooked-nosed, glass-eyed, wooden-legged, dirty, hideous old man, with the sham teeth, they have a queer taste. *That* is what I was thinking.

"Jack Wilks said the handsomest man in London had but half an hour's start of him. And without vanity, I am scarcely uglier than Jack Wilks. We were members of the same club at Medenham Abbey, Jack and I, and had many a merry night together. Well, sir, I—Mary of Scotland knew me but as a little hunch-backed music-master; and yet, and yet, I think, *she* was not indifferent to her David Riz—— and *she* came to misfortune. They all do —they all do!"

"Sir, you are wandering from your point!" I said, with some severity. For, really, for this old humbug to hint that he had been the baboon who frightened the club at Medenham, that he had been in the Inquisition at Valladolid—that under the name of D. Riz, as he called it, he had known the lovely Queen of Scots—was a *little* too much. "Sir," then I said, "you were speaking about a Miss de Béchamel. I really have not time to hear all your biography."

"Faith, the good wine gets into my head." (I should think so, the old toper! Four bottles all but two glasses.) "To return to poor Blanche. As I sat laughing, joking with her, she let slip a word, a little word, which filled me with dismay. Some one had told her a part of the Secret —the secret which has been divulged scarce thrice in three thousand years—the Secret of the Freemasons. Do you know what happens to those uninitiate who learn that secret? to those wretched men the initiate who reveal it?"

As Pinto spoke to me, he looked through and through me with his horrible piercing glance, so that I sate quite uneasily on my bench. He continued: "Did I question her awake? I knew she would lie to me. Poor child! I loved her no less because I did not believe a word she said. I loved her blue eye, her golden hair, her delicious voice, that was true in song, though when she spoke, false as Eblis! You are aware that I possess in rather a remarkable degree what we have agreed to call the mesmeric power. I set the unhappy girl to sleep. *Then* she was obliged to tell me all. It was as I had surmised. Goby de Mouchy, my wretched, besotted, miserable secretary, in his visits to the château of the old Marquis de Béchamel, who was one of our society, had seen Blanche. I suppose it was because she had been warned that he was worthless, and poor, artful, and a coward, she loved him. She wormed out of the besotted wretch the secrets of our Order. 'Did he tell you the NUMBER ONE?' I asked.

"She said, 'Yes.'

"'Did he,' I further inquired, 'tell you the——'

"'Oh, don't ask me, don't ask me!' she said, writhing on the sofa, where she lay in the presence of the Marquis de Béchamel, her most unhappy father. Poor Béchamel, poor Béchamel! How pale he looked as I spoke! 'Did he tell you,' I repeated with a dreadful calm, 'the NUMBER TWO?' She said, 'Yes.'

"The poor old marquis rose up, and clasping his hands, fell on his knees before Count Cagl—— Bah! I went by a different name then. Vat's in a name? Dat vich ve call a Rosicrucian by any other name vil smell as sveet. 'Monsieur,' he said, 'I am old—I am rich. I have five hundred thousand livres of rentes in Picardy. I have half as much in Artois. I have two hundred and eighty thousand on the Grand Livre. I am promised by my sovereign a dukedom and his orders, with a reversion to my heir. I am a Grandee of Spain of the First Class, and Duke of Volovento. Take my titles, my ready money, my life, my honour, everything I have in the world, but don't ask the THIRD QUESTION.'

"'Godefroid de Bouillon, Comte de Béchamel, Grandee

of Spain and Prince of Volovento, in our Assembly what was the oath you swore?'" The old man writhed as he remembered its terrific purport.

"Though my heart was racked with agony, and I would have died, ay, cheerfully" (died, indeed, as if *that* were a penalty!) "to spare yonder lovely child a pang, I said to her calmly, 'Blanche de Béchamel, did Goby de Mouchy tell you secret NUMBER THREE?'

"She whispered a *oui* that was quite faint, faint and small. But her poor father fell in convulsions at her feet.

"She died suddenly that night. Did I not tell you these I love come to no good? When General Bonaparte crossed the Saint Bernard, he saw in the convent an old monk with a white beard, wandering about the corridors, cheerful and rather stout, but mad—mad as a March hare. 'General,' I said to him, 'did you ever see that face before?' He had not. He had not mingled much with the higher classes of our society before the Revolution. *I* knew the poor old man well enough; he was the last of a noble race, and I loved his child."

"And did she die by——?"

"Man! did I say so? Do I whisper the secrets of the Vehmgericht? I say she died that night; and he—he, the heartless, the villain, the betrayer,—you saw him seated in yonder curiosity-shop, by yonder guillotine, with his scoundrelly head in his lap.

"You saw how slight that instrument was? It was one of the first which Guillotin made, and which he showed to private friends in a *hangar* in the Rue Picpus, where he lived. The invention created some little conversation amongst scientific men at the time, though I remember a machine in Edinburgh of a very similar construction, two hundred—well, many, many years ago—and at a breakfast which Guillotin gave he showed us the instrument, and much talk arose amongst us as to whether people suffered under it.

"And now I must tell you what befel the traitor who had caused all this suffering. Did he know that the poor

child's death was A SENTENCE? He felt a cowardly satisfaction that with her was gone the secret of his treason.
Then he began to doubt. I had MEANS to penetrate all his
thoughts, as well as to know his acts. Then he became a
slave to a horrible fear. He fled in abject terror to a convent. They still existed in Paris; and behind the walls of
Jacobins the wretch thought himself secure. Poor fool!
I had but to set one of my somnambulists to sleep. Her
spirit went forth and spied the shuddering wretch in his
cell. She described the street, the gate, the convent, the
very dress which he wore, and which you saw to-day.

"And now *this* is what happened. In his chamber in
the Rue St. Honoré, at Paris, sat a man *alone*—a man who
has been maligned, a man who has been called a knave and
charlatan, a man who has been persecuted even to the
death, it is said, in Roman Inquisitions, forsooth, and elsewhere. Ha! ha! A man who has a mighty will.

"And looking towards the Jacobin Convent (of which,
from his chamber, he could see the spires and trees), this
man WILLED. And it was not yet dawn. And he willed;
and one who was lying in his cell in the Convent of
Jacobins, awake and shuddering with terror for a crime
which he had committed, fell asleep.

"But though he was asleep his eyes were open.

"And after tossing and writhing, and clinging to the
pallet, and saying, 'No, I will not go,' he rose up and
donned his clothes—a grey coat, a vest of white piqué,
black satin small-clothes, ribbed silk stockings, and a white
stock with a steel buckle; and he arranged his hair, and he
tied his queue, all the while being in that strange somno-
lence which walks, which moves, which FLIES sometimes,
which sees, which is indifferent to pain, which OBEYS.
And he put on his hat, and he went forth from his cell;
and though the dawn was not yet, he trod the corridors as
seeing them. And he passed into the cloister, and then
into the garden where lie the ancient dead. And he came
to the wicket, which Brother Jerome was opening just at
the dawning. And the crowd was already waiting with

their cans and bowls to receive the alms of the good brethren.

"And he passed through the crowd and went on his way through, and the few people then abroad who marked him, said, 'Tiens! How very odd he looks! He looks like a man walking in his sleep!' This was said by various persons:—

"By milk-women, with their cans and carts, coming into the town.

"By roysterers who had been drinking at the taverns of the Barrier, for it was Mid-Lent.

"By the serjeants of the watch, who eyed him sternly as he passed near their halberds.

"But he passed on unmoved by the halberds,

"Unmoved by the cries of the roysterers,

"By the market-women coming with their milk and eggs,

"He walked through the Rue St. Honoré, I say:—

"By the Rue Rambuteau,

"By the Rue St. Antoine,

"By the King's Château of the Bastille,

"By the Faubourg St. Antoine.

"And he came to No. 29 in the Rue Picpus—a house which then stood between a court and garden—

"That is, there was a building of one story, with a great coach-door.

"Then there was a court, around which were stables, coach-houses, offices.

"Then there was a house—a two-storied house, with a *perron* in front.

"Behind the house was a garden—a garden of two hundred and fifty French feet in length.

"And as one hundred feet of France equal one hundred and six feet of England, this garden, my friends, equalled exactly two hundred and sixty-five feet of British measure.

"In the centre of the garden was a fountain and a statue —or, to speak more correctly, two statues. One was recumbent—a man. Over him, sabre in hand, stood a woman.

"The man was Olofernes. The woman was Judith. From the head, from the trunk, the water gushed. It was the taste of the doctor;—was it not a droll of taste?

"At the end of the garden was the doctor's cabinet of study. My faith, a singular cabinet, and singular pictures!—

"Decapitation of Charles Premier at Vitehall.

"Decapitation of Montrose at Edimbourg.

"Decapitation of Cinq Mars. When I tell you that he was a man of a taste charming!

"Through this garden, by these statues, up these stairs, went the pale figure of him who, the porter said, knew the way of the house. He did. Turning neither right nor left, he seemed to walk *through* the statues, the obstacles, the flower-beds, the stairs, the door, the tables, the chairs.

"In the corner of the room was THAT INSTRUMENT which Guillotin had just invented and perfected. One day he was to lay his own head under his own axe. Peace be to his name! With him I deal not!

"In a frame of mahogany, neatly worked, was a board with a half-circle in it, over which another board fitted. Above was a heavy axe, which fell—you know how. It was held up by a rope, and when this rope was untied, or cut, the steel fell.

"To the story which I now have to relate you may give credence, or not, as you will. The sleeping man went up to that instrument.

"He laid his head in it, asleep.

"Asleep!

"He then took a little penknife out of the pocket of his white dimity waistcoat.

"He cut the rope, asleep!

"The axe descended on the head of the traitor and villain. The notch in it was made by the steel buckle of his stock, which was cut through.

"A strange legend has got abroad that after the deed was done, the figure rose, took the head from the basket, walked forth through the garden, and by the screaming porters at the gate, and went and laid itself down at the Morgue. But for this I will not vouch. Only of this be sure. 'There are more things in heaven and earth, Horatio, than are dreamed of in your philosophy.' More and more the light peeps through the chinks. Soon, amidst music ravishing, the curtain **will** rise, and the glorious scene be displayed. Adieu! Remember me. Ha! 'tis dawn," Pinto said. And he was gone.

I am ashamed to say that my first movement was to clutch the cheque which he had left with me, and which I was determined to present the very moment the bank opened. I know the importance of these things, and that men *change their mind* sometimes. I sprang through the streets to the great banking house of Manasseh in Duke-street. It seemed to me as if I actually flew as I walked. As the clock struck ten I was at the counter and laid down my cheque.

The gentleman who received it, who was one of the Hebrew persuasion, as were the other two hundred clerks of the establishment, having looked at the draft with terror in his countenance, then looked at me, then called to himself two of his fellow clerks, and queer it was to see all their aquiline beaks over the paper.

"Come, come!" said I, "don't keep me here all day. Hand me over the money, short, if you please!" for I was, you see, a little alarmed, and so determined to assume some extra bluster.

"Will you have the kindness to step into the parlour to the partners?" the clerk said, and I followed him.

"What, *again?*" shrieked a bald-headed, red-whiskered gentleman, whom I knew to be Mr. Manasseh. "Mr. Salathiel, this is too bad! Leave me with this gentleman, S." And the clerk disappeared.

"Sir," he said, "I know how you came by this; the Count de Pinto gave it you. It is too bad! I honour my parents; I honour *their* parents; I honour their bills! But this one of grandma's is too bad—it is, upon my word, now! She've been dead these five-and-thirty years. And this last four months she has left her burial-place and took to drawing on our 'ouse! It's too bad, grandma; it is too bad!" and he appealed to me, and tears actually trickled down his nose.

"Is it the Countess Sidonia's check or not?" I asked, haughtily.

"But, I tell you, she's dead! It's a shame!—it's a shame!—it is, grandmamma!" and he cried, and wiped his great nose in his yellow pocket-handkerchief. "Look year —will you take pounds instead of guineas? She's dead, I tell you! It's no go! Take the pounds—one tausand pound!—ten nice, neat, crisp hundred-pound notes, and go away vid you, do?"

"I will have my bond, sir, or nothing," I said; and I put on an attitude of resolution which I confess surprised even myself.

"Wery vell," he shrieked, with many oaths, "then you shall have noting—ha, ha, ha!—noting but a policeman! Mr. Abednego, call a policeman! Take that, you humbug and impostor!" and here, with an abundance of frightful language which I dare not repeat, the wealthy banker abused and defied me.

Au bout du compte, what was I to do, if a banker did not choose to honour a cheque drawn by his dead grandmother? I began to wish I had my snuff-box back. I began to think I was a fool for changing that little old-fashioned gold for this slip of strange paper.

Meanwhile the banker had passed from his fit of anger to a paroxysm of despair. He seemed to be addressing some person invisible, but in the room: "Look here, ma'am, you've really been coming it too strong. A hundred thousand in six months, and now a thousand more! The 'ouse can't stand it; it *won't* stand it, I say! What? Oh! mercy, mercy!"

As he uttered these words, A HAND fluttered over the table in the air! It was a female hand: that which I had seen the night before. That female hand took a pen from the green baize table, dipped it in a silver inkstand, and wrote on a quarter of a sheet of foolscap on the blotting-book, "How about the diamond robbery? If you do not pay, I will tell him where they are."

What diamonds? what robbery? what was this mystery? That will never be ascertained, for the wretched man's demeanour instantly changed. "Certainly, sir;—oh, certainly," he said, forcing a grin. "How will you have the money, sir? All right, Mr. Abednego. This way out."

"I hope I shall often see you again," I said; on which I own poor Manasseh gave a dreadful grin, and shot back into his parlour.

I ran home, clutching the ten delicious, crisp hundred pounds, and the dear little fifty which made up the account. I flew through the streets again. I got to my chambers. I bolted the outer doors. I sank back in my great chair, and slept. * * *

My first thing on waking was to feel for my money. Perdition! Where was I? Ha!—on the table before me was my grandmother's snuff-box, and by its side one of those awful—those admirable—sensation novels, which I had been reading, and which are full of delicious wonder.

But that the guillotine is still to be seen at Mr. Gale's, No. 47, High Holborn, I give you MY HONOUR. I suppose I was dreaming about it. I don't know. What is dreaming? What is life? Why shouldn't I sleep on the ceiling?—and am I sitting on it now, or on the floor? I am puzzled. But enough. If the fashion for sensation novels goes on, I tell you I will write one in fifty volumes. For the present, DIXI. But between ourselves, this Pinto, who fought at the Colosseum, who was nearly being roasted by the Inquisition, and sang duets at Holyrood, I am rather sorry to lose him after three little bits of Roundabout Papers. *Et vous?*

DE FINIBUS.

WHEN Swift was in love with Stella, and despatching
her a letter from London thrice a month by the Irish
packet, you may remember how he would begin letter No.
XXIII., we will say, on the very day when XXII. had been
sent away, stealing out of the coffee-house or the assembly
so as to be able to prattle with his dear; "never letting go
her kind hand, as it were," as some commentator or other
has said in speaking of the Dean and his amour.   When
Mr. Johnson, walking to Dodsley's, and touching the posts
in Pall Mall as he walked, forgot to pat the head of one of
them, he went back and imposed his hands on it,—im-
pelled I know not by what superstition.   I have this I
hope not dangerous mania too.   As soon as a piece of work
is out of hand, and before going to sleep, I like to begin
another: it may be to write only half a dozen lines: but
that is something towards Number the Next.   The printer's
boy has not yet reached Green Arbour Court with the copy.
Those people who were alive half an hour since, Pendennis,
Clive Newcome, and (what do you call him? what was the
name of the last hero?   I remember now!) Philip Firmin,
have hardly drunk their glass of wine, and the mammas
have only this minute got the children's cloaks on, and
have been bowed out of my premises—and here I come
back to the study again: *tamen usque recurro*.   How lonely
it looks now all these people are gone!   My dear good
friends, some folks are utterly tired of you, and say,
"What a poverty of friends the man has!   He is always
asking us to meet those Pendennises, Newcomes, and so
forth.   Why does he not introduce us to some new characters?   Why is he not thrilling like Twostars, learned and
profound like Threestars, exquisitely humorous and human
like Fourstars?   Why, finally, is he not somebody else?"
My good people, it is not only impossible to please you all,

but it is absurd to try. The dish which one man devours, another dislikes. Is the dinner of to-day not to your taste? Let us hope to-morrow's entertainment will be more agreeble. * * * I resume my original subject. What an odd, pleasant, humorous, melancholy feeling it is to sit in the study, alone and quiet, now all these people are gone who have been boarding and lodging with me for twenty months! They have interrupted my rest: they have plagued me at all sorts of minutes: they have thrust themselves upon me when I was ill, or wished to be idle, and I have growled out a "Be hanged to you, can't you leave me alone now?" Once or twice they have prevented my going out to dinner. Many and many a time they have prevented my coming home, because I knew they were there waiting in the study, and a plague take them! and I have left home and family, and gone to dine at the Club and told nobody where I went. They have bored me, those people. They have plagued me at all sorts of uncomfortable hours. They have made such a disturbance in my mind and house, that sometimes I have hardly known what was going on in my family, and scarcely have heard what my neighbour said to me. They are gone at last; and you would expect me to be at ease? Far from it. I should almost be glad if Woolcomb would walk in and talk to me; or Twysden reappear, take his place in that chair opposite me, and begin one of his tremendous stories.

Madmen, you know, see visions, hold conversations with, even draw the likeness of, people invisible to you and me. Is this making of people out of fancy madness? and are novel-writers at all entitled to strait-waistcoats? I often forget people's names in life; and in my own stories contritely own that I make dreadful blunders regarding them; but I declare, my dear sir, with respect to the personages introduced into your humble servant's fables, I know the people utterly—I know the sound of their voices. A gentleman came in to see me the other day, who was so like the picture of Philip Firmin in Mr. Walker's charming drawings in the *Cornhill Magazine* that he was quite a curiosity to me. The same eyes, beard, shoulders, just as you have seen them from month to month. Well, he is not like the Philip Firmin in my mind. Asleep, asleep in the grave, lies the bold, the generous, the reckless, the tender-hearted creature whom I have made to pass through those adventures which have just been brought to an end. It is years since I heard the laughter ringing, or saw the bright blue eyes. When I knew him both were young. I become young as I think of him. And this morning he was alive again in this room, ready to laugh, to fight, to weep. As I write, do you know, it is the grey of evening; the house is quiet; everybody is out; the room is getting a little dark, and I look rather wistfully up from the paper with perhaps ever so little fancy that HE MAY COME IN.——No? No movement. No grey shade, growing more palpable, out of which at last look the well-known eyes. No, the printer came and took him away with the last page of the proofs. And with the printer's boy did the whole cortège of ghosts flit away, invisible? Ha! stay! what is this? Angels and ministers of grace! The door opens, and a dark form—enters, bearing a black—a black suit of clothes. It is John. He says it is time to dress for dinner.

    *   *   *   *   *

Every man who has had his German tutor, and has been coached through the famous Faust of Goethe (thou wert my instructor, good old Weissenborn, and these eyes beheld the great master himself in dear little Weimar town!) has read those charming verses which are prefixed to the drama, in which the poet reverts to the time when his work was first composed, and recalls the friends now departed, who once listened to his song. The dear shadows rise up around him, he says; he lives in the past again. It is to-day which appears vague and visionary. We humbler writers cannot create Fausts, or raise up monumental works that shall endure for all ages; but our books are diaries, in which our own feelings must of necessity be set down. As we look to the page written last month, or ten years ago, we remember the day and its events; the child ill, may-hap, in the adjoining room, and the doubts and fears which racked the brain as it still pursued its work; the dear old friend who read the commencement of the tale, and whose gentle hand shall be laid in ours no more.   I own for my part that, in reading pages which this hand penned formerly, I often lose sight of the text under my eyes.   It is not the words I see; but that past day; that bygone page of life's history; that tragedy, comedy it may be, which our little home company was enacting; that merry-making which we shared; that funeral which we followed; that bitter, bitter grief which we buried.

And, such being the state of my mind, I pray gentle readers to deal kindly with their humble servant's manifold short-comings, blunders, and slips of memory.   As sure as I read a page of my own composition, I find a fault or two, half-a-dozen.   Jones is called Brown.   Brown, who is dead, is brought to life.   Aghast, and months after the number was printed, I saw that I had called Philip Firmin, Clive Newcome.   Now Clive Newcome is the hero of another story by the reader's most obedient writer.   The two men are as different, in my mind's eye, as—as Lord Palmerston and Mr. Disraeli let us say.   But there is that blunder at page 990, line 76, volume 84 of the *Cornhill Magazine*, and it is past mending; and I wish in my life I had made no worse blunders or errors than that which is hereby acknowledged.

Another Finis written.   Another mile-stone passed on this journey from birth to the next world!   Sure it is a subject for solemn cogitation.   Shall we continue this story-telling business and be voluble to the end of our age?   Will it not be presently time, O prattler, to hold your tongue, and let younger people speak?   I have a friend, a painter, who, like other persons who shall be nameless, is growing old.   He has never painted with such laborious finish as his works now show.   This master is still the most humble and diligent of scholars.   Of Art, his mistress, he is always an eager, reverent pupil.   In his calling, in yours, in mine, industry and humility will help and comfort us. A word with you. In a pretty large experience I have not found the men who write books superior in wit or learning to those who don't write at all. In regard of mere information, non-writers must often be superior to writers. You don't expect a lawyer in full practice to be conversant with all kinds of literature; he is too busy with his law; and so a writer is commonly too busy with his own books to be able to bestow attention on the works of other people. After a day's work (in which I have been depicting, let us say, the agonies of Louisa on parting with the Captain, or the atrocious behaviour of the wicked Marquis to Lady Emily) I march to the Club, proposing to improve my mind and keep myself "posted up," as the Americans phrase it, with the literature of the day. And what happens? Given a walk after luncheon, a pleasing book, and a most comfortable arm-chair by the fire, and you know the rest. A doze ensues. Pleasing book drops suddenly, is picked up once with an air of some confusion, is laid presently softly in lap: head falls on comfortable arm-chair cushion: eyes close: soft nasal music is heard. Am I telling Club secrets? Of afternoons, after lunch, I say, scores of sensible fogies have a doze. Perhaps I have fallen asleep over that very book to which "Finis" has just been written. And if the writer sleeps, what happens to the readers? says Jones, coming down upon me with his lightning wit. What? You *did* sleep over it? And a very good thing too. These eyes have more than once seen a friend dozing over pages which this hand has written. There is a vignette somewhere in one of my books of a friend so caught napping with "Pendennis," or the "Newcomes," in his lap; and if a writer can give you a sweet soothing, harmless sleep, has he not done you a kindness? So is the author who excites and interests you worthy of your thanks and benedictions. I am troubled with fever and ague, that seizes me at odd intervals and prostrates me for a day. There is cold fit, for which, I am thankful to say, hot brandy-and-water is prescribed, and this induces hot fit, and so on. In one or two of these fits I have read novels with the most fearful contentment of mind. Once, on the Mississippi, it was my dearly beloved "Jacob Faithful:" once at Frankfort O.M., the delightful "Vingt Ans Après" of Monsieur Dumas: once at Tonbridge Wells, the thrilling "Woman in White:" and these books gave me amusement from morning till sunset. I remember those ague fits with a great deal of pleasure and gratitude. Think of a whole day in bed, and a good novel for a companion! No cares: no remorse about idleness: no visitors: and the Woman in White or the Chevalier d'Artagnan to tell me stories from dawn to night! "Please, ma'am, my master's compliments, and can he have the third volume?" (This message was sent to an astonished friend and neighbour who lent me, volume by volume, the "W. in W.") How do you like your novels? I like mine strong, "hot with," and no mistake: no love-making: no observations about society: little dialogue, except where the characters are bullying each other: plenty of fighting: and a villain in the cupboard, who is to suffer tortures just before Finis. I don't like your melancholy Finis. I never read the history of a consumptive heroine twice. If I might give a short hint to an impartial writer (as the *Examiner* used to say in old days), it would be to act, *not* à la mode le pays de Pole (I think that was the phraseology), but *always* to give quarter. In the story of Philip, just come to an end, I have the permission of the author to state that he was going to drown the two villains of the piece—a certain Doctor F—— and a certain Mr. T. H—— on board the *President*, or some other tragic ship—but you see I relented. I pictured to myself Firmin's ghastly face amid the crowd of shuddering people on that reeling deck in the lonely ocean, and thought, "Thou ghastly lying wretch, thou shalt not be drowned: thou shalt have a fever only; a knowledge of thy danger; and a chance—ever so small a chance—of repentance." I wonder whether he *did* repent when he found himself in the yellow-fever, in Virginia? The probability is, he fancied

that his son had injured him very much, and forgave him
on his deathbed. Do you imagine there is a great deal of
genuine right-down remorse in the world? Don't people
rather find excuses which make their minds easy; endeavour to prove to themselves that they have been lamentably belied and misunderstood; and try and forgive
the persecutors who *will* present that bill when it is due;
and not bear malice against the cruel ruffian who takes
them to the police-office for stealing the spoons? Years
ago I had a quarrel with a certain well-known person (I
believed a statement regarding him which his friends imparted to me, and which turned out to be quite incorrect).
To his dying day that quarrel was never quite made up. I
said to his brother, "Why is your brother's soul still dark
against me? It is I who ought to be angry and unforgiv-
ing: for I was in the wrong." In the region which they
now inhabit (for Finis has been set to the volumes of the
lives of both here below), if they take any cognizance of
our squabbles, and tittle-tattles, and gossips on earth here,
I hope they admit that my little error was not of a nature
unpardonable. If you have never committed a worse, my
good sir, surely the score against you will not be heavy.
Ha, *dilectissimi fratres!* It is in regard of sins *not* found
out that we may say or sing (in an under-tone, in a most
penitent and lugubrious minor key), *Miserere nobis miseris
peccatoribus.*

Among the sins of commission which novel-writers not
seldom perpetrate, is the sin of grandiloquence, or tall-talk-
ing, against which, for my part, I will offer up a special
libera me. This is the sin of schoolmasters, governesses,
critics, sermoners, and instructors of young or old people.
Nay (for I am making a clean breast, and liberating my
soul), perhaps of all the novel-spinners now extant, the
present speaker is the most addicted to preaching. Does
he not stop perpetually in his story and begin to preach to
you? When he ought to be engaged with business, is he
not forever taking the Muse by the sleeve, and plaguing
her with some of his cynical sermons? I cry *peccavi*

loudly and heartily. I tell you I would like to be able to write a story which should show no egotism whatever—in which there should be no reflections, no cynicism, no vulgarity (and so forth), but an incident in every other page, a villain, a battle, a mystery in every chapter. I should like to be able to feed a reader so spicily as to leave him hungering and thirsting for more at the end of every monthly meal.

Alexandre Dumas describes himself, when inventing the plan of a work, as lying silent on his back for two whole days on the deck of a yacht in a Mediterranean port. At the end of the two days he arose, and called for dinner. In those two days he had built his plot. He had moulded a mighty clay, to be cast presently in perennial brass. The chapters, the characters, the incidents, the combinations were all arranged in the artist's brain ere he set a pen to paper. My Pegasus won't fly, so as to let me survey the field below me. He has no wings, he is blind of one eye certainly, he is restive, stubborn, slow; crops a hedge when he ought to be galloping, or gallops when he ought to be quiet. He never will show off when I want him. Sometimes he goes at a pace which surprises me. Sometimes, when I most wish him to make the running, the brute turns restive, and I am obliged to let him take his own time. I wonder do other novel-writers experience this fatalism? They *must* go a certain way, in spite of themselves. I have been surprised at the observations made by some of my characters. It seems as if an occult Power was moving the pen. The personage does or says something, and I ask, how the Dickens did he come to think of that? Every man has remarked in dreams, the vast dramatic power which is sometimes evinced; I won't say the surprising power, for nothing does surprise you in dreams. But those strange characters you meet make instant observations of which you never can have thought previously. In like manner, the imagination foretells things. We spake anon of the inflated style of some writers. What also if there is an *afflated* style,—when a writer is like a Pythoness on her oracle tripod, and mighty words, words which he cannot help, come blowing, and bellowing, and whistling, and moaning through the speaking pipes of his bodily organ? I have told you it was a very queer shock to me the other day when, with a letter of introduction in his hand, the artist's (not my) Philip Firmin walked into this room, and sat down in the chair opposite. In the novel of "Pendennis," written ten years ago, there is an account of a certain Costigan, whom I had invented (as I suppose authors invent their personages out of scraps, heel-taps, odds and ends of characters). I was smoking in a tavern parlour one night—and this Costigan came into the room alive—the very man :—the most remarkable resemblance of the printed sketches of the man, of the rude drawings in which I had depicted him. He had the same little coat, the same battered hat, cocked on one eye, the same twinkle in that eye. "Sir," said I, knowing him to be an old friend whom I had met in unknown regions, "sir," I said, "may I offer you a glass of brandy-and-water?" "*Bedad, ye may*," says he, "*and I'll sing ye a song tu.*" Of course he spoke with an Irish brogue. Of course he had been in the army. In ten minutes he pulled out an army agent's account, whereon his name was written. A few months after we read of him in a police court. How had I come to know him, to divine him? Nothing shall convince me that I have not seen that man in the world of spirits. In the world of spirits and water I know I did: but that is a mere quibble of words. I was not surprised when he spoke in an Irish brogue. I had had cognizance of him before somehow. Who has not felt that little shock which arises when a person, a place, some words in a book (there is always a collocation) present themselves to you, and you know that you have before met the same person, words, scene, and so forth?

They used to call the good Sir Walter the "Wizard of the North." What if some writer should appear who can write so *enchantingly* that he shall be able to call into actual life the people whom he invents? What if Mignon, and Margaret, and Goetz von Berlichingen are alive now (though I don't say they are visible), and Dugald Dalgetty and Ivanhoe were to step in at that open window by the little garden yonder? Suppose Uncas and our noble old Leather Stocking were to glide silent in? Suppose Athos, Porthos, and Aramis should enter with a noiseless swagger, curling their mustachios? And dearest Amelia Booth, on Uncle Toby's arm; and Tittlebat Titmouse, with his hair dyed green; and all the Crummles company of comedians, with the Gil Blas troop; and Sir Roger de Coverley; and the greatest of all crazy gentlemen, the Knight of La Mancha, with his blessed squire? I say to you, I look rather wistfully towards the window, musing upon these people. Were any of them to enter, I think I should not be very much frightened. Dear old friends, what pleasant hours I have had with them! We do not see each other very often, but when we do, we are ever happy to meet. I had a capital half hour with Jacob Faithful last night; when the last sheet was corrected, when "Finis" had been written, and the printer's boy, with the copy, was safe in Green Arbour Court.

So you are gone, little printer's boy, with the last scratches and corrections on the proof, and a fine flourish by way of Finis at the story's end. The last corrections? I say those last corrections seem never to be finished. A plague upon the weeds! Every day, when I walk in my own little literary garden-plot, I spy some, and should like to have a spud, and root them out. Those idle words, neighbour, are past remedy. That turning back to the old pages produces anything but elation of mind. Would you not pay a pretty fine to be able to cancel some of them? Oh, the sad old pages, the dull old pages! Oh, the cares, the *ennui*, the squabbles, the repetitions, the old conversations over and over again! But now and again a kind thought is recalled, and now and again a dear memory. Yet a few chapters more, and then the last: after which, behold Finis itself come to an end, and the Infinite begun.

L

ON A PEAL OF BELLS.

As some bells in a church hard by are making a great
holiday clanging in the summer afternoon, I am reminded
somehow of a July day, a garden, and a great clanging of
bells years and years ago, on the very day when George
IV. was crowned. I remember a little boy lying in that
garden, reading his first novel. It was called the "Scottish Chiefs." The little boy (who is now ancient and not
little) read this book in the summer-house of his great
grandmamma. She was eighty years of age then. A most
lovely and picturesque old lady, with a long tortoiseshell
cane, with a little puff, or *tour*, of snow white (or was it
powdered?) hair under her cap, with the prettiest little
black velvet slippers and high heels you ever saw. She
had a grandson, a lieutenant in the navy; son of her son,
a captain in the navy; grandson of her husband, a captain
in the navy. She lived for scores and scores of years in a
dear little old Hampshire town inhabited by the wives,
widows, daughters of navy captains, admirals, lieutenants.
Dear me! Don't I remember Mrs. Duval, widow of Admiral Duval; and the Miss Dennets at the Great House at the
other end of the town, Admiral Dennet's daughters; and
the Miss Barrys, the late Captain Barry's daughters; and
the good old Miss Maskews, Admiral Maskews' daughter;
and that dear little Miss Norval, and the kind Miss Book-
ers, one of whom married Captain, now Admiral, Sir Henry
Excellent, K.C.B.? Far, far away into the past I look
and seek the little town with its friendly glimmer. That
town was so like a novel of Miss Austen's that I wonder
was she born and bred there? No, we should have known,
and the good old ladies would have pronounced her to be a
little idle thing, occupied with her silly books and neglecting her housekeeping. There were other towns in England,

no doubt, where dwelt the widows and wives of other navy captains, where they tattled, loved each other, and quarrelled; talked about Betty, the maid, and her fine ribbons, indeed! Took their dish of tea at six, played at quadrille every night till ten, when there was a little bit of supper, after which Betty came with the lanthorn; and next day came, and next, and next, and so forth, until a day arrived when the lanthorn was out, when Betty came no more; all that little company sank to rest under the daisies, whither some folks will presently follow them. How did they live to be so old, those good people? *Moi qui vous parle*, I perfectly recollect old Mr. Gilbert, who had been to sea with Captain Cook; and Captain Cook, as you justly observe, dear miss, quoting out of your "Mangnall's Questions," was murdered by the natives of Owhyhee, anno 1779. Ah! don't you remember his picture, standing on the seashore, in tights and gaiters, with a musket in his hand, pointing to his people not to fire from the boats, whilst a great tattooed savage is going to stab him in the back? Don't you remember those houris dancing before him and the other officers at the great Otaheite ball? Don't you know that Cook was at the siege of Quebec, with the glorious Wolfe, who fought under the Duke of Cumberland, whose royal father was a distinguished officer at Ramillies, before he commanded in chief at Dettingen? Huzzay! Give it them, my lads! My horse is down? Then I know I shall not run away. Do the French run? then I die content. Stop. Wo! *Quo me rapis?* My Pegasus is galloping off, goodness knows where, like his Majesty's charger at Dettingen.

How do these rich historical and personal reminiscences come out of the subject at present in hand? What *is* that subject, by the way? My dear friend, if you look at the last essaykin (though you may leave it alone, and I shall not be in the least surprised or offended), if you look at the last paper where the writer imagines Athos and Porthos, Dalgetty and Ivanhoe, Amelia and Sir Charles Grandison, Don Quixote and Sir Roger, walking in at the garden-window, you will at once perceive that Novels and their heroes and heroines are our present subject of discourse, into which we will presently plunge. Are you one of us, dear sir, and do you love novel-reading? To be reminded of your first novel will surely be a pleasure to you. Hush! I never read quite to the end of my first, the "Scottish Chiefs." I couldn't. I peeped in an alarmed furtive manner at some of the closing pages. Miss Porter, like a kind dear tender-hearted creature, would not have Wallace's head chopped off at the end of Vol. V. She made him die in prison,* and if I remember right (protesting I have not read the book for forty-two or three years), Robert Bruce made a speech to his soldiers, in which he said, "And Bannockburn shall equal Cambuskenneth." † But I repeat, I could not read the end of the fifth volume of that dear delightful book for crying. Good heavens! It was as sad, as sad as going back to school.

The glorious Scott cycle of romances came to me some four or five years afterwards; and I think boys of our year were specially fortunate in coming upon those delightful books at that special time when we could best enjoy them.

---

* I find, on reference to the novel, that Sir William died on the scaffold, not in prison. His last words were, "' My prayer is heard. Life's cord is cut by heaven. Helen! Helen! May heaven preserve my country, and——' He stopped. He fell. And with that mighty shock the scaffold shook to its foundation."

·† The remark of Bruce (which I protest I had not read for forty-two years), I find to be as follows:—" When this was uttered by the English heralds, Bruce turned to Ruthven, with an heroic smile. ' Let him come, my brave barons! and he shall find that Bannockburn shall page with Cambuskenneth!'" In the same amiable author's famous novel of "Thaddeus of Warsaw," there is more crying than in any novel I ever remember to have read. See, for example, the last page. * * * "Incapable of speaking, Thaddeus led his wife back to her carriage. * * * His tears gushed out in spite of himself, and mingling with hers, poured those thanks, those assurances, of animated approbation through her heart, which made it even ache with excess of happiness." * * * And a sentence or two further, "Kosciusko did bless him, and embalmed the benediction with a shower of tears."

Oh, that sunshiny bench on half-holidays, with Claver-house or Ivanhoe for a companion! I have remarked of very late days some little men in a great state of delecta-tion over the romances of Captain Mayne Reid, and Gus-tave Aimard's Prairie and Indian Stories, and during occa-sional holiday visits, lurking off to bed with the volume under their arms. But are those Indians and warriors so terrible as *our* Indians and warriors were? (I say, are they? Young gentlemen, mind, I do not say they are not.) But as an oldster I can be heartily thankful for the novels of the 1–10 Geo. IV., let us say, and so downward to a period not unremote. Let us see; there is, first, our dear Scott. Whom do I love in the works of that dear old master? Amo—

The Baron of Bradwardine, and Fergus. (Captain Wa-verley is certainly very mild.)

Amo Ivanhoe; LOCKSLEY; the Templar.

Amo Quentin Durward, and specially Quentin's uncle, who brought the Boar to bay. I forget the gentleman's name.

I have never cared for the Master of Ravenswood, or fetched his hat out of the water since he dropped it there when I last met him (circa 1825).

Amo SALADIN and the Scotch knight in the "Talisman." The Sultan best.

Amo CLAVERHOUSE.

Amo MAJOR DALGETTY. Delightful major! To think of him is to desire to jump up, run to the book, and get the volume down from the shelf. About all those heroes of Scott, what a manly bloom there is, and honourable modesty! They are not at all heroic. They seem to blush somehow in their position of hero, and as it were to say, "Since it must be done, here goes!" They are handsome, modest, upright, simple, courageous, not too clever. If I were a mother (which is absurd), I should like to be mother-in-law to several young men of the Walter-Scott-hero sort.

Much as I like those most unassuming, manly, unpre-

tending gentlemen, I have to own that I think the heroes
of another writer, viz.

LEATHER-STOCKING,

UNCAS,

HARDHEART,

TOM COFFIN,

are quite the equals of Scott's men; perhaps Leather-stocking is better than any one in "Scott's lot." *La Longue
Carabine* is one of the great prize-men of fiction. He
ranks with your Uncle Toby, Sir Roger de Coverley, Falstaff—heroic figures, all—American or British, and the
artist has deserved well of his country who devised them.

At school, in my time, there was a public day, when the
boys' relatives, an examining bigwig or two from the uni-
versities, old school-fellows, and so forth, came to the
place. The boys were all paraded; prizes were adminis-
tered; each lad being in a new suit of clothes—and magnificent dandies, I promise you, some of us were. Oh, the
chubby cheeks, clean collars, glossy new raiment, beaming
faces, glorious in youth—*fit tueri cœlum*—bright with
truth, and mirth, and honour! To see a hundred boys
marshalled in a chapel or old hall; to hear their sweet
fresh voices when they chant, and look in their brave calm
faces; I say, does not the sight and sound of them smite
you, somehow, with a pang of exquisite kindness? * * *
Well. As about boys, so about Novelists. I fancy the
boys of Parnassus School all paraded. I am a lower boy
myself in that academy. I like our fellows to look well,
upright, gentlemanlike. There is Master Fielding—he
with the black eye. What a magnificent build of a boy!
There is Master Scott, one of the heads of the school. Did
you ever see the fellow more hearty and manly? Yonder
lean, shambling, cadaverous lad, who is always borrowing
money, telling lies, leering after the housemaids, is Master
Laurence Sterne—a bishop's grandson, and himself intended for the Church; for shame, you little reprobate!
But what a genius the fellow has! Let him have a sound
flogging, and as soon as the young scamp is out of the

whipping-room, give him a gold medal.   Such would be my practice if I were Doctor Birch, and master of the school.

Let us drop this school metaphor, this birch and all pertaining thereto.   Our subject, I beg leave to remind the reader's humble servant, is novel heroes and heroines. How do you like your heroes, ladies? Gentlemen, what novel heroines do you prefer?   When I set this essay going, I sent the above question to two of the most inveterate novel-readers of my acquaintance.   The gentleman refers me to Miss Austen; the lady says Athos, Guy Livingston, and (pardon my rosy blushes) Colonel Esmond, and owns that in youth she was very much in love with Valancourt.

Valancourt, and who was he? cry the young people. Valancourt, my dears, was the hero of one of the most famous romances which ever was published in this country.   The beauty and elegance of Valancourt made your young grandmammas' gentle hearts to beat with respectful sympathy.   He and his glory have passed away.   Ah, woe is me that the glory of novels should ever decay; that dust should gather round them on the shelves; that the annual cheques from Messieurs the publishers should dwindle, dwindle!   Inquire at Mudie's, or the London Library, who asks for the "Mysteries of Udolpho" now? Have not even the "Mysteries of Paris" ceased to frighten? Alas, our novels are but for a season; and I know characters whom a painful modesty forbids me to mention, who shall go to limbo along with Valancourt and Doricourt, and Thaddeus of Warsaw.

A dear old sentimental friend, with whom I discoursed on the subject of novels yesterday, said that her favourite hero was Lord Orville, in "Evelina," that novel which Doctor Johnson loved so.   I took down the book from a dusty old crypt at a club, where Mrs. Barbauld's novelists repose: and this is the kind of thing, ladies and gentlemen, in which your ancestors found pleasure:—

"And here, whilst I was looking for the books, I was

followed by Lord Orville. He shut the door after he came in, and, approaching me with a look of anxiety, said, ' Is this true, Miss Anville—are you going?'

"' I believe so, my lord,' said I, still looking for the books.

"' So suddenly, so unexpectedly: must I lose you?'

"' No great loss, my lord,' said I, endeavouring to speak cheerfully.

"' Is it possible,' said he, gravely, ' Miss Anville can doubt my sincerity?'

"' I can't imagine,' cried I, ' what Mrs. Selwyn has done with those books.'

"' Would to heaven,' continued he, ' I might flatter myself you would allow me to prove it!'

"' I must run upstairs,' cried I, greatly confused, ' and ask what she has done with them.'

"' You are going then,' cried he, taking my hand, ' and you give me not the smallest hope of any return! Will you not, my too lovely friend, will you not teach me, with fortitude like your own, to support your absence?'

"' My lord,' cried I, endeavouring to disengage my hand, ' pray let me go!'

"' I will,' cried he, to my inexpressible confusion, dropping on one knee, ' if you wish me to leave you.'

"' Oh, my lord,' exclaimed I, ' rise, I beseech you; rise. Surely your lordship is not so cruel as to mock me.'

"' Mock you!' repeated he earnestly, ' no, I revere you. I esteem and admire you above all human beings! You are the friend to whom my soul is attached, as to its better half. You are the most amiable, the most perfect of women; and you are dearer to me than language has the power of telling.'

"I attempt not to describe my sensations at that moment; I scarce breathed; I doubted if I existed; the blood forsook my cheeks, and my feet refused to sustain me. Lord Orville hastily rising supported me to a chair upon which I sank almost lifeless.

"I cannot write the scene that followed, though every

word is engraven on my heart; but his protestations, his expressions, were too flattering for repetition; nor would he, in spite of my repeated efforts to leave him, suffer me to escape; in short, my dear sir, I was not proof against his solicitations, and he drew from me the most sacred secret of my heart! " *

Other people may not much like this extract, madam, from your favourite novel, but when you come to read it, *you* will like it. I suspect that when you read that book which you so love, you read it à deux. Did you not yourself pass a winter at Bath, when you were the belle of the assembly? Was there not a Lord Orville in your case too? As you think of him eleven lustres pass away. You look at him with the bright eyes of those days, and your hero stands before you, the brave, the accomplished,

---

* Contrast this old perfumed, powdered D'Arblay conversation with the present modern talk. If the two young people wished to hide their emotions now-a-days, and express themselves in modest language, the story would run:—

"Whilst I was looking for the books, Lord Orville came in. He looked uncommonly down in the mouth, as he said: 'Is this true, Miss Anville; are you going to cut?'

"'To absquatulate, Lord Orville,' said I, still pretending that I was looking for the books.

"'You're very quick about it,' said he.

"'Guess it's no great loss,' I remarked, as cheerfully as I could.

"'You don't think I'm chaffing?' said Orville, with much emotion.

"'What has Mrs. Selwyn done with the books?' I went on.

"'What, going?' said he, 'and going for good? I wish I was such a good-plucked one as you, Miss Anville,'" &c.

The conversation, you perceive, might be easily written down to this key; and if the hero and heroine were modern, they would not be suffered to go through their dialogue on stilts, but would converse in the natural graceful way at present customary. By the way, what a strange custom that is in modern lady novelists to make the men bully the women! In the time of Miss Porter and Madame D'Arblay, we have respect, profound bows and curtsies, graceful courtesy from men to women. In the time of Miss Brontë, absolute rudeness. Is it true, mesdames, that you like rudeness, and are pleased at being ill-used by men? I could point to more than one lady novelist who so represents you.

the simple, the true gentleman; and he makes the most elegant of bows to one of the most beautiful young women the world ever saw; and he leads you out to the cotillon, to the dear, unforgotten music. Hark to the horns of Elfland, blowing, blowing! *Bonne vieille*, you remember their melody, and your heart-strings thrill with it still.

Of your heroic heroes, I think our friend Monsigneur Athos, Count de la Fère, is my favourite. I have read about him from sunrise to sunset with the utmost contentment of mind. He has passed through how many volumes? Forty? Fifty? I wish for my part there were a hundred more, and would never tire of him rescuing prisoners, punishing ruffians, and running scoundrels through the midriff with his most graceful rapier. Ah, Athos, Porthos, and Aramis, you are a magnificent trio. I think I like d'Artagnan in his own memoirs best. I bought him years and years ago, price fivepence, in a little parchment-covered Cologne printed volume, at a stall in Gray's-inn-lane. Dumas glorifies him and makes a marshal of him; if I remember rightly, the original d'Artagnan was a needy adventurer, who died in exile very early in Louis XIV.'s reign. Did you ever read the "Chevalier d'Harmenthal"? Did you ever read the "Tulipe Noire," as modest as a story by Miss Edgeworth? I think of the prodigal banquets to which this Lucullus of a man has invited me, with thanks and wonder. To what a series of splendid entertainments he has treated me! Where does he find the money for these prodigious feasts? They say that all the works bearing Dumas's name are not written by him. Well? Does not the chief cook have *aides* under him? Did not Rubens's pupils paint on his canvases? Had not Lawrence assistants for his backgrounds? For myself, being also *du métier*, I confess I would often like to have a competent, respectable, and rapid clerk for the business part of my novels; and on his arrival, at eleven o'clock, would say, "Mr. Jones, if you please, the archbishop must die this morning in about five pages. Turn to article 'Dropsy' (or what you will) in Encyclopædia. Take care there are no medical blunders in his death. Group his daughters, physicians, and chaplains round him. In Wales' 'London,' letter B, third shelf, you will find an account of Lambeth, and some prints of the place. Colour in with local colouring. The daughter will come down, and speak to her lover in his wherry at Lambeth Stairs," &c. &c. Jones (an intelligent young man) examines the medical, historical, topographical books necessary; his chief points out to him in Jeremy Taylor (fol., London, MDCLV.) a few remarks, such as might befit a dear old archbishop departing this life. When I come back to dress for dinner, the archbishop is dead on my table in five pages; medicine, topography, theology, all right, and Jones has gone home to his family some hours. Sir Christopher is the architect of St. Paul's. He has not laid the stones or carried up the mortar. There is a great deal of carpenter's and joiner's work in novels which surely a smart professional hand might supply. A smart professional hand? I give you my word, there seem to me parts of novels—let us say the love-making, the "business," the villain in the cupboard, and so forth, which I should like to order John Footman to take in hand, as I desire him to bring the coals and polish the boots. Ask *me* indeed to pop a robber under a bed, to hide a will which shall be forthcoming in due season, or at my time of life to write a namby-pamby love conversation between Emily and Lord Arthur! I feel ashamed of myself, and especially when my business obliges me to do the love passages, I blush so, though quite alone in my study, that you would fancy I was going off in an apoplexy. Are authors affected by their own works? I don't know about other gentlemen, but if I make a joke myself I cry; if I write a pathetic scene I am laughing wildly all the time—at least Tomkins thinks so. You know I am such a cynic!

The editor of the *Cornhill Magazine* (no soft and yielding character like his predecessor, but a man of stern resolution) will only allow these harmless papers to run to a certain length. But for this veto I should gladly have prattled over half a sheet more, and have discoursed on many heroes and heroines of novels whom fond memory brings back to me. Of these books I have been a diligent student from those early days, which are recorded at the commencement of this little essay. Oh, delightful novels, well remembered! Oh, novels, sweet and delicious as the raspberry open-tarts of budding boyhood! Do I forget one night after prayers (when we under-boys were sent to bed) lingering at my cupboard to read one little half page more of my dear Walter Scott—and down came the monitor's dictionary upon my head! Rebecca, daughter of Isaac of York, I have loved thee faithfully for forty years! Thou wert twenty years old (say) and I but twelve, when I knew thee. At sixty odd, love, most of the ladies of thy Orient race have lost the bloom of youth, and bulged beyond the line of beauty; but to me thou art ever young and fair, and I will do battle with any felon Templar who assails thy fair name.

ON A PEAR-TREE.

A GRACIOUS reader no doubt has remarked that these humble sermons have for subjects some little event which happens at the preacher's own gate, or which falls under his peculiar cognizance. Once, you may remember, we discoursed about a chalk-mark on the door. This morning Betsy, the housemaid, comes with a frightened look, and says, " Law, mum! there's three bricks taken out of the garden-wall, and the branches broke, and all the pears taken off the pear-tree!" Poor peaceful suburban pear-tree! Gaol-birds have hopped about thy branches, and robbed them of their smoky fruit. But those bricks removed; that ladder evidently prepared, by which unknown marauders may enter and depart from my little Englishman's castle; is not this a subject of thrilling interest, and may it not *be continued in a future number?*—that is the terrible question. Suppose, having escaladed the outer wall, the miscreants take a fancy to storm the castle? Well—well! we are armed; we are numerous; we are men of tremendous courage, who will defend our spoons with our lives; and there are barracks close by (thank goodness!) whence, at the noise of our shouts and firing, at least a thousand bayonets will bristle to our rescue.

What sound is yonder? A church bell. I might go myself, but how listen to the sermon? I am thinking of those thieves who have made a ladder of my wall, and a prey of my pear-tree. They may be walking to church at this moment, neatly shaved, in clean linen, with every outward appearance of virtue. If I went, I know I should be watching the congregation, and thinking, " Is that one of the fellows who came over my wall?" If, after the reading of the eighth Commandment, a man sang out with particular energy, " Incline our hearts to keep this law," I should think, " Aha, Master Basso, did you have pears for breakfast this morning?" Crime is walking round me, that is clear. Who is the perpetrator? * * * What a changed aspect the world has, since these last few lines were written! I have been walking round about my premises, and in consultation with a gentleman in a single-breasted blue coat, with pewter buttons, and a tape ornament on the collar. He has looked at the holes in the wall, and the amputated tree. We have formed our plan of defence—*perhaps of attack.* Perhaps some day you may read in the papers, "DARING ATTEMPT AT BURGLARY— HEROIC VICTORY OVER THE VILLAINS," &c. &c. Rascals as yet unknown! perhaps you, too, may read these words, and may be induced to pause in your fatal intention. Take the advice of a sincere friend, and keep off. To find a man writhing in my man-trap, another mayhap impaled in my ditch, to pick off another from my tree (scoundrel! as though he were a pear) will give me no pleasure; but such things may happen. Be warned in time, villains! Or, if you *must* pursue your calling as cracksmen, have the goodness to try some other shutters. Enough! subside into your darkness, children of night! Thieves! we seek not to have *you* hanged—you are but as pegs whereon to hang others.

I may have said before, that if I were going to be hanged myself, I think I should take an accurate note of my sensations, request to stop at some public-house on the road to Tyburn, and be provided with a private room and writing materials, and give an account of my state of mind. Then, gee up, carter! I beg your reverence to continue your apposite, though not novel, remarks on my situation;—and so we drive up to Tyburn turnpike, where an expectant crowd, the obliging sheriffs, and the dexterous and rapid Mr. Ketch are already in waiting.

A number of labouring people are sauntering about our streets and taking their rest on this holyday—fellows who have no more stolen my pears than they have robbed the crown jewels out of the Tower—and I say I cannot help thinking in my own mind, "Are you the rascal who got over my wall last night? " Is the suspicion haunting my mind written on my countenance? I trust not. What if one man after another were to come up to me and say, "How dare you, sir, suspect me in your mind of stealing your fruit? Go be hanged, you and your jargonels! " You rascal thief! it is not merely three halfp'orth of sooty fruit you rob me of, it is my peace of mind—my artless innocence and trust in my fellow-creatures, my child-like belief that everything they say is true. How can I hold out the hand of friendship in this condition, when my first impression is, "My good sir, I strongly suspect that you were up my pear-tree last night? " It is a dreadful state of mind. The core is black; the death-stricken fruit drops on the bough, and a great worm is within—fattening, and feasting, and wriggling! Who stole the pears! I say. Is it you, brother? Is it you, madam? Come! are you ready to answer—*respondere parati et cantare pares?* (O shame! shame!)

Will the villains ever be discovered and punished who stole my fruit? Some unlucky rascals who rob orchards are caught up the tree at once. Some rob through life with impunity. If I, for my part, were to try and get up the smallest tree, on the darkest night, in the most remote orchard, I wager any money I should be found out—be caught by the leg in a man-trap, or have Towler fastening on me. I always am found out; have been; shall be. It's my luck. Other men will carry off bushels of fruit, and get away undetected, unsuspected; whereas I know woe and punishment would fall upon me were I to lay my hand on the smallest pippin. So be it. A man who has this precious self-knowledge will surely keep his hands from picking and stealing, and his feet upon the paths of virtue.

I will assume, my benevolent friend and present reader, that you yourself are virtuous, not from a fear of punishment, but from a sheer love of good: but as you and I walk through life, consider what hundreds of thousands of rascals we must have met, who have not been found out at all. In high places and low, in Clubs and on 'Change, at church or the balls and routs of the nobility and gentry, how dreadful it is for benevolent beings like you and me to have to think these undiscovered though not unsuspected scoundrels are swarming! What is the difference between you and a galley-slave? Is yonder poor wretch at the hulks not a man and a brother too? Have you ever forged, my dear sir? Have you ever cheated your neighbour? Have you ever ridden to Hounslow Heath and robbed the mail? Have you ever entered a first-class railway carriage, where an old gentleman sate alone in a sweet sleep, daintily murdered him, taken his pocket-book, and got out at the next station? You know that this circumstance occurred in France a few months since. If we have travelled in France this autumn we may have met the ingenious gentleman who perpetrated this daring and successful *coup*. We may have found him a well-informed and agreeable man. I have been acquainted with two or three gentlemen who have been discovered after—after the performance of illegal actions. What? That agreeable rattling fellow we met was the celebrated Mr. John Sheppard? Was that amiable quiet gentleman in spectacles the well-known Mr. Fauntleroy? In Hazlitt's admirable paper, "Going to a Fight," he describes a dashing sporting fellow who was in the coach, and who was no less a man than the eminent destroyer of Mr. William Weare. Don't tell me that you would not like to have met (out of business) Captain Sheppard, the Reverend Doctor Dodd, or others rendered famous by their actions and misfortunes, by their lives and their deaths. They are the subjects of ballads, the heroes of romance. A friend of mine had the house in May Fair, out of which poor Doctor Dodd was taken handcuffed. There was the paved hall over which he stepped. That little room at the side was, no doubt, the study where he composed his elegant sermons. Two years since I had the good fortune to partake of some admirable dinners in Tyburnia—magnificent dinners indeed; but rendered doubly interesting from the fact that the house was that occupied by the late Mr. Sadleir. One night the late Mr. Sadleir took tea in that dining-room, and, to the surprise of his butler, went out, having put into his pocket his own cream-jug. The next morning, you know, he was found dead on Hampstead Heath, with the cream-jug lying by him, into which he had poured the poison by which he died. The idea of the ghost of the late gentleman flitting about the room gave a strange interest to the banquet. Can you fancy him taking his tea alone in the dining-room? He empties that cream-jug and puts it in his pocket; and then he opens yonder door, through which he is never to pass again. Now he crosses the hall: and hark! the hall-door shuts upon him, and his steps die away. They are gone into the night. They traverse the sleeping city. They lead him into the fields, where the grey morning is beginning to glimmer. He pours something from a bottle into a little silver jug. It touches his lips, the lying lips. Do they quiver a prayer ere that awful draught is swallowed? When the sun rises they are dumb.

I neither knew this unhappy man, nor his countryman —Laërtes let us call him—who is at present in exile, having been compelled to fly from remorseless creditors. Laërtes fled to America, where he earned his bread by his pen. I own to having a kindly feeling towards this scapegrace, because, though an exile, he did not abuse the country whence he fled. I have heard that he went away taking no spoil with him, penniless almost; and on his voyage he made acquaintance with a certain Jew; and when he fell sick, at New York, this Jew befriended him, and gave him help and money out of his own store, which was but small. Now, after they had been awhile in the strange city, it happened that the poor Jew spent all his little money, and he too fell ill, and was in great penury. And now it was Laërtes who befriended that Ebrew Jew. He fee'd doctors; he fed and tended the sick and hungry. Go to, Laërtes! I know thee not. It may be thou art justly *exul patriæ*. But the Jew shall intercede for thee, thou not, let us trust, hopeless Christian sinner.

Another exile to the same shore I knew: who did not?

Julius Cæsar hardly owed more money than Cucedicus:
and, gracious powers! Cucedicus, how did you manage to
spend and owe so much?   All day he was at work for his
clients; at night he was occupied in the Public Council.
He neither had wife nor children.   The rewards which
he received from his orations were enough to maintain
twenty rhetoricians.   Night after night I have seen him
eating his frugal meal, consisting but of a fish, a small
portion of mutton, and a small measure of Iberian or Tri-
nacrian wine, largely diluted with the sparkling waters of
Rhenish Gaul.   And this was all he had; and this man
earned and paid away talents upon talents; and fled, owing
who knows how many more!   Does a man earn fifteen
thousand pounds a year, toiling by day, talking by night,
having horrible unrest in his bed, ghastly terrors at waking, seeing an officer lurking at every corner, a sword of
justice forever hanging over his head—and have for his
sole diversion a newspaper, a lonely mutton-chop, and a
little sherry and seltzer-water?   In the German stories we
read how men sell themselves to—a certain Personage, and
that Personage cheats them.   He gives them wealth; yes,
but the gold pieces turn into worthless leaves.   He sets
them before splendid banquets; yes, but what an awful
grin that black footman has who lifts up the dish-cover;
and don't you smell a peculiar sulphurous odour in the
dish?   Faugh! take it away; I can't eat.   He promises
them splendours and triumphs.   The conqueror's car rolls
glittering through the city, the multitudes shout and huz-
zah.   Drive on, coachman.   Yes, but who is that hanging
on behind the carriage?   Is this the reward of eloquence,
talents, industry?   Is this the end of a life's labour?
Don't you remember how, when the dragon was infesting
the neighbourhood of Babylon, the citizens used to walk
dismally out of evenings, and look at the valleys round
about strewed with the bones of the victims whom the monster had devoured?   O insatiate brute, and most disgusting, brazen, and scaly reptile!   Let us be thankful, children, that it has not gobbled us up too.   Quick.   Let us

turn away, and pray that we may be kept out of the reach
of his horrible maw, jaw, claw!

When I first came up to London, as innocent as Monsieur Gil Blas, I also fell in with some pretty acquaintances,
found my way into several caverns, and delivered my purse
to more than one gallant gentleman of the road. One I
remember especially—one who never eased me personally
of a single maravedi—one than whom I never met a bandit
more gallant, courteous, and amiable. Rob me? Rolando
feasted me; treated me to his dinner and his wine; kept a
generous table for his friends, and I know was most liberal
to many of them. How well I remember one of his specu-
lations! It was a great plan for smuggling tobacco. Rev-
enue officers were to be bought off; silent ships were to
ply on the Thames; cunning dépôts were to be established,
and hundreds of thousands of pounds to be made by the
coup. How his eyes kindled as he propounded the scheme
to me! How easy and certain it seemed! It might have
succeeded: I can't say: but the bold and merry, the hearty
and kindly Rolando came to grief—a little matter of imitated signatures occasioned a Bank persecution of Rolando
the Brave. He walked about armed, and vowed he would
never be taken alive: but taken he was; tried, condemned,
sentenced to perpetual banishment; and I heard that for
some time he was universally popular in the colony which
had the honour to possess him. What a song he could
sing! 'Twas when the cup was sparkling before us, and
heaven gave a portion of its blue, boys, blue, that I remember the song of Roland at the Old Piazza Coffee-
house. And now where is the Old Piazza Coffee-house?
Where is Thebes? where is Troy? where is the Colossus
of Rhodes? Ah, Rolando, Rolando! thou wert a gallant
captain, a cheery, a handsome, a merry. At *me* thou never
presentedst pistol. Thou badest the bumper of Burgundy
fill, fill for me, giving those who preferred it champagne.
Cœlum non animum, &c. Do you think he has reformed
now that he has crossed the sea, and changed the air? I
have my own opinion. Howbeit, Rolando, thou wert a

most kindly and hospitable bandit. And I love not to think of thee with a chain at thy shin.

Do you know how all these memories of unfortunate men have come upon me? When they came to frighten me this morning by speaking of my robbed pears, my perforated garden wall, I was reading an article in the *Saturday Review* about Rupilius. I have sate near that young man at a public dinner, and beheld him in a gilded uniform. But yesterday he lived in splendour, had long hair, a flowing beard, a jewel at his neck, and a smart surtout. So attired, he stood but yesterday in court; and to-day he sits over a bowl of prison cocoa, with a shaved head, and in a felon's jerkin.

That beard and head shaved, that gaudy deputy-lieutenant's coat exchanged for felon uniform, and your daily bottle of champagne for prison cocoa, my poor Rupilius, what a comfort it must be to have the business brought to an end! Champagne was the honourable gentleman's drink in the House of Commons dining-room, as I am informed. What uncommonly dry champagne that must have been! When we saw him outwardly happy, how miserable he must have been! when we thought him prosperous, how dismally poor! When the great Mr. Harker, at the public dinners, called out—"Gentlemen, charge your glasses, and please silence for the honourable Member for Lambeth!" how that honourable Member must have writhed inwardly! One day, when there was a talk of a gentleman's honour being questioned, Rupilius said, "If any man doubted mine, I would knock him down." But that speech was in the way of business. The Spartan boy, who stole the fox, smiled while the beast was gnawing him under his cloak: I promise you Rupilius had some sharp fangs gnashing under his. We have sate at the same feast, I say: we have paid our contribution to the same charity. Ah! when I ask this day for my daily bread, I pray not to be led into temptation, and to be delivered from evil.

DESSEIN'S.

I ARRIVED by the night-mail packet from Dover. The passage had been rough, and the usual consequences had ensued. I was disinclined to travel farther that night on my road to Paris, and knew the Calais hotel of old as one of the cleanest, one of the dearest, one of the most comfortable hotels on the continent of Europe. There is no town more French than Calais. That charming old Hôtel Dessein, with its court, its gardens, its lordly kitchen, its princely waiter—a gentleman of the old school, who has welcomed the finest company in Europe—have long been known to me. I have read complaints in the *Times*, more than once I think, that the Dessein bills are dear. A bottle of soda-water certainly costs——well, never mind how much. I remember as a boy, at the Ship at Dover (imperante Carolo Decimo), when, my place to London being paid, I had but 12s. left after a certain little Paris excursion (about which my benighted parents never knew anything), ordering for dinner a whiting, a beef-steak, and a glass of negus, and the bill was, dinner 7s., glass of negus, 2s. waiter 6d., and only half-a-crown left, as I was a sinner, for the guard and coachman on the way to London! And I *was* a sinner. I had gone without leave. What a long, dreary, guilty, forty hours' journey it was from Paris to Calais, I remember! How did I come to think of this escapade, which occurred in the Easter vacation of the year 1830? I always think of it when I am crossing to Calais. Guilt, sir, guilt remains stamped on the memory, and I feel easier in my mind now that it is liberated of this old peccadillo. I met my college tutor only yesterday. We were travelling, and stopped at the same hotel. He had the very next room to mine. After he had gone into his apartment, having shaken me quite kindly by the hand, I felt inclined to knock at his door, and say, "Doctor Bentley, I beg your pardon, but do you remember, when I was going down at the Easter vacation in 1830, you asked me where I was going to spend my vacation? And I said, with my friend Slingsby, in Huntingdonshire. Well, sir, I grieve to have to confess that I told you a fib. I had got 20*l.* and was going for a lark to Paris, where my friend Edwards was staying." There, it is out. The Doctor will read it, for I did not wake him up after all to make my confession, but protest he shall have a copy of this Roundabout sent to him when he returns to his lodge.

They gave me a bed-room there; a very neat room on the first floor, looking into the pretty garden. The hotel must look pretty much as it did a hundred years ago when he visited it. I wonder whether he paid his bill? Yes: his journey was just begun. He had borrowed or got the money somehow. Such a man would spend it liberally enough when he had it, give generously—nay, drop a tear over the fate of the poor fellow whom he relieved. I don't believe a word he says, but I never accused him of stinginess about money. That is a fault of much more virtuous people than he. Mr. Laurence is ready enough with his purse when there are anybody's guineas in it. Still, when I went to bed in the room, in *his* room; when I think how I admire, dislike, and have abused him, a certain dim feeling of apprehension filled my mind at the midnight hour. What if I should see his lean figure in the black satin breeches, his sinister smile, his long thin finger pointing to me in the moonlight (for I am in bed, and have popped my candle out), and he should say, "You mistrust me, you hate me, do you? And you, don't you know how Jack, Tom, and Harry, your brother authors, hate *you?*" I grin and laugh in the moonlight, in the midnight, in the silence. "O you ghost in black satin breeches and a wig! I like to be hated by some men," I say. "I know men whose lives are a scheme, whose laughter is a conspiracy, whose smile means something else, whose hatred is a cloak, and I had rather these men should hate me than not."

"My good sir," says he, with a ghastly grin on his lean face, "you have your wish."

"*Après?*" I say. "Please let me go to sleep. I shan't sleep any the worse because——"

"Because there are insects in the bed, and they sting you?" (This is only by way of illustration, my good sir; the animals don't bite me now. All the house at present seems to me excellently clean.) "'Tis absurd to affect this indifference. If you are thin-skinned, and the reptiles bite, they keep you from sleep."

"There are some men who cry out at a flea-bite as loud as if they were torn by a vulture," I growl.

"Men of the *genus irritabile*, my worthy good gentleman! —and you are one."

"Yes, sir, I am of the profession, as you say; and I daresay make a great shouting and crying at a small hurt."

"You are ashamed of that quality by which you earn your subsistence, and such reputation as you have? Your sensibility is your livelihood, my worthy friend. You feel a pang of pleasure or pain? It is noted in your memory, and some day or other makes its appearance in your manuscript. Why, in your last Roundabout rubbish you mention reading your first novel on the day when King George IV. was crowned. I remember him in his cradle at St. James's, a lovely little babe; a gilt Chinese railing was before him, and I dropped the tear of sensibility as I gazed on the sleeping cherub."

"A tear—a fiddlestick, Mr. STERNE," I growled out, for of course I knew my friend in the wig and satin breeches to be no other than the notorious, nay, celebrated Mr. Laurence Sterne.

"Does not the sight of a beautiful infant charm and melt you, *mon ami?* If not, I pity you. Yes, he was beautiful. I was in London the year he was born. I used to breakfast at the Mount Coffee-house. I did not become the fashion until two years later, when my 'Tristram' made his appearance, who has held his own for a hundred years. By the way, *mon bon monsieur*, how many authors

of your present time will last till the next century? Do
you think Brown will? "

I laughed with scorn as I lay in my bed (and so did the
ghost give a ghastly snigger).

"Brown!" I roared. "One of the most over-rated men
that ever put pen to paper!"

"What do you think of Jones? "

I grew indignant with this old cynic. "As a reasonable
ghost, come out of the other world, you don't mean," I
said, "to ask me a serious opinion of Mr. Jones? His books
may be very good reading for maid-servants and schoolboys, but you don't ask *me* to read them? As a scholar
yourself you must know that——"

"Well, then, Robinson? "

"Robinson, I am told, has merit. I daresay; I never
have been able to read his books, and can't, therefore, form
any opinion about Mr. Robinson. At least you will allow
that I am not speaking in a prejudiced manner about *him*."

"Ah! I see you men of letters have your cabals and
jealousies, as we had in my time. There was an Irish fellow by the name of Gouldsmith, who used to abuse me;
but he went into no genteel company—and faith! it mat-
tered little, his praise or abuse. I never was more surprised than when I heard that Mr. Irving, an American
gentleman of parts and elegance, had wrote the fellow's
life. To make a hero of that man, my dear sir, 'twas
ridiculous! You followed in the fashion, I hear, and chose
to lay a wreath before this queer little idol. Preposter-
ous! A pretty writer, who has turned some neat couplets.
Bah! I have no patience with Master Posterity, that has
chosen to take up this fellow, and make a hero of him!
And there was another gentleman of my time, Mr. Thief-
catcher Fielding, forsooth! a fellow with the strength, and
the tastes, and the manners of a porter! What madness
has possessed you all to bow before that Calvert Butt of a
man?—a creature without elegance or sensibility! The
dog had spirits, certainly. I remember my Lord Bathurst
praising them: but as for reading his books—*ma foi*, I

would as lief go and dive for tripe in a cellar. The man's vulgarity stifles me. He wafts me whiffs of gin. Tobacco and onions are in his great coarse laugh, which choke me, *pardi;* and I don't think much better of the other fellow —the Scots' gallipot purveyor—Peregrine Clinker, Humphrey Random—how did the fellow call his rubbish? Neither of these men had the *bel air,* the *bon ton,* the *je ne sçais quoy.* Pah! If I meet them in my walks by our Stygian river, I give them a wide berth, as that hybrid apothecary fellow would say. An ounce of civet, good apothecary; horrible, horrible! The mere thought of the coarseness of those men gives me the *chair de poule.* Mr. Fielding, especially, has no more sensibility than a butcher in Fleet Market. He takes his heroes out of ale-house kitchens, or worse places still. And this is the person whom Posterity has chosen to honour along with me—*me!* Faith, Monsieur Posterity, you have put me in pretty company, and I see you are no wiser than we were in our time. Mr. Fielding, forsooth! Mr. Tripe and Onions! Mr. Cowheel and Gin! Thank you for nothing, Monsieur Posterity!"

"And so," thought I, "even among these Stygians this envy and quarrelsomeness (if you will permit me the word) survive. What a pitiful meanness! To be sure, I can understand this feeling to a certain extent; a sense of justice will prompt it. In my own case, I often feel myself forced to protest against the absurd praises lavished on contemporaries. Yesterday, for instance, Lady Jones was good enough to praise one of my works. *Très bien.* But in the very next minute she began, with quite as great enthusiasm, to praise Miss Hobson's last romance. My good creature, what is that woman's praise worth who absolutely admires the writings of Miss Hobson? I offer a friend a bottle of '44 claret, fit for a pontifical supper. "This is capital wine," says he; "and now we have finished the bottle, will you give me a bottle of that ordinaire we drank the other day?" Very well, my good man. You are a good judge—of ordinaire, I daresay. Nothing so provokes

M

my anger, and rouses my sense of justice, as to hear other
men undeservedly praised. In a word, if you wish to remain friends with me, don't praise anybody. You tell me
that the Venus de' Medici is beautiful, or Jacob Omnium
is tall. *Que diable!* Can't I judge for myself? Haven't
I eyes and a foot-rule? I don't think the Venus *is* so
handsome, since you press me. She is pretty, but she has
no expression. And as for Mr. Omnium, I can see much
taller men in a fair for twopence."

"And so," I said, turning round to Mr. Sterne, "you
are actually jealous of Mr. Fielding? O you men of letters, you men of letters! Is not the world (your world, I
mean) big enough for all of you?"

I often travel in my sleep. I often of a night find myself walking in my night-gown about the grey streets. It
is awkward at first, but somehow nobody makes any remark. I glide along over the ground with my naked feet.
The mud does not wet them. The passers-by do not tread
on them. I am wafted over the ground, down the stairs,
through the doors. This sort of travelling, dear friends, I
am sure you have all of you indulged.

Well, on the night in question (and, if you wish to know
the precise date, it was the 31st of September last), after
having some little conversation with Mr. Sterne in our bed-
room, I must have got up, though I protest I don't know
how, and come downstairs with him into the coffee-room of
the Hôtel Dessein, where the moon was shining, and a cold
supper was laid out. I forget what we had—"vol au vent
d'œufs de Phénix—agneau aux pistaches à la Barmécide,"
—what matters what we had? As regards supper this is
certain, the less you have of it the better.

That is what one of the guests remarked,—a shabby old
man, in a wig, and such a dirty, ragged, disreputable
dressing-gown, that I should have been quite surprised at
him, only one never *is* surprised in dr—— under certain
circumstances.

"I can't eat 'em now," said the greasy man (with his
false old teeth, I wonder he could eat anything). "I re-

member Alvanley eating three suppers once at Carlton House—one night *de petite comité.*"

"*Petit comité,* sir," said Mr. Sterne.

"Dammy, sir, let me tell my own story my own way. I say, one night at Carlton House, playing at blind hookey with York, Wales, Tom Raikes, Prince Boothby, and Dutch Sam the boxer, Alvanley ate three suppers, and won three and twenty hundred pounds in ponies. Never saw a fellow with such an appetite except Wales in his *good* time. But he destroyed the finest digestion a man ever had with maraschino, by Jove—always at it."

"Try mine," said Mr. Sterne.

"What a doosid queer box," says Mr. Brummell.

"I had it from a Capuchin friar in this town. The box is but a horn one; but to the nose of sensibility Araby's perfume is not more delicate."

"I call it doosid stale old rappee," says Mr. Brummell —(as for me I declare I could not smell anything at all in either of the boxes). "Old boy in smockfrock, take a pinch?"

The old boy in the smockfrock, as Mr. Brummell called him, was a very old man, with long white beard, wearing, not a smockfrock, but a shirt; and he had actually nothing else save a rope round his neck, which hung behind his chair in the queerest way.

"Fair sir," he said, turning to Mr. Brummell, "when the Prince of Wales and his father laid siege to our town——"

"What nonsense are you talking, old cock?" says Mr. Brummell; "Wales was never here. His late Majesty George IV. passed through on his way to Hanover. My good man, you don't seem to know what's up at all. What is he talkin' about the siege of Calais? I lived here fifteen years! Ought to know. What's his old name?"

"I am Master Eustace, of Saint Peter," said the old gentleman in the shirt. "When my Lord King Edward laid siege to this city——"

"Laid siege to Jericho!" cries Mr. Brummell. "The old man is cracked—cracked, sir!"

"——laid siege to this city," continued the old man, "I and five more promised Messire Gautier de Mauny that we would give ourselves up as ransom for the place. And we came before our Lord King Edward, attired as you see, and the fair queen begged our lives out of her gramercy."

"Queen, nonsense! you mean the Princess of Wales— pretty woman, *petit nez retroussé*, grew monstrous stout?" suggested Mr. Brummell, whose reading was evidently not extensive. "Sir Sidney Smith was a fine fellow, great talker, hook nose, so has Lord Cochrane, so has Lord Wellington. She was very sweet on Sir Sidney."

"Your acquaintance with the history of Calais does not seem to be considerable," said Mr. Sterne to Mr. Brummell, with a shrug.

"Don't it, bishop?—for I conclude you are a bishop by your wig. I know Calais as well as any man. I lived here for years before I took that confounded consulate at Caen. Lived in this hotel, then at Leleux's. People used to stop here. Good fellows used to ask for poor George Brummell; Hertford did, so did the Duchess of Devonshire. Not know Calais indeed! That is a good joke. Had many a good dinner here: sorry I ever left it."

"My Lord King Edward," chirped the queer old gentleman in the shirt, "colonized the place with his English, after we had yielded it up to him. I have heard tell they kept it for nigh three hundred years, till my Lord de Guise took it from a fair Queen, Mary of blessed memory, a holy woman. Eh, but Sire Gautier of Mauny was a good knight, a valiant captain, gentle and courteous withal! Do you remember his ransoming the——"

"What is the old fellow twaddlin' about?" cries Brummell. "He is talking about some knight?—I never spoke to a knight, and very seldom to a baronet. Firkins, my butterman, was a knight—a knight and alderman. Wales knighted him once on going into the city."

"I am not surprised that the gentleman should not understand Messire Eustace of St. Peter's," said the ghostly individual addressed as Mr. Sterne. "Your reading doubt-less has not been very extensive?"

"Dammy, sir, speak for yourself!" cries Mr. Brummell, testily. "I never professed to be a reading man, but I was as good as my neighbours. Wales wasn't a reading man; York wasn't a reading man; Clarence wasn't a reading man; Sussex was, but he wasn't a man in society. I remember reading your 'Sentimental Journey,' old boy: read it to the duchess at Beauvoir, I recollect, and she cried over it. Doosid clever amusing book, and does you great credit. Birron wrote doosid clever books, too; so did Monk Lewis. George Spencer was an elegant poet, and my dear Duchess of Devonshire, if she had not been a grande dame, would have beat 'em all, by George. Wales couldn't write: he could sing, but he couldn't spell."

"Ah, you know the great world? so did I in my time, Mr. Brummell. I have had the visiting tickets of half the nobility at my lodgings in Bond Street. But they left me there no more cared for than last year's calendar," sighed Mr. Sterne. "I wonder who is the mode in London now? One of our late arrivals, my Lord Macaulay, has prodigious merit and learning, and, faith, his histories are more amus-ing than any novels, my own included."

"Don't know, I'm sure; not in my line. Pick this bone of chicken," says Mr. Brummell, trifling with a skeleton bird before him.

"I remember in this city of Calais worse fare than yon bird," said old Mr. Eustace, of Saint Peter. "Marry, sirs, when my Lord King Edward laid siege to us, lucky was he who could get a slice of horse for his breakfast, and a rat was sold at the price of a hare."

"Hare is coarse food, never tasted rat," remarked the Beau. "*Table-d'hôte* poor fare enough for a man like me, who has been accustomed to the best of cookery. But rat —stifle me! I couldn't swallow that: never could bear hardship at all."

"We had to bear enough when my Lord of England pressed us. 'Twas pitiful to see the faces of our women as the siege went on, and hear the little ones asking for dinner."

"Always a bore, children. At dessert, they are bad enough, but at dinner they're the deuce and all," remarked Mr. Brummell.

Messire Eustace, of St. Peter, did not seem to pay much attention to the Beau's remarks, but continued his own train of thought as old men will do.

"I hear," said he, "that there has actually been no war between us of France and you men of England for well nigh fifty year. Ours has ever been a nation of warriors. And besides her regular found men-at-arms, 'tis said the English of the present time have more than a hundred thousand of archers with weapons that will carry for half a mile. And a multitude have come amongst us of late from a great Western country, never so much as heard of in my time—valiant men and great drawers of the long-bow, and they say they have ships in armour that no shot can penetrate. Is it so? Wonderful; wonderful! The best armour, gossips, is a stout heart."

"And if ever manly heart beat under shirt-frill, thine is that heart, Sir Eustace!" cried Mr. Sterne, enthusiastically.

"We, of France, were never accused of lack of courage, sir, in so far as I know," said Messire Eustace. "We have shown as much in a thousand wars with you English by sea and land; and sometimes we conquered, and sometimes, as is the fortune of war, we were discomfited. And notably in a great sea-fight which befel off Ushant on the first of June—— Our amiral, Messire Villaret de Joyeuse, on board his galleon named the *Vengeur*, being sore pressed by an English bombard, rather than yield the crew of his ship to mercy, determined to go down with all on board of her: and, to the cry of Vive la Répub——or, I would say, of Nôtre Dame à la Rescousse, he and his crew all sank to an immortal grave——"

"Sir," said I, looking with amazement at the old gentleman, "surely, surely, there is some mistake in your state-

ment. Permit me to observe that the action of the first
of June took place five hundred years after your time,
and——"

"Perhaps I am confusing my dates," said the old gentleman, with a faint blush. "You say I am mixing up the
transactions of my time on earth with the story of my suc-
cessors? It may be so. We take no count of a few centuries more or less in our dwelling by the darkling Stygian
river. Of late, there came amongst us a good knight,
Messire de Cambronne, who fought against you English in
the country of Flanders, being captain of the guard of my
Lord the King of France, in a famous battle where you
English would have been utterly routed but for the succour
of the Prussian heathen. This Messire de Cambronne,
when bidden to yield by you of England, answered this,
'The guard dies, but never surrenders;' and fought a
long time afterwards, as became a good knight. In our
wars with you of England it may have pleased the Fates
to give you the greater success, but on our side, also,
there has been no lack of brave deeds performed by brave
men."

"King Edward may have been the victor, sir, as being
the strongest, but you are the hero of the siege of Calais!"
cried Mr. Sterne. "Your story is sacred, and your name
has been blessed for five hundred years. Wherever men
speak of patriotism and sacrifice, Eustace, of Saint Pierre,
shall be beloved and remembered. I prostrate myself before the bare feet which stood before King Edward. What
collar of chivalry is to be compared to that glorious order
which you wear? Think, sir, how out of the myriad millions of our race, you, and some few more, stand forth as
exemplars of duty and honour. *Fortunati nimium!*"

"Sir," said the old gentleman, "I did but my duty at a
painful moment; and 'tis matter of wonder to me that men
talk still, and glorify such a trifling matter. By our Lady's
grace, in the fair kingdom of France, there are scores of
thousands of men, gentle and simple, who would do as I
did. Does not every sentinel at his post, does not every

archer in the front of battle, brave it, and die where his captain bids him? Who am I that I should be chosen out of all France to be an example of fortitude? I braved no tortures, though these I trust I would have endured with a good heart. I was subject to threats only. Who was the Roman knight of whom the Latin clerk Horatius tells?"

"A Latin clerk? Faith, I forget my Latin," says Mr. Brummell. "Ask the parson here."

"Messire Regulus, I remember, was his name. Taken prisoner by the Saracens, he gave his knightly word, and was permitted to go seek a ransom among his own people. Being unable to raise the sum that was a fitting ransom for such a knight, he returned to Africa, and cheerfully submitted to the tortures which the Paynims inflicted. And 'tis said he took leave of his friends as gaily as though he were going to a village kermes, or riding to his garden house in the suburb of the city."

"Great, good, glorious man!" cried Mr. Sterne, very much moved. "Let me embrace that gallant hand, and bedew it with my tears! As long as honour lasts thy name shall be remembered. See this dew-drop twinkling on my cheek! 'Tis the sparkling tribute that Sensibility pays to Valour. Though in my life and practice I may turn from Virtue, believe me, I never have ceased to honour her! Ah, Virtue! Ah, Sensibility! Oh——"

Here Mr. Sterne was interrupted by a monk of the Order of St. Francis who stepped into the room, and begged us all to take a pinch of his famous old rappee. I suppose the snuff was very pungent, for, with a great start, I woke up; and now perceived that I must have been dreaming altogether. Dessein's of nowadays is not the Dessein's which Mr. Sterne, and Mr. Brummell, and I recollect in the good old times. The town of Calais has bought the old hotel, and Dessein has gone over to Quillacq's. And I was there yesterday. And I remember old diligences, and old postilions in pig-tails and jack-boots, who were once as alive as I am, and whose cracking whips I have heard in the midnight many and many a time. Now, where are they? Behold, they have been ferried over Styx, and have passed away into limbo.

I wonder what time does my boat go? Ah! Here comes the waiter bringing me my little bill.

ON SOME CARP AT SANS SOUCI.

WE have lately made the acquaintance of an old lady of ninety, who has passed the last twenty-five years of her old life in a great metropolitan establishment, the workhouse, namely, of the parish of Saint Lazarus. Stay—twenty-three or four years ago, she came out once, and thought to earn a little money by hop-picking: but being overworked, and having to lie out at night, she got a palsy which has incapacitated her from all further labour, and has caused her poor old limbs to shake ever since.

An illustration of that dismal proverb which tells us how poverty makes us acquainted with strange bed-fellows, this poor old shaking body has to lay herself down every night in her workhouse bed by the side of some other old woman with whom she may or may not agree. She herself can't be a very pleasant bed-fellow, poor thing! with her shaking old limbs and cold feet. She lies awake a deal of the night, to be sure, not thinking of happy old times, for hers never were happy; but sleepless with aches, and agues, and rheumatism of old age. "The gentleman gave me brandy-and-water," she said, her old voice shaking with rapture at the thought. I never had a great love for Queen Charlotte, but I like her better now from what this old lady told me. The Queen, who loved snuff herself, has left a legacy of snuff to certain poorhouses; and, in her watchful nights, this old woman takes a pinch of Queen Charlotte's snuff, "and it do comfort me, sir, that it do!" *Pulveris exigui munus.* Here is a forlorn aged creature, shaking with palsy, with no soul among the great struggling multitude of mankind to care for her, not quite trampled out of life, but past and forgotten in the rush, made a little happy, and soothed in her hours of unrest by this penny legacy. Let me think as I write. (The next month's sermon, thank goodness! is safe to press.) This discourse will appear at the season when I have read that wassail bowls make their appearance; at the season of pantomime, turkey and sausages, plum-puddings, jollifications for schoolboys; Christmas bills, and reminiscences more or less sad and sweet for elders. If we oldsters are not merry, we shall be having a semblance of merriment. We shall see the young folks laughing round the holly-bush. We shall pass the bottle round cosily as we sit by the fire. That old thing will have a sort of festival too. Beef, beer, and pudding will be served to her for that day also. Christmas falls on a Thursday. Friday is the workhouse day for coming out. Mary, remember that old Goody Twoshoes has her invitation for Friday, 26th December! Ninety, is she, poor old soul? Ah! what a bonny face to catch under a mistletoe! "Yes, ninety, sir," she says, "and my mother was a hundred, and my grandmother was a hundred and two."

Herself ninety, her mother a hundred, her grandmother a hundred and two? What a queer calculation!

Ninety! Very good, granny, you were born, then, in 1772.

Your mother, we will say, was twenty-seven when you were born, and was born therefore in 1745.

Your grandmother was thirty when her daughter was born, and was born therefore in 1715.

We will begin with the present granny first. My good old creature, you can't of course remember, but that little gentleman for whom your mother was laundress in the Temple was the ingenious Mr. Goldsmith, author of a "History of England," the "Vicar of Wakefield," and many diverting pieces. You were brought almost an infant to his chambers in Brick Court, and he gave you some sugar-candy, for the doctor was always good to children. That gentleman who well-nigh smothered you by sitting down on you as you lay in a chair asleep was the learned Mr. S. Johnson, whose history of "Rasselas" you have never read, my poor soul; and whose tragedy of "Irene" I don't believe any man in these kingdoms ever perused.

That tipsy Scotch gentleman who used to come to the chambers sometimes, and at whom everybody laughed, wrote a more amusing book than any of the scholars, your Mr. Burke and your Mr. Johnson, and your Doctor Goldsmith. Your father often took him home in a chair to his lodgings; and has done as much for Parson Sterne in Bond Street, the famous wit. Of course, my good creature, you remember the Gordon Riots, and crying No Popery before Mr. Langdale's house, the Popish distiller's, and that bonny fire of my Lord Mansfield's books in Bloomsbury Square? Bless us, what a heap of illuminations you have seen! For the glorious victory over the Americans at Breed's Hill; for the peace in 1814, and the beautiful Chinese bridge in St. James's Park; for the coronation of his Majesty, whom you recollect as Prince of Wales, Goody, don't you? Yes; and you went in a procession of laundresses to pay your respects to his good lady, the injured Queen of England, at Brandenburg House; and you remember your mother told you how she was taken to see the Scotch lords executed at the Tower. And as for your grandmother, she was born five months after the battle of Malplaquet. She was; where her poor father was killed, fighting like a bold Briton for the Queen. With the help of a Wade's "Chronology," I can make out ever so queer a history for you, my poor old body, and a pedigree as authentic as many in the peerage-books.

Peerage-books and pedigrees? What does she know about them? Battles and victories, treasons, kings, and beheadings, literary gentlemen, and the like, what have they ever been to her? Granny, did you ever hear of General Wolfe? Your mother may have seen him embark, and your father may have carried a musket under him. Your grandmother may have cried huzzay for Marlborough; but what is the Prince Duke to you, and did you ever so much as hear tell of his name? How many hundred or thousand of years had that toad lived who was in the coal at the defunct Exhibition?—and yet he was not a bit better informed than toads seven or eight hundred years younger.

"Don't talk to me your nonsense about Exhibitions, and Prince Dukes, and toads in coals, or coals in toads, or, what is it!" says granny. "I know there was a good Queen Charlotte, for she left me snuff; and it comforts me of a night when I lie awake."

To me there is something very touching in the notion of that little pinch of comfort doled out to granny, and gratefully inhaled by her in the darkness. Don't you remember what traditions there used to be of chests of plate, bulses of diamonds, laces of inestimable value, sent out of the country privately by the old Queen, to enrich certain relations in M-ckl-nb-rg Str-l-tz? Not all the treasure went. *Non omnis moritur.* A poor old palsied thing at midnight is made happy sometimes as she lifts her shaking old hand to her nose. Gliding noiselessly among the beds where lie the poor creatures huddled in their cheerless dormitory, I fancy an old ghost with a snuff-box that does not creak. "There, Goody, take of my rappee. You will not sneeze, and I shall not say 'God bless you.' But you will think kindly of old Queen Charlotte, won't you? Ah! I had a many troubles, a many troubles. I was a prisoner almost as much as you are. I had to eat boiled mutton every day: *entre nous*, I abominated it. But I never complained. I swallowed it. I made the best of a hard life. We have all our burdens to bear. But hark! I hear the cock crow, and snuff the morning air." And with this the royal ghost vanishes up the chimney—if there be a chimney in that dismal harem, where poor old Twoshoes and her companions pass their nights—their dreary nights, their restless nights, their cold long nights, shared in what glum companionship, illumined by what a feeble taper!

"Did I understand you, my good Twoshoes, to say that your mother was seven-and-twenty years old when you were born, and that she married your esteemed father when she herself was twenty-five? 1745, then, was the date of your dear mother's birth. I daresay her father was absent in the Low Countries, with his Royal Highness the Duke of Cumberland, under whom he had the honour of

carrying a halberd at the famous engagement of Fontenoy
—or if not there, he may have been at Preston Pans, under
General Sir John Cope, when the wild Highlanders broke
through all the laws of discipline and the English lines;
and, being on the spot, did he see the famous ghost which
didn't appear to Colonel Gardiner of the Dragoons?   My
good creature, is it possible you don't remember that Doctor Swift, Sir Robert Walpole (my Lord Orford, as you
justly say), old Sarah Marlborough, and little Mr. Pope,
of Twitnam, died in the year of your birth?   What a
wretched memory you have!   What? haven't they a
library, and the commonest books of reference at the old
convent of Saint Lazarus, where you dwell?"

"Convent of Saint Lazarus, Prince William, Dr. Swift,
Atossa, and Mr. Pope, of Twitnam!   What is the gentleman talking about?" says old Goody, with a "Ho! ho!"
and a laugh like an old parrot—you know they live to be
as old as Methuselah, parrots do, and a parrot of a hundred is comparrotively young (ho! ho! ho!).   Yes, and
likewise carps live to an immense old age.   Some which
Frederick the Great fed at Sans Souci are there now, with
great humps of blue mould on their old backs; and they
could tell all sorts of queer stories, if they chose to speak
—but they are very silent, carps are—of their nature *peu
communicatives*.   Oh! what has been thy long life, old
Goody, but a dole of bread and water and a perch on a
cage; a dreary swim round and round a Lethe of a pond?
What are Rossbach or Jena to those mouldy ones, and do
they know it is a grandchild of England who brings bread
to feed them?

No!   Those Sans Souci carps may live to be a thousand
years old and have nothing to tell but that one day is like
another; and the history of friend Goody Twoshoes has
not much more variety than theirs.   Hard labour, hard
fare, hard bed, numbing cold all night, and gnawing hunger most days.   That is her lot.   Is it lawful in my prayers to say, "Thank heaven, I am not as one of these?"   If
I were eighty, would I like to feel the hunger always gnaw-

ing, gnawing? to have to get up and make a bow when Mr. Bumble the beadle entered the common room? to have to listen to Miss Prim, who came to give me her ideas of the next world? If I were eighty, I own I should not like to have to sleep with another gentleman of my own age, gouty, a bad sleeper, kicking in his old dreams, and snoring; to march down my vale of years at word of command, accommodating my tottering old steps to those of the other prisoners in my dingy, hopeless old gang; to hold out a trembling hand for a sickly pittance of gruel, and say, "Thank you, mam," to Miss Prim, when she has done reading her sermon. John! when Goody Twoshoes comes next Friday, I desire she may not be disturbed by theological controversies. You have a very fair voice, and I heard you and the maids singing a hymn very sweetly the other night, and was thankful that our humble household should be in such harmony. Poor old Twoshoes is so old and toothless and quaky, that she can't sing a bit; but don't be giving yourself airs over her, because she can't sing and you can. Make her comfortable at our kitchen hearth. Set that old kettle to sing by our hob. Warm her old stomach with nut-brown ale and a toast laid in the fire. Be kind to the poor old school-girl of ninety, who has had leave to come out for a day of Christmas holiday. Shall there be many more Christmases for thee? Think of the ninety she has seen already; the four score and ten cold, cheerless, nipping New Years!

If you were in her place, would you like to have a remembrance of better early days, when you were young, and happy, and loving, perhaps; or would you prefer to have no past on which your mind could rest? About the year 1788, Goody, were your cheeks rosy, and your eyes bright, and did some young fellow in powder and a pigtail look in them? We may grow old, but to us some stories never are old. On a sudden they rise up, not dead, but living —not forgotten, but freshly remembered. The eyes gleam on us as they used to do The dear voice thrills in our hearts. The rapture of the meeting, the terrible, terrible

parting, again and again the tragedy is acted over. Yesterday, in the street, I saw a pair of eyes so like two which
used to brighten at my coming once, that the whole past
came back as I walked lonely, in the rush of the Strand,
and I was young again in the midst of joys and sorrows,
alike sweet and sad, alike sacred, and fondly remembered.

If I tell a tale out of school, will any harm come to my
old school-girl? Once, a lady gave her a half-sovereign,
which was a source of great pain and anxiety to Goody
Twoshoes. She sewed it away in her old stays somewhere,
thinking here at least was a safe investment—(vestis—a
vest—an investment,—pardon me, thou poor old thing,
but I cannot help the pleasantry). And what do you
think? Another pensionnaire of the establishment cut the
coin out of Goody's stays—*an old woman who went upon
two crutches!* Faugh, the old witch! What? Violence
amongst these toothless, tottering, trembling, feeble ones?
Robbery amongst the penniless? Dogs coming and snatching Lazarus's crumbs out of his lap? Ah, how indignant
Goody was as she told the story! To that pond at Pots-
dam where the carps live for hundreds of hundreds of
years, with hunches of blue mould on their back, I daresay the little Prince and Princess of Preussen-Britannien
come sometimes with crumbs and cakes to feed the mouldy
ones. Those eyes may have goggled from beneath the
weeds at Napoleon's jack-boots: they have seen Frederick's lean shanks reflected in their pool; and perhaps Monsieur de Voltaire has fed them—and now, for a crumb of
biscuit they will fight, push, hustle, rob, squabble, gobble,
relapsing into their tranquillity when the ignoble struggle
is over. Sans souci, indeed! It is mighty well writing
"Sans souci" over the gate; but where is the gate through
which Care has not slipped? She perches on the shoulders
of the sentry in the sentry-box: she whispers the porter
sleeping in his arm-chair: she glides up the staircase, and
lies down between the king and queen in their bed-royal:
this very night I daresay she will perch upon poor old
Goody Twoshoes's meagre bolster, and whisper, "Will the

gentleman and those ladies ask me again?   No, no; they
will forget poor old Twoshoes."   Goody!   For shame of
yourself!   Do not be cynical.   Do not mistrust your fellow-creatures.   What?   Has the Christmas morning dawned
upon thee ninety times?   For four score and ten years has
it been thy lot to totter on this earth, hungry and obscure?
Peace and goodwill to thee, let us say at this Christmas
season.   Come, drink, eat, rest awhile at our hearth, thou
poor old pilgrim!   And of the bread which God's bounty
gives us, I pray, brother reader, we may not forget to set
aside a part for those noble and silent poor, from whose
innocent hands war has torn the means of labour.   Enough!
As I hope for beef at Christmas, I vow a note shall be sent
to Saint Lazarus Union House, in which Mr. Roundabout
requests the honour of Mrs. Twoshoes's company on Friday,
26th December.

AUTOUR DE MON CHAPEAU.

NEVER have I seen a more noble tragic face. In the centre of the forehead there was a great furrow of care, towards which the brows rose piteously. What a deep solemn grief in the eyes! They looked blankly at the object before them, but through it, as it were, and into the grief beyond. In moments of pain, have you not looked at some indifferent object so? It mingles dumbly with your grief, and remains afterwards connected with it in your mind. It may be some indifferent thing—a book which you were reading at the time when you received her farewell letter (how well you remember the paragraph afterwards—the shape of the words, and their position on the page!); the words you were writing when your mother came in, and said it was all over—she was MARRIED—Emily married—to that insignificant little rival at whom you have laughed a hundred times in her company. Well, well: my friend and reader, whoe'er you be—old man or young, wife or maiden—you have had your grief-pang. Boy, you have lain awake the first night at school, and thought of home. Worse still, man, you have parted from the dear ones with bursting heart: and, lonely boy, recall the bolstering an unfeeling comrade gave you; and, lonely man, just torn from your children—their little tokens of affection yet in your pocket—pacing the deck at evening in the midst of the roaring ocean, you can remember how you were told that supper was ready, and how you went down to the cabin and had brandy-and-water and biscuit. You remember the taste of them. Yes; forever. You took them whilst you and your Grief were sitting together, and your Grief clutched you round the soul. Serpent, how you have writhed round me, and bitten me! Remorse, Remembrance, &c., come in the night season, and I feel you gnawing, gnawing! * * * I tell you that man's face was like Laocoon's (which, by the way, I always think over-rated. The real head is at Brussels, at the Duke Darem-berg's, not at Rome).

That man! What man? That man of whom I said that his magnificent countenance exhibited the noblest tragic woe. He was not of European blood. He was handsome, but not of European beauty. His face white—not of a Northern whiteness: his eyes protruding somewhat, and rolling in their grief. Those eyes had seen the Orient sun, and his beak was the eagle's. His lips were full. The beard, curling round them, was unkempt and tawny. The locks were of a deep, deep coppery red. The hands, swart and powerful, accustomed to the rough grasp of the wares in which he dealt, seemed unused to the flimsy artifices of the bath. He came from the Wilderness, and its sands were on his robe, his cheek, his tattered sandal, and the hardy foot it covered.

And his grief—whence came his sorrow? I will tell you. He bore it in his hand. He had evidently just con-cluded the compact by which it became his. His business was that of a purchaser of domestic raiment. At early dawn—nay, at what hour when the city is alive—do we not all hear the nasal cry of "Clo?" In Paris, *Habits Galons, Marchand d' habits*, is the twanging signal with which the wandering merchant makes his presence known. It was in Paris I saw this man. Where else have I not seen him? In the Roman Ghetto—at the Gate of David, in his fathers' once imperial city. The man I mean was an itinerant vendor and purchaser of wardrobes—what you call an * * * Enough! You know his name.

On his left shoulder hung his bag; and he held in that hand a white hat, which I am sure he had just purchased, and which was the cause of the grief which smote his noble features. Of course I cannot particularize the sum, but he had given too much for that hat. He felt he might have got the thing for less money. It was not the amount, I am sure it was the principle involved. He had given four-pence (let us say) for that which threepence would have

purchased. He had been done: and a manly shame was
upon him, that he, whose energy, acuteness, experience,
point of honour, should have made him the victor in any
mercantile duel in which he should engage, had been overcome by a porter's wife, who very likely sold him the old
hat, or by a student who was tired of it. I can understand his grief. Do I seem to be speaking of it in a dis-
respectful or flippant way? Then you mistake me. He
had been outwitted. He had desired, coaxed, schemed,
haggled, got what he wanted, and now found he had paid
too much for his bargain. You don't suppose I would ask
you to laugh at that man's grief? It is you, clumsy cynic,
who are disposed to sneer, whilst it may be tears of genuine
sympathy are trickling down this nose of mine. What do
you mean by laughing? If you saw a wounded soldier on
the field of battle, would you laugh? If you saw a ewe
robbed of her lamb, would you laugh, you brute? It is you
who are the cynic, and have no feeling: and you sneer because that grief is unintelligible to you which touches my
finer sensibility. The OLD CLOTHES' MAN had been defeated in one of the daily battles of his most interesting,
chequered, adventurous life.

Have you ever figured to yourself what such a life must
be? The pursuit and conquest of twopence must be the
most eager and fascinating of occupations. We might all
engage in that business if we would. Do not whist-players, for example, toil, and think, and lose their temper
over sixpenny points? They bring study, natural genius,
long forethought, memory, and careful historical experience to bear upon their favourite labour. Don't tell me
that it is the sixpenny points, and five shillings the rub,
which keeps them for hours over their painted pasteboard.
It is the desire to conquer. Hours pass by. Night glooms.
Dawn, it may be, rises unheeded; and they sit calling for
fresh cards at the Portland, or the Union, while waning
candles sputter in the sockets, and languid waiters snooze
in the ante-room. Sol rises. Jones has lost four pounds;
Brown has won two; Robinson lurks away to his family

house and (mayhap, indignant) Mrs. R. Hours of evening, night, morning, have passed away whilst they have been waging this sixpenny battle. What is the loss of four pounds to Jones, the gain of two to Brown? B. is, perhaps, so rich that two pounds more or less are as naught to him; J. is so hopelessly involved that to win four pounds cannot benefit his creditors, or alter his condition; but they play for that stake: they put forward their best energies: they ruff, finesse (what are the technical words, and how do I know?). It is but a sixpenny game if you like; but they want to win it. So as regards my friend yonder with the hat. He stakes his money: he wishes to win the game, not the hat merely. I am not prepared to say that he is not inspired by a noble ambition. Cæsar wished to be first in a village. If first of a hundred yokels, why not first of two? And my friend the old clothes' man wishes to win his game, as well as to turn his little sixpence.

Suppose in the game of life—and it is but a twopenny game after all—you are equally eager of winning. Shall you be ashamed of your ambition, or glory in it? There are games, too, which are becoming to particular periods of life. I remember in the days of our youth, when my friend Arthur Bowler was an eminent cricketer. Slim, swift, strong, well-built, he presented a goodly appearance on the ground in his flannel uniform. *Militâsti non sine gloria*, Bowler my boy! Hush! We tell no tales. Mum is the word. Yonder comes Charley, his son. Now Charley his son has taken the field, and is famous among the eleven of his school. Bowler, senior, with his capacious waistcoat, &c., waddling after a ball, would present an absurd object, whereas it does the eyes good to see Bowler, junior, scouring the plain—a young exemplar of joyful health, vigour, activity. The old boy wisely contents himself with amusements more becoming his age and waist; takes his sober ride; visits his farm soberly—busies himself about his pigs, his ploughing, his peaches, or what not. Very small *routiniers* amusements interest him; and (thank goodness!) nature provides very kindly for kindly-disposed fogies. We relish those things which we scorned in our lusty youth. I see the young folks of an evening kindling and glowing over their delicious novels. I look up and watch the eager eye flashing down the page, being, for my part, perfectly contented with my twaddling old volume of Howell's "Letters" or the *Gentleman's Magazine*. I am actually arrived at such a calm frame of mind that I like batter pudding. I never should have believed it possible; but it is so. Yet a little while, and I may relish water-gruel. It will be the age of *mon lait de poule et mon bonnet de nuit*. And then—the cotton extinguisher is pulled over the old noddle, and the little flame of life is popped out.

Don't you know elderly people who make learned notes in Army Lists, Peerages, and the like? This is the batter-pudding, water-gruel of old age. The worn-out old digestion does not care for stronger food. Formerly it could swallow twelve hours' tough reading, and digest an encyclopædia.

If I had children to educate, I would, at ten or twelve years of age, have a professor, or professoress, of whist for them, and cause them to be well grounded in that great and useful game. You cannot learn it well when you are old, any more than you can learn dancing or billiards. In our house at home we youngsters did not play whist because we were dear obedient children, and the elders said playing at cards was "a waste of time." A waste of time, my good people. *Allons!* What do elderly home-keeping people do of a night after dinner? Darby gets his newspaper; my dear Joan her *Missionary Magazine* or her volume of Cumming's Sermons—and don't you know what ensues? Over the arm of Darby's arm-chair the paper flutters to the ground unheeded, and he performs the trumpet obbligato *que vous savez* on his old nose. My dear old Joan's head nods over her sermon (awakening though the doctrine may be). Ding, ding, ding: can that be ten o'clock? It is time to send the servants to bed, my dear —and to bed master and mistress go too. But they have

not wasted their time playing at cards. Oh, no! I belong
to a club where there is whist of a night; and not a little
amusing is it to hear Brown speak of Thompson's play and
vice versâ. But there is one man—Greatorex let us call
him—who is the acknowledged captain and primus of all
the whist-players. We all secretly admire him. I, for
my part, watch him in private life, hearken to what he
says, note what he orders for dinner, and have that feeling
of awe for him that I used to have as a boy for the cock of
the school. Not play at whist? *Quelle triste vieillesse vous
vous préparez!* were the words of the great and good
Bishop of Autun. I can't. It is too late now. Too late!
too late! Ah! humiliating confession! That joy might
have been clutched, but the life-stream has swept us
by it —the swift life-stream rushing to the nearing sea.
Too late! too late! Twentystone, my boy! When you
read in the papers "Valse à deux temps," and all the
fashionable dances taught to adults by "Miss Lightfoots,"
don't you feel that you would like to go in and learn?
Ah, it is too late! You have passed the *choreas*, Master
Twentystone, and the young people are dancing without
you.

I don't believe much of what my Lord Byron, the poet,
says; but when he wrote, "So, for a good old gentlemanly
vice, I think I shall put up with avarice," I think his lordship meant what he wrote, and if he practised what he
preached, shall not quarrel with him. As an occupation
in declining years, I declare I think saving is useful, amusing, and not unbecoming. It must be a perpetual amusement. It is a game that can be played by day, by night,
at home and abroad, and at which you must win in the
long run. I am tired and want a cab. The fare to my
house, say, is two shillings. The cabman will naturally
want half-a-crown. I pull out my book. I show him the
distance is exactly three miles and fifteen hundred and
ninety yards. I offer him my card—my winning card.
As he retires with the two shillings, blaspheming inwardly,
every curse is a compliment to my skill. I have played

him and beat him; and a sixpence is my spoil, and just
reward. This is a game, by the way, which women play
far more cleverly than we do. But what an interest it im-
parts to life! During the whole drive home I know I shall
have my game at the journey's end; am sure of my hand,
and shall beat my adversary. Or I can play in another
way. I won't have a cab at all, I will wait for the omnibus: I will be one of the damp fourteen in that steaming
vehicle. I will wait about in the rain for an hour, and
'bus after 'bus shall 'pass, but I will not be beat. I *will*
have a place, and get it at length, with my boots wet
through, and an umbrella dripping between my legs. I
have a rheumatism, a cold, a sore-throat, a sulky evening,
—a doctor's bill to-morrow perhaps? Yes, but I have
won my game, and am gainer of a shilling on this rubber.

If you play this game all through life, it is wonderful
what daily interest it has, and amusing occupation. For
instance, my wife goes to sleep after dinner over her volume
of sermons. As soon as the dear soul is sound asleep, I
advance softly and puff out her candle. Her pure dreams
will be all the happier without that light; and, say she
sleeps an hour, there is a penny gained.

As for clothes, *parbleu!* There is not much money to
be saved in clothes, for the fact is, as a man advances in
life—as he becomes an *ancient Briton* (mark the pleasantry)
—he goes without clothes. When my tailor proposes something in the way of a change of raiment, I laugh in his
face. My blue coat and brass buttons will last these ten
years. It is seedy? What then? I don't want to charm
anybody in particular. You say that my clothes are
shabby? What do I care? When I wished to look well
in somebody's eyes, the matter may have been different.
But now, when I receive my bill of 10*l.* (let us say) at the
year's end, and contrast it with old tailors' reckonings, I
feel that I have played the game with master tailor; and
beat him, and my old clothes are a token of the victory.

I do not like to give servants board wages, though they
are cheaper than household bills: but I know they save out

of board wages, and so beat me. This shows that it is not the money but the game which interests me. So about wine. I have it good and dear. I will trouble you to tell me where to get it good and cheap. You may as well give me the address of a shop where I can buy meat for fourpence a pound, or sovereigns for fifteen shillings a-piece. At the game of auctions, docks, shy wine-merchants, depend on it there is *no* winning; and I would as soon think of buying jewellery at an auction in Fleet Street as of purchasing wine from one of your dreadful needy wine-agents such as infest every man's door. Grudge myself good wine? As soon grudge my horse corn. *Merci!* that would be a very losing game indeed, and your humble servant has no relish for such.

But in the very pursuit of saving there must be a hundred harmless delights and pleasures which we who are careless necessarily forego. What do you know about the natural history of your household? Upon your honour and conscience, do you know the price of a pound of butter? Can you say what sugar costs, and how much your family consumes and ought to consume? How much lard do you use in your house? As I think on these subjects I own I hang down the head of shame. I suppose for a moment that you, who are reading this, are a middle-aged gentleman, and paterfamilias. Can you answer the above questions? You know, sir, you cannot. Now turn round, lay down the book, and suddenly ask Mrs. Jones and your daughters if *they* can answer? They cannot. They look at one another. They pretend they can answer. They can tell you the plot and principal characters of the last novel. Some of them know something about history, geology, and so forth. But of the natural history of home—*Nichts*, and for shame on you all! *Honnis soyez!* For shame on you! for shame on us!

In the early morning I hear a sort of call or *jodel* under my window: and know 'tis the matutinal milkman leaving his can at my gate. O household gods! have I lived all these years and don't know the price or the quantity of the

N

milk which is delivered in that can?   Why don't I know?
As I live, if I live till to-morrow morning, as soon as I
hear the call of Lactantius I will dash out upon him. How
many cows?   How much milk, on an average, all the year
round?   What rent?   What cost of food and dairy servants?   What loss of animals, and average cost of purchase?   If I interested myself properly about my pint (or
hogshead, whatever it be) of milk, all this knowledge
would ensue; all this additional interest in life.   What is
this talk of my friend, Mr. Lewes, about objects at the
seaside, and so forth?   Objects at the seaside?   Objects at
the area-bell: objects before my nose: objects which the
butcher brings me in his tray: which the cook dresses and
puts down before me, and over which I say grace!   My
daily life is surrounded with objects which ought to interest me.   The pudding I eat (or refuse, that is neither here
nor there, and, between ourselves, what I have said about
batter pudding may be taken *cum grano*—we are not come
to *that* yet, except for the sake of argument or illustration)
—the pudding, I say, on my plate, the eggs that made it,
the fire that cooked it, the table-cloth on which it is laid,
and so forth—are each and all of these objects a knowledge of which I may acquire—a knowledge of the cost and
production of which I might advantageously learn?   To
the man who *does* know these things, I say the interest of
life is prodigiously increased.   The milkman becomes a
study to him; the baker a being he curiously and tenderly
examines.   Go, Lewes, and clap a hideous sea-anemone
into a glass: I will put a cabman under mine, and make a
vivisection of a butcher.   O Lares, Penates, and gentle
household gods, teach me to sympathize with all that comes
within my doors!   Give me an interest in the butcher's
book.   Let me look forward to the ensuing number of the
grocer's account with eagerness.   It seems ungrateful to
my kitchen-chimney not to know the cost of sweeping it;
and I trust that many a man who reads this, and muses
on it, will feel, like the writer, ashamed of himself, and
hang down his head humbly.

Now, if to this household game you could add a little money interest, the amusement would be increased far beyond the mere money value, as a game at cards for sixpence is better than a rubber for nothing. If you can interest yourself about sixpence, all life is invested with a new excitement. From sunrise to sleeping you can always be playing that game—with butcher, baker, coal-merchant, cabman, omnibus man—nay, diamond-merchant and stockbroker. You can bargain for a guinea over the price of a diamond necklace, or for a sixteenth per cent. in a transaction at the Stock Exchange. We all know men who have this faculty who are not ungenerous with their money. They give it on great occasions. They are more able to help than you and I who spend ours, and say to poor Prodigal who comes to us out at elbow, "My dear fellow, I should have been delighted: but I have already anticipated my quarter, and am going to ask Screwby if he can do anything for me."

In this delightful, wholesome, ever-novel twopenny game, there is a danger of excess, as there is in every other pastime or occupation of life. If you grow too eager for your twopence, the acquisition or the loss of it may affect your peace of mind, and peace of mind is better than any amount of twopences. My friend, the old clothes' man, whose agonies over the hat have led to this rambling disquisition, has, I very much fear, by a too eager pursuit of small profits, disturbed the equanimity of a mind that ought to be easy and happy. "Had I stood out," he thinks, "I might have had the hat for threepence," and he doubts whether, having given fourpence for it, he will ever get back his money. My good Shadrach, if you go through life passionately deploring the irrevocable, and allow yesterday's transactions to embitter the cheerfulness of to-day and to-morrow—as lieve walk down to the Seine, souse in, hats, body, clothes-bag and all, and put an end to your sorrow and sordid cares. Before and since Mr. Franklin wrote his pretty apologue of the Whistle have we not all made bargains of which we repented, and coveted and acquired objects for which we have paid too dearly? Who has not purchased his hat in some market or other? There is General M'Clellan's cocked hat for example: I daresay he was eager enough to wear it, and he has learned that it is by no means cheerful wear. There were the military beavers of Messeigneurs of Orleans: they wore them gallantly in the face of battle; but I suspect they were glad enough to pitch them into the James River and come home in mufti. Ah, *mes amis!* *à chacun son schakot!* I was looking at a bishop the other day, and thinking, "My right reverend lord, that broad-brim and rosette must bind your great broad forehead very tightly, and give you many a headache. A good easy wide-awake were better for you, and I would like to see that honest face with a cutty pipe in the middle of it." There is my Lord Mayor. My once dear lord, my kind friend, when your two years' reign was over, did not you jump for joy and fling your chapeau-bras out of window: and hasn't *that* hat cost you a pretty bit of money? There, in a splendid travelling chariot, in the sweetest bonnet, all trimmed with orange-blossoms and Chantilly lace, sits my Lady Rosa, with old Lord Snowden by her side. Ah, Rosa! what a price have you paid for that hat which you wear; and is your ladyship's coronet not purchased too dear? Enough of hats. Sir, or Madam, I take off mine, and salute you with profound respect.

ON ALEXANDRINES.

A LETTER TO SOME COUNTRY COUSINS.

DEAR COUSINS,—Be pleased to receive herewith a packet of Mayall's photographs, and copies of *Illustrated News, Illustrated Times, London Review, Queen,* and *Observer,* each containing an account of the notable festivities of the past week. If besides these remembrances of home you have a mind to read a letter from an old friend, behold here it is. When I was at school, having left my parents in India, a good-natured captain or colonel would come sometimes and see us Indian boys, and talk to us about papa and mamma, and give us coins of the realm, and write to our parents, and say, "I drove over yesterday and saw Tommy at Dr. Birch's. I took him to the George, and gave him a dinner. His appetite is fine. He states that he is reading Cornelius Nepos, with which he is much interested. His masters report," &c. And though Dr. Birch wrote by the same mail a longer, fuller, and official statement, I have no doubt the distant parents preferred the friend's letter, with its artless, possibly ungrammatical, account of their little darling.

I have seen the young heir of Britain. These eyes have beheld him and his bride—on Saturday in Pall Mall (when they stopped for awhile before the house of Smith, Elder and Co., and all within admired a lovely cloak of purple velvet and sable worn by a lady of whose appearance the photographers will enable you to judge), and on Tuesday in the nave of St. George's Chapel at Windsor, when the young Princess Alexandra of Denmark passed by with her blooming procession of bridesmaids; and half an hour later, when the Princess of Wales came forth from the chapel, her husband by her side robed in the purple mantle of the famous Order which his forefather established here five hundred years ago.   We were to see her yet once again, when her open carriage passed out of the Castle gate to the station of the near railway which was to convey her to Southampton.

Since womankind existed, has any woman ever had such a greeting?   At ten hours' distance, there is a city far more magnificent than ours.   With every respect for Kensington turnpike, I own that the Arc de l'Étoile at Paris is a much finer entrance to an imperial capital.   In our black, orderless, zigzag streets, we can show nothing to compare with the magnificent array of the Rue de Rivoli, that enormous regiment of stone stretching for five miles and presenting arms before the Tuileries.   Think of the late Fleet Prison and Waithman's Obelisk, and of the Place de la Concorde and the Luxor Stone!   "The finest site in Europe," as Trafalgar Square has been called by some obstinate British optimist, is disfigured by trophies, fountains, columns, and statues so puerile, disorderly, and hideous that a lover of the arts must hang the head of shame as he passes to see our dear old queen city arraying herself so absurdly; but when all is said and done, we can show one or two of the greatest sights in the world.   I doubt if any Roman festival was as vast or striking as the Derby day, or if any Imperial triumph could show such a prodigious muster of faithful people as our young Princess saw on Saturday, when the nation turned out to greet her.   The calculators are squabbling about the numbers of hundreds of thousands, of millions, who came forth to see her and bid her welcome.   Imagine beacons flaming, rockets blazing, yards manned, ships and forts saluting with their thunder, every steamer and vessel, every town and village from Ramsgate to Gravesend, swarming with happy gratulation; young girls with flowers, scattering roses before her; staid citizens and aldermen pushing and squeezing and panting to make the speech, and bow the knee, and bid her welcome!   Who is this who is honoured with such a prodigious triumph, and received with a welcome so astonishing?   A year ago we had never heard of her.   I think about her pedigree and family not a few of us are in the dark still, and I own, for my part, to be much puzzled by the allusions of newspaper genealogists and bards and skalds to "Vikings," Berserkers, and so forth. But it would be interesting to know how many hundreds of thousands of photographs of the fair bright face have by this time made it beloved and familiar in British homes. Think of all the quiet country nooks from Land's End to Caithness, where kind eyes have glanced at it. The farmer brings it home from market; the curate from his visit to the Cathedral town; the rustic folk peer at it in the little village shop window; the squire's children gaze on it round the drawing-room table; every eye that beholds it looks tenderly on its bright beauty and sweet artless grace, and young and old pray God bless her. We have an elderly friend (a certain Goody Twoshoes, who has been mentioned before in the pages of this Magazine), and who inhabits, with many other old ladies, the Union-house of the parish of St. Lazarus in Soho. One of your cousins from this house went to see her, and found Goody and her companion crones all in a flutter of excitement about the marriage. The whitewashed walls of their bleak dormitory were ornamented with prints out of the illustrated journals, and hung with festoons and true-lover's knots of tape and coloured paper; and the old bodies had had a good dinner, and the old tongues were chirping and clacking away, all eager, interested, sympathizing; and one very elderly and rheumatic Goody, who is obliged to keep her bed (and has, I trust, an exaggerated idea of the cares attending on royalty), said, "Pore thing, pore thing! I pity her." Yes, even in that dim place there was a little brightness and a quavering huzza, a contribution of a mite subscribed by those dozen poor old widows to the treasure of loyalty with which the nation endows the Prince's bride.

Three hundred years ago, when our dread Sovereign Lady Elizabeth came to take possession of her realm and capital city, Holingshed, if you please (whose pleasing history of course you carry about with you), relates in his

fourth volume folio, that—"At hir entring the citie, she
was of the people received maruellous intierlie, as appeared
by the assemblies, praiers, welcommings, cries, and all
other signes which argued a woonderfull earnest loue:"
and at various halting-places on the royal progress children
habited like angels appeared out of allegoric edifices and
spoke verses to her—

> Welcome, O Queen, as much as heart can think,
>   Welcome again, as much as tongue can tell,
> Welcome to joyous tongues and hearts that will not shrink.
>   God thee preserve, we pray, and wish thee ever well!

Our new Princess, you may be sure, has also had her
Alexandrines, and many minstrels have gone before her
singing her praises.   Mr. Tupper, who begins in very
great force and strength, and who proposes to give her no
less than eight hundred thousand welcomes in the first
twenty lines of his ode, is not satisfied with this most liberal amount of acclamation, but proposes at the end of his
poem a still more magnificent subscription.   Thus we begin,
"A hundred thousand welcomes, a hundred thousand welcomes."   (In my copy the figures are in the well-known
Arabic numerals, but let us have the numbers literally
accurate :)

> A hundred thousand welcomes!
> A hundred thousand welcomes!
>   And a hundred thousand more!
> O happy heart of England,
> Shout aloud and sing, land,
> As no land sang before;
> And let the pæans soar
> And ring from shore to shore,
> A hundred thousand welcomes,
> And a hundred thousand more;
>   And let the cannons roar,
>   The joy-stunned city o'er.
> And let the steeples chime it
> A hundred thousand welcomes
> And a hundred thousand more;
>   And let the people rhyme it

From neighbour's door to door,
From every man's heart's core,
A hundred thousand welcomes
And a hundred thousand more.

This contribution, in twenty not long lines, of 900,000
(say nine hundred thousand) welcomes is handsome indeed: and shows that when our bard is inclined to be liberal, he does not look to the cost. But what is a sum of
900,000 to his further proposal?—

O let all these declare it,
Let miles of shouting swear it,
  In all the years of yore,
  Unparalleled before:
And thou, most welcome Wand'rer
  Across the Northern Water,
Our England's Alexandra,
  Our dear adopted daughter—
Lay to thine heart, conned o'er and o'er,
  In future years remembered well,
  The magic fervour of this spell
That shakes the land from shore to shore,
And makes all hearts and eyes brim o'er;
  Our hundred thousand welcomes,
  Our fifty million welcomes,
And a hundred million more!

Here we have, besides the most liberal previous subscription, a further call on the public for no less than one
hundred and fifty million one hundred thousand welcomes
for her Royal Highness. How much is this per head for
all of us in the three kingdoms? Not above five welcomes
apiece, and I am sure many of us have given more than five
hurrahs to the fair young Princess.

Each man sings according to his voice, and gives in pro-
portion to his means. The guns at Sheerness "from their
adamantine lips" (which had spoken in quarrelsome old
times a very different language,) roared a hundred thundering welcomes to the fair Dane. The maidens of England
strewed roses before her feet at Gravesend when she landed.

Mr. Tupper, with the million and odd welcomes, may be compared to the thundering fleet; Mr. Chorley's song to the flowerets scattered on her Royal Highness's happy and carpeted path :—

> Blessings on that fair face!
>   Safe on the shore
> Of her home-dwelling place,
>   Stranger no more.
> Love, from her household shrine
>   Keep sorrow far!
> May, for her hawthorn twine,
> June, bring sweet eglantine,
> Autumn, the golden vine,
>   *Dear Northern Star!*

Hawthorn for May, eglantine for June, and in autumn a little tass of the golden vine for our Northern Star. I am sure no one will grudge the Princess these simple enjoyments, and of the produce of the last-named pleasing plant, I wonder how many bumpers were drunk to her health on the happy day of her bridal? As for the Laureate's verses, I would respectfully liken his Highness to a giant showing a beacon torch on "a windy headland." His flaring torch is a pine-tree, to be sure, which nobody can wield but himself. He waves it: and four times in the midnight he shouts mightily, "Alexandra!" and the Pontic pine is whirled into the ocean and Enceladus goes home.

Whose muse, whose cornemuse, sounds with such plaintive sweetness from Arthur's Seat, while Edinburgh and Musselburgh lie rapt in delight, and the mermaids come flapping up to Leith shore to hear the exquisite music? Sweeter piper Edina knows not than Aytoun, the Bard of the Cavaliers, who has given in his frank adhesion to the reigning dynasty. When a most beautiful, celebrated and unfortunate princess whose memory the Professor loves— when Mary, wife of Francis the Second, King of France, and by her own right proclaimed Queen of Scotland and England (poor soul!), entered Paris with her young bridegroom, good Peter Ronsard wrote of her—

Toi qui as veu l'excellence de celle
Qui rend le ciel de l'Escosse envieux,
Dy hardiment, contentez vous mes yeux,
Vous ne verrez jamais chose plus belle.*

Vous ne verrez jamais chose plus belle. Here is an Alexandrine written three hundred years ago, as simple as *bon jour.* Professor Aytoun is more ornate. After elegantly complimenting the spring, and a description of her Royal Highness's well-known ancestors, "the Berserkers," he bursts forth—

The Rose of Denmark comes, the Royal Bride!
O loveliest Rose! our paragon and pride—
Choice of the Prince whom England holds so dear—
What homage shall we pay
To one who has no peer?
What can the bard or wildered minstrel say
More than the peasant, who, on bended knee,
Breathes from his heart an earnest prayer for thee?
Words are not fair, if that they would express
Is fairer still; so lovers in dismay
Stand all abashed before that loveliness
They worship most, but find no words to pray.
Too sweet for incense! (bravo) Take our loves instead—
Most freely, truly, and devoutly given;
Our prayer for blessings on that gentle head,
For earthly happiness and rest in Heaven!
May never sorrow dim those dove-like eyes,
But peace as pure as reigned in Paradise,
Calm and untainted on creation's eve,
Attend thee still! May holy angels, &c.

This is all very well, my dear country cousins. But will you say "Amen" to this prayer? I won't. Assuredly our fair Princess will shed many tears out of the "dovelike eyes," or the heart will be little worth. Is she to know no parting, no care, no anxious longing, no tender watches by the sick, to deplore no friends and kindred, and feel no grief? Heaven forbid! When a bard or wildered minstrel writes so, best accept his own confession, that he is losing his head. On the day of her entrance into London

* Quoted in Mignet's "Life of Mary."

who looked more bright and happy than the Princess? On the day of the marriage, the fair face wore its mark of care already, and looked out quite grave, and frightened almost, under the wreaths and lace and orange-flowers. Would you have had her feel no tremor? A maiden on the bridegroom's threshold, a Princess led up to the steps of a throne? I think her pallor and doubt became her as well as her smiles. That, I can tell you, was *our* vote who sate in X compartment, let us say, in the nave of St. George's Chapel at Windsor, and saw a part of one of the brightest ceremonies ever performed there.

My dear cousin Mary, you have an account of the dresses; and I promise you there were princesses besides the bride whom it did the eyes good to behold. Around the bride sailed a bevy of young creatures so fair, white, and graceful that I thought of those fairy-tale beauties who are sometimes princesses, and sometimes white swans. The Royal Princesses and the Royal Knights of the Garter swept by in prodigious robes and trains of purple velvet, thirty shillings a yard, my dear, not of course including the lining, which, I have no doubt, was of the richest satin, or that costly "miniver" which we used to read about in poor Jerrold's writings. The young princes were habited in kilts; and by the side of the Princess Royal trotted such a little wee solemn Highlander! He is the young heir and chief of the famous clan of Brandenburg. His eyrie is amongst the Eagles, and I pray no harm may befall the dear little chieftain.

The heralds in their tabards were marvellous to behold, and a nod from Rouge Croix gave me the keenest gratification. I tried to catch Garter's eye, but either I couldn't or he wouldn't. In his robes, he is like one of the Three Kings in old missal illuminations. Gold Stick in waiting is even more splendid. With his gold rod and robes and trappings of many colours, he looks like a royal enchanter, and as if he had raised up all this scene of glamour by a wave of his glittering wand. The silver trumpeters wear such quaint caps, as those I have humbly tried to depict on the playful heads of children. Behind the trumpeters came a drum-bearer, on whose back a gold-laced drummer drubbed his march.

When the silver clarions had blown, and under a clear chorus of white-robed children chanting round the organ, the noble procession passed into the chapel, and was hidden from our sight for a while, there was silence, or from the inner chapel ever so faint a hum. Then hymns arose, and in the lull we knew that prayers were being said, and the sacred rite performed which joined Albert Edward to Alexandra his wife. I am sure hearty prayers were offered outside the gate as well as within for that princely young pair, and for their Mother and Queen. The peace, the freedom, the happiness, the order which her rule guarantees, are part of my birthright as an Englishman, and I bless God for my share. Where else shall I find such liberty of action, thought, speech, or laws which protect me so well? Her part of her compact with her people, what sovereign ever better performed? If ours sits apart from the festivities of the day, it is because she suffers from a grief so recent that the loyal heart cannot master it as yet, and remains *treu und fest* to a beloved memory. A part of the music which celebrates the day's service was composed by the husband who is gone to the place where the just and pure of life meet the reward promised by the Father of all of us to good and faithful servants who have well done here below. As this one gives in his account, surely we may remember how the Prince was the friend of all peaceful arts and learning; how he was true and fast always to duty, home, honour; how, through a life of complicated trials, he was sagacious, righteous, active and self-denying. And as we trace in the young faces of his many children the father's features and likeness, what Englishman will not pray that they may have inherited also some of the great qualities which won for the Prince Consort the love and respect of our country?

The papers tell us how, on the night of the marriage of the Prince of Wales, all over England and Scotland illuminations were made, the poor and children were feasted, and in village and city thousands of kindly schemes were devised to mark the national happiness and sympathy. "The bonfire on Coptpoint at Folkestone was seen in France," the *Telegraph* says, "more clearly than even the French marine lights could be seen at Folkestone." Long may the fire continue to burn! There are European coasts (and inland places) where the liberty light has been extinguished, or is so low that you can't see to read by it—there are great Atlantic shores where it flickers and smokes very gloomily. Let us be thankful to the honest guardians of ours, and for the kind sky under which it burns bright and steady.

ON A MEDAL OF GEORGE THE FOURTH.

BEFORE me lies a coin bearing the image and superscription of King George IV., and of the nominal value of two-and-sixpence. But an official friend at a neighbouring turnpike says the piece is hopelessly bad; and a chemist tested it, returning a like unfavourable opinion. A cabman, who had brought me from a club, left it with the club porter, appealing to the gent who gave it a pore cabby, at ever so much o'clock of a rainy night, which he hoped he would give him another. I have taken that cabman at his word. He has been provided with a sound coin. The bad piece is on the table before me, and shall have a hole drilled through it, as soon as this essay is written, by a loyal subject who does not desire to deface the Sovereign's fair image, but to protest against the rascal who has taken her name in vain. *Fid. Def.*, indeed! Is this what you call defending the faith? You dare to forge your Sovereign's name, and pass your scoundrel pewter as her silver? I wonder who you are, wretch and most consummate trickster? This forgery is so complete that even now I am deceived by it—I can't see the difference between the base and sterling metal. Perhaps this piece is a little lighter;—I don't know. A little softer:—is it? I have not bitten it, not being a connoisseur in the tasting of pewter or silver. I take the word of three honest men, though it goes against me: and though I have given two-and-sixpence worth of honest consideration for the counter, I shall not attempt to implicate anybody else in my misfortune, or transfer my ill-luck to a deluded neighbour.

I say the imitation is so curiously successful, the stamping, milling of the edges, lettering, and so forth, are so neat, that even now, when my eyes are open, I cannot see the cheat. How did those experts, the cabman, and pikeman, and tradesman, come to find it out? How do they happen to be more familiar with pewter and silver than I am? You see, I put out of the question another point which I might argue without fear of defeat, namely, the cabman's statement that I gave him this bad piece of money. Suppose every cabman who took me a shilling fare were to drive away and return presently with a bad coin and an assertion that I had given it to him? This would be absurd and mischievous; an encouragement of vice amongst men who already are subject to temptations. Being *homo*, I think if I were a cabman myself, I might sometimes stretch a furlong or two in my calculations of distance. But don't come *twice*, my man, and tell me I have given you a bad half-crown. No, no! I have paid once like a gentleman, and once is enough. For instance, during the Exhibition time I was stopped by an old country-woman in black, with a huge umbrella, who, bursting into tears, said to me, "Master, be this the way to Harlow, in Essex?" "This the way to Harlow? This is the way to Exeter, my good lady, and you will arrive there if you walk about 170 miles in your present direction," I answered courteously, replying to the old creature. Then she fell a-sobbing as though her old heart would break. She had a daughter a-dying at Harlow. She had walked already "vifty dree mile" that day. Tears stopped the rest of her discourse, so artless, genuine, and abundant that—I own the truth—I gave her, in I believe genuine silver, a piece of the exact size of that coin which forms the subject of this essay. Well. About a month since, near to the very spot where I had met my old woman, I was accosted by a person in black, a person in a large draggled cap, a person with a huge umbrella, who was beginning, "I say, master, can you tell me if this be the way to Har——" but here she stopped. Her eyes goggled wildly. She started from me, as Macbeth turned from Macduff. She would not engage with me. It was my old friend of Harlow, in Essex. I daresay she has informed many other people of her daughter's illness, and her anxiety to be put upon the right way to Harlow. Not long since a very gentlemanlike man, Major Delamere let us call him (I like the title of Major very much), requested to see me, named a dead gentleman who he said had been our mutual friend, and on the strength of this mutual acquaintance, begged me to cash his check for five pounds!

It is these things, my dear sir, which serve to make a man cynical. I do conscientiously believe that had I cashed the Major's cheque, there would have been a difficulty about payment on the part of the respected bankers on whom he drew. On your honour and conscience, do you think that old widow who was walking from Tunbridge Wells to Harlow had a daughter ill, and was an honest woman at all? The daughter couldn't always, you see, be being ill, and her mother on her way to her dear child through Hyde Park. In the same way some habitual sneerers may be inclined to hint that the cabman's story was an invention—or at any rate, choose to ride off (so to speak) on the doubt. No. My opinion, I own, is unfavourable as regards the widow from Tunbridge Wells, and Major Delamere; but, believing the cabman was honest, I am glad to think he was not injured by the reader's most humble servant.

What a queer, exciting life this rogue's march must be: this attempt of the bad half-crowns to get into circulation! Had my distinguished friend the Major knocked at many doors that morning, before operating on mine? The sport must be something akin to the pleasure of tiger or elephant hunting. What ingenuity the sportsman must have in tracing his prey—what daring and caution in coming upon him! What coolness in facing the angry animal (for, after all, a man on whom you draw a cheque *à bout portant* will be angry). What a delicious thrill of triumph, if you can bring him down! If I have money at the banker's and draw for a portion of it over the counter, that is mere prose—any dolt can do that. But, having no balance, say, I drive up in a cab, present a cheque at Coutts's, and, receiving the amount, drive off? What a glorious morning's sport that has been! How superior in excitement to the common transactions of every-day life! * * * I must tell a story; it is against myself, I know, but it *will* out, and perhaps my mind will be the easier.

More than twenty years ago, in an island remarkable for its verdure, I met four or five times one of the most agreeable companions with whom I have passed a night. I heard that evil times had come upon this gentleman; and, overtaking him in a road near my own house one evening, I asked him to come home to dinner. In two days, he was at my door again. At breakfast-time was this second appearance. He was in a cab (of course he was in a cab, they always are, these unfortunate, these courageous men). To deny myself was absurd. My friend could see me over the parlour blinds, surrounded by my family, and cheerfully partaking the morning meal. Might he have a word with me? and can you imagine its purport? By the most provoking delay—his uncle the admiral not being able to come to town till Friday—would I cash him a cheque? I need not say it would be paid on Saturday without fail. I tell you that man went away with money in his pocket, and I regret to add that his gallant relative has not *come to town yet!*

Laying down the pen, and sinking back in my chair, here, perhaps, I fall into a five minutes' reverie, and think of one, two, three, half-a-dozen cases in which I have been content to accept that sham promissory coin in return for sterling money advanced. Not a reader, whatever his age, but could tell a like story. I vow and believe there are men of fifty, who will dine well to-day, who have not paid their school debts yet, and who have not taken up their long-protested promises to pay. Tom, Dick, Harry, my boys, I owe you no grudge, and rather relish that wince with which you will read these meek lines and say, "He means me." Poor Jack in Hades! Do you remember a certain pecuniary transaction, and a little sum of money you borrowed "until the meeting of Parliament?" Parliament met often in your lifetime: Parliament has met since:

but I think I should scarce be more surprised if your ghost glided into the room now, and laid down the amount of our little account, than I should have been if you had paid me in your lifetime with the actual acceptances of the Bank of England. You asked to borrow, but you never intended to pay. I would as soon have believed that a promissory note of Sir John Falstaff (accepted by Messrs. Bardolph and Nym, and payable in Aldgate,) would be as sure to find payment, as that note of the departed—nay, lamented —Jack Thriftless.

He who borrows, meaning to pay, is quite a different person from the individual here described. Many—most, I hope—took Jack's promise for what it was worth—and quite well knew that when he said, "Lend me," he meant "Give me" twenty pounds. "Give me change for this half-crown," said Jack; I know it's a pewter piece, and you gave him the change in honest silver, and pocketed the counterfeit gravely.

What a queer consciousness that must be which accompanies such a man in his sleeping, in his waking, in his walk through life, by his fireside with his children round him! "For what we are going to receive," &c.—he says grace before his dinner. "My dears! Shall I help you to some mutton? I robbed the butcher of the meat. I don't intend to pay him. Johnson, my boy, a glass of champagne? Very good, isn't it? Not too sweet. Forty-six. I get it from So-and-so, whom I intend to cheat." As eagles go forth and bring home to their eaglets the lamb or the pavid kid, I say there are men who live and victual their nests by plunder. We all know highway robbers in white neckcloths, domestic bandits, marauders, passers of bad coin. What was yonder cheque which Major Delamere proposed I should cash but a piece of bad money? What was Jack Thriftless's promise to pay? Having got his booty, I fancy Jack or the Major returning home, and wife and children gathering round about him. Poor wife and children! They respect papa very likely. They don't know he is false coin. Maybe the wife has a dreadful inkling of the truth, and, sickening, tries to hide it from the daughters and sons. Maybe she is an accomplice: herself a brazen forgery. If Turpin and Jack Sheppard were married, very likely Mesdames Sheppard and Turpin did not know, at first, what their husbands' real profession was, and fancied, when the men left home in the morning, they only went away to follow some regular and honourable business. Then a suspicion of the truth may have come: then a dreadful revelation: and presently we have the guilty pair robbing together, or passing forged money each on his own account. You know Doctor Dodd? I wonder whether his wife knows that he is a forger, and scoundrel? Has she had any of the plunder, think you, and were the darling children's new dresses bought with it? The Doctor's sermon last Sunday was certainly charming, and we all cried. Ah, my poor Dodd! Whilst he is preaching most beautifully, pocket-handkerchief in hand, he is peering over the pulpit cushions, looking out piteously for Messrs. Peachum and Lockit from the police-office. By Doctor Dodd you understand I would typify the rogue of respectable exterior, not committed to gaol yet, but not undiscovered. We all know one or two such. This very sermon perhaps will be read by some, or more likely—for, depend upon it, your solemn hypocritic scoundrels don't care much for light literature—more likely, I say, this discourse will be read by some of their wives, who think, "Ah mercy! does that horrible cynical wretch know how my poor husband blacked my eye, or abstracted mamma's silver teapot, or forced me to write So-and-so's name on that piece of stamped paper, or what not?" My good creature, I am not angry with *you*. If your husband has broken your nose, you will vow that he had authority over your person, and a right to demolish any part of it: if he has conveyed away your mamma's teapot, you will say that she gave it to him at your marriage, and it was very ugly, and what not: if he takes your aunt's watch, and you love him, you will carry it ere long to the pawnbroker's, and perjure yourself—oh, how you will perjure yourself—

in the witness-box! I know this is a degrading view of woman's noble nature, her exalted mission, and so forth, and so forth. I know you will say this is bad morality. Is it? Do you, or do you not, expect your womankind to stick by you for better or for worse? Say I have committed a forgery, and the officers come in search of me, is my wife, Mrs. Dodd, to show them into the dining-room, and say, "Pray step in, gentlemen! My husband has just come home from church. That bill with my Lord Chesterfield's acceptance, I am bound to own, was never written by his lordship, and the signature is in the doctor's handwriting?" I say, would any man of sense or honour, or fine feeling, praise his wife for telling the truth under such circumstances? Suppose she made a fine grimace, and said, "Most painful as my position is, most deeply as I feel for my William, yet truth must prevail, and I deeply lament to state that the beloved partner of my life *did* commit the flagitious act with which he is charged, and is at this present moment located in the two-pair back, up the chimney, whither it is my duty to lead you." Why, even Dodd himself, who was one of the greatest humbugs who ever lived, would not have had the face to say that he approved of his wife telling the truth in such a case. Would you have had Flora Macdonald beckon the officers, saying, "This way, gentlemen! You will find the young chevalier asleep in that cavern." Or don't you prefer her to be *splendide mendax*, and ready at all risks to save him? If ever I lead a rebellion, and my women betray me, may I be hanged but I will not forgive them: and if ever I steal a teapot, and *my* women don't stand up for me, pass the articles under their shawls, whisk down the street with it, outbluster the policeman, and utter any amount of fibs before Mr. Beak; those beings are not what I take them to be, and—for a fortune—I won't give them so much as a bad half-crown.

Is conscious guilt a source of unmixed pain to the bosom which harbours it? Has not your criminal, on the contrary, an excitement, an enjoyment within quite unknown

to you and me who never did anything wrong in our lives?
The housebreaker must snatch a fearful joy as he walks
unchallenged by the policeman with his sack full of spoons
and tankards. Do not cracksmen, when assembled together, entertain themselves with stories of glorious old
burglaries which they or bygone heroes have committed?
But that my age is mature and my habits formed, I should
really just like to try a little criminality. Fancy passing
a forged bill to your banker; calling on a friend and sweeping his sideboard of plate, his hall of umbrellas and coats;
and then going home to dress for dinner, say—and to meet
a bishop, a judge, and a police magistrate or so, and talk
more morally than any man at table! How I should
chuckle (as my host's spoons clinked softly in my pocket)
whilst I was uttering some noble speech about virtue,
duty, charity! I wonder do we meet garotters in society?
In an average tea-party, now, how many returned convicts
are there? Does John Footman, when he asks permission
to go and spend the evening with some friends, pass his
time in thuggee; waylay and strangle an old gentleman or
two; let himself into your house, with the house-key of
course, and appear as usual with the shaving-water when
you ring your bell in the morning? The very possibility of
such a suspicion invests John with a new and romantic interest in my mind. Behind the grave politeness of his
countenance I try and read the lurking treason. Full of
this pleasing subject, I have been talking thief-stories with
a neighbour. The neighbour tells me how some friends of
hers used to keep a jewel-box under a bed in their room;
and, going into the room, they thought they heard a noise
under the bed. They had the courage to look. The cook
was under the bed—under the bed with the jewel-box.
Of course she said she had come for purposes connected
with her business; but this was absurd. A cook under a
bed is not there for professional purposes. A relation of
mine had a box containing diamonds under her bed, which
diamonds she told me were to be mine. Mine! One day,
at dinner-time, between the entrées and the roast, a cab

drove away from my relative's house containing the box wherein lay the diamonds. John laid the dessert, brought the coffee, waited all the evening—and oh, how frightened he was when he came to learn that his mistress's box had been conveyed out of her own room, and it contained diamonds—"Law bless us, did it now?" I wonder whether John's subsequent career has been prosperous? Perhaps the gentlemen from Bow Street were all in the wrong when they agreed in suspecting John as the author of the robbery. His noble nature was hurt at the suspicion. You conceive he would not like to remain in a family where they were mean enough to suspect him of stealing a jewel-box out of a bed-room—and the injured man and my relatives soon parted. But, inclining (with my usual cynicism) to think that he did steal the valuables, think of his life for the month or two whilst he still remains in the service! He shows the officers over the house, agrees with them that the *coup* must have been made by persons familiar with it; gives them every assistance; pities his master and mistress with a manly compassion; points out what a cruel misfortune it is to himself as an honest man, with his living to get and his family to provide for, that this suspicion should fall on him. Finally, he takes leave of his place, with a deep though natural melancholy that ever he had accepted it. What's a thousand pounds to gentlefolks? A loss certainly, but they will live as well without the diamonds as with them. But to John his Hhhonour was worth more than diamonds, his Hhonour was. Whohever is to give him back his character? Who is to prevent hany one from saying, "Ho yes. This is the butler which was in the family where the diamonds was stole?" &c.

I wonder has John prospered in life subsequently? If he is innocent, he does not interest me in the least. The interest of the case lies in John's behaviour, supposing him to be guilty. Imagine the smiling face, the daily service, the orderly performance of duty, whilst within John is suffering pangs lest discovery should overtake him. Every bell of the door which he is obliged to open may bring a police officer. The accomplices may peach. What an exciting life John's must have been for a while. And now, years and years after, when pursuit has long ceased, and detection is impossible, does he ever revert to the little transaction? Is it possible those diamonds cost a thousand pounds? What a rogue the fence must have been who only gave him so and so! And I pleasingly picture to myself an old ex-butler and an ancient receiver of stolen goods meeting and talking over this matter, which dates from times so early that the Queen's fair image could only just have begun to be coined or forged.

I choose to take John at the time when his little peccadillo is suspected, perhaps, but when there is no specific charge of robbery against him. He is not yet convicted: he is not even on his trial; how then can we venture to say he is guilty? Now think what scores of men and women walk the world in a like predicament; and what false coin passes current! Pinchbeck strives to pass off his history as sound coin. He knows it is only base metal, washed over with a thin varnish of learning. Poluphloisbos put his sermons in circulation: sounding brass, lackered over with white metal, and marked with the stamp and image of piety. What say you to Drawcansir's reputation as a military commander? to Tibbs's pretensions to be a fine gentleman? to Sapphira's claims as a poetess, or Rodoessa's as a beauty? His bravery, his piety, high birth, genius, beauty—each of these deceivers would palm his falsehood on us, and have us accept his forgeries as sterling coin. And we talk here, please to observe, of weaknesses rather than crimes. Some of us have more serious things to hide than a yellow cheek behind a raddle of rouge, or a white poll under a wig of jetty curls. You know, neighbour, there are not only false teeth in this world, but false tongues: and some make up a bust and an appearance of strength with padding, cotton, and what not; while another kind of artist tries to take you in by wearing under his waistcoat, and perpetually thumping, an immense sham heart. Dear sir, may yours and mine be found, at the right time, of the proper size and in the right place.

And what has this to do with half-crowns, good or bad? Ah, friend! may our coin, battered, and clipped, and defaced though it be, be proved to be Sterling Silver on the day of the Great Assay!

"STRANGE TO SAY, ON CLUB PAPER."

BEFORE the Duke of York's column, and between the
Athenæum and United Service Clubs, I have seen more
than once, on the esplanade, a preacher holding forth to a
little congregation of *badauds* and street-boys, whom he
entertains with a discourse on the crimes of a rapacious
aristocracy, or warns of the imminent peril of their own
souls. Sometimes this orator is made to "move on" by
brutal policemen. Sometimes, on a Sunday, he points to
a white head or two visible in the windows of the clubs to
the right and left of him, and volunteers a statement that
those quiet and elderly Sabbath-breakers will very soon be
called from this world to another, where their lot will by
no means be so comfortable as that which the reprobates
enjoy here, in their arm-chairs by their snug fires.

At the end of last month, had I been a Pall Mall preacher, I would have liked to send a whip round to all the
clubs in St. James's, and convoke the few members remaining in London to hear a discourse *sub Dio* on a text from
the *Observer* newspaper. I would have taken post under
the statue of Fame, say, where she stands distributing
wreaths to the three Crimean Guardsmen. (The crossing-
sweeper does not obstruct the path, and I suppose is away
at his villa on Sundays.) And, when the congregation was
pretty quiet, I would have begun:—

In the *Observer* of the 27th September, 1863, in the fifth
page and the fourth column, it is thus written:—

"The codicil appended to the will of the late Lord Clyde,
executed at Chatham, and bearing the signature of Clyde,
F.M., is written, strange to say, on a sheet of paper *bearing the Athenæum Club mark.*"

What the codicil is, my dear brethren, it is not our business to inquire. It conveys a benefaction to a faithful and

attached friend of the good field-marshal. The gift may be a lakh of rupees, or it may be a house and its contents —furniture, plate, and wine-cellar. My friends, I know the wine-merchant, and, for the sake of the legatee, hope heartily that the stock is large.

Am I wrong, dear brethren, in supposing that you expect a preacher to say a seasonable word on death here? If you don't, I fear you are but little familiar with the habits of preachers, and are but lax hearers of sermons. We might contrast the vault where the warrior's remains lie shrouded and coffined, with that in which his worldly provision of wine is stowed away. Spain and Portugal and France—all the lands which supplied his store—as hardy and obedient subaltern, as resolute captain, as colonel daring but prudent—he has visited the fields of all. In India and China he marches always unconquered; or at the head of his dauntless Highland brigade he treads the Crimean snow; or he rides from conquest to conquest in India once more; succouring his countrymen in the hour of their utmost need; smiting down the scared mutiny, and trampling out the embers of rebellion; at the head of a heroic army, a consummate chief. And now his glorious old sword is sheathed, and his honours are won; and he has bought him a house, and stored it with modest cheer for his friends (the good old man put water in his own wine, and a glass or two sufficed him)—behold the end comes, and his legatee inherits these modest possessions by virtue of a codicil to his lordship's will, written, "*strange to say, upon a sheet of paper bearing the Athenæum Club mark.*"

It is to this part of the text, my brethren, that I propose to address myself particularly, and if the remarks I make are offensive to any of you, you know the doors of our meeting-house are open, and you can walk out when you will. Around us are magnificent halls and palaces frequented by such a multitude of men as not even the Roman Forum assembled together. Yonder are the Martium and the Palladium. Next to the Palladium is the elegant Viatorium, which Barry gracefully stole from Rome. By

its side is the massive Reformatorium : and the—the Ultra-
torium rears its granite columns beyond.   Extending down
the street palace after palace rises magnificent, and under
their lofty roofs warriors and lawyers, merchants and nobles, scholars and seamen, the wealthy, the poor, the busy,
the idle assemble.   Into the halls built down this little
street and its neighbourhood the principal men of all London come to hear or impart the news ; and the affairs of the
state or of private individuals, the quarrels of empires or
of authors, the movements of the court or the splendid
vagaries of fashion, the intrigues of statesmen or of persons of another sex yet more wily, the last news of battles
in the great occidental continents, nay, the latest betting
for the horse-races, or the advent of a dancer at the theatre
—all that men do is discussed in these Pall Mall agoræ,
where we of London daily assemble.

Now, among so many talkers, consider how many false
reports must fly about : in such multitudes imagine how
many disappointed men there must be ; how many chatterboxes ; how many feeble and credulous (whereof I mark
some specimens in my congregation) ; how many mean,
rancorous, prone to believe ill of their betters, eager to find
fault ; and then, my brethren, fancy how the words of my
text must have been read and received in Pall Mall!   (I
perceive several of the congregation looking most uncomfortable.   One old boy with a dyed moustache turns purple
in the face, and struts back to the Martium : another, with
a shrug of the shoulder and a murmur of " Rubbish," slinks
away in the direction of the Togatorium, and the preacher
continues.)   The will of Field-Marshal Lord Clyde—signed
at Chatham, mind where his lordship died—is written,
strange to say, on a sheet of paper bearing the Athenæum
Club mark!

The inference is obvious.   A man cannot get Athenæum
paper except at the Athenæum.   Such paper is not sold at
Chatham, where the last codicil to his lordship's will is
dated.   And so the painful belief is forced upon us, that
a Peer, a Field-Marshal, wealthy, respected, illustrious,

could pocket paper at his club, and carry it away with him to the country. One fancies the hall porter conscious of the old lord's iniquity, and holding down his head as the marshal passes the door. What is that roll which his lordship carries? Is it his marshal's bâton gloriously won? No; it is a roll of foolscap conveyed from the club. What has he on his breast, under his great-coat? Is it his Star of India? No; it is a bundle of envelopes, bearing the head of Minerva, some sealing-wax, and a half-score of pens.

Let us imagine how in the hall of one or other of these clubs this strange anecdote will be discussed.

"Notorious screw," says Sneer. "The poor old fellow's avarice has long been known."

"Suppose he wishes to imitate the Duke of Marlborough," says Simper.

"Habit of looting contracted in India, you know; ain't so easy to get over, you know," says Snigger.

"When officers dined with him in India," remarks Solemn, "it was notorious that the spoons were all of a different pattern."

"Perhaps it isn't true. Suppose he wrote his paper at the club?" interposes Jones.

"It is dated at Chatham, my good man," says Brown. "A man if he is in London, says he is in London. A man if he is in Rochester, says he is in Rochester. This man happens to forget that he is using the club paper: and he happens to be found out: many men *don't* happen to be found out. I've seen literary fellows at clubs writing their rubbishing articles; I have no doubt they take away reams of paper. They crib thoughts: why shouldn't they crib stationery? One of your literary vagabonds who is capable of stabbing a reputation, who is capable of telling any monstrous falsehood to support his party, is surely capable of stealing a ream of paper."

"Well, well, we have all our weaknesses," sighs Robinson. "Seen that article, Thompson, in the *Observer* about Lord Clyde and the club paper? You'll find it upstairs.

In the third column of the fifth page towards the bottom of the page. I suppose he was so poor he couldn't afford to buy a quire of paper. Hadn't fourpence in the world. Oh, no!"

"And they want to get up a testimonial to this man's memory—a statue or something!" cries Jawkins. "A man who wallows in wealth and takes paper away from his club! I don't say he is not brave. Brutal courage most men have. I don't say he was not a good officer: a man with such experience *must* have been a good officer, unless he was born fool. But to think of this man loaded with honours—though of a low origin—so lost to self-respect as actually to take away the Athenæum paper! These parvenus, sir, betray their origin—betray their origin. I said to my wife this very morning, ' Mrs. Jawkins,' I said, ' there is talk of a testimonial to this man. I will not give one shilling. I have no idea of raising statues to fellows who take away club paper. No, by George, I have not. Why, they will be raising statues to men who take club spoons next! Not one penny of *my* money shall they have!' "

And now, if you please, we will tell the real story which has furnished this scandal to a newspaper, this tattle to club gossips and loungers. The field-marshal, wishing to make a further provision for a friend, informed his lawyer what he desired to do. The lawyer, a member of the Athenæum Club, there wrote the draft of such a codicil as he would advise, and sent the paper by the post to Lord Clyde at Chatham. Lord Clyde, finding the paper perfectly satisfactory, signed it and sent it back: and hence we have the story of "the codicil bearing the signature of Clyde, F.M., and written, strange to say, upon paper bearing the Athenæum Club mark."

Here I have been imagining a dialogue between a half-dozen gossips such as congregate round a club fire-place of an afternoon. I wonder how many people besides—whether any chance reader of this very page, has read and believed this story about the good old lord? Have the

country papers copied the anecdote, and our "own correspondents" made their remarks on it? If, my good sir,
or madam, you have read it and credited it, don't you own
to a little feeling of shame and sorrow, now that the trumpery little mystery is cleared? To "the new inhabitant of
light," passed away and out of reach of our censure, mis-
representation, scandal, dulness, malice, a silly falsehood
matters nothing. Censure and praise are alike to him—

> "The music warbling to the deafened ear,
> The incense wasted on the funeral bier,"

the pompous eulogy pronounced over the gravestone, or
the lie that slander spits on it. Faithfully though this
brave old chief did his duty, honest and upright though
his life was, glorious his renown—you see he could write
at Chatham on London paper; you see men can be found
to point out how "strange" his behaviour was.

And about ourselves? My good people, do you by
chance know any man or woman who has formed unjust
conclusions regarding his neighbour? Have you ever
found yourself willing, nay, eager to believe evil of some
man whom you hate? Whom you hate because he is successful, and you are not: because he is rich, and you are
poor: because he dines with great men who don't invite
you: because he wears a silk gown, and yours is still stuff:
because he has been called in to perform the operation,
though you lived close by: because his pictures have been
bought, and yours returned home unsold: because he fills
his church, and you are preaching to empty pews? If
your rival prospers, have you ever felt a twinge of anger?
If his wife's carriage passes you and Mrs. Tomkins, who
are in a cab, don't you feel that those people are giving
themselves absurd airs of importance? If he lives with
great people, are you not sure he is a sneak? And if you
ever felt envy towards another, and if your heart has ever
been black towards your brother, if you have been peevish
at his success, pleased to hear his merit depreciated, and
eager to believe all that is said in his disfavour—my good

sir, as you yourself contritely own that you are unjust,
jealous, uncharitable, so you may be sure, some men are
uncharitable, jealous, and unjust regarding *you.*

The proofs and manuscript of this little sermon have
just come from the printer's, and as I look at the writing,
I perceive, not without a smile, that one or two of the
pages bear, "strange to say," the mark of a club of which I
have the honour to be a member.   Those lines quoted in a
foregoing page are from some noble verses written by one of
Mr. Addison's men, Mr. Tickell, on the death of Cadogan,
who was amongst the most prominent "of Marlborough's
captains and Eugenio's friends."   If you are acquainted
with the history of those times, you have read how Cadogan had his feuds and hatreds too, as Tickell's patron had
his, as Cadogan's great chief had his.   "The Duke of
Marlborough's character has been so variously drawn"
(writes a famous contemporary of the duke's), "that it is
hard to pronounce on either side without the suspicion of
flattery or detraction.   I shall say nothing of his military
accomplishments, which the opposite reports of his friends
and enemies among the soldiers have rendered problemati-
cal.   Those maligners who deny him personal valour, seem
not to consider that this accusation is charged at a venture,
since the person of a general is too seldom exposed, and
that fear which is said sometimes to have disconcerted him
before action might probably be more for his army than
himself."   If Swift could hint a doubt of Marlborough's
courage, what wonder that a nameless scribe of our day
should question the honour of Clyde?

THE LAST SKETCH.

NOT many days since I went to visit a house where in former years I had received many a friendly welcome. We went in to the owner's—an artist's—studio. Prints, pictures, and sketches hung on the walls as I had last seen and remembered them. The implements of the painter's art were there. The light which had shone upon so many, many hours of patient and cheerful toil, poured through the northern window upon print and bust, lay figure and sketch, and upon the easel before which the good, the gentle, the beloved Leslie laboured. In this room the busy brain had devised, and the skilful hand executed, I know not how many of the noble works which have delighted the world with their beauty and charming humour. Here the poet called up into pictorial presence, and informed with life, grace, beauty, infinite friendly mirth and wondrous naturalness of expression, the people of whom his dear books told him the stories,—his Shakspeare, his Cervantes, his Molière, his Le Sage. There was his last work on the easel—a beautiful fresh smiling shape of Titania, such as his sweet guileless fancy imagined the "Midsummer Night's" queen to be. Gracious, and pure, and bright, the sweet smiling image glimmers on the canvas. Fairy elves, no doubt, were to have been grouped around their mistress in laughing clusters. Honest Bottom's grotesque head and form are indicated as reposing by the side of the consummate beauty. The darkling forest would have grown around them, with the stars glittering from the mid-summer sky: the flowers at the queen's feet, and the boughs and foliage about her, would have been peopled with gambolling sprites and fays. They were dwelling in the artist's mind no doubt, and would have been developed by that patient, faithful, admirable genius: but the busy brain stopped working, the skilful hand fell lifeless, the loving, honest heart ceased to beat. What was she to have been—that fair Titania—when perfected by the patient skill of the poet, who in imagination saw the sweet innocent figure, and with tender courtesy and caresses, as it were, posed and shaped and traced the fair form? Is there record kept anywhere of fancies conceived, beautiful, unborn? Some day will they assume form in some yet undeveloped light? If our bad unspoken thoughts are registered against us, and are written in the awful account, will not the good thoughts unspoken, the love and tenderness, the pity, beauty, charity, which pass through the breast, and cause the heart to throb with silent good, find a remembrance, too? A few weeks more, and this lovely offspring of the poet's conception would have been complete —to charm the world with its beautiful mirth. May there not be some sphere unknown to us where it may have an existence? They say our words, once out of our lips, go travelling in *omne œvum*, reverberating forever and ever. If our words, why not our thoughts? If the Has Been, why not the Might Have Been?

Some day our spirits may be permitted to walk in galleries of fancies more wondrous and beautiful than any achieved works which at present we see, and our minds to behold and delight in masterpieces which poets' and artists' minds have fathered and conceived only.

With a feeling much akin to that with which I looked upon the friend's—the admirable artist's—unfinished work, I can fancy many readers turning to these—the last pages which were traced by Charlotte Brontë's hand. Of the multitude that has read her books, who has not known and deplored the tragedy of her family, her own most sad and untimely fate? Which of her readers has not become her friend? Who that has known her books has not admired the artist's noble English, the burning love of truth, the bravery, the simplicity, the indignation at wrong, the eager sympathy, the pious love and reverence, the passionate honour, so to speak, of the woman? What a story is that of that family of poets in their solitude yonder on the gloomy northern moors! At nine o'clock at night, Mrs. Gaskell tells, after evening prayers, when their guardian and relative had gone to bed, the three poetesses—the three maidens, Charlotte, and Emily, and Anne—Charlotte being the "motherly friend and guardian to the other two"— "began, like restless wild animals, to pace up and down their parlour, 'making out' their wonderful stories, talking over plans and projects, and thoughts of what was to be their future life."

One evening, at the close of 1854, as Charlotte Nicholls sat with her husband by the fire, listening to the howling of the wind about the house, she suddenly said to her husband, "If you had not been with me, I must have been writing now." She then ran upstairs, and brought down, and read aloud, the beginning of a new tale. When she had finished, her husband remarked, "The critics will accuse you of repetition." She replied, "Oh! I shall alter that. I always begin two or three times before I can please myself." But it was not to be. The trembling little hand was to write no more. The heart, newly awakened to love and happiness, and throbbing with maternal hope, was soon to cease to beat; that intrepid outspeaker and champion of truth, that eager, impetuous redresser of wrong, was to be called out of the world's fight and struggle, to lay down the shining arms, and to be removed to a sphere where even a noble indignation *cor ulterius nequit lacerare,* and where truth complete, and right triumphant, no longer need to wage war.

I can only say of this lady, *vidi tantum.* I saw her first just as I rose out of an illness from which I had never thought to recover. I remember the trembling little frame, the little hand, the great honest eyes. An impetuous honesty seemed to me to characterize the woman. Twice I recollect she took me to task for what she held to be errors in doctrine. Once about Fielding we had a disputation. She spoke her mind out. She jumped too rapidly to conclusions. (I have smiled at one or two passages in the "Biography," in which my own disposition or behaviour forms the subject of talk.) She formed conclusions that might be wrong, and built up whole theories of character upon them. New to the London world, she entered it with an independent, indomitable spirit of her own; and judged of contemporaries, and especially spied out arrogance or affectation, with extraordinary keenness of vision. She was angry with her favourites if their conduct or conversation fell below her ideal. Often she seemed to me to be judging the London folk prematurely: but perhaps the city is rather angry at being judged. I fancied an austere little Joan of Arc marching in upon us, and rebuking our easy lives, our easy morals. She gave me the impression of being a very pure, and lofty, and high-minded person. A great and holy reverence of right and truth seemed to be with her always. Such, in our brief interview, she appeared to me. As one thinks of that life so noble, so lonely—of that passion for truth—of those nights and nights of eager study, swarming fancies, invention, depression, elation, prayer; as one reads the necessarily incomplete, though most touching and admirable history of the heart that throbbed in this one little frame—of this one amongst the myriads of souls that have lived and died on this great earth—this great earth?—this little speck in the infinite universe of God,—with what wonder do we think of to-day, with what awe await to-morrow, when that which is now but darkly seen shall be clear! As I read this little fragmentary sketch, I think of the rest. Is it? And where is it? Will not the leaf be turned some day, and the story be told? Shall the deviser of the tale somewhere perfect the history of little Emma's griefs and troubles? Shall Titania come forth complete with her sportive court, with the flowers at her feet, the forest around her, and all the stars of summer glittering overhead?

How well I remember the delight, and wonder, and pleasure with which I read "Jane Eyre," sent to me by an author whose name and sex were then alike unknown to me; the strange fascinations of the book; and how with my own work pressing upon me, I could not, having taken the volumes up, lay them down until they were read through! Hundreds of those who, like myself, recognized and admired that master-work of a great genius, will look with a mournful interest and regard and curiosity upon this, the last fragmentary sketch from the noble hand which wrote "Jane Eyre." W. M. T.

EMMA.

(A FRAGMENT OF A STORY BY THE LATE CHARLOTTE BRONTË.)

CHAPTER I.

WE all seek an ideal in life. A pleasant fancy began to visit me in a certain year, that perhaps the number of human beings is few who do not find their quest at some era of life for some space more or less brief. I had certainly not found mine in youth, though the strong belief I held of its existence sufficed through all my brightest and freshest time to keep me hopeful. I had not found it in maturity. I was become resigned never to find it. I had lived certain dim years entirely tranquil and unexpectant. And now I was not sure but something was hovering round my hearth which pleased me wonderfully.

Look at it, reader. Come into my parlour and judge for yourself whether I do right to care for this thing. First, you may scan me, if you please. We shall go on better together after a satisfactory introduction and due apprehension of identity. My name is Mrs. Chalfont. I am a widow. My house is good, and my income such as need not check the impulse either of charity or a moderate hospitality. I am not young, nor yet old. There is no silver yet in my hair, but its yellow lustre is gone. In my face wrinkles are yet to come, but I have almost forgotten the days when it wore any bloom. I married when I was very young. I lived for fifteen years a life which, whatever its trials, could not be called stagnant. Then for five years I was alone, and, having no children, desolate. Lately Fortune, by a somewhat curious turn of her wheel, placed in my way an interest and a companion.

The neighbourhood where I live is pleasant enough, its scenery agreeable, and its society civilized, though not numerous. About a mile from my house there is a ladies' school, established but lately—not more than three years since. The conductresses of this school were of my acquaintances; and though I cannot say that they occupied the very highest place in my opinion—for they had brought back from some months' residence abroad, for finishing purposes, a good deal that was fantastic, affected, and pretentious—yet I awarded them some portion of that respect which seems the fair due of all women who face life bravely, and try to make their own way by their own efforts.

About a year after the Misses Wilcox opened their school, when the number of their pupils was as yet exceedingly limited, and when, no doubt, they were looking out anxiously enough for augmentation, the entrance-gate to their little drive was one day thrown back to admit a carriage—"a very handsome, fashionable carriage," Miss Mabel Wilcox said, in narrating the circumstance afterwards—and drawn by a pair of really splendid horses. The sweep up the drive, the loud ring at the door-bell, the bustling entrance into the house, the ceremonious admission to the bright drawing-room, roused excitement enough in Fuchsia Lodge. Miss Wilcox repaired to the reception-room in a pair of new gloves, and carrying in her hand a handkerchief of French cambric.

She found a gentleman seated on the sofa, who, as he rose up, appeared a tall, fine-looking personage; at least she thought him so, as he stood with his back to the light. He introduced himself as Mr. Fitzgibbon, inquired if Miss Wilcox had a vacancy, and intimated that he wished to intrust to her care a new pupil in the shape of his daughter. This was welcome news, for there was many a vacancy in Miss Wilcox's schoolroom; indeed, her establishment was as yet limited to the select number of three, and she and her sisters were looking forward with anything but confidence to the balancing of accounts at the close of their first half-year. Few objects could have been more agreeable to her then than that to which, by a wave of the hand, Mr. Fitzgibbon now directed her attention—the figure of a child standing near the drawing-room window.

Had Miss Wilcox's establishment boasted fuller ranks—had she indeed entered well on that course of prosperity which in after years an undeviating attention to externals enabled her so triumphantly to realize—an early thought with her would have been to judge whether the acquisition now offered was likely to answer well as a show-pupil. She would have instantly marked her look, dress, &c., and inferred her value from these indicia. In those anxious commencing times, however, Miss Wilcox could scarce afford herself the luxury of such appreciation : a new pupil represented 40*l.* a year, independently of masters' terms —and 40*l.* a year was a sum Miss Wilcox needed and was glad to secure; besides, the fine carriage, the fine gentleman, and the fine name gave gratifying assurance, enough and to spare, of eligibility in the proffered connection. It was admitted, then, that there were vacancies in Fuchsia Lodge; that Miss Fitzgibbon could be received at once; that she was to learn all that the school prospectus proposed to teach; to be liable to every extra; in short, to be as expensive, and consequently as profitable a pupil, as any directress's heart could wish. All this was arranged as upon velvet, smoothly and liberally. Mr. Fitzgibbon showed in the transaction none of the hardness of the bargain-making man of business, and as little of the penurious anxiety of the straitened professional man. Miss Wilcox felt him to be "quite the gentleman." Everything disposed her to be partially inclined towards the little girl whom he, on taking leave, formally committed to her guardianship; and as if no circumstance should be wanting to complete her happy impression, the address left written on a card served to fill up the measure of Miss Wilcox's satisfaction—Conway Fitzgibbon, Esq., May Park, Midland County. That very day three decrees were passed in the new-comer's favour :—

1st. That she was to be Miss Wilcox's bed-fellow.

2nd. To sit next her at table.

3rd. To walk out with her.

In a few days it became evident that a fourth secret

clause had been added to these, viz., that Miss Fitzgibbon was to be favoured, petted, and screened on all possible occasions.

An ill-conditioned pupil, who before coming to Fuchsia Lodge had passed a year under the care of certain old-fashioned Misses Sterling, of Hartwood, and from them had picked up unpractical notions of justice, took it upon her to utter an opinion on this system of favouritism.

"The Misses Sterling," she injudiciously said, "never distinguished any girl because she was richer or better dressed than the rest. They would have scorned to do so. *They* always rewarded girls according as they behaved well to their school-fellows and minded their lessons, not according to the number of their silk dresses, and fine laces and feathers."

For it must not be forgotten that Miss Fitzgibbon's trunks, when opened, disclosed a splendid wardrobe; so fine were the various articles of apparel, indeed, that instead of assigning for their accommodation the painted deal drawers of the school bedroom, Miss Wilcox had them arranged in a mahogany bureau in her own room. With her own hands, too, she would on Sundays array the little favourite in her quilted silk pelisse, her hat and feathers, her ermine boa, and little French boots and gloves. And very self-complacent she felt when she led the young heiress (a letter from Mr. Fitzgibbon, received since his first visit, had communicated the additional particulars that his daughter was his only child, and would be the inheritress of his estates, including May Park, Midland County)— when she led her, I say, into the church, and seated her stately by her side at the top of the gallery-pew. Unbiassed observers might, indeed, have wondered what there was to be proud of, and puzzled their heads to detect the special merits of this little woman in silk—for, to speak truth, Miss Fitzgibbon was far from being the beauty of the school: there were two or three blooming little faces amongst her companions lovelier than hers. Had she been a poor child, Miss Wilcox herself would not have liked her physiognomy at all: rather, indeed, would it have repelled than attracted her; and, moreover—though Miss Wilcox hardly confessed the circumstance to herself, but, on the contrary strove hard not to be conscious of it—there were moments when she became sensible of a certain strange weariness in continuing her system of partiality. It hardly came natural to her to show this special distinction in this particular instance. An undefined wonder would smite her sometimes that she did not take more real satisfaction in flattering and caressing this embryo heiress—that she did not like better to have her always at her side, under her special charge. On principle Miss Wilcox continued the plan she had begun. On *principle*, for she argued with herself: This is the most aristocratic and richest of my pupils; she brings me the most credit and the most profit: therefore, I ought in justice to show her a special indulgence; which she did—but with a gradually increasing peculiarity of feeling.

Certainly, the undue favours showered on little Miss Fitzgibbon brought their object no real benefit. Unfitted for the character of playfellow by her position of favourite, her fellow-pupils rejected her company as decidedly as they dared. Active rejection was not long necessary; it was soon seen that passive avoidance would suffice; the pet was not social. No; even Miss Wilcox never thought her social. When she sent for her to show her fine clothes in the drawing-room when there was company, and especially when she had her into her parlour of an evening to be her own companion, Miss Wilcox used to feel curiously perplexed. She would try to talk affably to the young heiress, to draw her out, to amuse her. To herself the governess could render no reason why her efforts soon flagged; but this was invariably the case. However, Miss Wilcox was a woman of courage; and be the *protégée* what she might, the patroness did not fail to continue on *principle* her system of preference.

A favourite has no friends; and the observation of a gentleman, who about this time called at the Lodge and chanced to see Miss Fitzgibbon, was, "That child looks consummately unhappy:" he was watching Miss Fitzgibbon, as she walked, by herself, fine and solitary, while her schoolfellows were merrily playing.

"Who is the miserable little wight?" he asked.

He was told her name and dignity.

"Wretched little soul!" he repeated; and he watched her pace down the walk and back again; marching upright, her hands in her ermine muff, her fine pelisse showing a gay sheen to the winter's sun, her large Leghorn hat shading such a face as fortunately had not its parallel on the premises.

"Wretched little soul!" reiterated this gentleman. He opened the drawing-room window, watched the bearer of the muff till he caught her eye, and then summoned her with his finger. She came; he stooped his head down to her; she lifted her face up to him.

"Don't you play, little girl?"

"No, sir."

"No! why not? Do you think yourself better than other children?"

No answer.

"Is it because people tell you you are rich, you won't play?"

The young lady was gone. He stretched his hand to arrest her, but she wheeled beyond his reach, and ran quickly out of sight.

"An only child," pleaded Miss Wilcox; "possibly spoiled by her papa, you know; we must excuse a little pettishness."

"Humph! I am afraid there is not a little to excuse."

CHAPTER II.

MR. ELLIN—the gentleman mentioned in the last chapter—was a man who went where he liked, and being a gossiping, leisurely person, he liked to go almost anywhere. He could not be rich, he lived so quietly; and yet he must have had some money, for, without apparent profession, he continued to keep a house and a servant. He always spoke of himself as having once been a worker; but if so, that could not have been very long since, for he still looked far from old. Sometimes of an evening, under a little social conversational excitement, he would look quite young; but he was changeable in mood, and complexion, and expression, and had chameleon eyes, sometimes blue and merry, sometimes grey and dark, and anon green and gleaming. On the whole he might be called a fair man, of average height, rather thin and rather wiry. He had not resided more than two years in the present neighbourhood; his antecedents were unknown there; but as the Rector, a man of good family and standing, and of undoubted scrupulousness in the choice of acquaintance, had introduced him, he found everywhere a prompt reception, of which nothing in his conduct had yet seemed to prove him unworthy. Some people, indeed, dubbed him "a character," and fancied him "eccentric;" but others could not see the appropriateness of the epithets. He always seemed to them very harmless and quiet, not always perhaps so perfectly unreserved and comprehensible as might be wished. He had a discomposing expression in his eye; and sometimes in conversation an ambiguous diction; but still they believed he meant no harm.

Mr. Ellin often called on the Misses Wilcox; he sometimes took tea with them; he appeared to like tea and muffins, and not to dislike the kind of conversation which usually accompanies that refreshment; he was said to be a good shot, a good angler.—He proved himself an excellent gossip—he liked gossip well. On the whole he liked women's society, and did not seem to be particular in requiring difficult accomplishments or rare endowments in his female acquaintance. The Misses Wilcox, for instance, were not much less shallow than the china saucer which held their teacups; yet Mr. Ellin got on perfectly well with them, and had apparently great pleasure in hearing them discuss all the details of their school. He knew the

names of all their young ladies too, and would shake
hands with them if he met them walking out; he knew
their examination days and gala days, and more than once
accompanied Mr. Cecil, the curate, when he went to examine in ecclesiastical history.

This ceremony took place weekly, on Wednesday afternoons, after which Mr. Cecil sometimes stayed to tea, and
usually found two or three lady parishioners invited to
meet him. Mr. Ellin was also pretty sure to be there.
Rumour gave one of the Misses Wilcox in anticipated wed-
lock to the curate, and furnished his friend with a second
in the same tender relation; so that it is to be conjectured
they made a social, pleasant party under such interesting circumstances. Their evenings rarely passed without
Miss Fitzgibbon being introduced—all worked muslin and
streaming sash and elaborated ringlets; others of the pupils would also be called in, perhaps to sing, to show off a
little at the piano, or sometimes to repeat poetry. Miss
Wilcox conscientiously cultivated display in her young ladies, thinking she thus fulfilled a duty to herself and to
them, at once spreading her own fame and giving the children self-possessed manners.

It was curious to note how, on these occasions, good,
genuine natural qualities still vindicated their superiority
to counterfeit, artificial advantages. While "dear Miss
Fitzgibbon," dressed up and flattered as she was, could
only sidle round the circle with the crestfallen air which
seemed natural to her, just giving her hand to the guests,
then almost snatching it away, and sneaking in unmannerly
haste to the place allotted to her at Miss Wilcox's side,
which place she filled like a piece of furniture, neither
smiling nor speaking the evening through — while such
was *her* deportment, certain of her companions, as Mary
Franks, Jessy Newton, &c., handsome, open-countenanced
little damsels—fearless because harmless—would enter
with a smile of salutation and a blush of pleasure, make
their pretty reverence at the drawing-room door, stretch a
friendly little hand to such visitors as they knew, and sit

down to the piano to play their well-practised duet with an innocent, obliging readiness which won all hearts.

There was a girl called Diana—the girl alluded to before as having once been Miss Sterling's pupil—a daring, brave girl, much loved and a little feared by her comrades. She had good faculties, both physical and mental—was clever, honest, and dauntless. In the schoolroom she set her young brow like a rock against Miss Fitzgibbon's pretensions; she found also heart and spirit to withstand them in the drawing-room. One evening, when the curate had been summoned away by some piece of duty directly after tea, and there was no stranger present but Mr. Ellin, Diana had been called in to play a long, difficult piece of music which she could execute like a master. She was still in the midst of her performance, when—Mr. Ellin having for the first time, perhaps, recognized the existence of the heiress by asking if she was cold—Miss Wilcox took the opportunity of launching into a strain of commendation on Miss Fitzgibbon's inanimate behaviour, terming it lady-like, modest, and exemplary. Whether Miss Wilcox's constrained tone betrayed how far she was from really feeling the approbation she expressed, how entirely she spoke from a sense of duty, and not because she felt it possible to be in any degree charmed by the personage she praised —or whether Diana, who was by nature hasty, had a sudden fit of irritability—is not quite certain, but she turned on her music-stool :—

"Ma'am," said she to Miss Wilcox, "that girl does not deserve so much praise. Her behaviour is not at all exemplary. In the schoolroom she is insolently distant. For my part I denounce her airs; there is not one of us but is as good or better than she, though we may not be as rich."

And Diana shut up the piano, took her music-book under her arm, curtsied, and vanished.

Strange to relate, Miss Wilcox said not a word at the time; nor was Diana subsequently reprimanded for this outbreak. Miss Fitzgibbon had now been three months in the school, and probably the governess had had leisure to wear out her early raptures of partiality.

Indeed, as time advanced, this evil often seemed likely to right itself; again and again it seemed that Miss Fitzgibbon was about to fall to her proper level, but then, somewhat provokingly to the lovers of reason and justice, some little incident would occur to invest her insignificance with artificial interest. Once it was the arrival of a great basket of hothouse fruit—melons, grapes, and pines—as a present to Miss Wilcox in Miss Fitzgibbon's name. Whether it was that a share of these luscious productions was imparted too freely to the nominal donor, or whether she had had a surfeit of cake on Miss Mabel Wilcox's birthday, it so befell, that in some disturbed state of the digestive organs Miss Fitzgibbon took to sleep-walking. She one night terrified the school into a panic by passing through the bedrooms, all white in her night-dress, moaning and holding out her hands as she went.

Dr. Percy was then sent for; his medicines, probably, did not suit the case; for within a fortnight after the somnambulistic feat, Miss Wilcox going upstairs in the dark, trod on something which she thought was the cat, and on calling for a light, found her darling Matilda Fitzgibbon curled round on the landing, blue, cold, and stiff, without any light in her half-open eyes, or any colour in her lips, or movement in her limbs. She was not soon roused from this fit; her senses seemed half scattered; and Miss Wilcox had now an undeniable excuse for keeping her all day on the drawing-room sofa, and making more of her than ever.

There comes a day of reckoning both for petted heiresses and partial governesses.

One clear winter morning, as Mr. Ellin was seated at breakfast, enjoying his bachelor's easy chair and damp, fresh London newspaper, a note was brought to him marked "private," and "in haste." The last injunction was vain, for William Ellin did nothing in haste—he had no haste in him; he wondered anybody should be so foolish as to hurry; life was short enough without it. He looked at the little note—three-cornered, scented, and feminine. He knew the handwriting; it came from the very lady Rumour had so often assigned him as his own. The bachelor took out a morocco case, selected from a variety of little instruments a pair of tiny scissors, cut round the seal, and read: —"Miss Wilcox's compliments to Mr. Ellin, and she should be truly glad to see him for a few minutes, if at leisure. Miss W. requires a little advice. She will reserve explanations till she sees Mr. E."

Mr. Ellin very quietly finished his breakfast; then, as it was a very fine December day—hoar and crisp, but serene, and not bitter—he carefully prepared himself for the cold, took his cane, and set out. He liked the walk; the air was still; the sun not wholly ineffectual; the path firm, and but lightly powdered with snow. He made his journey as long as he could by going round through many fields, and through winding, unfrequented lanes. When there was a tree in the way conveniently placed for support, he would sometimes stop, lean his back against the trunk, fold his arms, and muse. If Rumour could have seen him, she would have affirmed that he was thinking about Miss Wilcox; perhaps when he arrives at the Lodge his demeanour will inform us whether such an idea be warranted.

At last he stands at the door and rings the bell; he is admitted, and shown into the parlour—a smaller and a more private room than the drawing-room. Miss Wilcox occupies it; she is seated at her writing-table; she rises— not without air and grace—to receive her visitor. This air and grace she learnt in France; for she was in a Parisian school for six months, and learnt there a little French, and a stock of gestures and courtesies. No: it is certainly not impossible that Mr. Ellin may admire Miss Wilcox. She is not without prettiness, any more than are her sisters; and she and they are one and all smart and showy. Bright stone-blue is a colour they like in dress; a crimson bow rarely fails to be pinned on somewhere to give contrast; positive colours generally—grass-greens, red violets, deep yellows—are in favour with them; all harmonies are at a discount. Many people would think Miss Wilcox, standing there in her blue merino dress and pomegranate ribbon, a very agreeable woman. She has regular features; the nose is a little sharp, the lips a little thin, good complexion, light red hair. She is very business-like, very practical; she never in her life knew a refinement of feeling or of thought; she is entirely limited, respectable, and self-satisfied. She has a cool, prominent eye; sharp and shallow pupil, unshrinking and inexpansive; pale irid; light eyelashes, light brow. Miss Wilcox is a very proper and decorous person; but she could not be delicate or modest, because she is naturally destitute of sensitiveness. Her voice, when she speaks, has no vibration; her face no expression; her manner no emotion. Blush or tremor she never knew.

"What can I do for you, Miss Wilcox?" says Mr. Ellin, approaching the writing-table, and taking a chair beside it.

"Perhaps you can advise me," was the answer; "or perhaps you can give me some information. I feel so thoroughly puzzled, and really fear all is not right."

"Where? and how?"

"I will have redress if it be possible," pursued the lady; "but how to set about obtaining it! Draw to the fire, Mr. Ellin; it is a cold day."

They both drew to the fire. She continued:—

"You know the Christmas holidays are near?"

He nodded.

"Well, about a fortnight since, I wrote, as is customary, to the friends of my pupils, notifying the day when we break up, and requesting that, if it was desired that any girl should stay the vacation, intimation should be sent accordingly. Satisfactory and prompt answers came to all the notes except one—that addressed to Conway Fitzgibbon, Esquire, May Park, Midland County—Matilda Fitzgibbon's father, you know."

"What? won't he let her go home?"

"Let her go home, my dear sir! you shall hear. Two

P

weeks elapsed, during which I daily expected an answer; none came. I felt annoyed at the delay, as I had particularly requested a speedy reply. This very morning I had made up my mind to write again, when—what do you think the post brought me? "

" I should like to know."

" My own letter—actually my own—returned from the post-office, with an intimation—such an intimation!—but read for yourself."

She handed to Mr. Ellin an envelope; he took from it the returned note and a paper—the paper bore a hastily-scrawled line or two. It said, in brief terms, that there was no such place in Midland County as May Park, and that no such person had ever been heard of there as Conway Fitzgibbon, Esquire.

On reading this, Mr. Ellin slightly opened his eyes.

" I hardly thought it was so bad as this," said he.

" What? you did think it was bad then? You suspected that something was wrong? "

" Really! I scarcely knew what I thought or suspected. How very odd, no such place as May Park! The grand mansion, the grounds, the oaks, the deer, vanished clean away. And then Fitzgibbon himself! But you saw Fitzgibbon—he came in his carriage? "

" In his carriage! " echoed Miss Wilcox; " a most stylish equipage, and himself a most distinguished person. Do you think, after all, there is some mistake? "

" Certainly, a mistake; but when it is rectified I don't think Fitzgibbon or May Park will be forthcoming. Shall I run down to Midland County and look after these two precious objects? "

" Oh! would you be so good, Mr. Ellin? I knew you would be so kind; personal inquiry, you know—there's nothing like it."

" Nothing at all. Meantime, what shall you do with the child—the pseudo-heiress, if pseudo she be? Shall you correct her—let her know her place? "

" I think," responded Miss Wilcox, reflectively—" I

think not exactly as yet; my plan is to do nothing in a hurry; we will inquire first. If after all she should turn out to be connected as was at first supposed, one had better not do anything which one might afterwards regret. No; I shall make no difference with her till I hear from you again."

"Very good. As you please," said Mr. Ellin, with that coolness which made him so convenient a counsellor in Miss Wilcox's opinion. In his dry laconism she found the response suited to her outer worldliness. She thought he said enough if he did not oppose her. The comment he stinted so avariciously she did not want.

Mr. Ellin "ran down," as he said, to Midland County. It was an errand that seemed to suit him; for he had curious predilections as well as peculiar methods of his own. Any secret quest was to his taste; perhaps there was something of the amateur detective in him. He could conduct an inquiry and draw no attention. His quiet face never looked inquisitive, nor did his sleepless eye betray vigilance.

He was away about a week. The day after his return, he appeared in Miss Wilcox's presence as cool as if he had seen her but yesterday. Confronting her with that fathomless face he liked to show her, he first told her he had done nothing.

Let Mr. Ellin be as enigmatical as he would, he never puzzled Miss Wilcox. She never saw enigma in the man. Some people feared, because they did not understand, him; to her it had not yet occurred to begin to spell his nature or analyze his character. If she had an impression about him, it was, that he was an idle but obliging man, not aggressive, of few words, but often convenient. Whether he were clever and deep, or deficient and shallow, close or open, odd or ordinary, she saw no practical end to be answered by inquiry, and therefore did not inquire.

"Why had he done nothing?" she now asked.

"Chiefly because there was nothing to do."

"Then he could give her no information?"

"Not much: only this, indeed—Conway Fitzgibbon was a man of straw; May Park a house of cards. There was no vestige of such man or mansion in Midland County, or in any other shire in England. Tradition herself had nothing to say about either the name or the place. The Oracle of old deeds and registers, when consulted, had not responded.

"Who can he be, then, that came here, and who is this child?"

"That's just what I can't tell you:—an incapacity which makes me say I have done nothing."

"And how am I to get paid?"

"Can't tell you that either."

"A quarter's board and education owing, and masters' terms besides," pursued Miss Wilcox. "How infamous! I can't afford the loss."

"And if we were only in the good old times," said Mr. Ellin, "where we ought to be, you might just send Miss Matilda out to the plantations in Virginia, sell her for what she is worth, and pay yourself."

"Matilda, indeed, and Fitzgibbon! A little impostor! I wonder what her real name is?"

"Betty Hodge? Poll Smith? Hannah Jones?" suggested Mr. Ellin.

"Now," cried Miss Wilcox, "give me credit for sagacity! It's very odd, but try as I would—and I made every effort —I never could really like that child. She has had every indulgence in this house; and I am sure I made great sacrifice of feeling to principle in showing her much attention; for I could not make any one believe the degree of antipathy I have all along felt towards her."

"Yes. I can believe it. I saw it."

"Did you? Well—it proves that my discernment is rarely at fault. Her game is up now, however; and time it was. I have said nothing to her yet; but now——"

"Have her in whilst I am here," said Mr. Ellin. "Has she known of this business? Is she in the secret? Is she herself an accomplice, or a mere tool? Have her in."

Miss Wilcox rang the bell, demanded Matilda Fitzgibbon, and the false heiress soon appeared. She came in her ringlets, her sash, and her furbelowed dress adornments—alas! no longer acceptable.

"Stand there!" said Miss Wilcox, sternly, checking her as she approached the hearth. "Stand there on the farther side of the table. I have a few questions to put to you, and your business will be to answer them. And mind—let us have the truth. *We will not endure lies.*"

Ever since Miss Fitzgibbon had been found in the fit, her face had retained a peculiar paleness and her eyes a dark orbit. When thus addressed, she began to shake and blanch like conscious guilt personified.

"Who are you?" demanded Miss Wilcox. "What do you know about yourself?"

A sort of half-interjection escaped the girl's lips; it was a sound expressing partly fear, and partly the shock the nerves feel when an evil, very long expected, at last and suddenly arrives.

"Keep yourself still, and reply, if you please," said Miss Wilcox, whom nobody should blame for lacking pity, because nature had not made her compassionate. "What is your name? We know you have no right to that of Matilda Fitzgibbon."

She gave no answer.

"I do insist upon a reply. Speak you shall, sooner or later. So you had better do it at once."

This inquisition had evidently a very strong effect upon the subject of it. She stood as if palsied, trying to speak, but apparently not competent to articulate.

Miss Wilcox did not fly into a passion, but she grew very stern and urgent; spoke a little loud; and there was a dry clamour in her raised voice which seemed to beat upon the ear and bewilder the brain. Her interest had been injured —her pocket wounded—she was vindicating her rights— and she had no eye to see, and no nerve to feel, but for the point in hand. Mr. Ellin appeared to consider himself strictly a looker-on; he stood on the hearth very quiet.

At last the culprit spoke.   A low voice escaped her lips.
"Oh, my head!" she cried, lifting her hands to her forehead.   She staggered, but caught the door and did not fall.
Some accusers might have been startled by such a cry—
even silenced; not so Miss Wilcox.   She was neither cruel
nor violent; but she was coarse, because insensible.   Having just drawn breath, she went on, harsh as ever.

Mr. Ellin, leaving the hearth, deliberately paced up the
room as if he were tired of standing still, and would walk
a little for a change.   In returning and passing near the
door and the criminal, a faint breath seemed to seek his
ear, whispering his name—

"Oh, Mr. Ellin!"

The child dropped as she spoke.   A curious voice—not
like Mr. Ellin's, though it came from his lips—asked Miss
Wilcox to cease speaking, and say no more.   He gathered
from the floor what had fallen on it.   She seemed overcome, but not unconscious.   Resting beside Mr. Ellin, in
a few minutes she again drew breath.   She raised her eyes
to him.

"Come, my little one; have no fear," said he.

Reposing her head against him, she gradually became
reassured.   It did not cost him another word to bring her
round; even that strong trembling was calmed by the mere
effects of his protection.   He told Miss Wilcox, with remarkable tranquillity, but still with a certain decision, that
the little girl must be put to bed.   He carried her upstairs,
and saw her laid there himself.   Returning to Miss Wilcox, he said:

"Say no more to her.   Beware, or you will do more mis-
chief than you think or wish.   That kind of nature is very
different from yours.   It is not possible that you should
like it; but let it alone.   We will talk more on the subject
to-morrow.   Let me question her."

THE SECOND FUNERAL OF NAPOLEON.

THE SECOND FUNERAL OF NAPOLEON.

(BY MICHAEL ANGELO TITMARSH.)

I.—ON THE DISINTERMENT OF NAPO-LEON AT ST. HELENA.

MY DEAR,—It is no easy task in this world to distinguish between what is great in it, and what is mean; and many and many is the puzzle that I have had in reading History (or the works of fiction which go by that name), to know whether I should laud **up to the** skies, and endeavour, to the best of my small capabilities, to imitate the remarkable character about whom I was reading, or whether I should fling aside the book and the hero of it, as things altogether base, unworthy, laughable, and get a novel, or a game of billiards, or a pipe of tobacco, or the report of the last de-bate in the House, or any other employment which would leave the mind in a state of easy vacuity, rather than pes-ter it with a vain set of dates relating to actions which are in themselves not worth a fig, or with a parcel of names of people whom it can do one no earthly good to remember.

It is more than probable, my love, that you are acquainted with what is called Grecian and Roman history, chiefly from perusing, in very early youth, the little sheepskin-bound volumes of the ingenious Dr. Goldsmith, and have been indebted for your knowledge of our English annals to a subsequent study of the more voluminous works of Hume and Smollett. The first and the last-named authors, dear Miss Smith, have written each an admirable history,—that of the Reverend Dr. Primrose, Vicar of Wakefield, and that of Mr. Robert Bramble, of Bramble Hall—in both of which works you will find true and instructive pictures of human life and which you may always think over with advantage.   But let me caution you against putting any considerable trust in the other works of these authors, which were placed in your hands at school and afterwards, and in which you were taught to believe.   Modern historians, for the most part, know very little, and, secondly, only tell a little of what they know.

As for those Greeks and Romans whom you have read of in "sheepskin," were you to know really what those monsters were, you would blush all over as red as a hollyhock, and put down the history book in a fury.   Many of our English worthies are no better.   You are not in a situation to know the real characters of any one of them.   They appear before you in their public capacities, but the individuals you know not.   Suppose, for instance, your mamma had purchased her tea in the Borough from a grocer living there by the name of Greenacre: suppose you had been asked out to dinner, and the gentleman of the house had said: "Ho! François! a glass of champagne for Miss Smith;"—Courvoisier would have served you just as any other footman would; you would never have known that there was anything extraordinary in these individuals, but would have thought of them only in their respective public characters of Grocer and Footman.   This, Madam, is History, in which a man always appears dealing with the world in his apron, or his laced livery, but which has not the power or the leisure, or, perhaps, is too high and mighty to condescend to follow and study him in his privacy.   Ah, my dear, when big and little men come to be measured rightly, and great and small actions to be weighed properly, and people to be stripped of their royal robes, beggars' rags, generals' uniforms, seedy out-at-elbowed coats, and the like—or the contrary, say, when souls come to be stripped of their wicked deceiving bodies, and turned out stark naked as they were before they were born—what a strange startling sight shall we see, and what a pretty figure shall some of us cut! Fancy how we shall see Pride, with his Stulz-clothes and padding pulled off, and dwindled down to a forked radish! Fancy some Angelic Virtue, whose white raiment is suddenly whisked over his head, showing us cloven feet and a tail! Fancy Humility, eased of its sad load of cares and want and scorn, walking up to the very highest place of all, and blushing as he takes it! Fancy,—but we must not fancy such a scene at all, which would be an outrage on public decency. Should we be any better than our neighbours? No, certainly. And as we can't be virtuous, let us be decent. Fig-leaves are a very decent, becoming wear, and have been now in fashion for four thousand years. And so, my dear, History is written on fig-leaves. Would you have anything further? O fie!

Yes, four thousand years ago, that famous tree was planted. At their very first lie, our first parents made for it, and there it is still the great Humbug Plant, stretching its wide arms, and sheltering beneath its leaves, as broad and green as ever, all the generations of men. Thus, my dear, coquettes of your fascinating sex cover their persons with figgery, fantastically arranged, and call their masquerading, modesty. Cowards fig themselves out fiercely as "salvage men," and make us believe that they are warriors. Fools look very solemnly out from the dusk of the leaves, and we fancy in the gloom that they are sages. And many a man sets a great wreath about his pate and struts abroad a hero, whose claims we would all of us laugh at, could we but remove the ornament and see his numskull bare.

And such—(excuse my sermonizing)—such is the constitution of mankind, that men have as it were entered into a compact among themselves to pursue the fig-leaf system à l'outrance, and to cry down all who oppose it. Humbug they will have. Humbugs themselves, they will respect humbugs. Their daily victuals of life must be seasoned with humbug. Certain things are there in the world that they will not allow to be called by their right names, and will insist upon our admiring, whether we will or no. Woe be to the man who would enter too far into the recesses of that magnificent temple where our Goddess is enshrined, peep through the vast embroidered curtains indiscreetly, penetrate the secret of secrets, and expose the Gammon of Gammons! And as you must not peer too curiously within, so neither must you remain scornfully without. Humbug-worshippers, let us come into our great temple regularly and decently; take our seats, and settle our clothes decently; open our books, and go through the service with decent gravity; listen, and be decently affected by the expositions of the decent priest of the place; and if by chance some straggling vagabond, loitering in the sunshine out of doors, dares to laugh or to sing, and disturb the sanctified dulness of the faithful;—quick! a couple of big beadles rush out and belabour the wretch, and his yells make our devotions more comfortable.

Some magnificent religious ceremonies of this nature are at present taking place in France; and thinking that you might perhaps while away some long winter evening with an account of them, I have compiled the following pages for your use. Newspapers have been filled, for some days past, with details regarding the Saint Helena expedition, many pamphlets have been published, men go about crying little books and broadsheets filled with real or sham particulars: and from these scarce and valuable documents the following pages are chiefly compiled.

We must begin at the beginning, premising, in the first place, that Monsieur Guizot, when French ambassador at London, waited upon Lord Palmerston with a request that the body of the Emperor Napoleon should be given up to the French nation, in order that it might find a final resting-place in French earth. To this demand the English Government gave a ready assent; nor was there any particular explosion of sentiment upon either side, only some pretty cordial expressions of mutual good-will. Orders were sent out to St. Helena that the corpse should be disinterred in due time when the French expedition had ar-

rived in search of it, and that every respect and attention should be paid to those who came to carry back to
their country the body of the famous dead warrior and
sovereign.

This matter being arranged in very few words (as in
England upon most points is the laudable fashion), the
French Chambers began to debate about the place in which
they should bury the body when they got it; and numberless pamphlets and newspapers out of doors joined in the
talk. Some people there were who had fought and conquered and been beaten with the great Napoleon, and loved
him and his memory. Many more were there who, because of his great genius and valour, felt excessively proud
in their own particular persons, and clamoured for the return of their hero. And if there was some few individuals
in this great, hot-headed, gallant, boasting, sublime, absurd
French nation, who had taken a cool view of the dead Emperor's character; if, perhaps, such men as Louis Philippe,
and Monsieur A. Thiers, Minister and Deputy, and Monsieur François Guizot, Deputy and Excellency, had, from
interest or conviction, opinions at all differing from those
of the majority; why, they knew what was what, and kept
their opinions to themselves, coming with a tolerably good
grace and flinging a few handfuls of incense upon the altar
of the popular idol.

In the succeeding debates, then, various opinions were
given with regard to the place to be selected for the Emperor's sepulture. "Some demanded," says an eloquent
anonymous Captain in the Navy who has written an "Itin-
erary from Toulon to St. Helena," "that the coffin should
be deposited under the bronze taken from the enemy by the
French army—under the Column of the Place Vendôme.
The idea was a fine one. This is the most glorious monument that was ever raised in a conqueror's honour. This
column has been melted out of foreign cannon. These
same cannons have furrowed the bosoms of our braves with
noble cicatrices; and this metal—conquered by the soldier
first, by the artist afterwards—has allowed to be imprinted

on its front its own defeat and our glory. Napoleon might sleep in peace under this audacious trophy. But, would his ashes find a shelter sufficiently vast beneath this pedestal? And his puissant statue dominating Paris, beams with sufficient grandeur on this place: whereas the wheels of carriages and the feet of passengers would profane the funereal sanctity of the spot in trampling on the soil so near his head."

You must not take this description, dearest Amelia, "at the foot of the letter," as the French phrase it, but you will here have a masterly exposition of the arguments for and against the burial of the Emperor under the Column of the Place Vendôme. The idea was a fine one, granted; but, like all other ideas, it was open to objections. You must not fancy that the cannon, or rather the cannon-balls, were in the habit of furrowing the bosoms of French braves, or any other braves, with cicatrices: on the contrary, it is a known fact that cannon-balls make wounds, and not cicatrices (which, my dear, are wounds partially healed); nay, that a man generally dies after receiving one such projectile on his chest, much more after having his bosom furrowed by a score of them. No, my love; no bosom, however heroic, can stand such applications, and the author only means that the French soldiers faced the cannon and took them. Nor, my love, must you suppose that the column was melted; it was the cannon was melted, not the column; but such phrases are often used by orators when they wish to give a particular force and emphasis to their opinions.

Well, again, although Napoleon might have slept in peace under this audacious trophy, how could he do so and carriages go rattling by all night, and people with great iron heels to their boots pass clattering over the stones? Nor indeed could it be expected that a man whose reputation stretches from the Pyramids to the Kremlin, should find a column of which the base is only five-and-twenty feet square, a shelter vast enough for his bones. In a word, then, although the proposal to bury Napoleon under the column was ingenious, it was found not to suit; whereupon somebody else proposed the Madelaine.

"It was proposed," says the before-quoted author with his usual felicity, "to consecrate the Madelaine to his exiled manes"—that is, to his bones when they were not in exile any longer. "He ought to have, it was said, a temple entire. His glory fills the world. His bones could not contain themselves in the coffin of a man—in the tomb of a king!" In this case what was Mary Magdalen to do? "This proposition, I am happy to say, was rejected, and a new one—that of the President of the Council—adopted. Napoleon and his braves ought not to quit each other. Under the immense gilded dome of the Invalides he would find a sanctuary worthy of himself. A dome imitates the vault of heaven, and that vault alone" (meaning of course the other vault) "should dominate above his head. His old mutilated Guard shall watch around him: the last veteran, as he has shed his blood in his combats, shall break his last sigh near his tomb, and all these tombs shall sleep under the tattered standards that have been won from all the nations of Europe."

The original words are "sous les lambeaux criblés des drapeaux cueillis chez toutes les nations;" in English, "under the riddled rags of the flags that have been culled or plucked" (like roses or buttercups) "in all the nations." Sweet, innocent flowers of victory! there they are, my dear, sure enough, and a pretty considerable *hortus siccus* may any man examine who chooses to walk to the Invalides. The burial-place being thus agreed on, the expedition was prepared, and on the 7th July the *Belle Poule* frigate, in company with *La Favorite* corvette, quitted Toulon harbour. A couple of steamers, the *Trident* and the *Ocean*, escorted the ships as far as Gibraltar, and there left them to pursue their voyage.

The two ships quitted the harbour in the sight of a vast concourse of people, and in the midst of a great roaring of cannons. Previous to the departure of the *Belle Poule*, the Bishop of Fréjus went on board, and gave to the cenotaph, in which the Emperor's remains were to be deposited, his episcopal benediction.   Napoleon's old friends and followers, the two Bertrands, Gourgaud, Emanuel Las Cases, "companions in exile, or sons of the companions in exile of the prisoner of the *infâme* Hudson," says a French writer, were passengers on board the frigate. Marchand, Denis, Pierret, Novaret, his old and faithful servants, were likewise in the vessel. It was commanded by his Royal Highness Francis Ferdinand Philip Louis Marie d'Orleans, Prince de Joinville, a young prince two-and-twenty years of age, who was already distinguished in the service of his country and king.

On the 8th of October, after a voyage of six-and-sixty days, the *Belle Poule* arrived in James Town harbour, and on its arrival, as on its departure from France, a great firing of guns took place.   First, the *Oreste* French brig-of-war began roaring out a salutation to the frigate; then the *Dolphin* English schooner gave her one-and-twenty guns; then the frigate returned the compliment of the *Dolphin* schooner; then she blazed out with one-and-twenty guns more, as a mark of particular politeness to the shore —which kindness the forts acknowledged by similar detonations.

These little compliments concluded on both sides, Lieutenant Middlemore, son and aide-de-camp of the Governor of St. Helena, came on board the French frigate, and brought his father's best respects to his Royal Highness. The Governor was at home ill, and forced to keep his room; but he had made his house at James Town ready for Captain Joinville and his suite, and begged that they would make use of it during their stay.

On the 9th, H. R. H. the Prince of Joinville put on his full uniform and landed, in company with Generals Bertrand and Gourgaud, Messrs. Las Cases, Marchand, M. Coquereau, the chaplain of the expedition, and M. de Rohan Chabot, who acted as chief mourner.   All the garrison was under arms to receive the illustrious Prince and the other members of the expedition—who forthwith re-

paired to Plantation House, and had a conference with the
Governor regarding their mission.

On the 10th, 11th, 12th, these conferences continued:
the crews of the French ships were permitted to come on
shore and see the tomb of Napoleon. Bertrand, Gourgaud,
Las Cases wandered about the island and revisited the spots
to which they had been partial in the lifetime of the
Emperor.

The 15th October was fixed on for the day of the ex-
humation: that day five-and-twenty years, the Emperor
Napoleon first set his foot upon the island.

On the day previous all things had been made ready:
the grand coffins and ornaments brought from France, and
the articles necessary for the operation were carried to the
valley of the Tomb.

The operations commenced at midnight. The well-
known friends of Napoleon before named, and some other
attendants of his, the chaplain and his acolytes, the doctor
of the *Belle Poule*, the captains of the French ships, and
Captain Alexander of the Engineers, the English Commissioner, attended the disinterment. His Royal Highness
Prince de Joinville could not be present because the workmen were under English command.

The men worked for nine hours incessantly, when at
length the earth was entirely removed from the vault, all
the horizontal strata of masonry demolished, and the large
slab which covered the place where the stone sarcophagus
lay, removed by a crane. This outer coffin of stone was
perfect, and could scarcely be said to be damp.

"As soon as the Abbé Coquereau had recited the prayers,
the coffin was removed with the greatest care, and carried
by the engineer-soldiers, bareheaded, into a tent that had
been prepared for the purpose. After the religious ceremonies, the inner coffins were opened. The outermost
coffin was slightly injured: then came one of lead, which
was in good condition, and enclosed two others—one of
tin and one of wood. The last coffin was lined inside
with white satin, which, having become detached by the

effect of time, had fallen upon the body and enveloped it like a winding-sheet, and had become slightly attached to it.

"It is difficult to describe with what anxiety and emotion those who were present waited for the moment which was to expose to them all that death had left of Napoleon. Notwithstanding the singular state of preservation of the tomb and coffins, we could scarcely hope to find anything but some misshapen remains of the least perishable part of the costume to evidence the identity of the body. But when Doctor Guillard raised the sheet of satin, an indescribable feeling of surprise and affection was expressed by the spectators, many of whom burst into tears. The Emperor was himself before their eyes! The features of the face, though changed, were perfectly recognized; the hands extremely beautiful; his well-known costume had suffered but little, and the colours were easily distinguished. The attitude itself was full of ease, and but for the fragments of the satin lining which covered, as with a fine gauze, several parts of the uniform, we might have believed we still saw Napoleon before us lying on his bed of state. General Bertrand and M. Marchand, who were both present at the interment, quickly pointed out the different articles which each had deposited in the coffin, and remained in the precise position in which they had previously described them to be.

"The two inner coffins were carefully closed again; the old leaden coffin was strongly blocked up with wedges of wood, and both were once more soldered up with the most minute precautions, under the direction of Dr. Guillard. These different operations being terminated, the ebony sarcophagus was closed as well as its oak case. On delivering the key of the ebony sarcophagus to Count de Chabot, the King's Commissioner, Captain Alexander declared to him, in the name of the Governor, that this coffin, containing the mortal remains of the Emperor Napoleon, was considered as at the disposal of the French Government, from that day and from the moment at which it should arrive at the place of embarkation, towards which it was about to be sent under the orders of General Middlemore. The King's Commissioner replied that he was charged by his Government, and in its name, to accept the coffin from the hands of the British authorities, and that he and the other persons composing the French mission were ready to follow it to James Town, where the Prince de Joinville, superior commandant of the expedition, would be ready to receive it and conduct it on board his frigate. A car drawn by four horses, decked with funereal emblems, had been prepared before the arrival of the expedition, to receive the coffin, as well as a pall, and all the other suitable trappings of mourning. When the sarcophagus was placed on the car, the whole was covered with a magnificent imperial mantle brought from Paris, the four corners of which were borne by Generals Bertrand and Gourgaud, Baron Las Cases and M. Marchand. At half-past three o'clock the funeral car began to move, preceded by a chorister bearing the cross, and by the Abbé Coquereau. M. de Chabot acted as chief mourner. All the authorities of the island, all the principal inhabitants, and the whole of the garrison, followed in procession from the tomb to the quay. But with the exception of the artillerymen necessary to lead the horses, and occasionally support the car when descending some steep parts of the way, the places nearest the coffin were reserved for the French mission. General Middlemore, although in a weak state of health, persisted in following the whole way on foot, together with General Churchill, chief of the staff in India, who had arrived only two days before from Bombay. The immense weight of the coffins, and the unevenness of the road, rendered the utmost carefulness necessary throughout the whole distance. Colonel Trelawney commanded in person the small detachment of artillerymen who conducted the car, and, thanks to his great care, not the slightest accident took place. From the moment of departure to the arrival at the quay, the cannons of the forts and the *Belle Poule* fired minute-guns. After an hour's march the rain ceased for the first time since the commencement of the operations, and on

arriving in sight of the town we found a brilliant sky and
beautiful weather. From the morning the three French
vessels of war had assumed the usual signs of deep mourning: their yards crossed and their flags lowered. Two
French merchantmen, *Bonne Amie* and *Indien*, which had
been in the roads for two days, had put themselves under
the Prince's orders, and followed during the ceremony all
the manœuvres of the *Belle Poule*. The forts of the town
and the houses of the consuls, had also their flags half-
mast high.

"On arriving at the entrance of the town, the troops of
the garrison and the militia formed in two lines as far as
the extremity of the quay. According to the order for
mourning prescribed for the English army, the men had
their arms reversed and the officers had crape on their
arms, with their swords reversed. All the inhabitants had
been kept away from the line of march, but they lined the
terraces commanding the town, and the streets were occupied only by the troops, the 91st Regiment being on the
right and the militia on the left. The cortége advanced
slowly between two ranks of soldiers to the sound of a
funeral march, while the cannons of the forts were fired,
as well as from the *Belle Poule* and the *Dolphin*, the echoes
being repeated a thousand times by the rocks above James
Town. After two hours' march the cortége stopped at the
end of the quay, where the Prince de Joinville had stationed himself at the head of the officers of the three
French ships of war. The greatest official honours had
been rendered by the English authorities to the memory of
the Emperor—the most striking testimonials of respect had
marked the adieu given by St. Helena to his coffin; and
from this moment the mortal remains of the Emperor were
about to belong to France. When the funeral-car stopped,
the Prince de Joinville advanced alone, and in presence of
all around, who stood with their heads uncovered, received,
in a solemn manner, the imperial coffin from the hands of
General Middlemore. His Royal Highness then thanked
the Governor, in the name of France, for all the testimo-

nials of sympathy and respect with which the authorities and inhabitants of St. Helena had surrounded the memorable ceremonial. A cutter had been expressly prepared to receive the coffin. During the embarkation, which the Prince directed himself, the bands played funeral airs, and all the boats were stationed round with their oars shipped. The moment the sarcophagus touched the cutter, a magnificent royal flag, which the ladies of James Town had embroidered for the occasion, was unfurled, and the *Belle Poule* immediately squared her masts and unfurled her colours. All the manœuvres of the frigate were immediately followed by the other vessels. Our mourning had ceased with the exile of Napoleon, and the French naval division dressed itself out in all its festal ornaments to receive the imperial coffin under the French flag. The sarcophagus was covered in the cutter with the imperial mantle. The Prince de Joinville placed himself at the rudder, Commandant Guyet at the head of the boat; Generals Bertrand and Gourgaud, Baron de Las Cases, M. Marchand, and the Abbé Coquereau occupied the same places as during the march. Count Chabot and Commandant Hernoux were astern, a little in advance of the Prince. As soon as the cutter had pushed off from the quay, the batteries ashore fired a salute of twenty-one guns, and our ships returned the salute with all their artillery. Two other salutes were fired during the passage from the quay to the frigate, the cutter advancing very slowly, and surrounded by the other boats. At half-past six o'clock it reached the *Belle Poule*, all the men being on the yards with their hats in their hands. The Prince had had arranged on the deck a chapel, decked with flags and trophies of arms, the altar being placed at the foot of the mizzenmast. The coffin, carried by our sailors, passed between two ranks of officers with drawn swords, and was placed on the quarter-deck. The absolution was pronounced by the Abbé Coquereau the same evening. Next day, at ten o'clock, a solemn mass was celebrated on the deck, in presence of the officers and part of the crews of the ships. His

Royal Highness stood at the foot of the coffin. The cannon of the *Favorite* and *Oreste* fired minute-guns during this ceremony, which terminated by a solemn absolution; and the Prince de Joinville, the gentlemen of the mission, the officers, and the *premiers mâitres* of the ship, sprinkled holy water on the coffin. At eleven, all the ceremonies of the church were accomplished, all the honours done to a sovereign had been paid to the mortal remains of Napoleon. The coffin was carefully lowered between decks, and placed in the *chapelle ardente* which had been prepared at Toulon for its reception. At this moment, the vessels fired a last salute with all their artillery, and the frigate took in her flags, keeping up only her flag at the stern, and the royal standard at the maintopgallant-mast. On Sunday, the 18th, at eight in the morning, the *Belle Poule* quitted St. Helena with her precious deposit on board.

"During the whole time that the mission remained at James Town, the best understanding never ceased to exist between the population of the island and the French. The Prince de Joinville and his companions met in all quarters and at all times with the greatest good-will and the warmest testimonials of sympathy. The authorities and the inhabitants must have felt, no doubt, great regret at seeing taken away from their island the coffin that had rendered it so celebrated; but they repressed their feelings with a courtesy that does honour to the frankness of their character."

II.—ON THE VOYAGE FROM ST. HELENA
TO PARIS

ON the 18th October the French frigate quitted the island with its precious burden on board.

His Royal Highness the Captain acknowledged cordially the kindness and attention which he and his crew had received from the English authorities and the inhabitants of the Island of St. Helena; nay, promised a pension to an old soldier who had been for many years the guardian of the imperial tomb, and went so far as to take into consideration the petition of a certain lodging-house keeper, who prayed for a compensation for the loss which the removal of the Emperor's body would occasion to her. And although it was not to be expected that the great French nation should forego its natural desire of recovering the remains of a hero so dear to it for the sake of the individual interest of the landlady in question, it must have been satisfactory to her to find that the peculiarity of her position was so delicately appreciated by the august Prince who commanded the expedition, and carried away with him *animæ dimidium suæ*—the half of the genteel independence which she derived from the situation of her hotel. In a word, politeness and friendship could not be carried farther. The Prince's realm and the landlady's were bound together by the closest ties of amity. M. Thiers was Minister of France, the great patron of the English alliance. At London M. Guizot was the worthy representative of the French good-will towards the British people; and the remark frequently made by our orators at public dinners, that "France and England, while united, might defy the world," was considered as likely to hold good for many years to come,—the union that is. As for defying the world, that was neither here nor there; nor did English politicians ever dream of doing any such thing, except perhaps at the tenth glass of port at Freemason's Tavern.

Little, however, did Mrs. Corbett, the Saint Helena landlady, little did his Royal Highness Prince Ferdinand Philip Marie de Joinville know what was going on in Europe all this time (when I say in Europe, I mean in Turkey, Syria, and Egypt); how clouds, in fact, were gathering upon what you call the political horizon; and how tempests were rising that were to blow to pieces our Anglo-Gallic temple of friendship. Oh, but it is sad to think that a single wicked old Turk should be the means of setting our two Christian nations by the ears!

Yes, my love, this disreputable old man had been for some time past the object of the disinterested attention of the great sovereigns of Europe. The Emperor Nicholas (a moral character, though following the Greek superstition, and adored for his mildness and benevolence of disposition), the Emperor Ferdinand, the King of Prussia, and our own gracious Queen, had taken such just offence at his conduct and disobedience towards a young and interesting sovereign, whose authority he had disregarded, whose fleet he had kidnapped, whose fair provinces he had pounced upon, that they determined to come to the aid of Abdul Medjid the First, Emperor of the Turks, and bring his rebellious vassal to reason. In this project the French nation was invited to join, but they refused the invitation, saying, that it was necessary for the maintenance of the balance of power in Europe that his Highness Mehemet Ali should keep possession of what by hook or by crook he had gotten, and that they would have no hand in injuring him. But why continue this argument, which you have read in the newspapers for many months past? You, my dear, must know as well as I, that the balance of power in Europe could not possibly be maintained in any such way; and though, to be sure, for the last fifteen years, the progress of the old robber has not made much difference to us in the neighbourhood of Russell Square, and the battle of

Nezib did not in the least affect our taxes, our homes, our institutions, or the price of butcher's meat, yet there is no knowing what *might* have happened had Mehemet Ali been allowed to remain quietly as he was: and the balance of power in Europe might have been—the deuce knows where.

Here, then, in a nutshell, you have the whole matter in dispute. While Mrs. Corbett and the Prince de Joinville were innocently interchanging compliments at Saint Helena, —bang! bang! Commodore Napier was pouring broadsides into Tyre and Sidon; our gallant navy was storming breaches and routing armies; Colonel Hodges had seized upon the green standard of Ibrahim Pacha; and the powder-magazine of Saint John of Acre was blown up sky-high, with eighteen hundred Egyptian soldiers in company with it. The French said that *l'or Anglais* had achieved all these successes, and no doubt believed that the poor fellows at Acre were bribed to a man.

It must have been particularly unpleasant to a high-minded nation like the French—at the very moment when the Egyptian affair and the balance of Europe had been settled in this abrupt way—to find out all of a sudden that the Pasha of Egypt was their dearest friend and ally. They had suffered in the person of their friend; and though, seeing that the dispute was ended, and the territory out of his hand, they could not hope to get it back for him, or to aid him in any substantial way, yet Monsieur Thiers determined, just as a mark of politeness to the Pasha, to fight all Europe for maltreating him,—all Europe, England included. He was bent on war, and an immense majority of the nation went with him. He called for a million of soldiers, and would have had them too, had not the King been against the project and delayed the completion of it at least for a time.

Of these great European disputes Captain Joinville received a notification while he was at sea on board his frigate, as we find by the official account which has been published of his mission.

"Some days after quitting Saint Helena," says that

Q

document, "the expedition fell in with a ship coming from Europe, and was thus made acquainted with the warlike rumours then afloat, by which a collision with the English marine was rendered possible. The Prince de Joinville immediately assembled the officers of the *Belle Poule*, to deliberate on an event so unexpected and important.

"The council of war having expressed its opinion that it was necessary at all events to prepare for an energetic defence, preparations were made to place in battery all the guns that the frigate could bring to bear against the enemy. The provisional cabins that had been fitted up in the battery were demolished, the partitions removed, and, with all the elegant furniture of the cabins, flung into the sea.   The Prince de Joinville was the first ' to execute himself,' and the frigate soon found itself armed with six or eight more guns.

"That part of the ship where these cabins had previously been, went by the name of Lacedæmon : everything luxurious being banished to make way for what was useful.

"Indeed, all persons who were on board agree in saying that Monseigneur the Prince de Joinville most worthily acquitted himself of the great and honourable mission which had been confided to him.   All affirm not only that the commandant of the expedition did everything at St. Helena which as a Frenchman he was bound to do in order that the remains of the Emperor should receive all the honours due to them, but moreover that he accomplished his mission with all the measured solemnity, all the pious and severe dignity, that the son of the Emperor himself would have shown upon a like occasion.   The commandant had also comprehended that the remains of the Emperor must never fall into the hands of the stranger, and being himself decided rather to sink his ship than to give up his precious deposit, he had inspired every one about him with the same energetic resolution that he had himself taken ' *against an extreme eventuality.*' "

Monseigneur, my dear, is really one of the finest young fellows it is possible to see.   A tall, broad-chested, slim-waisted, brown-faced, dark-eyed young prince, with a great beard (and other martial qualities no doubt) beyond his years. As he strode into the Chapel of the Invalides on Tuesday at the head of his men, he made no small impression, I can tell you, upon the ladies assembled to witness the ceremony. Nor are the crew of the *Belle Poule* less agreeable to look at than their commander. A more clean, smart, active, well-limbed set of lads never "did dance" upon the deck of the famed *Belle Poule* in the days of her memorable combat with the *Saucy Arethusa*. "These five hundred sailors," says a French newspaper, speaking of them in the proper French way, "sword in hand, in the severe costume of board-ship (*la sevère tenue du bord*), seemed proud of the mission that they had just accomplished. Their blue jackets, their red cravats, the turned-down collars of blue shirts edged with white, *above all* their resolute appearance and martial air, gave a favourable specimen of the present state of our marine—a marine of which so much might be expected and from which so little has been required."—*Le Commerce:* 16th December.

There they were, sure enough; a cutlass upon one hip, a pistol on the other—a gallant set of young men indeed. I doubt, to be sure, whether the *sevère tenue du bord* requires that the seaman should be always furnished with these ferocious weapons, which in sundry maritime manœuvres, such as going to sleep in your hammock for instance, or twinkling a binnacle, or luffing a marlinspike, or keelhauling a maintopgallant (all naval operations, my dear, which any seafaring novelist will explain to you)— I doubt, I say, whether these weapons are *always* worn by sailors, and have heard that they are commonly, and very sensibly too, locked up until they are wanted. Take another example: suppose artillerymen were incessantly compelled to walk about with a pyramid of twenty-four-pound shot in one pocket, a lighted fuse and a few barrels of gunpowder in the other—these objects would, as you may imagine, greatly inconvenience the artilleryman in his peaceful state.

The newspaper writer is therefore most likely mistaken in saying that the seamen were in the *sevère tenue du bord*, or by "*bord*" meaning "*abordage*"—which operation they were not, in a harmless church, hung round with velvet and wax-candles, and filled with ladies, surely called upon to perform. Nor indeed can it be reasonably supposed that the picked men of the crack frigate of the French navy are a "good specimen" of the rest of the French marine, any more than a cuirassed colossus at the gate of the Horse Guards can be considered a fair sample of the British soldier of the line. The sword and pistol, however, had no doubt their effect—the former was in its sheath, the latter not loaded, and I hear that the French ladies are quite in raptures with these charming *loups-de-mer*.

Let the warlike accoutrements then pass. It was necessary, perhaps, to strike the Parisians with awe, and therefore the crew was armed in this fierce fashion; but why should the Captain begin to swagger as well as his men? and why did the Prince de Joinville lug out sword and pistol so early? or why, if he thought fit to make preparations, should the official journals brag of them afterwards as proofs of his extraordinary courage?

Here is the case. The English Government makes him a present of the bones of Napoleon: English workmen work for nine hours without ceasing, and dig the coffin out of the ground: the English Commissioner hands over the key of the box to the French representative, Monsieur Chabot: English horses carry the funeral-car down to the sea-shore, accompanied by the English Governor, who has actually left his bed to walk in the procession and to do the French nation honour.

After receiving and acknowledging these politenesses, the French Captain takes his charge on board, and the first thing we afterwards hear of him is the determination "*qu'il a su faire passer*" into all his crew, to sink rather than yield up the body of the Emperor *aux mains de l'étranger* —into the hands of the foreigner. My dear Monseigneur, is not this *par trop fort?* Suppose "the foreigner" had wanted the coffin, could he not have kept it? Why show this uncalled-for valour, this extraordinary alacrity at sinking? Sink or blow yourself up as much as you please, but your Royal Highness must see that the genteel thing would have been to wait until you were asked to do so, before you offended good-natured, honest people, who—heaven help them!—have never shown themselves at all murderously inclined towards you. A man knocks up his cabins forsooth, throws his tables and chairs overboard, runs guns into the portholes, and calls *le quartier du bord où existaient ces chambres, Lacedæmon.* Lacedæmon! There is a province, O Prince, in your royal father's dominions, a fruitful parent of heroes in its time, which would have given a much better nickname to your *quartier du bord :* you should have called it Gascony.

> Sooner than strike we'll all ex-pi-er
> On board of the Bell-e Pou-le.

Such fanfaronnading is very well on the part of Tom Dibdin, but a person of your Royal Highness's "pious and severe dignity" should have been above it. If you entertained an idea that war was imminent, would it not have been far better to have made your preparations in quiet, and when you found the war-rumour blown over, to have said nothing about what you intended to do? Fie upon such cheap Lacedæmonianism! There is no poltroon in the world but can brag about what he *would* have done; however, to do your Royal Highness's nation justice, they brag and fight too.

This narrative, my dear Miss Smith, as you will have remarked, is not a simple tale merely, but is accompanied by many moral and pithy remarks which form its chief value in the writer's eyes at least, and the above account of the sham Lacedæmon on board the *Belle Poule* has a double-barrelled morality, as I conceive. Besides justly reprehending the French propensity towards braggadocio, it proves very strongly a point on which I am the only statesman in Europe who has strongly insisted. In the

"Paris Sketch Book" (*one* copy, I believe, is still to be had at the publisher's)—in the "Paris Sketch Book" it was stated that *the French hate us*. They hate us, my dear, profoundly and desperately, and there never was such a hollow humbug in the world as the French alliance. Men get a character for patriotism in France merely by hating England. Directly they go into strong opposition (where, you know, people are always more patriotic than on the ministerial side), they appeal to the people, and have their hold on the people by hating England in common with them. Why? it is a long story, and the hatred may be accounted for by many reasons, both political and social. Any time these eight hundred years this ill-will has been going on, and has been transmitted on the French side from father to son. On the French side, not on ours: we have had no, or few, defeats to complain of, no invasions to make us angry; but you see that to discuss such a period of time would demand a considerable number of pages, and for the present we will avoid the examination of the question.

But they hate us, that is the long and short of it, and you see how this hatred has exploded just now, not upon a serious cause of difference, but upon an argument; for what is the Pasha of Egypt to us or them but a mere abstract opinion? For the same reason the Littleendians in Lilliput abhorred the Bigendians; and I beg you to remark how his Royal Highness Prince Ferdinand Mary, upon hearing that this argument was in the course of debate between us, straightway flung his furniture overboard and expressed a preference for sinking his ship rather than yielding it to the *étranger*. Nothing came of this wish of his, to be sure; but the intention is everything. Unlucky circumstances denied him the power, but he had the will.

Well, beyond this disappointment, the Prince de Joinville had nothing to complain of during the voyage, which terminated happily by the arrival of the *Belle Poule* at Cherbourg, on the 30th of November, at five o'clock in the morning. A telegraph made the glad news known at

Paris, where the Minister of the Interior, Tanneguy-Duchâtel (you will read the name, Madam, in the old Anglo-French wars), had already made "immense preparations" for receiving the body of Napoleon.

The entry was fixed for the 15th of December.

On the 8th of December at Cherbourg the body was transferred from the *Belle Poule* frigate to the *Normandie* steamer.   On which occasion, the mayor of Cherbourg deposited, in the name of his town, a gold laurel branch upon the coffin—which was saluted by the forts and dikes of the place with ONE THOUSAND GUNS!   There was a treat for the inhabitants.

There was on board the steamer a splendid receptacle for the coffin: "a temple with twelve pillars and a dome to cover it from the wet and moisture, surrounded with velvet hangings and silver fringes.   At the head was a gold cross, at the foot a gold lamp: other lamps were kept constantly burning within, and vases of burning incense were hung around.   An altar, hung with velvet and silver, was at the mizzen-mast of the vessel, *and four silver eagles at each corner of the altar.*"   It was a compliment at once to Napoleon and—excuse me for saying so, but so the facts are—to Napoleon and to God Almighty.

Three steamers, the *Normandie*, the *Véloce*, and the *Courrier*, formed the expedition from Cherbourg to Havre, at which place they arrived on the evening of the 9th of November, and where the *Véloce* was replaced by the Seine steamer, having in tow one of the state-coasters, which was to fire the salute at the moment when the body was transferred into one of the vessels belonging to the Seine.

The expedition passed Havre the same night, and came to anchor at Val de la Haye on the Seine, three leagues below Rouen.

Here the next morning (10th), it was met by the flotilla of steamboats of the Upper Seine, consisting of the three *Dorades*, the three *Étoiles*, the *Elbeuvien*, the *Parisien*, the *Parisienne*, and the *Zampa*.   The Prince de Joinville, and the persons of the expedition, embarked immediately in the flotilla, which arrived the same day at Rouen.

At Rouen salutes were fired, the National Guard on both sides of the river paid military honours to the body; and over the middle of the suspension-bridge a magnificent cenotaph was erected, decorated with flags, fasces, violet hangings, and the imperial arms. Before the cenotaph the expedition stopped, and the absolution was given by the archbishop and the clergy. After a couple of hours' stay, the expedition proceeded to Pont de l'Arche. On the 11th it reached Vernon, on the 12th Mantes, on the 13th Maisons-sur-Seine.

"Everywhere," says the official account from which the above particulars are borrowed, "the authorities, the National Guard, and the people flocked to the passage of the flotilla, desirous to render the honours due to his glory, which is the glory of France. In seeing its hero return, the nation seemed to have found its Palladium again,—the sainted relics of victory."

At length, on the 14th, the coffin was transferred from the *Dorade* steamer on board the imperial vessel arrived from Paris. In the evening, the imperial vessel arrived at Courbevoie, which was the last stage of the journey.

Here it was that M. Guizot went to examine the vessel, and was very nearly flung into the Seine, as report goes, by the patriots assembled there. It is now lying on the river, near the Invalides, amidst the drifting ice, whither the people of Paris are flocking out to see it.

The vessel is of a very elegant antique form, and I can give you on the Thames no better idea of it than by requesting you to fancy an immense wherry, of which the stern has been cut straight off, and on which a temple on steps has been elevated. At the figure-head is an immense gold eagle, and at the stern is a little terrace, filled with evergreens and a profusion of banners. Upon pedestals along the sides of the vessel are tripods in which incense was burned, and underneath them are garlands of flowers called here "immortals." Four eagles surmount the temple, and a great scroll or garland, held in their beaks, surrounds it. It is hung with velvet and gold; four gold caryatides support the entry of it; and in the midst, upon a large platform hung with velvet, and bearing the imperial arms, stood the coffin. A steamboat, carrying two hundred musicians playing funereal marches and military symphonies, preceded this magnificent vessel to Courbevoie, where a funereal temple was erected, and "a statue of Notre Dame de Grâce, before which the seamen of the *Belle Poule* inclined themselves, in order to thank her for having granted them a noble and glorious voyage."

Early on the morning of the 15th December, amidst clouds of incense, and thunder of cannon, and innumerable shouts of people, the coffin was transferred from the barge, and carried by the seamen of the *Belle Poule* to the Imperial Car.

And now having conducted our hero almost to the gates of Paris, I must tell you what preparations were made in the capital to receive him.

Ten days before the arrival of the body, as you walked across the Deputies' Bridge, or over the Esplanade of the Invalides, you saw on the bridge eight, on the esplanade thirty-two, mysterious boxes erected, wherein a couple of score of sculptors were at work night and day.

In the middle of the Invalid Avenue, there used to stand, on a kind of shabby fountain or pump, a bust of Lafayette, crowned with some dirty wreaths of "immortals," and looking down at the little streamlet which occasionally dribbled below him. The spot of ground was now clear, and Lafayette and the pump had been consigned to some cellar, to make way for the mighty procession that was to pass over the place of their habitation.

Strange coincidence! If I had been Mr. Victor Hugo, my dear, or a poet of any note, I would, in a few hours, have made an impromptu concerning that Lafayette-crowned pump, and compared its lot now to the fortune of its patron some fifty years back. From him then issued, as from his fountain now, a feeble dribble of pure words; then, as now, some faint circle of disciples were willing to admire him.   Certainly in the midst of the war and storm without, this pure fount of eloquence went dribbling, dribbling on, till of a sudden the revolutionary workmen knocked down statue and fountain, and the gorgeous imperial cavalcade trampled over the spot where they stood.

As for the Champs Elysées, there was no end to the preparations: the first day you saw a couple of hundred scaffoldings erected at intervals between the handsome gilded gas-lamps that at present ornament that avenue; next day, all these scaffoldings were filled with brick and mortar. Presently, over the bricks and mortar rose pediments of statues, legs of urns, legs of goddesses, legs and bodies of goddesses, legs, bodies, and busts of goddesses.   Finally, on the 13th December, goddesses complete.   On the 14th, they were painted marble-colour; and the basements of wood and canvas on which they stood were made to resemble the same costly material.   The funereal urns were ready to receive the frankincense and precious odours which were to burn in them.   A vast number of white columns stretched down the avenue, each bearing a bronze buckler on which was written, in gold letters, one of the victories of the Emperor, and each decorated with enormous imperial flags.   On these columns golden eagles were placed; and the newspapers did not fail to remark the ingenious position in which the royal birds had been set: for while those on the right-hand side of the way had their heads turned *towards* the procession, as if to watch its coming, those on the le*f*t were looking exactly the other way, as if to regard its progress.   Do not fancy I am joking: this point was gravely and emphatically urged in many newspapers; and I do believe no mortal Frenchman ever thought it anything but sublime.

Do not interrupt me, sweet Miss Smith.   I feel that you are angry.   I can see from here the pouting of your lips, and know what you are going to say.   You are going to say, "I will read no more of this Mr. Titmarsh; there is no subject, however solemn, but he treats it with flippant irreverence, and no character, however great, at whom he does not sneer."

Ah, my dear! you are young now and enthusiastic; and your Titmarsh is old, very old, sad, and grey-headed. I have seen a poor mother buy a halfpenny wreath at the gate of Montmartre burying-ground, and go with it to her little child's grave, and hang it there over the little humble stone; and if ever you saw me scorn the mean offering of the poor shabby creature, I will give you leave to be as angry as you will. They say that on the passage of Napoleon's coffin down the Seine, old soldiers and country-people walked miles from their villages just to catch a sight of the boat which carried his body, and to kneel down on the shore and pray for him. God forbid that we should quarrel with such prayers and sorrow, or question their sincerity. Something great and good must have been in this man, something loving and kindly, that has kept his name so cherished in the popular memory, and gained him such lasting reverence and affection.

But, Madam, one may respect the dead without feeling awe-stricken at the plumes of the hearse; and I see no reason why one should sympathize with the train of mutes and undertakers, however deep may be their mourning. Look, I pray you, at the manner in which the French nation has performed Napoleon's funeral. Time out of mind, nations have raised, in memory of their heroes, august mausoleums, grand pyramids, splendid statues of gold or marble, sacrificing whatever they had that was most costly and rare, or that was most beautiful in art, as tokens of their respect and love for the dead person. What a fine example of this sort of sacrifice is that (recorded in a book of which Simplicity is the great characteristic) of the poor woman who brought her pot of precious ointment—her all, and laid it at the feet of the Object which, upon earth, she most loved and respected. "Economists and calculators" there were even in those days who quarrelled with the manner in which the poor woman lavished so much "capital;" but you will remember how nobly and generously the sacrifice was appreciated, and how the economists were put to shame.

With regard to the funeral ceremony that has just been performed here, it is said that a famous public personage and statesman, Monsieur Thiers indeed, spoke with the bitterest indignation of the general style of the preparations, and of their mean and tawdry character. He would have had a pomp as magnificent, he said, as that of Rome at the triumph of Aurelian: he would have decorated the bridges and avenues through which the procession was to pass, with the costliest marbles and the finest works of art, and have had them to remain there forever as monuments of the great funeral.

The economists and calculators might here interpose with a great deal of reason (for, indeed, there was no reason why a nation should impoverish itself to do honour to the memory of an individual for whom, after all, it can feel but a qualified enthusiasm): but it surely might have employed the large sum voted for the purpose more wisely and generously, and recorded its respect for Napoleon by some worthy and lasting memorial, rather than have erected yonder thousand vain heaps of tinsel, paint, and plaster, that are already cracking and crumbling in the frost, at three days old.

Scarcely one of the statues, indeed, deserves to last a month: some are odious distortions and caricatures, which never should have been allowed to stand for a moment. On the very day of the fête, the wind was shaking the canvas pedestals, and the flimsy wood-work had begun to gape and give way. At a little distance, to be sure, you could not see the cracks, and pedestals and statues *looked* like marble. At some distance you could not tell but that the wreaths and eagles were gold embroidery, and not gilt paper—the great tricolour flags damask, and not striped calico. One would think that these sham splendours betokened sham respect, if one had not known that the name of Napoleon is held in real reverence, and observed somewhat of the character of the nation.   Real feelings they have, but they distort them by exaggeration; real courage, which they render ludicrous by intolerable braggadocio; and I think the above official account of the Prince de Joinville's proceedings, of the manner in which the Emperor's remains have been treated in their voyage to the capital, and of the preparations made to receive him in it, will give, my dear Miss Smith, some means of understanding the social and moral condition of this worthy people of France.

III.—ON THE FUNERAL CEREMONY.

SHALL I tell you, my dear, that when François woke me at a very early hour on this eventful morning, while the keen stars were still glittering overhead, a half-moon, as sharp as a razor, beaming in the frosty sky, and a wicked north wind blowing, that blew the blood out of one's fingers and froze your leg as you put it out of bed;—shall I tell you, my dear, that when François called me, and said, "V'là vot' café, Monsieur Titemasse, buvez-le, tiens, il est tout chaud," I felt myself, after imbibing the hot breakfast, so comfortable under three blankets and a mackintosh, that for at least a quarter-of-an-hour no man in Europe could say whether Titmarsh would or would not be present at the burial of the Emperor Napoleon.

Besides, my dear, the cold, there was another reason for doubting. Did the French nation, or did they not, intend to offer up some of us English over the imperial grave? And were the games to be concluded by a massacre? It was said in the newspapers that Lord Granville had despatched circulars to all the English resident in Paris, begging them to keep their homes. The French journals announced this news, and warned us charitably of the fate intended for us. Had Lord Granville written? Certainly not to me. Or had he written to all *except me?* And was I *the victim*—the doomed one?—to be seized directly I showed my face in the Champs Elysées, and torn in pieces by French Patriotism to the frantic chorus of the Marseillaise? Depend on it, Madam, that high and low in this city on Tuesday were not altogether at their ease, and that the bravest felt no small tremor. And be sure of this, that as his Majesty Louis Philippe took his nightcap off his royal head that morning, he prayed heartily that he might, at night, put it on in safety.

Well, as my companion and I came out of doors, being

bound for the Church of the Invalides, for which a Deputy had kindly furnished us with tickets, we saw the very prettiest sight of the whole day, and I can't refrain from mentioning it to my dear tender-hearted Miss Smith.

In the same house where I live (but about five stories nearer the ground), lodges an English family, consisting of —1. A great-grandmother, a hale, handsome old lady of seventy, the very best-dressed and neatest old lady in Paris. 2. A grandfather and grandmother, tolerably young to bear that title. 3. A daughter. And 4. Two little great-grand, or grand children, that may be of the age of three and one, and belong to a son and daughter who are in India. The grandfather, who is as proud of his wife as he was thirty years ago when he married, and pays her compliments still twice or thrice in a day, and when he leads her into a room looks round at the persons assembled, and says in his heart, "Here, gentlemen, here is my wife—show me such another woman in England,"—this gentleman had hired a room on the Champs Elysées, for he would not have his wife catch cold by exposing her to the balconies in the open air.

When I came to the street, I found the family assembled in the following order of march :—

—— No. 1, the great-grandmother walking daintily along, supported by No. 3, her granddaughter.

—— A nurse carrying No. 4. junior, who was sound asleep: and a huge basket containing saucepans, bottles of milk, parcels of infants' food, certain dimity napkins, a child's coral, and a little horse belonging to No. 4 senior.

—— A servant bearing a basket of condiments.

—— No. 2, grandfather, spick and span, clean shaved, hat brushed, white buckskin gloves, bamboo cane, brown great-coat, walking as upright and solemn as may be, having his lady on his arm.

—— No. 4 senior, with mottled legs and a tartan costume, who was frisking about between his grandpapa's legs, who heartily wished him at home.

"My dear," his face seemed to say to his lady, "I think you might have left the little things in the nursery, for we shall have to squeeze through a terrible crowd in the Champs Elysées."

The lady was going out for a day's pleasure, and her face was full of care: she had to look first after her old mother who was walking ahead, then after No. 4 junior with the nurse—he might fall into all sorts of danger, wake up, cry, catch cold, nurse might slip down, or heaven knows what. Then she had to look her husband in the face, who had gone to such expense and been so kind for her sake, and make that gentleman believe she was thoroughly happy; and, finally, she had to keep an eye upon No. 4 senior, who, as she was perfectly certain, was about in two minutes to be lost forever or trampled to pieces in the crowd.

These events took place in a quiet little street leading into the Champs Elysées, the entry of which we had almost reached by this time. The four detachments above described, which had been straggling a little in their passage down the street, closed up at the end of it, and stood for a moment huddled together. No. 3, Miss X—, began speaking to her companion the great-grandmother.

"Hush, my dear," said that old lady, looking round alarmed at her daughter. "*Speak French.*" And she straightway began nervously to make a speech which she supposed to be in that language, but which was as much like French as Iroquois. The whole secret was out: you could read it in the grandmother's face, who was doing all she could to keep from crying, and looked as frightened as she dared to look. The two elder ladies had settled between them that there was going to be a general English slaughter that day, and had brought the children with them, so that they might all be murdered in company.

God bless you, O women, moist-eyed and tender-hearted! In those gentle silly tears of yours there is something touches one, be they never so foolish. I don't think there were many such natural drops shed that day as those which just made their appearance in the grandmother's eyes, and then went back again as if they had been ashamed of them-

selves, while the good lady and her little troop walked
across the road.   Think how happy she will be when night
comes, and there has been no murder of English, and the
brood is all nestled under her wings sound asleep, and she
is lying awake, thanking God that the day and its pleasures
and pains are over.   Whilst we were considering these
things, the grandfather had suddenly elevated No. 4 senior
upon his left shoulder, and I saw the tartan hat of that
young gentleman, and the bamboo cane which had been
transferred to him, high over the heads of the crowd on the
opposite side through which the party moved.

After this little procession had passed away—you may
laugh at it, but upon my word and conscience, Miss Smith,
I saw nothing in the course of the day which affected me
more—after this little procession had passed away, the
other came, accompanied by gun-banging, flag-waving,
incense-burning, trumpets pealing, drums rolling, and at
the close, received by the voice of six hundred choristers,
sweetly modulated to the tones of fifteen score of fiddlers.
Then you saw horse and foot, jack-boots and bearskin,
cuirass and bayonet, national guard and line, marshals and
generals all over gold, smart aides-de-camp galloping about
like mad, and high in the midst of all, riding on his golden
buckler, Solomon in all his glory forsooth—Imperial Cæsar
with his crown over his head, laurels and standards waving
about his gorgeous chariot, and a million of people looking
on in wonder and awe.

His Majesty the Emperor and King reclined on his
shield, with his head a little elevated.   His Majesty's skull
is voluminous, his forehead broad and large.   We remarked
that his Imperial Majesty's brow was of a yellowish colour,
which appearance was also visible about the orbits of the
eyes.   He kept his eyelids constantly closed, by which we
had the opportunity of observing that the upper lids were
garnished with eye-lashes.   Years and climate have effected
upon the face of this great monarch only a trifling alteration; we may say, indeed, that Time has touched his Im-

perial and Royal Majesty with the lightest feather in his wing. In the nose of the Conqueror of Austerlitz we remarked very little alteration: it is of the beautiful shape which we remember it possessed five-and-twenty years since, ere unfortunate circumstances induced him to leave us for a while. The nostril and the tube of the nose appear to have undergone some slight alteration, but in examining a beloved object the eye of affection is perhaps too critical. *Vive l'Empereur!* the soldier of Marengo is among us again. His lips are thinner, perhaps, than they were before! how white his teeth are! you can just see three of them pressing his under lip; and pray remark the fulness of his cheeks and the round contour of his chin. Oh, those beautiful white hands! many a time have they patted the cheek of poor Josephine, and played with the black ringlets of her hair. She is dead now and cold, poor creature; and so are Hortense and bold Eugene, "than whom the world never saw a curtier knight," as was said of King Arthur's Sir Lancelot. What a day would it have been for those three could they but have lived until now, and seen their hero returning! Where's Ney? His wife sits looking out from M. Flahaut's window yonder, but the bravest of the brave is not with her. Murat too is absent: honest Joachim loves the Emperor at heart, and repents that he was not at Waterloo: who knows but that at the sight of the handsome swordsman those stubborn English "canaille" would have given way? A king, Sire, is, you know, the greatest of slaves—State affairs of consequence— his Majesty the King of Naples is detained no doubt. When we last saw the King, however, and his Highness the Prince of Elchingen, they looked to have as good health as ever they had in their lives, and we heard each of them calmly calling out "*Fire!*" as they have done in numberless battles before.

Is it possible? can the Emperor forget? We don't like to break it to him, but has he forgotten all about the farm at Pizzo, and the garden of the Observatory? Yes, truly: there he lies on his golden shield, never stirring, never so much as lifting his eyelids, or opening his lips any wider.

O vanitas vanitatum ! Here is our Sovereign in all his glory, and they fired a thousand guns at Cherbourg and never woke him!

However, we are advancing matters by several hours, and you must give just as much credence as you please to the subjoined remarks concerning the Procession, seeing that your humble servant could not possibly be present at it, being bound for the church elsewhere.

Programmes, however, have been published of the affair, and your vivid fancy will not fail to give life to them, and the whole magnificent train will pass before you.

Fancy then, that the guns are fired at Neuilly: the body landed at daybreak from the funereal barge, and transferred to the car; and fancy the car, a huge Juggernaut of a machine, rolling on four wheels of an antique shape, which supported a basement adorned with golden eagles, banners, laurels, and velvet hangings. Above the hangings stand twelve golden statues with raised arms supporting a huge shield, on which the coffin lay. On the coffin was the imperial crown, covered with violet velvet crape, and the whole vast machine was drawn by horses in superb housings, led by valets in the imperial livery.

Fancy at the head of the procession first of all—

The Gendarmerie of the Seine, with their trumpets and Colonel.

The Municipal Guard (horse), with their trumpets, standard, and Colonel.

Two squadrons of the 7th Lancers, with Colonel, standard, and music.

The Commandant of Paris and his Staff.

A battalion of Infantry of the Line, with their flag, sappers, drums, music, and Colonel.

The Municipal Guard (foot), with flag, drums, and Colonel.

The Sapper-pumpers, with ditto.

Then picture to yourself more squadrons of Lancers and Cuirassiers.

The General of the Division, and his Staff; all officers of all arms employed at Paris, and unattached; the Military School of Saint Cyr, the Polytechnic School, the School of the État-Major; and

the Professors and Staff of each.   Go on imagining more battal-
ions of Infantry, of Artillery, companies of Engineers, squadrons
of Cuirassiers, ditto of the Cavalry, of the National Guard, and
the first and second legions of ditto.

Fancy a carriage, containing the Chaplain of the St. Helena expedition, the only clerical gentleman that formed a part of the procession.

Fancy you hear the funereal music, and then figure in your mind's
eye—

THE EMPEROR'S CHARGER, that is, Napoleon's own saddle and
bridle (when First Consul) upon a white horse.   The saddle (which
has been kept ever since in the Garde Meuble of the Crown) is of
amaranth velvet, embroidered in gold: the holsters and housings
are of the same rich material.   On them you remark the attributes
of War, Commerce, Science, and Art.   The bits and stirrups are
silver-gilt chased.   Over the stirrups, two eagles were placed at
the time of the empire; the horse was covered with a violet crape
embroidered with golden bees.

After this, came more Soldiers, General Officers, Sub-Officers, Marshals, and what was said to be the prettiest sight almost of the
whole, the banners of the eighty-six Departments of France.
These are due to the invention of M. Thiers, and were to have
been accompanied by federates from each Department.   But the
Government very wisely mistrusted this and some other projects
of Monsieur Thiers, and as for a federation, my dear, *it has been
tried*.   Next comes—

His Royal Highness the Prince de Joinville.

The 500 sailors of the *Belle Poule* marching in double files on each
side of

THE CAR.

[Hush! the enormous crowd thrills as it passes, and only some few
voices cry *Vive l'Empereur*. Shining golden in the frosty sun—with
hundreds of thousands of eyes upon it, from houses and housetops,
from balconies, black, purple, and tricolor, from tops of leafless trees,
from behind long lines of glittering bayonets under schakos and
bearskin caps, from behind the Line and the National Guard
again, pushing, struggling, heaving, panting, eager, the heads of
an enormous multitude stretching out to meet and follow
it, amidst long avenues of columns and statues gleaming white, of standards rainbow-coloured, of golden
eagles, of pale funereal urns, of discharging odours
amidst huge volumes of pitch-black smoke,

THE GREAT IMPERIAL CHARIOT

ROLLS MAJESTICALLY ON.

The cords of the pall are held by two Marshals, an Admiral, and
General Bertrand; who are followed by—
The Prefects of the Seine and Police, &c.
The Mayors of Paris, &c.
The Members of the Old Guard, &c.
A Squadron of Light Dragoons, &c.
Lieutenant-General Schneider, &c.
More cavalry, more infantry, more artillery, more everybody; and
as the procession passes, the Line and the National Guard forming
line on each side of the road fall in and follow it, until it arrives
at the Church of the Invalides, where the last honours are to be
paid to it.

Among the company assembled under the dome of that
edifice, the casual observer would not perhaps have remarked a gentleman of the name of Michael Angelo Titmarsh, who nevertheless was there. But as, my dear Miss
Smith, the descriptions in this letter, from the words in
page 399, line 11—*the party moved*—up to the words *paid
to it*, in the last period, have purely emanated from your
obedient servant's fancy, and not from his personal observation (for no being on earth, except a newspaper re-
porter, can be in two places at once), permit me now to
communicate to you what little circumstances fell under
my own particular view on the day of the 15th of December.

As we came out, the air and the buildings round about
were tinged with purple, and the clear sharp half-moon
before-mentioned was still in the sky, where it seemed to
be lingering as if it would catch a peep of the commencement of the famous procession. The Arc de Triomphe was
shining in a keen frosty sunshine, and looking as clean and
rosy as if it had just made its toilette. The canvas or
pasteboard image of Napoleon, of which only the gilded
legs had been erected the night previous, was now visible,
body, head, crown, sceptre and all, and made an imposing
show. Long gilt banners were flaunting about, with the
imperial cipher and eagle, and the names of the battles
and victories glittering in gold. The long avenues of the
Champs Elysées had been covered with sand for the con-
venience of the great procession that was to tramp across

it that day.   Hundreds of people were marching to and
fro, laughing, chattering, singing, gesticulating as happy
Frenchmen do.   There is no pleasanter sight than a French
crowd on the alert for a festival, and nothing more catching than their good-humour.   As for the notion which has
been put forward by some of the opposition newspapers
that the populace were on this occasion unusually solemn
or sentimental, it would be paying a bad compliment to the
natural gaiety of the nation to say that it was, on the
morning at least of the 15th of December, affected in any
such absurd way.   Itinerant merchants were shouting out
lustily their commodities of cigars and brandy, and the
weather was so bitter cold, that they could not fail to find
plenty of customers.   Carpenters and workmen were still
making a huge banging and clattering among the sheds
which were built for the accommodation of the visitors.
Some of these sheds were hung with black, such as one
sees before churches in funerals; some were robed in violet,
in compliment to the Emperor whose mourning they put
on.   Most of them had fine tricolour hangings with appropriate inscriptions to the glory of the French arms.

All along the Champs Elysées were urns of plaster-of-
Paris destined to contain funereal incense and flames: columns decorated with huge flags of blue, red, and white,
embroidered with shining crowns, eagles, and N's in gilt
paper, and statues of plaster representing Nymphs, Triumphs, Victories, or other female personages, painted in
oil so as to represent marble.   Real marble could have had
no better effect, and the appearance of the whole was lively
and picturesque in the extreme.   On each pillar was a
buckler of the colour of bronze, bearing the name and date
of a battle in gilt letters: you had to walk through a mile-
long avenue of these glorious reminiscences, telling of spots
where, in the great imperial days, throats had been victori-
ously cut.

As we passed down the avenue, several troops of soldiers met us: the *garde-municipale à cheval*, in brass hel-
mets and shining jack-boots, noble-looking men, large, on

large horses, the pick of the old army, as I have heard, and armed for the special occupation of peace-keeping: not the most glorious, but the best part of the soldier's duty, as I fancy. Then came a regiment of Carabineers, one of Infantry—little, alert, brown-faced, good-humoured men, their band at their head playing sounding marches. These were followed by a regiment or detachment of the Municipals on foot—two or three inches taller than the men of the Line, and conspicuous for their neatness and discipline. By-and-by came a squadron or so of dragoons of the National Guards: they are covered with straps, buckles, aiguillettes, and cartouche-boxes, and made under their tricolour cocks' plumes a show sufficiently warlike. The point which chiefly struck me on beholding these military men of the National Guard and the Line, was the admirable manner in which they bore a cold that seemed to me as sharp as the weather in the Russian retreat, through which cold the troops were trotting without trembling and in the utmost cheerfulness and good-humour. An aide-de-camp galloped past in white pantaloons. By heavens! it made me shudder to look at him.

With this profound reflection, we turned away to the right towards the hanging-bridge (where we met a detachment of young men of the École de l'État Major, fine-looking lads, but sadly disfigured by the wearing of stays or belts, that make the waists of the French dandies of a most absurd tenuity), and speedily passed into the avenue of statues leading up to the Invalides. All these were statues of warriors from Ney to Charlemagne, modelled in clay for the nonce, and placed here to meet the corpse of the greatest warrior of all. Passing these, we had to walk to a little door at the back of the Invalides, where was a crowd of persons plunged in the deepest mourning, and pushing for places in the chapel within.

The chapel is spacious and of no great architectural pretensions, but was on this occasion gorgeously decorated in honour of the great person to whose body it was about to give shelter.

We had arrived at nine: the ceremony was not to begin, they said, till two: we had five hours before us to see all that from our places could be seen.

We saw that the roof, up to the first lines of architecture, was hung with violet; beyond this with black. We saw N.'s, eagles, bees, laurel wreaths, and other such imperial emblems, adorning every nook and corner of the edifice. Between the arches, on each side of the aisle, were painted trophies, on which were written the names of some of Napoleon's Generals and of their principal deeds of arms—and not their deeds of arms alone, *pardi*, but their coats-of-arms too. O stars and garters! but this is too much. What was Ney's paternal coat, prythee, or honest Junot's quarterings, or the venerable escutcheon of King Joachim's father, the innkeeper?

You and I, dear Miss Smith, know the exact value of heraldic bearings. We know that though the greatest pleasure of all is to *act* like a gentleman, it is a pleasure, nay a merit, to *be* one—to come of an old stock, to have an honourable pedigree, to be able to say that centuries back our fathers had gentle blood, and to us transmitted the same. There *is* a good in gentility: the man who questions it is envious, or a coarse dullard, not able to perceive the difference between high breeding and low. One has in the same way heard a man brag that he did not know the difference between wines, not he—give him a good glass of port and he would pitch all your claret to the deuce. My love, men often brag about their own dulness in this way.

In the matter of gentlemen, democrats cry, "Psha! Give us one of Nature's gentlemen, and hang your aristocrats." And so indeed Nature does make *some* gentlemen—a few here and there. But Art makes most. Good birth, that is, good handsome well-formed fathers and mothers, nice cleanly nursery-maids, good meals, good physicians, good education, few cares, pleasant easy habits of life, and luxuries not too great or enervating, but only refining—a course of these going on for a few generations are the best gentlemen-makers in the world, and beat Nature hollow.

If, respected Madam, you say that there is something *better* than gentility in this wicked world, and that honesty and personal worth are more valuable than all the politeness and high breeding that ever wore red-heeled pumps, knights' spurs, or Hoby's boots, Titmarsh for one is never going to say you nay. If you even go so far as to say that the very existence of this super-genteel society among us, from the slavish respect that we pay to it, from the dastardly manner in which we attempt to imitate its airs and ape its vices, goes far to destroy honesty of intercourse, to make us meanly ashamed of our natural affections and honest, harmless usages, and so does a great deal more harm than it is possible it can do good by its example—perhaps, Madam, you speak with some sort of reason. Potato myself, I can't help seeing that the tulip yonder has the best place in the garden, and the most sunshine, and the most water, and the best tending—and not liking him over well. But I can't help acknowledging that Nature has given him a much finer dress than ever I can hope to have, and of this, at least, must give him the benefit.

Or say, we are so many cocks and hens, my dear (*sans arrière pensée*), with our crops pretty full, our plumes pretty sleek, decent picking here and there in the straw-yard, and tolerable snug roosting in the barn : yonder on the terrace, in the sun, walks Peacock, stretching his proud neck, squealing every now and then in the most pert fashionable voice and flaunting his great supercilious dandified tail. Don't let us be too angry, my dear, with the useless, haughty, insolent creature, because he despises us. *Something* is there about Peacock that we don't possess. Strain your neck ever so, you can't make it as long or as blue as his—cock your tail as much as you please, and it will never be half so fine to look at. But the most absurd, disgusting, contemptible sight in the world would you and I be, leaving the barn-door for my lady's flower garden, forsaking our natural sturdy walk for the peacock's genteel rickety stride, and adopting the squeak of his voice in the place of our gallant lusty cock-a-doodle-dooing.

R

Do you take the allegory? I love to speak in such, and
the above types have been presented to my mind while sitting opposite a gimcrack coat-of-arms and coronet that are
painted in the Invalides Church, and assigned to one of the
Emperor's Generals.

Ventrebleu ! Madam, what need have *they* of coats-of-
arms and coronets, and wretched imitations of old exploded
aristocratic gewgaws that they had flung out of the country
—with the heads of the owners in them sometimes, for indeed they were not particular—a score of years before?
What business, forsooth, had they to be meddling with
gentility and aping its ways, who had courage, merit, daring, genius sometimes, and a pride of their own to support,
if proud they were inclined to be? A clever young man
(who was not of high family himself, but had been bred
up genteelly at Eton and the university)—young Mr. George
Canning, at the commencement of the French Revolution,
sneered at "Roland the Just, with ribbons in his shoes,"
and the dandies, who then wore buckles, voted the sarcasm
monstrous killing. It was a joke, my dear, worthy of a
lackey, or of a silly smart parvenu, not knowing the society
into which his luck had cast him (God help him! in later
years, they taught him what they were!), and fancying in
his silly intoxication that simplicity was ludicrous and
fashion respectable. See, now, fifty years are gone, and
where are shoebuckles? Extinct, defunct, kicked into
the irrevocable past off the toes of all Europe!

How fatal to the parvenu, throughout history, has been
this respect for shoebuckles. Where, for instance, would
the Empire of Napoleon have been, if Ney and Lannes had
never sported such a thing as a coat-of-arms, and had
only written their simple names on their shields, after the
fashion of Desaix's scutcheon yonder?—the bold republican who led the crowning charge at Marengo, and sent the
best blood of the Holy Roman Empire to the right-about,
before the wretched misbegotten imperial heraldry was
born, that was to prove so disastrous to the father of it. It
has always been so. They won't amalgamate. A country

must be governed by the one principle or the other. But give, in a republic, an aristocracy ever so little chance, and it works and plots and sneaks and bullies and sneers itself into place, and you find democracy out of doors. Is it good that the aristocracy should so triumph?—that is a question that you may settle according to your own notions and taste; and permit me to say, I do not care twopence how you settle it. Large books have been written upon the subject in a variety of languages, and coming to a variety of conclusions. Great statesmen are there in our country, from Lord Londonderry down to Mr. Vincent, each in his degree maintaining his different opinion. But here, in the matter of Napoleon, is a simple fact: he founded a great, glorious, strong, potent republic, able to cope with the best aristocracies in the world, and perhaps to beat them all; he converts his republic into a monarchy, and surrounds his monarchy with what he calls aristocratic institutions; and you know what becomes of him. The people estranged, the aristocracy faithless (when did they ever pardon one who was not of themselves?)—the imperial fabric tumbles to the ground. If it teaches nothing else, my dear, it teaches one a great point of policy—namely, to stick by one's party.

While these thoughts (and sundry others relative to the horrible cold of the place, the intense dulness of delay, the stupidity of leaving a warm bed and a breakfast in order to witness a procession that is much better performed at a theatre)—while these thoughts were passing in the mind, the church began to fill apace, and you saw that the hour of the ceremony was drawing near.

Imprimis, came men with lighted staves, and set fire to at least ten thousand of wax-candles that were hanging in brilliant chandeliers in various parts of the chapel. Curtains were dropped over the upper windows as these illuminations were effected, and the church was left only to the funereal light of the spermaceti. To the right was the dome, round the cavity of which sparkling lamps were set, that designed the shape of it brilliantly against the dark-

ness.   In the midst, and where the altar used to stand, rose
the catafalque.   And why not?   Who is God here but
Napoleon? and in him the sceptics have already ceased
to believe; but the people does still somewhat.   He and
Louis XIV. divide the worship of the place between them.

As for the catafalque, the best that I can say for it is
that it is really a noble and imposing-looking edifice, with
tall pillars supporting a grand dome, with innumerable
escutcheons, standards, and allusions military and funereal.
A great eagle of course tops the whole: tripods burning
spirits of wine stand round this kind of dead-man's throne,
and as we saw it (by peering over the heads of our neighbours in the front rank), it looked, in the midst of the
black concave, and under the effect of half-a-thousand flashing cross-lights, properly grand and tall.   The effect of
the whole chapel, however (to speak the jargon of the
painting-room), was spoiled by being *cut up ;* there were
too many objects for the eye to rest upon; the ten thousand
wax candles, for instance, in their numberless twinkling
chandeliers, the raw *tranchant* colours of the new banners,
wreaths, bees, N.'s, and other emblems dotting the place
all over, and incessantly puzzling, or rather *bothering* the
beholder.

High overhead, in a sort of mist, with the glare of their
original colours worn down by dust and time, hung long
rows of dim ghostly-looking standards, captured in old
days from the enemy.   They were, I thought, the best and
most solemn part of the show.

To suppose that the people were bound to be solemn
during the ceremony is to exact from them something quite
needless and unnatural.   The very fact of a squeeze dissi-
pates all solemnity.   One great crowd is always, as I imagine, pretty much like another.   In the course of the last
few years I have seen three : that attending the coronation
of our present sovereign, that which went to see Courvoisier
hanged, and this which witnessed the Napoleon ceremony.
The people so assembled for hours together are jocular
rather than solemn, seeking to pass away the weary time

with the best amusements that will offer.   There was, to
be sure, in all the scenes above alluded to, just one moment—one particular moment—when the universal people
feels a shock and is for that second serious.

But except for that second of time, I declare I saw no
seriousness here beyond that of ennui.   The church began
to fill with personages of all ranks and conditions.   First,
opposite our seats came a company of fat grenadiers of the
National Guard, who presently, at the word of command,
put their muskets down against benches and wainscots,
until the arrival of the procession.   For seven hours these
men formed the object of the most anxious solicitude of all
the ladies and gentlemen seated on our benches: they began to stamp their feet, for the cold was atrocious, and we
were frozen where we sate.   Some of them fell to blowing
their fingers; one executed a kind of dance, such as one
sees often here in cold weather—the individual jumps repeatedly upon one leg, and kicks out the other violently,
meanwhile his hands are flapping across his chest.   Some
fellows opened their cartouche-boxes, and from them drew
eatables of various kinds.   You can't think how anxious
we were to know the qualities of the same.   "Tiens, ce
gros qui mange une cuisse de volaille!"—"Il a du jambon,
celui-là."   "I should like some, too," growls an Englishman, "for I hadn't a morsel of breakfast," and so on.   This
is the way, my dear, that we see Napoleon buried.

Did you ever see a chicken escape from clown in a pantomime, and hop over into the pit, or amongst the fiddlers?
and have you not seen the shrieks of enthusiastic laughter that the wondrous incident occasions?   We had our
chicken, of course: there never was a public crowd without
one.   A poor unhappy woman in a greasy plaid cloak, with
a battered rose-coloured plush bonnet, was seen taking her
place among the stalls allotted to the grandees.   "Voyez
donc l'Anglaise," said everybody, and it was too true.
You could swear that the wretch was an Englishwoman—a
bonnet was never made or worn so in any other country.
Half-an-hour's delightful amusement did this lady give us

all. She was whisked from seat to seat by the *huissiers*, and at every change of place woke a peal of laughter. I was glad, however, at the end of the day to see the old pink bonnet over a very comfortable seat, which somebody had not claimed and she had kept.

Are not these remarkable incidents? The next wonder we saw was the arrival of a set of tottering old Invalids, who took their places under us with drawn sabres. Then came a superb drum-major, a handsome smiling good-humoured giant of a man, his breeches astonishingly embroidered with silver lace. Him a dozen little drummer-boys followed—"the little darlings!" all the ladies cried out in a breath: they were indeed pretty little fellows, and came and stood close under us: the huge drum-major smiled over his little red-capped flock, and for many hours in the most perfect contentment twiddled his moustaches and played with the tassels of his cane.

Now the company began to arrive thicker and thicker. A whole covey of *Conseillers-d'État* came in, in blue coats, embroidered with blue silk: then came a crowd of lawyers in toques and caps, among whom were sundry venerable Judges in scarlet, purple velvet, and ermine—a kind of Bajazet costume. Look there! there is the Turkish Ambassador in his red cap, turning his solemn brown face about and looking preternaturally wise. The Deputies walk in in a body. Guizot is not there: he passed by just now in full ministerial costume. Presently little Thiers saunters back: what a clear, broad, sharp-eyed face the fellow has, with his grey hair cut down so demure! A servant passes, pushing through the crowd a shabby wheel-chair. It has just brought old Monçey, the Governor of the Invalids, the honest old man who defended Paris so stoutly in 1814. He has been very ill, and is worn down almost by infirmities: but in his illness he was perpetually asking, "Doctor, shall I live till the 15th? Give me till then, and I die contented?" One can't help believing that the old man's wish is honest, however one may doubt the piety of another illustrious Marshal, who once carried a candle before

Charles X. in a procession, and has been this morning to
Neuilly to kneel and pray at the foot of Napoleon's coffin.
He might have said his prayers at home, to be sure, but
don't let us ask too much; that kind of reserve is not a
Frenchman's characteristic.

Bang—bang! At about half-past two a dull sound of
cannonading was heard without the church, and signals
took place between the Commandant of the Invalids, of
the National Guard, and the big drum-major.   Looking to
these troops (the fat Nationals were shuffling into line
again) the two Commandants uttered, as nearly as I could
catch them, the following words—

"HARRUM HUMP!"

At once all the National bayonets were on the present,
and the sabres of the old Invalids up.   The big drum-
major looked round at the children, who began very slowly
and solemnly on their drums, Rub-dub-dub—rub-dub-dub
—(count two between each)—rub-dub-dub, and a great procession of priests came down from the altar.

First, there was a tall handsome cross-bearer, bearing a
long gold cross, of which the front was turned towards his
grace the Archbishop.   Then came a double row of about
sixteen incense boys, dressed in white surplices: the first
boy, about six years old, the last with whiskers and of the
height of man.   Then followed a regiment of priests in
black tippets and white gowns: they had black hoods, like
the moon when she is at her third quarter, wherewith those
who were bald (many were, and fat too) covered themselves.   All the reverend men held their heads meekly
down, and affected to be reading in their breviaries.

After the Priests came some Bishops of the neighbouring
districts, in purple, with crosses sparkling on their episcopal
bosoms.

Then came, after more priests, a set of men whom I
have never seen before—a kind of ghostly heralds, young
and handsome men, some of them in stiff tabards of black
and silver, their eyes to the ground, their hands placed at
right angles with their chests.

Then came two gentlemen bearing remarkable tall candlesticks, with candles of corresponding size.   One was burning brightly, but the wind (that chartered libertine) had blown out the other, which nevertheless kept its place in the procession—I wondered to myself whether the reverend gentleman who carried the extinguished candle, felt disgusted, humiliated, mortified—perfectly conscious that the eyes of many thousands of people were bent upon that bit of refractory wax.   We all of us looked at it with intense interest.

Another cross-bearer, behind whom came a gentleman carrying an instrument like a bedroom candlestick.

His Grandeur Monseigneur Affre, Archbishop of Paris: he was in black and white, his eyes were cast to the earth, his hands were together at right angles from his chest: on his hands were black gloves, and on the black gloves sparkled the sacred episcopal—what do I say?—archiepiscopal ring. On his head was the mitre.   It is unlike the godly coronet that figures upon the coach-panels of our own Right Reverend Bench.   The Archbishop's mitre may be about a yard high: formed within probably of consecrated pasteboard, it is without covered by a sort of watered silk of white and silver.   On the two peaks at the top of the mitre are two very little spangled tassels, that frisk and twinkle about in a very agreeable manner.

Monseigneur stood opposite to us for some time, when I had the opportunity to note the above remarkable phenomena.   He stood opposite me for some time, keeping his eyes steadily on the ground, his hands before him, a small clerical train following after.   Why didn't they move? There was the National Guard keeping on presenting arms, the little drummers going on rub-dub-dub—rub-dub-dub—in the same steady, slow way, and the Procession never moved an inch.   There was evidently, to use an elegant phrase, a hitch somewhere.

[*Enter a fat priest, who bustles up to the drum-major.*]

Fat priest—" Taisez-vous."

Little drummer—Rub-dub-dub—rub-dub-dub—rub-dub-dub, &c.

Drum-major—" Qu'est-ce donc? "

Fat priest—"Taisez-vous, vous dis-je; ce n'est pas le corps. Il n'arrivera pas—pour une heure."

The little drums were instantly hushed, the procession turned to the right about, and walked back to the altar again, the blown-out candle that had been on the near side of us before was now on the off side, the National Guards set down their muskets and began at their sandwiches again. We had to wait an hour and a half at least before the great procession arrived. The guns without went on booming all the while at intervals, and as we heard each, the audience gave a kind of "*ahahah !*" such as you hear when the rockets go up at Vauxhall.

At last the real Procession came.

Then the drums began to beat as formerly, the Nationals to get under arms, the clergymen were sent for and went, and presently—yes there was the tall cross-bearer at the head of the procession, and they came *back !*

They chanted something in a weak, snuffling, lugubrious manner, to the melancholy bray of a serpent.

Crash! however. Mr. Habeneck and the fiddlers in the organ-loft pealed out a wild shrill march, which stopped the reverend gentlemen, and in the midst of this music—

And of a great trampling of feet and clattering,

And of a great crowd of Generals and Officers in fine clothes,

With the Prince de Joinville marching quickly at the head of the procession,

And while everybody's heart was thumping as hard as possible,

NAPOLEON'S COFFIN PASSED.

It was done in an instant. A box covered with a great red cross—a dingy-looking crown lying on the top of it—Seamen on one side and Invalids on the other—they had passed in an instant and were up the aisle.

A faint snuffling sound, as before, was heard from the

officiating priests, but we knew of nothing more. It is said that old Louis Philippe was standing at the cata-falque, whither the Prince de Joinville advanced and said, "Sire, I bring you the body of the Emperor Napoleon."

Louis Philippe answered, "I receive it in the name of France." Bertrand put on the body the most glorious vic-torious sword that ever has been forged since the apt descendants of the first murderer learned how to hammer steel; and the coffin was placed in the temple prepared for it.

The six hundred singers and the fiddlers now commenced the playing and singing of a piece of music; and a part of the crew of the *Belle Poule* skipped into the places that had been kept for them under us, and listened to the music, chewing tobacco. While the actors and fiddlers were going on, most of the spirits-of-wine lamps on altars went out.

When we arrived in the open air we passed through the court of the Invalides, where thousands of people had been assembled, but where the benches were not quite bare. Then we came on to the terrace before the place: the old soldiers were firing off the great guns, which made a dread-ful stunning noise, and frightened some of us, who did not care to pass before the cannon and be knocked down even by the wadding. The guns were fired in honour of the King, who was going home by a back door. All the forty thousand people who covered the great stands before the Hôtel had gone away too. The Imperial Barge had been dragged up the river, and was lying lonely along the Quay, examined by some few shivering people on the shore.

It was five o'clock when we reached home: the stars were shining keenly out of the frosty sky, and François told me that dinner was just ready.

In this manner, my dear Miss Smith, the great Napoleon was buried.

Farewell.

THE END.